The Sister Pact

The Sister Pact

Lisa Swift

hera

First published in the United Kingdom in 2021 by

Hera Books
28b Cricketfield Road
London, E5 8NS
United Kingdom

A CIP catalogue record for this book is available from the British Library.

Print ISBN 978 1 80032 610 1
Ebook ISBN 978 1 912973 77 4

Look for more great books at www.herabooks.com

Printed and bound in Great Britain by Clays Ltd, Elcograf S.p.A.

1

For my ever-supportive mum Sandra Firth, to go alongside her well-earned World's Best Mum mug

Chapter One

It was another quiet night in The Highwayman's Drop. Morgue quiet.

But it would pick up later, Brooke Padgett told herself as she wiped down the bar. Sunday night was quiz night: that'd pull in all the usual suspects. Plus they'd got some fresh guest ales on, so the CAMRA fanatics would be in, and with the new food menu...

Oh, who was she kidding? Brooke had seen more life on a dog than there was in the pub tonight. She threw down the towel and dropped her chin onto her fist.

Business had been dwindling for over a year now. Brooke and her mum Janey had tried everything to get the place back to its former glory – live music, new beers, putting a bit of food on, even a monthly book club – yet trade remained stubbornly low.

She just couldn't figure it out. Nothing had really changed – well, one thing had changed, one pretty big thing as far as she personally was concerned, but in terms of the pub itself, it was the same traditional country inn it had been since dinosaurs walked the earth. It had a dartboard and a beer garden and a pool table. It had today's papers, an open fire, a fruit machine and shelves of books and board games. It had photos of the village from the dim and distant past on the walls, horse brasses, Toby jugs, the good sort of crisps. The door was always open, offering those Yorkshire specialities: a friendly welcome and a reasonably priced pint. The ingredients were all there for the perfect pub. It was just that a little of its heart had been chipped away that nothing seemed able to repair.

Brooke summoned her best barmaid smile as Martin Brady, a long-time regular, walked in.

'Heyup, here's trouble.' She greeted him with a friendly nod and started pouring him a pint of the usual.

'Hiya, Brooke love.' He glanced around. 'Bit dead in here, isn't it?'

Brooke sighed. 'Tell me about it.'

'Ah well. Happen it'll pick up,' he said soothingly, registering her glum expression.

'Where's the rest of the boys?' Brooke asked, summoning a joviality she didn't feel as she watched tawny liquid slosh against the sides of the pint glass.

'They'll be on their way. You know we never miss the quiz.' Martin peered over the bar. 'No Janey?'

'Her shift started ten minutes ago. She's fallen asleep watching *Pointless*, I bet.'

Martin's eyes took on a dreamy quality. 'Nice-looking woman, your mam.'

'Runs in the family, eh?'

'Couldn't have put it better myself.' He eyed the glass of beer she put in front of him reverently. 'Ah, there we go, the perfect pint. You'll make some young lad a lovely wife one of these days, Brooke Padgett.'

Brooke laughed. 'Plus you should see the right hook I've got on me after twelve years behind the pumps. Dad always said he never worried about me being out at night as long as I had my trusty pint-pulling arm with me.' She glanced around the thin scattering of customers. 'Marty, would you mind keeping an eye on the bar? I'd better go wake Mum up before I'm needed for quizmaster duties.'

Martin saluted. 'No problem.'

'If anyone wants a drink, tell them I won't be five minutes.' She took another gloomy look at the few occupied tables. 'Not that I'm expecting a sudden mad rush. Back in a bit.'

She left the bar under Martin's watchful eye and headed upstairs to the apartment she shared with her mum.

There were voices coming from the living room – one male, one female. Brooke frowned. Who else was here? There were two entrances to the flat, one inside the pub and a fire escape round the back. Had her mum been sneaking men up on the quiet?

She peeped around the living room door. Janey was on the sofa, sipping a cup of tea as she listened to the man sitting opposite her.

'I'm afraid I don't have much bar experience,' he was saying in an apologetic tone. 'But I'm a fast learner, and dead keen. If you give me a chance then I swear you won't be sorry, Mrs Padgett.'

Oh God. How had her mum managed to arrange this without her knowing? Brooke was sure she'd talked Janey out of it the last time she'd brought up the idea of taking on more staff. Already they'd had to adjust the pub's opening times so they could cut the hours of the two bar staff who worked afternoon shifts for them. What were they planning to pay this guy in, salted peanuts and out-of-date schnapps?

'Call me Janey, please,' her mum said, with a warm smile for the prospective barman. 'I wouldn't worry about experience, Hayden. You've got plenty of qualities to make up for that. A handsome, personable lad like you

3

is just what we need to breathe a bit of sex appeal into the old place.'

Brooke could only see the back of Hayden's head, but she could tell from the pinkness creeping up the back of his neck to meet his dark curls that he wasn't sure quite how to respond to that comment. She cleared her throat, and two pairs of eyes swivelled in her direction.

'Oh, hello, love,' her mum said easily, not at all abashed at being caught out. 'This is Hayden. Hayden, my daughter Brooke, the junior landlady.'

'The younger landlady,' Brooke corrected her. 'What's going on in here?'

'Hayden came in response to our ad. Carmel in the post office was kind enough to put it in the window for us.'

'Was she indeed? For us? Well, bully for Carmel.'

'I'd have called you up but I knew you'd be rushed off your feet,' Janey said innocently. 'Anyway, I don't think we need to see anyone else. Hayden seems perfect.'

Hayden nodded vigorously. 'I'm very enthusiastic, Miss Padgett, and I'm a hard worker. Honestly, whatever evening shifts you've got, I'll take them all.'

Miss Padgett. Brooke almost snorted out loud at that. They were nearly exactly the same age. The lad obviously didn't remember, but he'd been in her class at Leyholme Primary. Brooke wasn't sure she could take a 'Miss Padgett' from Hayden Bailey: not after the little scrote had put frogspawn in her PE pumps as a dare in Year Four.

She turned to Janey, fixing her face into a bright, dangerous smile. 'Mother dearest, may I have a word in private?'

'Now?' Janey said, looking nervous. 'I think you ought to be getting back to the bar, don't you?'

'I do not. Martin Brady's watching it for me.' She pointed to the other door. 'Kitchen.'

Janey sighed and put down her tea. 'Sorry about this, Hayden.'

'All right, Mum, what the hell?' Brooke demanded when they were alone. 'We talked about this. We can't afford more staff right now, and we certainly don't need them. There isn't enough for an extra person to do.'

'There's plenty for Hayden to do.'

'You know there isn't. How can we justify taking him on when we just cut Mark and Fiona's hours?'

'All right, so afternoons are pretty quiet these days,' Janey conceded. 'But we do need someone who can take shifts in the evenings. Mark and Fiona have got young families, they don't want night shifts.' She turned to the draining board to start putting away the washing-up. 'You've been working too hard, Brooke. A night off every once in a while would do you the world of good. Anyway, having someone else available to mind the bar gives me more time for chef duties, doesn't it? We could expand the menu.'

'Right. And did you tell Hayden he'd be working for pork scratchings and tummy rubs, or does the poor deluded boy think he might be getting actual cash in his pay packet?'

'Oh, things aren't all that bad.' Janey opened a drawer and took out her vape. 'Hayden's just what we need, a bit of eye candy to bring in the ladies. It's like Peperami Central down there with only me and you behind the bar.'

'You can't be saying stuff like that to him either,' Brooke whispered. 'Christ, Mum, we haven't even taken him on yet and he's got grounds for a sexual harassment claim.'

'Don't be daft, he's a man. It doesn't count that way round, they enjoy it. It's a compliment to their virility.'

'It bloody does count! Phrases like "eye candy", "sex appeal" and – can I particularly stress this one – "Peperami Central" are right off the menu.' She wrinkled her nose as her mum exhaled and the kitchen filled with a cloud of sickly-sweet blueberry fog. 'Do you have to do that indoors? I'm probably getting passive popcorn lung.'

'Oh, for God's sake. Right little killjoy you are tonight.' Janey turned off her vape and put it away. 'Anyway, you've got to agree Hayden's a good-looking lad. It's no use pretending you think different, I saw you sneaking a look.'

Brooke snorted. 'Young enough to be your son is what he is, Janey Padgett.'

Her mum shrugged. 'My appreciation is strictly from a business point of view. He'd be a draw, wouldn't he?'

'Mum, we're running a pub, not a knocking shop for randy middle-aged women.' Brooke cast a look at the door. 'And keep your voice down, he might be able to hear. Has he got any bar experience at all?'

'Well, all right, no,' Janey admitted. 'But he's wearing very tight jeans. That's a damn sight more use to us than bar experience.'

'Huh. You know he's the little git who put frogspawn in my pumps?'

Janey laughed. 'Oh, was that him? That was hilarious.' She forced her face straight when she noticed her daughter's expression. 'I mean, of course it wasn't hilarious, it was awful for you. Poor little Brooke. Still, it feels mean to hold it against him twenty-odd years later. He's ever so keen.'

'I'd noticed,' Brooke said drily. 'Why? This can't possibly be his dream job, pulling pints at a failing pub.'

'We're not failing. We're just… going through a fallow period. Every business has those.'

'When Dad was alive we never had them.'

'Yes, well, things are different now. There's the economy and… you know, things,' Janey said. 'Anyway, to answer your question, I'm sensing he might need the money. It felt a bit rude to ask why.'

'Oh, so *now* she knows what constitutes socially acceptable chitchat,' Brooke muttered. 'You were too busy asking him if he's got any even tighter jeans he can wear for his first shift, I suppose.'

'Now you're being daft,' Janey said loftily. She took an envelope from the counter. 'This came, by the way. From that bloke at Willowtree Taverns again. I suppose your sister got one too.'

Brooke glared at it before stuffing it in the pocket of her jeans.

'Not going to read it?' her mum asked.

'Not now.' She patted her mum's shoulder. 'I better get back to the bar. You never know, we might actually have such a thing as a customer.'

'I'll just tell Hayden he's got the job then I'll join you. He can cut his teeth next week with the Friday night crowd.'

Brooke shook her head. 'I told you, Mum, we can't afford another person. It's a nice idea, but we're not going to suddenly find the place heaving just because we've got some new totty behind the bar.'

'Brooke, I'm doing this for you,' Janey said earnestly. 'You've been going full pelt ever since we lost your dad, and God knows I'm too old at sixty-two to be lugging barrels around the cellar. You need another young pair of hands.'

'I don't. I like doing it all myself, it keeps me busy.'

'Yes, too busy. You used to be all about having fun; now you spend every night here, hiding behind a grin while old men flirt with you. You're wasting your youth on this place. When was the last time you saw your friends? Went out on a date?'

'I go on dates. I've got one on Friday actually.'

Janey blinked. 'Have you? You never said.'

'This is… kind of a blind date,' Brooke said. 'I don't know what he's going to be like, a mutual friend arranged it.'

'You want me to do your hair for you?'

'Thanks, I'd like that. It's just an afternoon drink so nothing too fancy. And don't worry, I'll be back for my shift.'

'You won't need to be if we take Hayden on,' her mum said. 'If he's on bar then there's no need to rush back if you fancy this boy you're out with, is there? I mean, if you decide to take the date somewhere else afterwards.'

Brooke stared at her.

'You know, like his bedroom,' Janey added helpfully.

'I got it, Mum, thanks.' Brooke shook her head. 'No, there'll be none of that going on. I can't be arsed with sex if I'm going to be working.'

'I told you, if we hire Hayden then there'll be no need—'

'All right, fine.' Brooke sighed. 'Since you're obviously not going to let it drop, he can have a trial period to see if he's capable of earning his keep. Two weeks, that's all. I'll be here Friday night to start his training – tell Frogspawn Boy not to cock it up.'

8

As she headed back to the bar, Brooke pulled the letter from Willowtree Taverns out of her pocket, ripped the envelope open and skimmed the contents. She scowled darkly at it before tearing it into pieces.

Chapter Two

Janey perched on the edge of her daughter's bed while Brooke sat cross-legged at her feet in front of the full-length mirror. A wave of nostalgia carried her as she ran her fingers through Brooke's thick blonde hair. She could almost forget she was on hairstyling duties for a thirty-year-old and not the child her daughter had once been.

When Brooke had been small, just getting a brush through her bird's-nest tangle had been a struggle. At first Janey had let Brooke's hair grow long like her sister's, which fell in a copper sheen to Rhianna's waist. Long hairstyles had gone out of the window not long after Brooke started Beavers though, when she'd fallen in with a bunch of roaring, jumping, climbing boys who liked to spend their time building dens in the woods. After Janey had cut an irremovable twig out of her youngest daughter's hair for the third time and a wriggly green caterpillar had poked its little face out from the severed locks, she'd finally admitted defeat and got out the pudding bowl. It felt like Rhianna had never lost her baby hair; it had stayed so soft and fine. Whereas after the caterpillar incident, Brooke had spent most of her childhood looking like one of the kids from *The Village of the Damned*.

'What's up, Mum?' Brooke asked, noticing that her mother's hand had stilled.

'Hmm?' Janey forced herself back into the present. 'Oh, nothing. Off with the pixies. What are we doing for you then, my love?'

'Can you curl it for me? I can never get it right on my own.'

'It always goes huge with a curl. You'll look like '80s Jon Bon Jovi.'

'Just a little wave. You know, like you did for me when we went to Nell and Xander's wedding.'

'All right.' Janey turned on the straighteners. 'So, are you going to tell me anything about him?'

'I told you, I can't. It's a blind date.'

'Yes, but I assume this friend of yours thought you'd be a good match for a reason.'

Brooke shrugged. 'When you get to thirty, I think your friends think "single" is reason enough.'

Janey started twisting Brooke's hair into loose waves with the straighteners. 'You know, I can never help wondering—'

'—why my hair's so much thicker than Rhianna's,' Brooke said, smiling. 'I know, Mum. You mention it every time.'

'It's just a source of constant amazement to me that two sisters ended up with such different heads on their shoulders. Rhia was always jealous of how thick and blonde your hair was.'

'Yeah, because she never knew the pain of you yanking a brush through the knots,' Brooke said, laughing. 'I feel like Nature cursed us by deliberately giving us the other sister's hair. I'd have killed for some I could brush without bringing tears to my eyes, and Rhia always dreamed of being blonde like Disney Cinderella.'

'Did you call her about that letter from Willowtree?'

Brooke pressed her eyes closed. 'No. But I will. Tomorrow.'

'You've been saying that all week.'

'I know. I want to get this date out of the way first, that's all.'

'You make it sound like a chore, Brooke.'

'Well, first dates are chores, aren't they? Just an ordeal you have to go through to get to the better bits later on.'

'It's been so long I hardly remember,' Janey said, smiling wistfully. 'I do remember the excitement of it, the tummy butterflies, but the rest… I suppose the world of dating's changed a lot since I was a young thing. Back then it was all flicking through *Jackie* to get ideas for outfits and hoping when I got to the pictures that it'd be David Essex or one of the Bay City Rollers who'd show up to sweep me off my feet.'

Brooke laughed. 'I hope that's not a jinx. If my date turns up with a perm and flares, it's on you.'

'Don't worry, I'm sure he won't have a perm. Although I'll wish on a star for you that he's got David's lovely bum.'

'You and your men in tight trousers.' Brooke glanced over her shoulder. 'Were you disappointed when you met Dad? I mean, that he wasn't David Essex.'

Janey smiled. 'Your dad was more in the Oliver Reed mould. The bad boy you wanted to tame, all leather jacket and come-hither grin.'

'What, Dad?'

'Hard to believe, I know. It was just an act to impress girls, though. I'd worked out what a big softie he was by the end of our first conversation.' She stared dreamily at her reflection, so very different from the nineteen-year-old she'd been then. 'There wasn't a bad bone in that man's body, Brooke.'

'I know there wasn't.'

'We were very lucky to have him.' Janey sprayed some mousse into the now wavy hair and scrunched it a bit. 'There you go, chickie. Ready to knock him dead.'

'Thanks, Mum.' Brooke got to her feet and kissed the top of her mum's head. 'You know, you're all right.'

'Ta. Does that mean I'm forgiven for Haydengate?'

'Hmm. I'll tell you after his first shift tonight.'

-

Brooke was meeting Nick at a bar in Halifax, La Hacienda. She'd been torn between power-dressing – heels, suit, no-nonsense hair; hopefully give off a bit of that *Devil Wears Prada*, crush-your-balls-with-a-stiletto vibe – or going glam in the hope he'd think she was the sort of modern, go-getting urbanite who frequented posh wine bars all the time. In the end, she'd decided there wasn't much point in trying to intimidate someone like Nick Weyborough and split the difference: suit jacket with full-length sleeves to hide her tattoos, jeans and a sparkly top.

Brooke reached up to pat her moussed waves as she glanced around. At least she could be sure her hair looked all right. Her mum always knew the best way to tame the beast, even on those humid days when it trebled in size. Still, Brooke couldn't help feeling that even with her best hair on, she really didn't belong in this sort of place.

She recognised Nick from his photo on the Willowtree Taverns website, although his hair had crept back a few inches since it had been taken. Despite the receding hairline, though, Brooke was forced to admit he wasn't unattractive. That was as much down to tailoring and attitude as appearance – the guy oozed confidence and class. He was seated at a table, flicking through a magazine. Brooke threw back her shoulders and went to join him.

'Hi,' she said. 'Nick, isn't it? You're expecting me.'

Nick Weyborough looked up from his mag and cast a quick but appraising glance over her figure, lingering on her breasts, before he stood up to shake her hand.

'Sit down, Miss Padgett. Let me get you a drink.' He indicated a seat, then waved to get the attention of a waitress.

'That's fine, I'll get my own. I mean, it's hardly a date, is it?' Brooke laughed then stopped suddenly, wincing.

'Please. This place is one of ours. If you're with me, your drinks are on Willowtree Taverns.'

'Well, all right.' Brooke glanced up as the waitress approached. 'I'm driving though, so just a sparkling water.'

The waitress went to fetch her drink. Nick Weyborough, meanwhile, steepled his fingers and looked at her over the top. Brooke shifted uncomfortably.

'OK, is this a power play thing?' she asked him when the waitress returned to deliver her drink and Nick still hadn't spoken a word. 'Because it isn't working.'

'It isn't a power play,' Nick said. 'Although if it were, the way your hands are shaking would tend to suggest it is working.'

Brooke laughed, taking a sip of water to cool her heated cheeks. 'You're calling me out on being nervous? OK, so I'm nervous. I'm not going to sign my pub away because of an evolutionary response designed to stop me being gobbled up by a sabre-toothed tiger, Nick.'

'I wouldn't have expected it of you, Miss Padgett.'

'It's just Brooke,' she said. 'Why did you want to meet me? I told you when I wrote to you, I won't change my mind.'

'We've upped our offer since then. Haven't you been getting my letters?'

Brooke shrugged. 'I got them. I didn't see that the new letters needed any new answer. I told you: you can offer any price and the answer will still be no.'

Nick smiled as he sipped some sort of cocktail, his diamond-studded cufflinks glinting in the sunshine that streamed through the almost cathedral-like stained glass windows of the wine bar.

'You own one-third?' he said.

'That's right. The pub's been in my dad's family for four generations. When he died, he left equal shares to me, my mum and sister.' Brooke met his eye. 'But that doesn't matter. I can speak for all of us. We won't sell.'

'Your sister feels differently.'

Brooke stared at him. 'What?'

'Mrs Garrett, isn't it? Rhianna Garrett. I spoke with her yesterday and she seemed keen to strike a deal.'

'She wouldn't say that. Not without consulting me.'

Nick's mouth flickered. 'And yet, here I am telling you that she did.'

Bloody Rhianna! Brooke should've known she wasn't to be trusted. If it were up to Rhia, she'd have flogged the pub for twenty quid and a complimentary radio alarm clock. She always had been ashamed to admit The Highwayman's Drop was where she came from.

But it wasn't Plummy Mummy's bloody livelihood, was it? She had her rich husband and her posh house and the portfolio of stocks and shares James managed for them. She didn't need The Highwayman's. Brooke needed it.

'Well, that… that doesn't matter,' she said, folding her arms. 'You can't just buy her share. Me and Mum won't sell and that's that.'

'You're speaking for both of you?' Nick said. 'I did extend the drinks invitation to your mother as well.'

'She couldn't make it. Rest assured we're of one mind.'

Brooke stifled a burp and hoped Nick hadn't noticed. Ugh, why the hell hadn't she asked for tap water instead of sparkling? She had to keep up the strong, confident woman act. The last thing she wanted this slimeball to think was that she was the sort of stuttering, terrified country mouse who could be pushed around by him and his sharp suit.

'That being the case, I wonder you're here at all,' Nick observed, sipping his cocktail.

'I'm here because you apparently find it impossible to take no for an answer in writing and continue to harass my family.'

'Very few people would consider an offer of £750,000 harassment, Brooke,' he said quietly.

'I told you, it doesn't matter what you—' She broke off. 'Sorry, how much?'

'Didn't you read our most recent letter?'

'I skimmed it. I didn't notice...' She gave him a sharp look. 'Anyway, that's irrelevant. We won't sell. The Highwayman's has always been a freehold and I'm determined it'll remain one.'

'Why are you so dead set against it?'

'Why are you so dead set on having it?'

Nick shrugged. 'I'm perfectly happy to answer that. Willowtree Taverns now have twenty pubs in the Airedale and Calderdale region, mostly old coaching inns amid gorgeous rural scenery. The Highwayman's Drop fits our Best of British profile perfectly.'

'So do lots of places. Go buy them up.'

He smiled. 'Weren't you listening? We already did.'

She shook her head. 'You see, this is my issue, Nick. Identical bloody pubs that look like they came out of a build-your-own-licensed-premises kit, with the same IKEA showroom decor, the same overpriced beers, the same nauseating "Live, Laugh, Love," calligraphy and uniformed staff. Places that ought to be the hearts of their communities, getting absorbed into these flat, faceless chains.'

'Many of our establishments were in decline and would have closed if we hadn't bought them, like so many pubs around the country. Willowtree Taverns have allowed them a second life. Not to mention saving numerous jobs.'

Brooke ignored him. 'I was born in The Highwayman's; so was my dad, and his mum before him. It's the place in the village where people go when they're lonely and want to see a friendly face, or to enjoy the company of their friends and family. It's at the centre of our community in Leyholme. We can't sacrifice that; it'd be devastating.'

'And yet your turnover has been falling for well over a year.'

'That's… a temporary setback. You think I could bear to see my pub transformed into something with no soul?'

Nick pushed his drink to one side so he could lean towards her. His eyes weren't unfriendly, exactly, or unsympathetic either. Brooke would probably have described them as shrewd: grey, bright and piercing.

'I'm impressed by your passion, Brooke,' he said in a quiet, earnest tone, almost as if he meant it. 'You can rest assured communities are at the heart of our ethos at Willowtree Taverns too. Our pubs are often in small villages, and we're well aware of the role they play for the people there. You wouldn't lose that.'

'Huh. I've been to some of your pubs. Paint-by-numbers places with no character. I couldn't even tell you which was which.'

'But if you and your mum were to stay on as our tenants, then it would still be your pub. You'd be responsible for hiring staff and making all day-to-day decisions. What's more, you'd have the security of the company behind you – not to mention a tidy fee from the sale of the premises to set aside for a rainy day.'

Right. Of course someone like Nick Weyborough would see a quarter of a million quid as just 'rainy day' money...

'You'd keep us on as landladies?' Brooke asked suspiciously.

'Absolutely.'

'And you'd guarantee you wouldn't change anything? The drinks, the decor, the name, everything that's part of the place: we'd have final say?'

Nick hesitated. 'Well, I'm not in a position to promise that. At the end of the day, we do have a brand to maintain. People need to know what they're going to get when they enter a Willowtree Tavern.'

'See, Nick, that's my problem. The Highwayman's isn't a brand. It's a pub.' Brooke finished her drink and stood up. 'Thanks for seeing me. I appreciate the offer, but it's still a no.'

'Brooke, please.' Nick stood too, smiling with all the charm he could muster. 'Stay. Have another drink with me. I'm sure we can find a compromise.'

'I'm sorry, but I know we can't.'

'I refuse to believe that. In all my years in this industry, I've learnt it's a truism that everyone has their price.'

'The Highwayman's is my price.' Brooke shook his hand firmly. 'Now let's call that the end of negotiations, shall we? Goodbye.'

Chapter Three

When Brooke got home, she went up to the flat by the back entrance – through the beer garden and up the metal steps of the fire escape – hoping her mum would be downstairs in the pub. However, she found Janey on the landline in the hallway.

'I know, love,' she was saying in her best maternal croon, the one she saved for cut knees, scumbag boyfriends and really bad period pains. 'I know. Well, James has got a very demanding… mmm. Yes, I know. It's not your fault, but… yes, I know.'

Brooke rolled her eyes at the soothing, constantly interrupted singsong, knowing that on the other end of the line, Rhianna was pulling her usual poor-little-rich-girl woe-is-me crap. What in her perfect life was she complaining about today?

Spoilt. That was Rhianna's problem. Always getting her own way, whether it was from their mum and dad, her husband James or just Lady Luck, who'd smiled on her like a favourite pet at every stage of her blessed exist-ence. Rhianna, who was born with all the looks and all the brains, leaving none left to go around for her little sister. Then there was the scholarship to St Mary's, giving her free access to the best education money could buy, followed by a place at Cambridge to study law – for all the bloody use she'd made of her fancy education, when she'd never worked a day in her life. James had already been a wealthy man when Rhianna had met him at twenty-one, and she'd quickly found herself elevated to a comfortable, easy life as a housewife and mother in his luxurious home in the poshest part of Cheshire. It was all she'd ever wanted, which of course meant it had landed in her lap with no effort on her part whatsoever.

It didn't piss Brooke off that her sister believed the world revolved around her. It pissed Brooke off that, in a lot of ways, it felt like the world actually did.

How dare she speak to Nick behind Brooke's back? How *dare* she? Rhianna, who'd never had to work for her living, while Brooke was here day in, day out, trying to keep the family business afloat. It wasn't like she needed the money. A quarter of a million quid was chicken feed to her and James. It was spite; that was all. A deliberate attempt to get one over on the sister she'd spent her life looking down on.

'Is that Rhianna?' Brooke asked Janey. Her mum jumped.

'Oh. Brooke,' she said. 'I hadn't expected you back so soon. How was your date, chick?'

'Give me the phone.'

'What?'

'Just give it here.'

Brooke practically snatched it from her mum's hand.

'All right, Rhia, what the hell are you playing at?'

'I'm sorry?' Rhianna said. Those polished vowels, so carefully rounded; every trace of accent gone. God forbid her sister actually remembered where she'd come from.

'Don't pretend you don't know what I mean,' Brooke snapped. 'You spoke to Nick Weyborough behind my back. You told him you wanted to sell.'

'Well, I… all right, I did. He telephoned me yesterday. What's wrong with that?'

'Christ, Rhianna!' Brooke gave a harsh laugh. 'You know the only way to see those bastards off is by putting on a united front, and you're there wiggling up Nick's trouser leg like the little snake in the grass you are. Why? To get one over on me? I didn't think you were that petty.'

'I wasn't trying to get one over on anyone,' Rhianna said quietly. 'All I said was, I might – *might* – be interested in selling if you and Mum were. But if you weren't, then that was that.'

'You had no call saying anything to that slimy yuppie twat! You should've told him to sod off until you'd discussed it with the rest of the family.'

'Perhaps I ought to have, yes, but…' She sighed. 'Brooke, I do wish you'd consider selling. That sort of money could make a real difference to us. To you and to me.'

Brooke laughed. 'Are you kidding me? James's car must be worth more than Nick's offer.'

'I'm not talking about James, I'm talking about me. I could really use that money, Brooke.' She let out a little sob.

'You're serious?' Brooke said in a gentler tone. 'You need cash? Why?'

'It would be a big help. Things… things aren't so good.'

'You and James aren't having money problems?'

'Not exactly,' Rhianna murmured. 'Look, I can't talk now. The children are home. I wish you'd think about it though, please.' She hung up.

'What was that all about?' Brooke asked, turning to Janey. 'Are Rhianna and James struggling for money? I thought they had pots of the stuff.'

'I don't know anything about that,' Janey said. 'All she told me was that they'd had a big row.'

'Over money?'

'She didn't say. James has been working long hours lately. I suppose she's feeling neglected.' Janey quirked an eyebrow. 'So you've been to see Nick Weyborough, have you?'

Brooke grimaced. 'Yeah.'

Her mum flicked her ear. 'That's for getting me to give you date hair under false pretences. Why didn't you tell me?'

'Because I know what you're like. All he'd have to do is turn up in a pair of skintight trousers and you'd be offering him the pub for the price of a pickled egg. You're not to be trusted around charming men.'

'Was he charming?'

'He thought so.' Brooke slipped an arm around her mum's shoulders. 'I'm sorry, Mum. I just thought I'd have a better chance of pulling off the tough guy act on my own. You'd only make me giggle.'

'Well, that makes us one-all. No more telling me off about hiring Hayden.'

'Oh yeah, him,' Brooke said, pulling a face. 'Is he here yet?'

'I told him five o'clock, after Fiona finishes.' Janey shot her an arch look. 'You should sort yourself out with a real date, Brooke. One with a decent possibility of some rumpy-pumpy at the end of it.'

Brooke laughed. 'You'd better not be talking about Hayden Bailey.'

'Why not? He's your age. Handsome. No wedding ring, I had a look.'

'No wedding ring is not the same as available. Besides, I'd probably get back to his place to discover it was all a prank and he'd filled the bed with frogspawn.'

–

The twins were eating their tea when Hayden got home from his last job of the day and dumped his toolbox on the worktop in their bungalow's open-plan kitchenette. Darcie was still in her uniform: the navy blue blazer and striped white blouse of St Mary's. Cara had thrown off her charcoal Ravenswood Secondary blazer and was stuffing her face with chips.

'Dad, guess what?' she mumbled through a gobful of half-chewed potato.

'Welcome home, Father dearest,' Hayden said. 'How are you this fine afternoon? I hope your day at work wasn't too irksome.'

'Wassa irksome?'

'It means annoying,' Darcie told her. 'Like you.'

'Like your face.'

'Oi. No arguing when I've just got through the door.' Hayden planted a kiss on the top of each little head, both covered in dark curls like his own, but Cara's just a shade fairer. 'What's the news then, Car?'

'I got made captain of the football team.'

'Wow, did you? Well done, honey.' He ruffled her hair. 'We'll have to do something tomorrow to celebrate. Where's Nan?'

'Here!' a voice called from one of the bedrooms. 'Out in a minute, Hayd. I'm straight from work myself. Just grabbed a shower while the girls were eating.'

'What an industrious bunch we are at Chez Bailey.' Hayden leaned over Darcie to nick one of her chips. 'So what did you learn at school today, Darce?'

'We learnt that if you pinch people's chips, you go to prison,' she said, glaring at him as she drew her plate to one side.

'I'm glad they're instilling you with such a strong moral compass. Obviously you're now ready for the intermediate Ethics course, "Dads, And Why They Don't Count". What about you, Car? Good day at school?'

She shrugged. 'Drama was OK. Maths was rubbish. Dad, can you help me with my homework later? It's stupid equations.'

'Your dad can't tonight,' Hayden's mum Pam said as she came in, a towel wrapped round her hair. She caught sight of the toolbox on the kitchen worktop and shook her head. 'Hayden, can we not have that dirty thing on the counter? We have to eat what comes off that.'

'We'll get botulism, won't we, Nan?' Darcie said.

Pam nodded. 'It's a very real possibility, Darce.'

'What's botchylism?' Cara asked.

Darcie giggled. 'It's where you're sick everywhere and you poo everywhere and you can't stop.'

'Eurghhh!' Cara exclaimed gleefully as she popped another chip in her mouth. 'That's gross. Dad, why can't you do my homework?'

Hayden raised an eyebrow. '*Do* your homework? It was help you with it a minute ago.'

'Yeah, that's what I said. Are you going out?'

'Yep. I'm going to work.'

'You've just been to work.' Darcie pointed an accusing finger at the toolbox. 'See?'

'I'm going to different work. I start my new job tonight.'

'What will you have to do?' Cara asked.

'Give people beer in exchange for money. I think even a cotton-headed ninnymuggins like your dad should be able to manage that, don't you?'

Cara looked unconvinced.

'Maybe,' she said. 'Don't spill it though or they won't give you money.'

'Sage advice.' Hayden clapped them both on the shoulder. 'Right, I'd better change into something a bit less filthy. I'm sure Nan can help with homework while I'm out.'

Pam followed him out of the room and closed the door.

'Have you eaten?' she said in a low voice.

'I grabbed a Mars bar from the vending machine.'

'You can't survive on that. I'll make you a sandwich for the walk over.' She cast a concerned eye over his features. 'I don't like you burning the candle at both ends like this, Hayd. You're already taking on every job God sends during the day, and now working night shifts at the pub… it isn't good for you.'

'What choice have I got?' he said, looking away. 'Darcie needs so much – they both do, but everything for St Mary's seems to cost a small fortune. Darcie's uniform was three times what Cara's cost, and then there's the trips, the books… I guess it's small change to the other parents: doctors and lawyers or whatever. To a jobbing electrician on a single parent's income, it equals a hell of a lot of hours.'

'It's a great opportunity for her, though.'

'Yeah, fantastic,' he muttered. 'These independent schools chuck a few scholarships in the way of people like us and call it meritocracy. It never occurs to them that fees aren't the only thing putting an education like that out of our reach.'

'But she loves it. The place is really testing her. That makes it worthwhile, eh?'

'I know.' He sighed. 'I know. Thanks for picking them up from school again, Mum, and minding them tonight. Thanks for everything you do for us.'

'Well. You're all I've got, aren't you?' she said, giving his arm a squeeze.

He smiled. 'Unfortunately for you. Reckon you can manage some homework help? Sorry, I was a bit quick to volunteer you.'

Pam grimaced. 'Maybe with some assistance from my pal Mr Google. Cara's homework's been beyond me since about Year Three. As for Darcie, I can't even spell half the words she's been throwing at me since she started at St Mary's.'

'Tell me about it,' Hayden said. 'Look, I'd better get ready or I'll be late. That young landlady's already looking daggers at me. I'm sensing I've got a lot to do to prove myself.'

Chapter Four

'You're late,' Brooke told Hayden when he joined her behind the bar.

'Sorry,' he said, slightly breathless from his brisk walk over. 'Got held up on a job.'

'And you decided that job was more important to you than this one, did you?'

'No. I'd never have booked a job in so close to a shift if I'd known about it in advance.' He took off his jacket and glanced around for somewhere to stash it. 'You only hired me on Sunday, remember?'

'What is it you do when you're not rocking up here at all hours, then?'

'I'm an electrician.' He nodded to the coat in his arms. 'Are you going to tell me where to put this or shall I just stand here hugging it all night?'

Her lips twitched. 'You want me to tell you where to put it?'

'Yeah yeah, I know. Up my arse on the second shelf.' Deciding this was probably some sort of initiative test, Hayden lighted on a cubby hole next to a dishwasher for dirty glasses and shoved the bundled jacket in there. 'You don't like me much, do you?'

Brooke shrugged. 'It's nothing personal. I'm doubtful about your ability to do the job. You're lacking the qualities I'd associate with a really top-quality barman.'

'Your mum didn't think so.'

'I'm less easily impressed than she is. It takes more than a decent lunchbox to get round me.'

'Thanks. I'm flattered you noticed.'

'I meant in general.' She nodded a greeting to a group of three men who'd just come in. 'It'll fill up steadily as people get out of work. Friday's our busiest night.'

'Where's your mum?'

'In the kitchen, cooking.'

'What, this place does food? It never used to.'

'Well, now it does.'

Brooke turned a steely gaze on him, her arms folded, and Hayden tried not to smile. There was something about Brooke in a grump that made her look kind of cute, like a little tattooed Barbie. Not that he'd ever tell her that. He remembered what used to happen to lads who made that mistake at school, and it'd always been short, sharp and painful.

'Well you'll never know if I'm a barman in the making until you put me through my paces, will you?' he said. 'Come on, Brooke, Yoda me.'

'What happened to "Miss Padgett"? At your interview you were all snivelling subservience. I was almost warming to you back then.'

'Yeah, well, I've got the job now, haven't I?'

'You've got a trial of the job,' she told him. 'I wouldn't get cheeky.'

'All right. Still, it seems daft keeping up that level of formality when you've frogspawned with a woman.'

She jabbed a finger at him. 'I bloody knew you remembered me!'

He grinned. 'Come on. You never really thought I'd forgotten.'

'Mate, have you got any idea what it feels like to have frogspawn jelly squelching through your bare toes? Not to mention the fact I was haunted for months by the inadvertent tadpolicide.'

They heard a throat clear and turned to face the bar. Theo Blake, who ran the village's 1940s cafe with his fiancée, was waiting to be served.

'Not interrupting anything, am I?' he said.

'Just the floorshow. All part of the service.' Brooke nudged Hayden. 'Watch and learn, Junior,' she said in an undertone.

'Pint of Best please, Brooke, and an orange juice for Lexie,' Theo said.

'Poor lass, I bet she's gagging for a glass of wine.' Brooke started pulling his pint. 'Not long left, is there?'

'Six weeks. I'm nervous as hell.'

'Oh, you'll be brilliant. Don't forget to bring the new arrival to meet us, will you? I'll give you a free drink to wet her head.'

Hayden couldn't help being impressed as he watched Brooke chat with her customer, a warm smile on her face and her eyes crinkling with humour – very different to the prickly person she was with him. Talking to Theo, she sounded genuinely interested in everything he had to tell her about his fiancée's pregnancy; business at The Blue Parrot; his godson's GCSE revision woes. Then she did it again with the next customer, making them, too, feel that no one's life or welfare was as important to Brooke as theirs was. Even Ryan Theakston, a villager Hayden remembered as being notoriously hard to like, smiled when he chatted to Brooke.

'Well?' she said when there was a lull. 'Learn anything?'

Hayden shook his head. 'How do you do that?'

'There's no trick to it. You care. You come to care about all your regulars, even the awkward ones.'

'So when you said I didn't have the qualities needed in an ideal barman, what are they exactly?'

'Pulling a decent pint isn't the only skill you need to work here,' she told him as she started unloading clean glasses from the dishwasher. 'You have to be a people person, even when you don't feel like being one. You have to be skilled in conflict resolution, and you have to know the most appropriate way to respond to flirting and when to put your foot down if it crosses the line. You need to know when to tell someone they've had enough, and what to do if they don't like being told they've had enough. To use the words my mum used to me when I first started working the bar, you need tits, teeth and toughness like you wouldn't believe.' She looked up to meet his eye. 'Still think you want the job, Hayden Bailey?'

'I need the job.'

'OK then, show me what you've got. Pour me a pint of Golden Best. Spout in all the way so the sparkler's touching the bottom; nice, firm pull until you feel it resist, then a second pull to fill. Let it settle, top up if you need to so the head sits just proud of the rim, then serve. I'm just going to change the Boltmaker barrel then I'll be back to see how you've done.'

'Right.' Hayden turned to the bar as Brooke disappeared through the door to the cellar. 'Right,' he muttered to himself.

He took down one of the pint glasses and put it under the pump Brooke had pointed to.

What had she said: spout... all the way in? Halfway in? Glass straight, or tilted?

God, he should be able to do this. He'd drunk enough pints in his life to have seen it done more times than he could count; he just hadn't been paying attention.

Still, how difficult could it be? He rolled up his sleeves, lifted the glass and started to pump.

Bloody hell. It was harder than it looked, this. Hayden could feel the muscles in his arm tightening as he guided the pump towards him. At least he'd be getting a decent workout in this job. It was as good as weight training.

'What the hell is *that*?' Brooke said when she came back from the cellar, pointing to the pint he'd poured.

He grimaced. 'Sorry.'

'You've got more head than beer in that, Hayden. I mean, would you pay £3.60 for that? It's barely a half.'

'I know, I know. I panicked and forgot what you said.'

'Did you tilt the glass?'

'Yeah. I thought that's how I'd seen it done. Is that wrong?'

'It is for cask ale – unless the pump's got a short spout, which they don't tend to have up north. For lager, cider or Guinness you need a forty-five-degree tilt, then you gradually bring it straight. Ale, keep it straight throughout.' She took down another pint glass. 'Here, watch me.'

Hayden watched as Brooke expertly manipulated the Best pump and golden liquid filled the glass – lapping deliciously at the sides, smooth and silky, before she let it settle to a perfect half-inch foam head. It made him feel sort of funny. He couldn't help dwelling on the way Brooke gripped the top of the pump as she slowly, skilfully pulled it towards her body, biting her bottom lip in concentration.

'There,' she said, putting the finished pint down in front of him. 'That wasn't hard, was it?'

His head jerked up. 'What?'

'Come on, Bailey, wake up.' She nudged him as another customer approached. 'Here's Stevie Madeleine. Hers is a medium pinot grigio with a dash of soda, and a pint of Landlord for her missus. I'll pour the pint and you do the wine. That should be nice and easy for you.'

'How can you remember everyone's drink order like that?'

She tapped her head. 'Like a steel trap, mate.'

Hayden managed Stevie's spritzer OK, although he suspected he'd put a bit more soda in than she would've liked. Still, she was polite enough to keep schtum. Brooke turned a benevolent smile on him, like someone who'd just taught their particularly dim puppy its first trick.

'Well done,' she said. 'That's lesson one. Just around eight hundred more to go and you might be halfway ready.'

'Gee, thanks,' he said drily, taking a sip of the dodgy pint he'd poured before.

'Oi. Who said you could have that?'

'What else are you going to do with it? You've been drinking the good one, I saw you.'

'Yeah, well. It's my pub.' She examined him through one narrowed eye. 'What're you doing here anyway?'

'Um, you offered me a job?'

'I mean, here. In Leyholme. I thought you and your mum moved away when we were teenagers.'

He flushed slightly. 'We… did. My nan was still here though, till she died last year. Me and Mum moved back six months ago, into her old bungalow.'

Brooke snorted. 'Seriously, you still live with your mum?'

'Er, you live with your mum, Mrs Pot.'

'That's different. We're business partners.'

Hayden shook his head. 'How come you can be such a charmer with the customers and yet you're such a mean son of a bitch with your staff?'

'I only charm when I'm getting paid,' she said with a tight smile. 'So why do you live with your mum then?'

'Bad break-up.' He swiftly changed the subject. 'How about you? The number of lads you used to have running after you, I'd have thought you'd be married with fifteen bouncing babies by now.'

She shuddered. 'You must be joking. That was my sister's dream, not mine. Kids aren't for me.'

'You don't like them?'

'It's unfair to say I don't like them. I just... don't get them.'

'What don't you get about them?'

'Babies are all right. I never quite know how to talk to them once they're past the incomprehensible babbling stage. They put me on edge.' She shot him a sharp look. 'Why are you so interested?'

He shrugged. 'Just making small talk, since we're going to be stuck behind this bar together all night. Don't worry, I promise not to impregnate you when you're not looking.'

'What about you? Did you do the marriage and kids thing?'

'Who, me?' he said, trying not to flinch. 'No. No, I never got married.'

'How come?'

'I guess I haven't met the right person yet.'

34

Brooke smiled. 'It's tough dating with your mum at home, right?'

He laughed. 'You have that problem too?'

'It causes occasional complications.'

'Well, I do all right for myself, considering. No one serious, but I manage to avoid living a completely monastic life.'

They were interrupted by Hayden's mobile phone. He took it out and glanced at the screen.

'You should turn that off while you're at work, you know,' Brooke said.

'Yeah, sorry, I forgot to put it on silent. Look, let me just… I won't be a second.' He swiped to answer. 'What's up, sweetheart?'

'Daaaaad!' Cara wailed. 'I can't dooooo them!'

'Do what? Car, I'm working here.'

'The equations! Dad, they're properly evil. Nan says they didn't have them when she was at school and I don't get how they wooooork!'

'Look, I can't do anything about that now. We'll do it tomorrow, OK? Me and you.'

She sniffed. 'You promise?'

'I promise. We've got the whole weekend we can spend together.'

'Yeah, OK,' she said, appeased. 'Bye, Dad. Hope work's good.'

'Thanks, honey. See you later.'

He turned to find Brooke watching him with one eyebrow raised.

'Well,' she said. 'You really do do all right for yourself, don't you?'

He grimaced. 'Sorry about that.'

'Hayden, look, my mum was keen to take you on for this role,' Brooke said in a low voice. 'Against my better judgement, I promised her you could have a two-week trial to see how it works out. But if you can't get here on time and you can't keep your love life confined to leisure hours, maybe we should call it a day now, eh?'

'Don't be like that. I need this job, Brooke.' He sighed. 'I'm sorry. I thought it might be an emergency, but... well, it won't happen again.'

'And you won't be late again. Will you?'

'No, Miss.'

'Good. Because two-week trial or not, Hayden Bailey, three strikes and you're out.'

-

By the time Hayden was walking home later that night, he was aching all over. Between pulling pints and shifting barrels, he felt like he'd been trampled by a herd of obese elephants. Never again would he take bar staff for granted.

Automatically, his hand slid into his jacket pocket. He swore as it came out empty again. Hayden hadn't smoked since the twins were toddlers, but at times of stress he always found himself instinctively reaching for a cigarette.

Still, he'd enjoyed tonight, for all that it had been harder work than he'd expected. Brooke's prickliness had eased slightly as she'd relaxed around him, and he'd enjoyed reminiscing about schooldays and catching up on what old pals were up to. Brooke was forthright, fiery and no-nonsense in a way that, if he was being completely honest, he found a bit of a turn-on. She made him laugh. It had been nice to make a friend, if you could call Brooke that. Hayden's few mates were all over in Leeds, where he and his family had been living before they'd moved back to Leyholme six months ago, and it was tough to meet people your age socially when you were a young dad.

It was tough to meet women especially; the right kind of women. The ones who wouldn't mind his family set-up, and who'd be willing to get to know not only him but his girls too if the relationship progressed to that point. Women Hayden's age weren't usually interested in potentially having to play stepmum to a couple of eleven-year-olds. They were quite often interested in him, and there'd been a few fuck-buddies and casual flings over the years, but he could count the number of proper girlfriends he'd had on the fingers of… on two fingers.

Hayden wondered fleetingly if Carol-Ann, the girls' mum, was seeing anyone at the moment. What a different life she led from his! She seemed to have a new boyfriend every time he spoke to her. She was like a big kid herself, forever attaching herself to someone new because she felt she couldn't cope on her own. Hayden didn't hate her for walking out on him and the girls – a kid of eighteen who'd come through the care system, with no family for support – but he did feel a certain sadness that they hadn't been able to make things work. Cara and Darcie had no relationship with their mum at all now, and every day Hayden regretted her absence in their lives.

He wasn't sure what had possessed him to hide the fact he was a dad from Brooke tonight. He'd tried to convince himself he was just worried about his position – that if she knew he had family commitments, she'd have yet another reason to be wary of his ability to do the job. But that wasn't it. Brooke had said she wasn't keen on kids, and, well… Hayden had kind of instinctively wanted her to think well of him. To respect him; not to think he was the sort of pillock who'd got his girlfriend pregnant at eighteen and ended up a single dad of twins.

And… there was something else. Hayden loved being a dad. He was extraordinarily proud of his girls; they were his whole world. But tonight, for the first time since they'd been born, he'd regretted not being the sort of carefree bachelor that someone like Brooke Padgett would find attractive. Just for a moment he'd wanted her to see him that way, even though he knew it couldn't last.

Obviously he'd have to come clean eventually, but it would be nice to get to know Brooke a bit better first, without her regarding him with that wary look he'd seen countless times in the eyes of women when he'd mentioned he was a dad. It was a long time since he'd met someone he wanted to get to know better. And once Brooke did find out about the girls… well, he'd play that by ear.

–

When she'd sent Hayden home to his mum, Brooke locked all the doors and started collecting the empties.

She frowned as she dumped a load of glasses on the bar. There was a smartphone lying on the polished mahogany. Had a customer left it?

Brooke picked it up, instantly recognising the metallic case. This was Hayden's, wasn't it? He must've left it on the bar after he finished his shift.

She glanced at the screen. One missed call from the girl he'd been talking to earlier, Cara, and one from some woman called Darcie – he was certainly a busy boy. Brooke felt a stab of envy.

A social life: she remembered having one of those. She even, just barely, remembered what it was like to have a sex life. Hers had been pretty active, once. A couple of years ago she would've finished her shift and headed out with friends to a club, or on a hot date with some lad. But when her dad had died of a heart attack eighteen months ago, so had Brooke Padgett: Party Girl. The only place she ever wanted to be nowadays was behind the bar. It made her feel close to her dad, working in the pub.

A smile flickered as she caught her reflection in the polished wood, remembering how, when she was a kid, her dad used to sit her on the bar and she'd watch with fascination as he showed her the proper way to pull a pint. 'This'll be you one day, nibbler,' he'd tell her. It hadn't occurred to Brooke that he hadn't meant she'd be joining him behind the bar but taking his place.

She tucked Hayden's phone into her pocket, making a mental note to stick it in a padded envelope and drop it through his letterbox tomorrow. His nan's old place, he'd said. That was one of the bungalows on Chester Street, wasn't it? Not exactly a bachelor pad – especially with his mum living there – but if his call log was anything to go by, it obviously wasn't putting off his booty calls. Maybe her mum was right; maybe he would bring in more female customers. Not that Brooke approved of using staff as sexy, tight-trouser-wearing bait, but she had to face facts: they needed all the customers they could get.

Brooke was forced to confess that her mum hadn't been entirely wrong: it had been nice having someone else helping out. She felt almost relaxed after tonight's shift. Once Hayden had got the hang of pouring a proper pint he hadn't done badly, and he was so keen to learn that he'd served nearly every customer himself.

She was even half ready to admit she'd enjoyed the company. Friday nights were the nights people came in with their friends and loved ones; husbands and wives, parents, siblings. Watching them enjoy themselves had a nasty habit of making Brooke feel lonely.

When she'd finished clearing up, she flicked off the lights and headed upstairs.

God, had there really been a time she would've gone clubbing after working a shift? Now she could barely keep her eyes open. She must be getting old.

'Mum,' she said when she walked into their apartment, blinking at Janey pulling sheets and pillow cases out of the airing cupboard. 'What're you doing?'

Janey gestured to indicate Brooke should lower her voice.

'Something's come up,' she said quietly.

'Eh? What has?'

'You'd better go into the living room. Be gentle, love.'

Bewildered, Brooke opened the living room door. She was met by the sight of her six-year-old niece Livvy sobbing quietly on the pouffe. Ten-year-old Max was standing behind the armchair as if he didn't know what to do with himself, looking confused and frightened. And on the sofa was Rhianna with her hair all dishevelled, sitting behind two large suitcases.

Chapter Five

'Sorry to just turn up like this,' Rhianna muttered. The vacant expression in her eyes made it clear half her brain was somewhere else.

'Rhia, what the fuck?' Brooke glanced at the children and grimaced. 'Sorry, I didn't mean to – it was a shock, that's all. What're you doing here?'

'Daddy's a scum,' Max told her.

'Daddy is *not* a scum,' Livvy said, giving her brother's leg a weak push.

'He is. Mummy said so.'

'Children, please,' Rhianna said wearily. 'Livvy, you're right. I shouldn't have called Daddy names. That was wrong.'

'Then can we go home now?' Livvy asked.

'No... no, not tonight. Tonight we're going to stay with Grandma and Aunty Brooke.'

'It's just Brooke,' Brooke said automatically. 'Rhia, what's this all about?'

Rhianna cast a wary look at the children. Janey, who must have been eavesdropping, poked her head around the door.

'Now then, you two,' she said to the kids. 'Who wants to come help Nana make up some beds?'

Max glanced at his mum. 'Do we have to?'

'It's polite to help when we're asked, Maxie.' She summoned a smile. 'Besides, I need to have a grown-up talk with Aun— with Brooke.'

Max looked doubtful, but he nodded. 'OK. Liv, come on. I can help you make yours.'

'Mature for his age, isn't he?' Brooke said when the kids had left the room, as much for something to say as anything. She was defaulting to barmaid mode; the instinct which told her that when you're stuck for conversation, just say something flattering about someone's children or grandchildren and they'll soon be chattering away.

'Yes,' Rhianna said in a faraway voice. 'Max is the best reader in his year. His vocabulary's already... already... oh, Brooke.' She broke off into sobs.

Brooke sat by her sister on the sofa. 'Rhianna, what is it? Tell me what happened.'

'I had to get out,' she whispered. 'Did Mum tell you James has been working late?'

'She mentioned it. Is this connected with what you told me on the phone – the money problems?'

'Yes and no.' She took out her mobile and passed it to Brooke. 'What do you think of this?'

Brooke frowned. 'What am I supposed to think of it? It's an iPhone.'

'It's James's. I mean, it used to be. He passed it on to me when he upgraded.'

'OK. So?'

'Only, he forgot to uninstall his Fitbit app. He synched his watch with his new phone but it was still synching to mine too. Then last week I opened the app by mistake and...' She gave a hard laugh. 'It's all in there, Brooke. All his statistics. Every evening about six, when he's supposed to be working late, you should see the way his heart starts to race.'

'What, you mean...' Brooke's eyes widened. 'You're kidding!'

'Nope. On Monday, when he rang to say he was staying late at the office yet again, I left the kids with the au pair and drove to his work to see if my suspicions were justified. Of course they were, right? I found him trousers down with some girl from accounts.'

'Oh my God! The *shit*!' Brooke rubbed her sister's back. 'What did he say?'

'He gave me the usual lines: "It's not what it looks like, it was just one time," et cetera. But eventually he confessed everything. It's been going on for months.' She snorted. 'He tried to blame stress brought on by overwork. I didn't know one of the side effects of stress was forgetting who you're allowed to have sex with.'

'And so you told him you were leaving him.'

Rhianna smiled wryly. 'Oh, no, I told him I understood and we could go to couples' counselling to work it out.'

'What?'

Rhianna took out a starched handkerchief and blew her nose. 'I knew he'd do everything to talk me out of it if I announced I was leaving, and I didn't trust myself not to give in, like I always have done. So I... I pretended I'd try to put the affair behind us, but I never really intended to. I'm not a complete pushover, Brooke, despite what you think.'

'I never said that,' Brooke said. 'So that's why you wanted cash?'

She nodded. 'I won't get anything from James in a divorce except what he legally has to pay to support the children. The prenup he made me sign was iron-clad. A quarter of a million would've been enough for me, Max and Livvy to make a new start so we'd never have to be dependent on that bastard again.'

Brooke blinked. Her sister very rarely used bad language, not even during times of great stress. Even when Brooke had rung to tell her their dad was on end-of-life care in hospital, Rhianna hadn't been able to summon anything stronger than an 'oh my gosh!'.

'It's not like you to swear.'

Rhianna smiled bleakly. 'Sometimes there's no other word that'll do.'

'You're not wrong.' Brooke shook her head. 'God, what a *prick!* I can't believe he'd do that. I admit I found him hard work, but he seemed devoted to you and the kids.'

'Yes, well. Things aren't always what they seem.' Rhianna glanced at the door. 'Don't say anything to Max and Livvy, will you? About the girl from accounts, I mean. I suppose they'll have to be told some version of the story, but I don't want them to be completely alienated from their father, no matter how much of a sleaze he is.'

'Whatever you want, Rhia.' Brooke absorbed her sister into a rare hug, all differences momentarily forgotten. 'You stay here as long as you need, eh? Me and Mum'll do whatever we can for you.'

Rhianna smiled. 'Thanks, Brooke. It's good to be home.'

—

The next morning when Brooke ventured into the living room, Rhianna and the kids were already there. Livvy and

Max were sitting with their hands folded in their laps, as if not quite sure what to do with themselves, while Rhianna sat between them staring vacantly at the blank television screen.

Brooke took in the pale faces of the kids and experienced a surge of pity. Janey had put Livvy in with Rhianna in the spare room while Max had a room to himself in what was usually the office. Brooke, just the other side of a thin wall, had been able to hear the little boy's soft sobs all through the night. His eyes were red-raw this morning and framed by dark semicircles as he huddled close to his mum on the sofa. No child should have a face like that.

'Good morning.' Rhianna smiled weakly at her sister.

'Morning,' Brooke said, trying to fake a joviality she didn't feel. She nodded to the TV. 'You know, you can put that on if you want.'

'Oh, no, thank you. No TV in the mornings. Livvy and Max have got a strict limit on screen time.'

Brooke felt that if she were in Rhianna's situation, she'd bin the usual rules and do whatever she could to make the bereft children's lives momentarily brighter. But her sister was still in shock, clearly. Perhaps clinging to routine was the only thing keeping her sane right now.

'All right,' Brooke said. 'Have you guys had breakfast?'

'No, not yet.'

'It's French Day today, Mummy,' Livvy reminded her.

'Yes. It is, isn't it?' Rhianna glanced at Brooke. 'We do themed breakfasts at weekends. To teach the children about different cuisines around the world.'

Brooke blinked. 'Right. What, like, brie baguettes or something?'

'No, croissants will be fine,' Rhianna said, leaning wearily against the sofa.

'Croissants?'

'Or brioche. Whatever there is.'

'What there *is* is Shreddies or cereal bars.'

Rhianna curled her lip. 'Oh, no. Those boxed cereals are nothing but salt and e-numbers.'

'It's no unhealthier than croissants, is it? They're about ninety per cent butter.'

'We don't eat anything processed,' Rhianna said, a note of stubbornness creeping into her tone.

Brooke felt a twinge of annoyance, but, reminding herself that her sister was going through a difficult time, she pushed it down.

'What about toast?' she said. 'There's marge and raspberry jam to go on it, and a banana for one of your five a day. Sorry it's not French.'

Rhianna smiled gratefully. 'That'll be fine. Thanks, Brooke.'

'I'll put the toast on then. You want a coffee too?'

'Fresh?'

'Instant, sorry.'

'Oh. No thanks. I'll just have a chai tea or something.'

Brooke stared at her, and Rhianna ran flustered fingers through her unbrushed hair. 'Right. None of that either. In that case I won't bother. Thanks anyway.'

Brooke headed into the kitchen, wondering how a query about whether they'd had breakfast had somehow morphed into the understanding that she was going to make it for them.

She put a couple of slices in the toaster, trying to suppress the simmering annoyance that was always the outcome of any significant period in her sister's company.

God knew Brooke wanted to be a good, supportive sibling, and she was trying, really she was. She knew she just needed to grin and bear it for a while – after all, Rhianna probably wouldn't be here for long. It was just a stopgap until she found a place of her own – or until James wheedled her into going back to him. Brooke sincerely hoped that wouldn't happen, but she suspected her sister would be a soft touch in that respect. After a fortnight squashed into the little flat, without her au pair or her Nespresso coffee machine or her Paris-trained manicurist, Brooke could just see Rhianna running back into that cheating scumbag's arms.

The toast popped up and Brooke put it on a plate before shoving in another couple of slices.

French Day, honestly. Did Rhianna think everyone kept loaves of brioche lying about for themed breakfast mornings? Brooke slapped margarine roughly on the first slice of toast, causing it to break.

It hadn't always been this way. There had been a time when the sisters were close. When Brooke was small, she'd admired Rhianna like no one else in her little world. Her pretty, clever big sister, who played with her despite being older by two years, and stuck up for her when the other kids teased her about her pudding bowl haircut or her boyish ways or her littleness. Brooke remembered Rhianna actually pushing Hayden Bailey over in the play-ground when she heard about the frogspawn incident, shoving him face-first into a puddle and earning herself the first and only punishment of her well-behaved little life.

It was that awful school that had ruined her. The schol-arship to St Mary's had seemed like a blessing, at the time. Mum and Dad had been so proud of their clever daughter, and excited for what Rhianna's future might hold – a top university, a professional career. Brooke, on the other hand, had felt wary for reasons she hadn't fully understood at nine years old. She knew her sister was going to a special new school, one where she'd learn different, harder lessons, and sensed that the place was somehow destined to take Rhianna away from her. And she'd been right.

Just a month after her sister started at St Mary's, Brooke noticed the change. She was less interested suddenly in spending time with her little sister, or her old friends from Leyholme Primary. She had new friends: friends who invited her to their posh homes to play in their large gardens, but who Brooke never met because Rhianna never invited them back to The Highwayman's in return. Brooke had wondered why it always took her sister so long to get home from school, and one day when she went to investigate, she found out that Rhianna was getting off her school bus three stops early so her new friends wouldn't discover where she lived.

Then she started changing how she talked, and rolling her eyes at the broader Yorkshire accents of her parents and sister. She sulked because their mum and dad couldn't afford to buy her the things she now wanted – the things her new friends had. Gradually she stopped being the Rhianna Padgett her sister had known and became a stranger; one who belonged to a world Brooke could never be a part of. God, she'd spent so many nights as a child crying for what she'd lost – for that little girl she'd loved so much – that even as an adult she could never quite forgive Rhianna for being complicit in the death of her old self.

Ugh, she was getting mawkish now. Sisters were sisters, blood was thick, and Rhianna and the kids needed her. Brooke brushed away a silly little tear, arranged the toast and fruit on a tray and took it into the living room.

She handed Livvy a plate of jam-smeared toast and the little girl glanced enquiringly at her mum.

'Is it all right, Mummy?'

'Is what all right?' Brooke asked.

Rhianna smiled apologetically. 'We don't let them eat at home unless they're at the table.'

'Oh. Right. Well, sorry, Livvy, we don't have room for a dining table here,' Brooke said. 'You'll have to make do with your knees, I'm afraid.'

'Why is your house so small, Aunty Brooke?' Livvy asked as she tucked in.

'It's just Brooke. And it's small because there's only me and Nana living here usually.'

'Grandma,' Rhianna corrected her.

Brooke frowned. 'Mum prefers Nana.'

'I know, but it's so…'

'Common?' Brooke suggested, raising an eyebrow.

'I just don't like it.' Rhianna took a listless look at her toast. 'I don't think I can eat this.'

'Then why did you ask for it?'

'I didn't want to be rude after you offered.'

Except Brooke hadn't offered, had she? She'd been instructed, like a replacement for the au pair who presumably usually did this stuff for Rhianna. Mentally Brooke counted to ten, before she ended up saying something she'd regret.

'That's fine,' she said, forcing a smile. 'I'll have it. Where's Mum?'

'Down in the pub, cleaning.'

'Right. I just need to go ask her something. Help yourself to more toast if you want, kids.'

Brooke took Rhianna's unwanted plate of toast and went to seek out Janey. As she left, she heard Max ask his mum if he could phone a friend later.

'Of course, sweetheart.' Rhianna lowered her voice. 'But don't tell him where you're staying, will you?'

Yes, God forbid little Maxie's well-off prep school friends should find out he was staying in a vulgar Yorkshire pub. Brooke dug her fingernails into her palm.

She found Janey sucking on her vape behind the bar. Brooke sat down at a table, dropped her head onto her arms and groaned.

'She's driving me round the bend, Mum,' she said in a muffled voice. 'She's not been here twelve hours and I'm having to count to ten in my head so I won't throttle her.'

Janey put her vape down and went to rest a hand on Brooke's shoulder.

'I know it's hard, five of us in a little flat. But be patient, chick. Your sister's having a rough time.'

'I know she is.' Brooke lifted her head. 'And I'm trying, Mum, honestly, but she's such a snotty cow. It's like she's spent so long inhabiting that fake bloody Stepford suburbia, she's forgotten how to talk like a real person.'

'I'm well aware that a little of Rhianna goes a long way, hence why I'm down here getting my nicotine fix. Still, she needs us right now, Brooke.'

Brooke sighed. 'It's hard, that's all. You know, I just heard her tell Max not to let his friend know where they're staying. Still ashamed of us, even while she's happy to use this place to hide out.'

'She's probably worried Max's friend's parents will tell James she's here.'

'I'm pretty sure James can work that out on his own. She's obviously got nowhere else to go, or she wouldn't be back here.' Brooke took a piece of toast and nibbled on it half-heartedly. 'How long do you think she'll stay?'

'As long as she needs to, I suppose. Don't forget she owns a share in this place as well as us.'

'Huh. I can't exactly see her rolling up her sleeves and pulling a few pints, can you?'

'Perhaps not. Still, we need to be wearing our kid gloves with her, Brooke. I mean, after eleven years of marriage! Those poor kiddies too.'

Brooke thought back to Max's soft sobs all through the night: the muffled tears of a child desperate not to upset his mum any further. Poor little soul. How would she have coped at ten years old if, in the dead of night, her mum had pulled her away from her home for reasons she was too young to understand and thrust her on unsympathetic relatives?

It had been true, what she'd told Hayden. Brooke found it hard to be comfortable around children. She didn't dislike them exactly, but their unpredictability, their refusal to follow the rules of the adult world, freaked her out. She was always on the edge of her nerves around them; hyper-aware that she needed to act like the grown-up she didn't really feel she was, and terrified of saying or doing the wrong thing. Nevertheless, there was something about the way Max obviously wanted to protect his mum that hit her right in the heart.

'Well, you're right.' Brooke stood up and gave her mum a kiss. 'I'll try to do better. Thanks for the pep talk, Mum.'

Janey patted her arm. 'There's my girl. We all just need to try to keep our tempers, that's all.'

Chapter Six

Janey was folding towels in the bathroom when she became aware of heated voices coming from the living room.

'Why the hell were you in my room in the first place?' she heard Brooke demand.

'You think I wanted to be in that sty?' Rhianna shot back. 'It's worse than when you were a teenager. I don't know how an adult woman can live like that and keep her self-respect.'

'My self— you're such a cowbag, you know that? How is my room any of your business? How is my *life* any of your business? God, Rhianna!'

'I was looking for my children's missing clothes, if you must know,' Rhianna said. 'Every time I put things in the laundry, items go astray. I just know they've been bundled into your wardrobe unironed along with all your manky Primark crap.'

Brooke laughed. 'You *put* them in the laundry? For the magic laundry fairy to do, right? Speaking of living like an adult woman, Rhia, maybe you could do your own bloody washing instead of expecting me and Mum to do it for you.'

'Keep your voice down if you're going to swear,' Rhianna hissed. 'The children must be learning all sorts of choice language from you. And I dread to think how their table manners are suffering, eating off their laps in front of the television every evening.'

'Yeah, well it's my home and this is how things are in it. If you don't like it, feel free to sod off.'

Sighing, Janey left the towels and went to poke her head around the living room door.

Rhianna's lip was wobbling now. 'You would throw the fact I've got nowhere else to go in my face, wouldn't you?'

Brooke shook her head. 'Spare me the emotional blackmail, can you? You've been here two weeks, Rhia. You can't expect us to tiptoe around you forever and then play the pity card whenever you don't get your own way.'

'Oh, I'm sorry if after a whole fortnight I'm not quite over my husband of eleven years having an affair.'

OK. Enough was enough. Janey strode into the room and put her hands on her hips in best mum fashion.

'All right, what's going on in here?' she demanded. 'The children are in their bedrooms and they can hear every damn word you two are spitting at each other.'

Brooke pointed at her sister. 'She's been going through my stuff, Mum! I caught her ransacking my cupboard.'

'Because I needed to find all Livvy's clean underwear ready for her to start school tomorrow,' Rhianna said. 'If *she* checked her stinking laundry before she put it away instead of shoving it in the cupboard in a pile, I wouldn't have to go through it.'

'You wouldn't have to go through it if you did your own sodding washing, either.'

'Enough!' Janey marched between them. 'God almighty. I had enough of this shit the first time around.'

Rhianna threw herself down on the sofa. 'She started it.'

Brooke rolled her eyes. 'Jesus, Rhia, grow up, can you?'

'You can both grow up,' Janey said firmly. 'Like it or not, you two have to live together. What's more, there are two little people here who are frightened and disoriented and looking to the adults for comfort. And what do they see? Their mum and their aunt bickering like a pair of schoolgirls.'

Brooke took a deep breath and exhaled slowly. 'Sorry, Mum. She winds me up, that's all.'

'What we need here is a bit of mutual respect.' Janey turned to Rhianna. 'Rhia, you know we both love you, and this is your home as much as ours. But it's been over a fortnight, and it's time you stopped acting like a guest.'

Rhianna blinked. 'What?'

'You're the only adult here not earning her keep. From now on, you take your turn to cook the meals. You can do your own washing, and you can help out in the pub tonight.'

Janey couldn't tell whose face looked more horrified, Brooke's or Rhianna's.

'We can't have her in the pub!' Brooke spluttered. 'We're struggling enough for customers without her sour chops sneering at people over the pumps.'

'Max and Livvy are starting at the primary school tomorrow!' Rhianna protested. 'I'll be so humiliated if the other parents think I'm some barmaid.'

'Like me and Mum, you mean,' Brooke said.

'Yes, well, that's all right for you, isn't it? You don't have children. Besides, people expect you to be behind a bar.'

'Whereas they expect you to be the queen of bloody Spain, I suppose.'

'So it's come to this, has it?' Janey rolled up her sleeves. 'Jesus, I never thought I'd have to say this again. The pair of you, go to your rooms.'

'Me?' Brooke said. 'What did I do?'

'It doesn't matter what anyone did. You two need a time out: far, far away from each other. Go to your rooms, go for a walk, go to bloody Timbuctoo if you like, I'm past caring. Just get the hell away from each other. When you're ready to say sorry and behave like adults again, let me know.'

'Fine.' Brooke glared at Rhianna. 'She'll have to do the apologising, though. I'm going to walk to Morton and cool off.'

'Do I still have to go to my room?' Rhianna asked her mum when Brooke had marched out.

'You ought to be talking to your children,' Janey told her sternly. 'They're starting a new school tomorrow, they must be scared stiff. Well, are you ashamed of yourself?'

Rhianna sighed. 'I'm sorry, Mum. I don't know why it's so hard for us to get along. Brooke just makes me feel so… lesser, you know?'

'Lesser?'

'Like I'm nobody, just some snivelling little worm. It's an effect she always seems to have on me.'

Janey sat down next to her eldest daughter.

'You could try a bit harder with her though, Rhia,' she said in a gentler voice. 'She loves you, but you do make it difficult for her to like you sometimes.'

'She just seems to bring out the worst in me,' Rhianna murmured. 'Whenever we're together, I feel like we're back to being teenagers again.'

'Anything more from James?'

'Another barrage of texts this morning. He's still pressing me to go home and talk about it.'

'Did you speak to him?'

'Not yet. I can't face it. I texted and said the children had got emergency places at the local primary school, which he was pretty horrified by, and that we'd discuss access arrangements when everything was a bit more settled.' She pressed her eyes closed. 'They cry for him every day, Mum. I am doing the right thing, aren't I?'

'Absolutely,' Janey said firmly. 'A cheat once is a cheat forever. If you stayed with him for the children's sake, that'd damage Livvy and Max as well as you.'

'I really thought James was the one, you know?' Rhianna whispered. 'That we had something like you and Dad had. Mum, I feel such a fool.'

'He's the fool for throwing away the best thing that ever happened to him for the sake of some cheap nookie.'

'Thank you,' Rhianna said with a watery smile. 'And I'm sorry if I didn't always seem grateful for everything you and Dad did for me. I know you had to sacrifice a lot so I could take the place at St Mary's.'

'You were worth it, eh?' Janey said, giving her a jiggle.

Rhianna gave a wet laugh. 'I don't know about that.'

She rested her head on her mum's shoulder, and Janey kissed the top of her hair.

'Do you know why your dad left you a share of the pub, Rhianna?' she said softly.

'I've often wondered. The Highwayman's was always Brooke's thing, and it wasn't like I needed it. I suppose he didn't want me to feel he didn't care about me as much as her.'

Janey shook her head. 'He left it so you'd never be completely dependent on James. Your dad was always wary of him – ever since he made you sign that contract thing.'

'Lots of rich people have prenups before they get married, though.'

'Your dad believed marriage ought to be about partnership. Share and share alike.'

'I never knew that was why he left me a share,' Rhianna said in a dreamy voice. 'Good old Dad. Still, the pub's no help to me now, is it? I can't provide for the children with a building, and God knows it isn't earning much.'

'That'll change.'

Rhianna lifted her head to look at her mum. 'There was another letter this morning. From Nick Weyborough.'

'I saw. One million quid, final offer. It's a very generous figure.'

'I mean, in other circumstances I wouldn't even consider selling,' Rhianna said. 'But The Highwayman's seems to be haemorrhaging customers, to the extent it might end up closing in a few years if things don't improve. And here's Willowtree Taverns offering silly money for it, and me desperate for cash... the timing alone feels like fate.'

'Three hundred grand is pretty small fry to you, isn't it?'

Rhianna snorted. 'Yeah, when I was a millionaire's wife it was. Now I'm a broke, jobless slob, it's wealth beyond measure. More than enough to get me and the children set up in our own place.' She glanced up. 'It does feel foolish to turn it down, don't you think? Just imagine what Brooke could do with that kind of money – you too, Mum. You could retire and really start enjoying life. Travel the world, like you always wanted to.'

Janey sighed. 'That doesn't sound at all bad. I used to love being behind the bar when it was Eddie and me, but it's not the same without your dad. I spend most of my time in the kitchen nowadays anyway, never seeing anyone.'

'Would you sell? If it was up to you alone?'

'I'd rather not, but let's face it, this isn't the place it was two years ago. I'm starting to wonder if we can ever get back what we had.'

'What do you think Dad would want us to do?'

'I think he'd want us to remember that we're a family, and there's nothing more important than that. Not even The Highwayman's.' Janey gave her a last squeeze and stood up. 'But that doesn't mean you're getting out of working a shift tonight.'

Rhianna grimaced. 'Do I have to?'

'Yes you do. You ought to be earning your keep. Besides, it'll help you understand your sister better.'

'I have to take care of the children though.'

'I'll take care of the children. It's quiz night tonight, which means the kitchen closes early.' She held up a hand as Rhianna opened her mouth to protest. 'No, Rhia, it's no good trying to talk me out of it. Now go see if the kids need anything, eh? I'll be in my room, getting changed. I'm on cooking duty soon.'

–

When Janey was alone in her bedroom, she let out a long sigh.

It pained her to see her girls going for each other's jugulars, which they invariably did after more than ten minutes in one another's company. She knew they loved each other, but there just seemed to be this total clash of personalities. Rhianna only had to give the impression she looked down on Brooke's job or manners and Brooke would bristle like an angry cat. Rhianna, always fastidious and neat, couldn't bear her sister's slap-dash approach to life, and felt cowed by Brooke's confidence. Put them together in a small flat with two young kids and an old lady, and it was a recipe for frayed nerves. Tempers had been stretched to breaking point over the last fortnight.

God knew how they were going to cope over the coming months. While Brooke remained optimistic that her sister wouldn't be with them for long, Janey felt sure she'd be there for some time. Rhianna was flat broke, and her mum certainly wasn't going to let her go back to that cheating bastard for the sake of his house and money. That was how men like him got women in their power. Well, he wasn't having her daughter.

She opened her cupboard to pick something to wear for her shift. It didn't matter what, really, when she'd be stuck in the kitchen most of the day.

It had been a good idea of Brooke's, introducing a limited menu of pub grub, but Janey missed serving customers. Still, it was better to hand that over to the younger ones: Brooke and that lad Hayden. People liked to see a young, smiling face when they went for their drinks, and Janey's glory days as a draw behind the bar were long gone.

Rhianna's talk of early retirement had got her thinking about something that had been on her mind recently. There were certainly things Janey wanted to do in her life while she still could. Let's face it, she thought as she caught sight of her reflection in the mirror, she wasn't getting any younger.

She moved closer to the mirror and pinched her cheeks to bring some colour into them.

'Well, old man, what do you think?' she asked the photo of her husband on the chest of drawers. 'Am I ready for the knacker's yard?'

Eddie didn't answer. He just smiled at her from the frame. That was all right, though, because Janey knew what he'd say. 'Haven't aged a day, our lass.' He'd been the best sort of big fat liar.

She wasn't a complete wreck anyway. Her hair was still thick, and a deep, rich chestnut thanks to the skill of her hairdresser. The face underneath was lined, yes, but it was fine-featured and not entirely hideous. And after all, sixty-two wasn't *old* old – not these days. No one could take Eddie's place in her heart, naturally, but it would be nice to have a companion to spend the remainder of her life with. Someone to snuggle up to in the night. That was what Janey missed most of all: the feeling of a pair of loving arms around her.

Was it too late to start again? To find someone?

She wouldn't even know where to begin, these days. Her mobile phone was one of the old ones, with just a basic screen and push buttons. Janey had no idea how to operate one of these smartphones – when she saw the girls on theirs, how fast their fingers moved, it frightened her. Computers she could do the most basic things on, like type a letter, but they were generally a mystery. She had an email address she never used and a Facebook account she barely knew how to manage. Janey felt guilty, now, for the times she'd rolled her eyes at her own parents because they didn't know how to operate a pocket calculator or cassette player.

But that was how dating worked nowadays, wasn't it? You sent pictures of yourself to some website – in your birthday suit, probably – and ten minutes later, a handsome man would send you an email asking if you'd like to come over to his place for oysters and sex. Then he'd chop you up and bury you out in the woods. Janey had seen a lot of true-crime documentaries.

Did anyone still do it the old-fashioned way? Just hang out at a pub or nightclub and wait for someone they liked to ask for their phone number? At her age, probably not.

She narrowed her eyes at her reflection as she tried to see herself the way others might. She wasn't a complete hag, was she? What's more she was lonely, and bored, and, not to put too fine a point on it, frustrated. As complicated as modern dating was, Janey wasn't quite ready to write off any thought of romance just yet – or sex, for that matter.

Why shouldn't she have her share of fun as well as the young ones? If love, libido and laughter didn't halt at sixty, who said life had to? She was free, single and with plenty of years to enjoy yet – she hoped – and she knew it was what Eddie would want. Her husband had been seven years older than her, and well aware he might be the first to go. 'Don't wait too long, Janey,' he'd said to her once, a few years before the end. 'You always were too good to keep to myself.'

Yes, Janey decided as she cast a fond look at his photo. Eddie was right: it was time. Time to get out there and start looking for husband number two.

Chapter Seven

Brooke tried to rearrange her face from a scowl to some-thing a bit more pleasant as she strode through Leyholme's park. She could see four little dots on leads yanking a dark-haired woman in her direction: local dog-walker Deb Whiley and her charges. The way Brooke looked following her row with Rhianna, the dogs were likely to take one look at her and run whimpering in the other direction.

She summoned a smile as Deb reached her, bending to stroke Red, Deb's wife Stevie's mischievous spaniel.

'Afternoon. Nice day to be a dog-walker.' It was a warm mid-April day. The cherry blossoms were starting to open, and a carpet of bluebells had transformed the park.

'Nice day to get out into the fresh air,' Deb said, laughing. 'We've got a houseful at home. Stevie invited Xander and Nell with her dad and stepmum for Sunday dinner, plus we've got Freddie and his girlfriend over, and there's Milly and the baby. There was barely room for me, let alone the doggies. Families, right?'

'Huh. Tell me about it.' Brooke nodded goodbye and continued with her walk.

At least Deb got on with Stevie's family, even if they were a bit on the sprawling side. Brooke's cheeks, already pink with anger when she'd left the house, coloured even deeper with a feeling of shame. Another row, after all her promises to herself! How hard was it to just keep her temper?

This was the most time she'd spent in Rhianna's company since they'd been kids. Rhianna used to phone her family once a week on a Sunday, but the sisters' exchanges generally amounted to no more than a few words. The Garrett family's royal visits, as Brooke termed them, occurred no more than annually. Rhianna would roll up with the kids around Easter, rarely accompanied by her husband – James usually had some vague excuse about 'work' keeping him at home. Garretts and Padgetts would be packed into the flat for an uncomfortable weekend, then Rhianna would take the kids home with a look of relief on her face, knowing the ritual was over for another year. The next time they all saw each other, the children had invariably half-forgotten who their aunt and grandparents were.

And now Brooke, her sister and the niece and nephew she'd viewed as virtual strangers were seeing each other every day. Dad had been the peacemaker, always able to alleviate tension with a joke that would get them all laughing, but Dad wasn't here. How the hell were they going to stand it?

Brooke's attention was caught by the former Scout hut as she passed it. Poor old thing. The troop had moved their meetings to the mechanics' institute now, and the hut where Brooke had gone to Beavers, then to Cubs and Scouts, had fallen into disrepair. The door was hanging off, rotten and graffiti-covered, and a sign warned of 'DANGER – falling objects'.

Brooke wondered why no one did anything about it. There always used to be some proactive villager who'd start haranguing the parish council to tidy up eyesores or corralling volunteers to get it fixed up. Her dad, for a start. As a third-generation Leyholmer and a source of boundless energy and enthusiasm, he couldn't bear to be sitting still when he could be sorting something out.

That was the answer, wasn't it? That was why the Scout hut languished in its dismal state. It was why the pensioners' luncheon club had recently had to close, and why the community post office was struggling for volunteers. The old guard, the ones who'd got things done around here, was dying out. The Eddie Padgetts of the world were fewer, and the younger generation who occupied Leyholme now lived more isolated lives, never knowing their neighbours' names.

Brooke left the park and took a detour down Jubilee Street, glancing along the neat little sandstone houses with their well-pruned gardens. She remembered a time she could name every family who lived along here. Now… there were at least five households she didn't know, new young residents; commuters. They didn't come in the pub often, preferring, presumably, to do their wining and dining in the modern nightspots near where they worked. Leyholme was still a lovely place to live, but every year there were more people Brooke didn't know; pleasant enough but mostly keeping themselves to themselves. And every year, the pub lost a little bit of its role as the village's heart.

It'd make her dad sad to see how far business had dropped off. Brooke tried to imagine what he'd tell her, and smiled as his voice echoed in her head. 'No good crying about it, is it? Roll your sleeves up and get it sorted.' And he'd have a plan too. She wished she knew what it was.

When Brooke got back from her walk, there was a delivery driver hovering at the door of the pub.

'Can I help you?' she asked. 'I live here.'

He glanced at the device in his hand. 'You Mrs Garrett?'

'No, I'm Ms Padgett, but I can sign for a parcel if you want. She's my sister.'

'Right.' The man held out his scanner for her to sign, then went to the van and produced a huge flower arrangement of red and white roses in a silver vase. Brooke blinked at it.

'My condolences,' the man said as he plonked it at her feet.

Brooke shook her head. 'Good guess, but no. This is the guilty husband arrangement.'

'Ah. Yeah, that'll do it.' He nodded matily and got back into his van.

Brooke struggled up the fire escape with the flowers and put them down in the living room, where Livvy and Max were watching cartoons. Two pairs of big brown eyes turned to look at her as she came in.

'Wow!' Livvy breathed. 'Those are big flowers.'

'They're for your mum,' Brooke said.

'Who from?' Max asked.

'Just... a friend.' Brooke examined the bouquet for a card and pocketed it before the children were able to read it. 'Where is she anyway?'

'Nana asked her to go to the supermarket,' Max said. 'Nana's downstairs with the pub people so she says I'm in charge till Mummy gets back.'

'Oh. OK.' Brooke paused, feeling awkward at being left alone with them. 'So, um… are you both looking forward to school tomorrow?'

'I suppoooose so,' Livvy said in a glum little singsong voice. 'It won't be like at Ferndene though.'

'That was your old school?'

She nodded, not taking her eyes off the colourful figures on the TV. 'Mummy says the children there won't be like my Ferndene friends. She says there'll be boys as well as girls, and they'll talk differently to me.'

'Did she indeed?' Brooke muttered.

Livvy nodded again. 'Like you and Nana. I don't mind though. I think you sound funny.' She turned to look at her aunt. 'Can you give us something to do, Brooke? We're super bored.'

'You shouldn't say that, Liv,' Max said. 'Nana says the b-word's a swear.'

Brooke laughed. 'Yeah, she used to say that to me and your mum too. She doesn't mean it's a proper swear. She means there's no excuse for complaining about being bored when there's so much fun stuff you could do.'

'What fun stuff?' Livvy asked.

Brooke shrugged. 'Read a book. Play a game. Do a jigsaw.'

Livvy perked up. 'Ooh, I like jigsaws! I'm good at jigsaws, aren't I, Maxie?'

'You're all right. For a little kid,' Max conceded graciously.

'Mummy says a kid's a baby goat.'

'Yeah, well you look like a baby goat.'

'You do!' Livvy yelled delightedly. 'A really super ugly one.'

'At least I don't *smell* like one,' Max said, wafting a hand in front of his nose as if his sister's goaty pong was stinking out the room.

Brooke smiled. They'd been so quiet and gloomy since they arrived, it was refreshing to hear them teasing each other.

'I know where there's some jigsaws,' she said. 'They might be a bit hard though, Livvy. They're for bigger ki— er, baby goats than you.'

The little girl puffed herself up. 'That's all right, I like hard ones. I can even do grown-up ones like Avril does.' Avril, Brooke had learned, was the children's much-missed twenty-year-old Belgian au pair.

'OK, hang on.' Brooke went into the hall and hunted in a cupboard until she found a box containing old board games, jigsaws and other toys. She dragged it into the living room.

'There you go,' she said to the children. 'You can play with anything you want in there.'

Livvy dived for the box and started rooting through.

'Are all these things yours?' she asked, turning big eyes up to Brooke.

'They were mine and your mum's when we were little.'

Silence fell as Livvy explored the box. Brooke stood over her, wondering what to say next.

'Um… have you eaten tea yet?' she asked. 'I could probably cook you something.'

'You mean dinner,' Max told her. 'Tea's what you drink.'

Brooke didn't feel nearly as irritated by Max correcting how she spoke as when Rhianna did it. Perhaps it was because he did it with such a comical expression on his face. Still, someone really ought to have a word with him about manners. He wasn't going to make friends easily if he behaved that way with the other kids at Leyholme Primary.

'Here, dinner is what we have in the middle of the day,' Brooke told him. 'Tea's what we call the evening meal.'

'Then if tea's what you eat, what do you call the stuff you drink?'

'We call that tea too. They're both called tea.'

Max cocked his head. 'Then if someone says "please may I have some tea?", how do you know whether they're hungry or thirsty?'

Brooke laughed. 'I suppose we just work it out.'

'But if you called it dinner, you wouldn't have to work it out.'

'True. But if we renamed the drink tea as "steamy brown stuff", we wouldn't have to work it out then either. We could just say "hey, you want a cup of steamy brown stuff?"'

Max giggled. 'And if they said yes, you could give them gravy and they'd have to drink it.'

Brooke nodded. 'I like your thinking, Max.'

Max rearranged his face into its usual serious expression. 'Yes please then, Aunty Brooke. I'd like some food tea.'

'It's just Brooke,' she said. 'Fish finger sandwiches OK?'

He hesitated. 'We don't normally eat those. I don't know if they're allowed.'

'Well, it's all I've got time for, I'm afraid. Our barmaid's going to finish her shift soon so I need to get ready for work.'

'I suppose it's OK,' he said cautiously.

'Right.' Brooke glanced at Livvy tipping a box of jigsaw pieces onto the carpet. 'You help your sister with her jigsaw and it'll be ready in about quarter of an hour.'

But she'd no sooner closed the door to the kitchen when it opened again and Max appeared with an eager expression on his small, pale face.

'I don't want to do jigsaws,' he said. 'I want to help you please.'

'I don't really need any help, Max,' Brooke said, crouching to take a packet of Captain Birdseye's finest out of the freezer.

'Mummy says we should help if we're guests.'

Brooke couldn't help thinking Mummy could do with spending a bit less time preaching and a bit more time practising, but she held her tongue.

'Aren't you a bit big for saying Mummy and Daddy?' Brooke asked as she took a loaf from the breadbin.

The boy looked puzzled. 'Why?'

'When kids get to your age, they usually…' She caught sight of his serious little face and trailed off. 'It doesn't matter. Yes, you can help me if you like.'

She took out the margarine and set Max to work buttering pieces of bread.

'What's that?' Max asked, pointing to one of her tattoos.

'This?' She held her arm out for him to look at it. 'It's a flower. A rose.'

'Does it come off?'

'No, it's there forever.'

'Why did you want it to be there forever?'

Brooke looked at the rose on its thorny briar, depicted in black ink. 'Well, because I think it's beautiful, and I like to have beautiful things on my body. And I suppose it reminds me of something too. All my tattoos remind me of something.'

'What does it remind you of?'

She traced the picture with the tip of one finger, following the briars to the rose interwoven with them. 'I think it reminds me that things which are beautiful can hurt you,' she said quietly. 'Like life, I suppose.'

Max blinked. 'Life?'

Brooke shook her head, smiling. 'Oh, ignore me, I'm talking daft. Let's get this tea on, eh?'

Max's gaze was still transfixed by the rose tattoo. 'If I had a picture of a rose on me, I'd want it to be red with green leaves, not boring black.'

'I like it black,' Brooke said absently as she put the fish fingers under the grill.

'Could I have a red one?'

'You could have any colours you like.' She glanced at him. 'You'd have to be eighteen though, Max, and I doubt your mum would be too impressed. I wouldn't mention it to her if I were you, she'll go apeshi— er, she'll go ape.'

'What does that mean, go ape?'

'Well, it means to be very angry. Like a big angry ape.'

See, this was what unnerved her about children. It was so easy to get things wrong around them. Brooke wondered if there was such a thing as an anti-Brownie point, and how many she'd earned during this conversation with her nephew.

'What were you and my mummy shouting at each other for?' Max asked while he smeared margarine over a slice of bread. 'Were you going ape then?'

'You always ask this many questions?'

He blinked. 'Is asking questions bad?'

'No, it's not bad,' Brooke said. 'We weren't going ape. We were just... having a discussion.'

'If you weren't going ape, why could I hear you from my bedroom?'

'It was... a bit of a loud discussion.'

'Why?'

'Well, do you ever argue with your sister?'

Max nodded. 'Yeah, loads. Avril says brothers and sisters are supposed to love each other. I think we do love each other, but Livvy's still a pain.'

Brooke laughed. 'I think you just answered your own question, Max.'

'Is my mummy a pain?' he asked, looking up at her.

Brooke was silent, focusing on checking the fish fingers.

'I think we might both be a pain to each other, sometimes,' she said at last. 'That's just what it's like to have brothers and sisters.'

'Even when you're grown up?'

'Especially when you're grown up.'

'You still love each other though, don't you?'

'I guess we do.' Brooke heard the front door being unlocked. 'Things can just be a bit complicated when you're adults.'

'Like with Mummy and Daddy? She says that's complicated.'

'That's... a different sort of complicated.' Brooke forced a smile as her sister came in with the shopping. 'Hi, Rhia.'

'Hi.'

There was silence for a moment as they looked at each other.

'Look, about earlier—' Brooke began.

71

Rhianna dumped the shopping on the worktop and waved a hand. 'Oh, don't say anything. We were both crazy. Cabin fever.'

'Now you have to say sorry for being a pain,' Max told his mum. 'And Brooke has to say sorry for being a pain too.'

Rhianna smiled. 'Is that right?'

He nodded. 'And shake hands, like you make me and Livvy do after a fight.'

Brooke laughed. She held out her hand and Rhianna, laughing too, gave it a firm shake.

'I'm sorry. I should have asked before hunting for the children's things in your room,' Rhianna said.

'And I had no cause to fly off the handle about it.'

'Well, let's say no more about it.' Rhianna nodded towards the living room. 'Did you buy the flowers? I could barely squeeze into the room.'

'Oh. No. A delivery man brought them.' Brooke handed her the card from her pocket. *From James*, she mouthed.

Rhianna's expression hardened as she read the card. She crumpled it and threw it in the bin.

'He's got some nerve,' she muttered. 'He's been haranguing me ever since he found out the children were taking up school places here. Does he really think he can win me back with Interflora, after what he—' She caught sight of Max's brown eyes blinking at her and stopped short.

'Who's got nerves, Mummy?' he asked.

'No one, sweetie.' She forced a smile and nodded to the grill. 'So, what's cooking?'

'Max and me were just making a batch of fish finger sandwiches,' Brooke said, smiling down at her little assistant.

Rhianna's eye twitched. 'Fish fingers?'

Max nodded. 'For tea.'

'Dinner, sweetie,' Rhianna corrected him, drawing him to her.

'No, Mummy, that's wrong,' he told her in a tone glowing with newfound knowledge. 'That was only for where we lived before. Here they have food tea and drink tea, and this is food tea.'

'It's all right, isn't it?' Brooke said, meeting her sister's eye. 'They said they were hungry and I didn't have time to make anything else.'

'Of course,' Rhianna said with a strained smile. 'We wouldn't normally... but that's fine. If it's all there was time for.' She nodded to one of the bags. 'But, um, I did buy the ingredients for avocado egg salad. You know, if it happens again. Avril always said that took no time to make.'

Brooke willed her smile to stay in place.

'Right,' she said. 'Thanks, I'll remember that. No idea how to make it, but I'm sure it can't be too hard.'

'I could make some up now quickly.' Rhianna looked at Max. 'Wouldn't you rather have that, Maxie?'

He shook his head. 'I want fish finger sandwiches. I helped make them, Mummy. I did the really hard bit.'

'Plus I'd rather they didn't go in the bin after I've cooked them,' Brooke said, trying to keep any suggestion of reproach out of her voice.

'I suppose so,' Rhianna said. 'All right, Max. Just this once.'

'You'd better get changed for your shift, Rhia,' Brooke said.

Rhianna glanced at her clothes. 'Why, what's wrong with these?'

Brooke nodded to Max. 'All right, kid, good job buttering. Go help your sister with her jigsaw now, eh? I'll bring your food in in a minute.'

When Max had run off, Brooke turned her attention back to Rhianna.

'We normally smarten up for working behind the bar.'

'Dress up just to spill beer all over myself?' Rhianna said, curling her lip. 'Whatever for?'

'The customers like to see a bit of glam in the staff. We need to keep them happy if we want to keep them coming back.'

'Our job's to serve them drinks, not turn them on.'

'It's just the way things are, Rhia,' Brooke said, digging her fingernails into her palms.

'Well it shouldn't be. I'll pull pints if I must, but I'm not dolling myself up like a Hooters girl to do it.'

'Fine,' Brooke muttered, her jaw clenching. 'Fine. Go as you are then. Whatever you like.'

Chapter Eight

'What time does Brooke start work?' Hayden asked Janey as they watched the teams start to arrive for the weekly quiz. In the fortnight he'd been working at The Highwayman's, he'd learnt that other than Fridays and Saturdays, the Sunday quiz night was the busiest of the week.

Still, the old place wasn't like he remembered it when he'd lived in the village growing up. It looked the same – he doubted even the wallpaper had changed – but the atmosphere felt different, somehow. Perhaps it was because he'd only ever visited for family events, but he was sure it used to be packed out. Now, even the busy nights were barely full enough to need two of them on the bar. He could see why Brooke had been wary about taking on more staff.

Janey had let Fiona go half an hour early, and had already been behind the bar when Hayden arrived. She seemed to prefer pulling pints to working in the kitchen, and often found an excuse to sneak out. Like Brooke, she had that natural rapport with people. It was a shame the pub couldn't hire a chef so she could be freed from cooking duty to do what she did best.

'She'll be down any minute.' Janey lifted an eyebrow. 'Why do you ask?'

He shrugged. 'Just wondering. Not that you're not scintillating company yourself, Mrs P.'

'But I can't compete with Brooke's charms. That's fair enough,' she said, laughing. 'You know what today is, Hayden?'

He smiled. 'The last day of my trial period. Have I made it, do you think?'

'I'll certainly be voting for you,' Janey said, patting him on the back. 'I should warn you though, you'll have double trouble tonight. I've recruited Rhianna to work a shift.'

'Rhianna? I thought she didn't have much to do with the business side of things.'

'That's why I'm making her do it.' Janey nodded to Martin Brady as he came in with his team, and he winked at her. 'Help cure that princess complex of hers.'

'Huh. There was nothing princess-like about the way she shoved me into a puddle for putting frogspawn in Brooke's pumps. Why do you say that, then?'

'You'll see for yourself,' Janey said. 'I've always been proud of what Rhia achieved at St Mary's, but it hasn't half made her an uppity little madam. I can see you having a tough shift with her and Brooke bickering all night.'

Hayden frowned. 'What, St Mary's for girls, the independent school? Was that where Rhianna went after Leyholme Primary?'

'Yes, she was a scholarship girl.' Janey inflated slightly, the way parents do when they talk about their children's achievements. 'She's a clever cookie, our Rhianna. Aced her exams, got a place at Cambridge to study law. God knows where she got the brainy gene.'

'What, she's a lawyer?'

'No.' Janey turned to wipe under the spirit optics. 'She always talked about qualifying as a barrister but she met her husband right after graduating and... well, that was that. She was married at twenty-one. He had enough money that she didn't need to work, so Rhianna dedicated herself to the house and kids instead. Nothing wrong with that, if it's what she wants.'

'Still, it seems a shame she never got any use out of her degree.'

'Three weeks ago, I'd have said all that mattered was that she was happy in life. Now we know what we know about her hubby, I'm tempted to agree with you.'

'You know, my— um, a mate of mine has a daughter at St Mary's,' Hayden said. 'She's a scholarship kid too.'

'Clever little thing, is she?'

'Like you wouldn't believe.'

'How many children does he have?'

'Two. Twin girls. The other's at Ravenswood.'

'Hmm. I'd advise him to keep an eye on them. The biggest tragedy that came from Rhianna's scholarship was what it did to her relationship with her sister.' Janey fixed on a warm smile as Martin Brady stepped up to the bar. 'Now then, love. The usual, is it?'

'Evening, beautiful,' Martin said. 'Yes please, pint of Boltmaker. Nice to see you back where you belong instead of shut up in that kitchen.'

'Well, I have to keep growing lads like you fed as well as watered, don't I?' Janey said with an arch look at his beer belly. She nodded to the door, where more people were entering. 'Family group, Hayden. Can you tell them they're fine for a bit, but it's no children after seven?'

Hayden's eyes widened. 'Shit!'

Janey cast him a surprised look. 'What's up, lad?'

'Nothing.' He grimaced. 'Nothing. Just realised, um…
I forgot to pay the milk bill. Yes, that's fine; I'll go let them
know.'

He approached his mum and the girls, who were
claiming themselves a table.

'Hi Dad!' Cara said. 'We asked Nan if we could come
see where you work. Isn't it cool?'

'Very cool,' he said. 'But we're not really supposed to
have kids in, sweetheart.'

Pam blinked. 'Aren't you? It said on the website
families were welcome until seven.'

He glanced at the bar. Brooke had appeared and Janey
was preparing to hand over to her.

'Er, yes,' he said. 'Well, they are most days, but, um, it's
quiz night.'

Darcie looked interested. 'Quizzes? I'm good at
quizzes. Can I do the quiz, Dad?'

'This is a grown-up quiz, Darce. Sorry.'

She looked put out. 'I bet I could still do it. I get loads
of answers when we watch quizzes on TV, don't I, Nan?
I could totally win.'

'I could win if it's about animals,' Cara said. 'I know
everything about animals. More than Darce.'

'Do not!'

'Do so.'

'Girls, please,' Pam said. 'We've just come to say hello
to Dad, that's all. We can do our own quiz at home.'

'But then there'll be nobody to beat,' Darcie muttered.

'Quizzes aren't about winning. They're about…
learning.'

One of the quiz hounds at a neighbouring table
snorted. 'Not at this pub, love.'

'Can I have a word, Mum?' Hayden said from behind a fixed grin.

'All right.'

Hayden took her elbow and guided her out of earshot of the girls.

'Mum, you can't bring them here!' he hissed.

Pam frowned. 'Why not? I thought you'd be dying to show your lovely daughters off to the people you work with.'

'It's the last day of my trial period. I can't have family dropping in.'

'They missed you, Hayden,' she said quietly. 'They're not used to seeing so little of you.'

Hayden sighed. 'I know, I feel awful not being around in the evenings. It won't be forever. Just for a little while so the bank account's shored up against any more unexpected expenses.'

'Can't we just stay for a little bit?'

'It's really not a good time, Mum.' He nodded to Brooke, who was glaring at him while she pulled a pint. 'That's my boss. You see that face she's got on? That's the special face she saves just for me. It means "stop slacking and get back to work, Bailey".'

'Well, go back to work then. I'm sure she won't mind us stopping in to have a drink. We're paying customers.'

'You don't understand.' He grimaced. 'I kind of… fibbed to her a bit. About having kids.'

'Eh? What for? Normally you can't shut up about them.'

'Because I wanted to impress her, didn't I? I needed the job, she told me she hates kids, so… I conveniently forgot to mention I had a couple.'

'Hates kids, does she?' Pam looked at Brooke chatting to the customer she was serving. 'You were at school with her, weren't you? The tomboy with the David Hockney haircut. I can't believe she doesn't like kids. She looks so sweet.'

'She is. Sometimes. And sometimes she's an absolute bastard,' Hayden said. 'Brooke already thinks I'm an idiot; I wasn't mad about her thinking I was also the sort of idiot who'd managed to get his girlfriend pregnant at eighteen.'

Pam narrowed one eye at him. 'Aaaah. I see.'

'What do you see?'

'You're keen on her, aren't you?'

'Keen on her not sacking me? Bloody right I am. I need to hang on to this job, Mum.'

'Come on, Hayden, I wasn't born yesterday. You like the girl.'

'That's... neither here nor there,' Hayden said, flushing. 'The girl doesn't like me – not like that, anyway. I just want to keep my home and work lives separate.'

Pam winked. 'All right, sunshine. Whatever you say.'

'Seriously, Mum. Enough with the winking.'

'Fine, fine.' She nudged him in the ribs. 'Your secret's safe with me, our Hayden.'

'Look, stop, can you? I told you, Brooke hates kids. Whereas I've got a couple of eleven-year-olds that, as you know, I'm pretty attached to. Even if I did like her, that's a pretty big stumbling block to anything serious happening between us, wouldn't you say?'

'Mmhmm. That's your story and you're sticking to it, eh?' Pam looked back at the twins, who were playing some sort of clapping game. 'OK, if it's what you want I'll take them back home. They'll be happy they've seen inside the place.'

He exhaled with relief. 'Right, great.'

'I promised them a Fruit Shoot each though. And a bag of crisps.'

'All right, all right. Just a sec.'

He darted to the bar and grabbed a couple of blackcurrant Fruit Shoots and two bags of cheese and onion crisps while Brooke watched him curiously.

'Sorry,' he said. 'I'll pay for these. Back in a sec.'

He dashed back and bundled the drinks and crisps into his mum's arms. 'There.'

He was about to kiss the girls goodbye when he noticed Brooke watching him.

'See you, girls. See you, Mum,' he said, keeping his distance while he waved them off. 'Have a good night.'

He headed back behind the bar, breathing a sigh of relief as he watched his family leave.

'OK, Bailey, what was that all about?' Brooke asked.

'Er, customer who didn't know the rule about no families. I was just filling her in.'

'Families are fine till seven, you didn't need to hurry them out. That was your mum, wasn't it?'

'Yeah.' He laughed nervously. 'But, you know, can't have any nepotism in the ranks. Rules are rules, right?'

Brooke blinked. 'OK. Whose are the kids, then?'

'No one's.'

'What, so your mum just kidnapped them from the nearest orphanage for an evening at the pub?'

'Well, obviously they're someone's. Just not right now.' He grimaced. 'Er, what I mean is, she's babysitting them for a mate.'

'Someone in the village?'

'No, no one you know. They live miles away. Miles and miles and miles.'

'Why're you being strange?'

'I'm just a bit wired. Overdosed on coffee.' He forced himself to relax, letting the hands that had tightened into fists unclench along with his buttocks. 'Sorry, Brooke.'

She smiled. 'Well, for the first time I'm glad I'll have you here tonight. Did my mum tell you we'll have the Sloane Ranger sharing our shift?'

'Your sister, you mean? Yeah, she mentioned it. As long as she's got no plans to shove me face-first into a puddle again.'

'You had that coming, to be fair,' Brooke said, laughing. 'Who was it dared you to put frogspawn in my pumps in the first place? They deserved a dunking just as much as you.'

'Oh. No one.'

'Eh? When I grassed you up, you told Mrs Rhodes another boy put you up to it.'

'Yeah, that was a fib. It was all my own work.'

'So why did you do it?'

Hayden shrugged. 'Because you were sort of cool, I guess.'

She snorted. 'Come on. You're not going to tell me you were mean to me because you secretly liked me; that old chestnut?'

'No,' he said, smiling. 'I didn't know girls were something to like in that way at eight. If you really want to know, I was jealous of you.'

'Jealous? Why?'

'Well, you were so good at everything.'

She shook her head. 'Are you confusing me with my sister? I wasn't good at anything. The only talent I've ever had is pouring a good pint, and it was another ten years until I discovered that.'

'You were good at all the things I thought counted at eight years old,' Hayden told her. 'You could kick my arse at everything. Climbing, footie, tig, conkers. I thought you were awesome, and consequently was jealous as hell of you. I think I kind of wanted to be you.'

For the first time since he'd met her again, Brooke seemed to be speechless.

'You know, Hayden,' she said after a minute, 'that's the single sweetest, creepiest thing a lad's ever said to me.'

'It did come out a bit more Buffalo Bill than I was aiming for.' He met her eye. 'So your sister working in the pub – is that going to be a regular thing?'

'Huh. Not if I have anything to do with it. Pub brawls aren't supposed to happen this side of the bar.'

'Only, if it is then I guess you won't need me any more, will you?'

'What, swap you for Rhianna? I think that's just about my worst nightmare.'

He smiled. 'Brooke Padgett, you're making me blush.'

'If you saw me and Rhianna together, you'd be a bit less flattered.' She nodded towards Rhianna coming down the stairs. 'Speaking of the Queen Mum, here she comes. Now we just need to try and not murder her for the next couple of hours.'

Chapter Nine

Rhianna had reconsidered changing her clothes before working behind the bar, but she'd dressed down, not up. She was now in the grey sweatpants and hoodie she wore to go jogging. Her hair was scraped back into a tight ponytail, and she'd scrubbed her face free of make-up. If Brooke and her mum would force her to go slumming behind the bar, then slum it she would. Her current plan was to make such a bad job of the business, they'd never ask her again. She only hoped no parents of the other children who'd be in Max or Livvy's class at Leyholme Primary School would come in for a drink tonight.

'Hiya,' the young man behind the bar greeted her. He smiled in a friendly way, as if they knew each other.

He was sort of boyish-looking and well-built, like a builder or something. Perhaps he was a builder. Rhianna supposed he must have a daytime job as well, unless he was on benefits. Anyway, whatever he did for a living, his fingernails were filthy.

'Um, hello,' she said cautiously. 'Where's Brooke?'

'Over there, setting up for the quiz.' He nodded to her sister, who was wrestling with a microphone stand, then grinned at Rhianna. 'You don't remember me, do you?'

She blinked. 'Ought I to?'

'You certainly ought,' he said, mimicking her RP accent. 'You once shoved me into a muddy puddle.'

'Me? I wouldn't.'

'You did, you know,' Brooke said as she joined them. 'It's Hayden Bailey, Rhia. Remember? He was in my class at Leyholme Primary.'

'I… yes. Yes, I remember,' Rhianna said slowly. 'He put frogspawn in your shoes.'

'In my pumps, actually. A fact I didn't discover until I stuck my feet in them getting changed for PE.' Brooke examined her sister's sweatpants and hoodie. 'Speaking of PE, what're you wearing that gear for?'

'I didn't want to get beer all over my designer things, did I?' Rhianna said, shrugging. 'They're dry clean only.'

'You can't work the bar dressed like that. Go get changed.'

Rhianna frowned. 'Look, Brooke, I'm here to help, but that hardly gives you the right to boss me around. I own a share of this place too, remember?'

'*Me* remember? I'm the one who's here every day. We hadn't seen you and the kids for six months when you turned up two weeks ago.'

'Perhaps I didn't want my children here socialising with all the village drunks, ruining their health with junk food and turning the air blue with the language they pick up in this place,' Rhianna snapped, the always uneasy truce between the sisters disintegrating again as tempers flared. 'You know what Max just told me? That he wants to get a tattoo! "A rose like Brooke's," he said. What the heck have you been saying to him?'

'Nothing controversial. He asked what my rose meant and I told him.'

'You should cover those up around the children. Ten years old, and my son's talking about mutilating himself for life thanks to you.' Rhianna curled her lip at the black tattoos that decorated her sister's arms. 'I don't know why you do that to yourself. Don't you ever consider how they'll look when you're eighty? What people will think of you?'

'Yeah, they'll think I'm a seriously badass old lady who's had a hell of a fun time living. Which beats getting patronised and helped across the road by Scouts, if you ask me.'

'Tattoos are awful. Especially on women.'

'Is that you talking or James, Rhianna? Or is it basically the same thing now?'

'I'm quite capable of thinking for myself, thank you.' Rhianna cast another scornful glance at Brooke's arms. 'They make you look rough.'

'Maybe I am rough,' Brooke snapped. 'Certainly by your standards, Mrs Bucket. And what about what you're teaching your own kids? Why do you let Max correct people without telling him it's bad manners?'

'It's not poor manners to inform people about correct speech. Should I teach him to just accept bad habits without challenging them?'

'There is no "correct" speech, Rhianna. There's just different speech.' Brooke sounded suddenly weary. 'And I can tell you now, if Max starts giving the other children at school lectures on how to talk properly, he's going to have a tough time of it. Not to mention the "Mummy" thing. It might be all the rage at his old school, but here it'll just make him sound babyish and coddled. The other kids'll take the piss something chronic.'

'Why should Max have to change how he speaks for other people's benefit? He fitted in perfectly at Abbotleigh.'

'Yeah, well, this is the real world. He's not going to prep school now.'

'Don't I know it,' Rhianna muttered. 'You don't think he'll get bullied, do you?'

'I hope not, but you know how kids are. If you want him to make friends at Leyholme, you ought to talk to him about accepting other people's differences so they'll be happy to accept his. People shouldn't have to change how they speak for Max's benefit either.'

'Are you saying I'm a bad mother?'

'I'm saying you ought to prepare your son for what's coming so he won't be miserable at his new school. I'm saying that basic good manners will get him a long way.'

'Jesus, Mrs P was right,' Hayden said. 'Are you two going to bicker like this all night?'

Brooke turned to glare at him. 'Like what?'

'Like five-year-olds. God, if my— if I had daughters who behaved like you two, I'd lock them in a room together until they'd learnt to be civil.' He lowered his voice. 'Look, here's a customer. For Christ's sake, some-body serve him so this conversation can end.'

'All right, Rhia, watch me and see what you can learn,' Brooke said, stepping forward to smile at the man.

Rhianna tried not to curl her lip as she watched her sister pour a pint, chatting easily to the customer as she did so.

'Why are you always like that with men?' she asked when he'd taken his drink back to his table.

Brooke frowned. 'Like what with men?'

Hayden rolled his eyes. 'Here we go.'

'Simpering and flirting like that,' Rhianna said. 'So desperate for his approval. It sets feminism back decades.'

Brooke laughed. 'You're lecturing *me* on feminism? You're like one of these bloody tradwives. When have you ever done a day's work in your life?'

'That man must've been seventy, and you're sticking your chest out and giggling like a schoolgirl. You might as well strip to your underwear and ask him to pay for his drink by tucking the money into your knickers.'

'Whereas his friends'll be rushing to check this place out when he tells them about the mardy-arsed scruffbag glaring at him over the Budweiser pump.'

'God almighty,' Hayden muttered. 'I should've phoned in sick.'

'At least I don't need to cheapen myself to earn a living,' Rhianna said.

'Because you've never had to earn a bloody living,' Brooke shot back. 'And for your information, that was not flirting, it was old-fashioned friendliness. You should give it a go sometime, love.'

'Why do you always pretend to be something you're not, Brooke? Why can't you just be yourself?'

'*Why can't you just be yourself?*' Brooke mimicked. 'What the hell happened to your accent then, while we're on the subject of faking it?'

'Look, let's just get this over with,' Rhianna muttered through clenched teeth. 'Show me what I have to do.'

'Right.' Brooke nodded to a man approaching them. 'Here's a customer. Rhia, you take this one.'

Rhianna's eyes widened, and she dropped to her haunches behind the bar.

'All right,' Hayden said, blinking as he looked down at her. 'This is new. What're you doing down there, Rhianna?'

'Brooke, that's the headteacher of the school!' she hissed to her sister. 'I had a meeting with him about the children starting there.'

'I know, it's Xander,' Brooke said. 'What about it?'

'I can't let him see me! Cover for me, please.'

'Eh? Why?'

'Because I don't want him to think I work here, that's why!'

'Hiya, Brooke,' Rhianna heard Xander say. 'Everything OK?'

'Um, yeah. Fine,' Brooke said, on the back foot for a moment. 'How's the little one?'

'Keeping us busy. Nell's got her family visiting so they're babysitting Florrie while we have a rare date night,' Xander said. 'Pint of Doom Bar and a white wine please, plus whatever you're having.'

'Thanks, that's very kind.' Brooke looked down at Rhianna, who was trying not to make a sound as she huddled against the bar. 'Doom Bar, you say?'

'That's right. It's still one of the guest ales, isn't it?'

'Er, yes.' Surreptitiously, Brooke poked at Rhianna with her foot. Her sister eyed the shoe resentfully before shuffling aside so Brooke could get to the beer pump she needed. A blob of beer dripped onto her head and Rhianna huffed as she brushed it away.

'Oh. Hello, Mrs Garrett. I didn't see you down there.'

Rhianna looked up at the head peering down at her over the bar.

'Mr Scott.' She summoned a smile. 'What a surprise. I'm just down here… examining the floor.'

'Examining it?'

'Yes. For, er… peanuts. They're a health and safety risk.' She got to her feet and dusted herself off.

'Do you work here then?' Xander asked.

'Oh, no. I'm just helping out as a favour,' Rhianna told him breezily.

'You're a friend of Brooke's?'

'She's my sister, more's the pity,' Brooke said as she poured his drinks. 'Her and the kids are staying with me and Mum for a while.'

'Rhianna Padgett... oh! That was stupid of me,' Xander said, beaming at Rhianna. 'I never put two and two together when you came to see me. Of course we know each other already, don't we?'

Rhianna stared at him. 'Do we?'

'Well, we used to. You were two years below me at Leyholme Primary.'

'Oh. Was I? Sorry, I, er... I didn't realise.'

'Anyway, tell Livvy and Max we can't wait to welcome them tomorrow,' Xander said. 'It's a very friendly environment, I'm sure they'll be happy with us.'

'Thank you,' Rhianna said, blinking. 'I hope they fit in all right.'

'I'm certain they will. Come and see me any time if you have concerns.' Xander took his drinks and headed back to his wife.

'See?' Brooke said in a low voice. 'No one cares if you work in the pub, Rhianna. No one cares where you work. People aren't like that here.'

'No,' Rhianna said, watching Xander as he took a seat beside his wife. 'No, I... guess not.'

'I need to hand out the quiz papers. Hayden, you're in charge here.' Brooke held up a hand to Rhianna as she opened her mouth to object. 'Yes, I know it's your pub, but he's got more experience so just do what he says, OK?'

After the quiz had ended and the last customers had gone home to bed, Brooke began collecting up the abandoned papers and pens.

'Where's Rhianna?' she asked Hayden, who was unloading glasses from the dishwasher.

'I sent her back upstairs. Poor lass looked exhausted. Plus I couldn't cope with much more, if I'm honest.'

Brooke snorted. 'Poor lass my arse. Has she been giving you grief?'

'No, she was friendly enough once we got chatting about her kids, but your sister's not exactly a natural behind the bar. Tonight's shift set this place back by two broken glasses, about four pints' worth of wasted beer as she tried to master the art of the perfect pint, and, er, one nearly poisoned customer.'

Brooke's eyes widened. 'Poisoned?'

'Nearly poisoned,' Hayden corrected her. 'Ryan Theakston. She tried to serve him a pint of Landlord when I'd just changed the barrel without pouring off the gassy beer first. He'd have been burping for a week if he'd drunk it.'

Brooke shook her head, scowling. 'For God's sake. Can't she be trusted with the simplest thing?'

'Oh, she didn't do it on purpose. We were all new to this once, weren't we? Even you, barmaid extraordinaire.'

'She bloody did do it on purpose. I bet it's part of her plan to run this place into the ground so she can force me to—' Brooke broke off, casting him a wary look.

'Force you to what?'

'Nothing.'

Hayden came out from behind the bar, sat down at one of the tables and stretched out his long legs.

She smiled. 'All right, what're you doing?'

'Having a nice sit down.' He nodded to the seat next to him. 'Come join me. It's ever so refreshing.'

'I've got to tidy up.'

'You can do that in a minute. I want to talk to you.'

Brooke hesitated, then went to sit down.

'What's with you and your sister, Brooke?' he asked. 'I've spent all night with her, and yeah, she can be hard work, but it sounds like she's having a tough time of things. Why not cut her some slack and see what happens?'

'Easy for you to say, from the privileged position of an only child,' Brooke muttered. 'She's just… infuriating. The way she looks down on everyone.'

'You mean on you.' He dipped his head to look into her eyes. 'That's what it's all about, isn't it?'

'It's more than that.' Brooke sighed. 'When we were kids we used to be so close, you know? Then when I was nine, Rhianna started at her fancy new school and suddenly she was this stranger who lied to her friends about where she lived and pulled a face every time I glottal-stopped a T. I just… can't forgive her for it. Changing on me like that.'

'After she went to St Mary's, you mean?'

'Yeah.'

Hayden felt a stab of worry as he thought of his own girls. Darcie had been at St Mary's over seven months. He hadn't noticed any deterioration in her relationship with Cara, but then again, he hadn't been at home much recently to see it, had he?

'Why would you think your sister wants to run this place into the ground?' he asked.

Brooke squinted at him. She seemed to be examining his face, as if trying to make up her mind about something. Eventually, she made a decision.

'Rhianna wants to sell the pub,' she told him.

'Sell The Highwayman's!'

Brooke nodded. 'There's a chain wants to buy it. They're offering a small fortune, and she's desperate for cash so her and the kids can make a new start.'

'But you don't want to sell, right?'

'Well, no. This is the family business; it has been for nearly a century. I get that Rhianna needs money, but I need The Highwayman's. It was my dad's.'

Her eyes were wet with a film of tears. She turned her face away so he wouldn't see, not realising it was too late. Hayden shuffled closer.

'I've never heard you open up like that before,' he said softly.

She gave a wet laugh. 'Me neither.'

He smiled. 'You know, Brooke, you've gone out of your way to make me think you're this hard, cynical person but I'm not buying it.'

'Well, you should. I'm tough as old boots.'

'Nope. Don't believe a word.'

She looked up at him, and her face looked different. More vulnerable than he'd seen it before, behind its protective mask of wry cynicism. Soft; full of need.

'Why are you so nice to me?' she asked quietly. 'I don't deserve it after two weeks of being the bitch boss from hell.'

'You haven't been the bitch boss from hell. You know, you're actually sort of adorable when you're trying extra hard to be a dick.'

She laughed. 'Shut your face. How dare you.'

'Sorry,' he said, smiling. 'It's true, though. No offence, Brooke, but you suck at being mean.'

'Hayd, I'm worried,' she whispered. 'I'm seriously worried.'

'About the pub?'

She nodded. 'I'm worried that we've tried everything to improve business and nothing's worked. I'm worried the chain will talk my mum into selling, and her and Rhianna will outvote me, and I'll be forced into giving it up. I'm worried the chain *won't* talk my mum into selling and we'll go bust within a few years and I'll be responsible for losing us all that money. I'm worried Rhianna'll go back to that piece of shit who cheated on her and it'll be my fault because no matter how hard I try to be a supportive sister, we always end up fighting and eventually I'll drive her away. I'm worried about Max and Livvy starting at Leyholme Primary tomorrow. I'm worried—'

Without fully processing what he was doing, Hayden leaned forward and instinctively stopped her lips with a kiss. Brooke looked shocked for a moment. Then her eyes closed, and her arms wrapped around his neck.

'Sorry,' he said when he pulled away, slightly breathless. 'I don't know what made me do that. You just, um… you were upset and I… sorry.'

'That's OK.' Brooke looked a little lost, taken by surprise by the kiss and her own response to it. 'So, er… you'd better go home, I guess. I need to lock up.'

'Right. Yes.'

They both stood up, their eyes fixed on each other. Hayden took a step towards her.

Should he hold her? He wanted to. She looked like she wanted him to. But something held him back.

'So could we… you know, see each other outside work sometime?' he asked, suddenly shy.

Brooke smiled. 'Haven't you got enough women on the go?'

He blinked. 'Who, me?'

'What about Cara? And Darcie?'

'Darcie?'

'I saw those missed calls on your phone when you left it here, Hayden. I mean, don't think I'm jealous; you're entitled to enjoy yourself. I used to be a bit of a player myself in my misspent youth. I just don't know how you'll be able to fit me in, with the two jobs and what looks to be an already bulging little black book.'

She turned towards the kitchen to go make sure everything was switched off.

'Brooke, wait!' Hayden said.

'What?'

'It isn't… I'm not…' He pressed his eyes closed. 'Nothing.'

'All right. See you then.'

'But what if I can fit you in?' he said, realising he sounded slightly desperate. 'That kiss felt good, didn't it? I enjoyed it anyway.'

'Yes, it felt good. I'm still your boss though, Hayd.'

'All right, I resign.'

She smiled. 'Cute, but I know you can't afford to. I'll think about it, OK? See you tomorrow.'

Brooke walked off, but halfway to the kitchen, she stopped.

'Hayden?' she said without turning around. 'Those kids who came in earlier with your mum.'

Hayden closed his eyes, knowing what was coming. He'd been expecting it to click all night, to be honest. Oh well, at least he'd have one kiss to remember her by...

'What about them?' he asked quietly.

'What are they called?'

'What are they called?'

'Yeah.'

'Well, one of them's called, er...' He grimaced. 'I guess one of them's called Cara.'

'And the other one's called...'

'Darcie.'

'Darcie Bailey.'

He sighed. 'Yes.'

Brooke turned back to face him, her expression a mixture of bemusement and irritation. 'For God's sake, Hayden. Why didn't you tell me?'

'Well, you said you weren't keen on kids and I... I wanted you to like me.' He met her eyes. 'Brooke, I was eighteen years old when I found out my girlfriend Carol-Ann was pregnant. With twins, as if one baby wasn't scary enough. I suppose it's not surprising she freaked out and took off before the girls were six months old. Since then, it's just been us.'

Brooke's expression softened. 'You brought them up all on your own?'

'Not all on my own. My mum was always there for us. But it's been tough, and money's a constant worry. Even more so since Carol-Ann lost her job and stopped paying child support, and then Darcie got offered a scholarship to St Mary's. I guess you know what that's like in a family with limited means.'

'I do. And I'm sorry,' Brooke said. 'That must've been rough on you. Still, I don't like being lied to, Hayden.'

'No,' he said, bowing his head. 'Will you still think about it? A date, I mean.'

'I'm not sure that's a good idea, are you? You're a dad. OK, we could have some fun, but there'll come a time when your kids are going to be an issue for us. You know that as well as I do.'

'Maybe,' he admitted. 'It's just been a long time since I met anyone I really liked. I tried to talk myself out of it, but... well, it didn't work.'

'I think it's simpler all round if we stay just friends. My life's complicated enough right now, not to mention busy as fuck, and yours doesn't sound much better.' Brooke looked as if she was about to go, then hesitated. 'That's why you needed the job so badly? To pay for your kid's school stuff?'

'Yeah. Just my luck to father a child who turns out to be a bloody genius.'

'You must be proud of her.'

'I am, of both of them. It's hard to believe sometimes that they could've come from me.' He paused. 'So... we're friends though, right?'

'Course we are.' She summoned a smile. 'And I'm happy to say you've come through your trial period with flying colours too. Welcome to the team, Hayden.'

Chapter Ten

When Brooke went upstairs Rhianna was in the living room, flicking through a notebook. The roses that had been delivered earlier were gone, Brooke noticed. She'd hazard a guess she'd find them in the kitchen bin.

Rhianna closed the notebook when her sister came in. 'Hey.'

Brooke grunted a greeting, which was all she felt her sister deserved after her behaviour in the pub.

'Look, Brooke, about tonight,' Rhianna said. 'I'm sorry. I did it again, didn't I?'

'If by "it", you mean acted like a toffee-nosed cow who's above the sort of thing the rest of us have to do to make money, then yes, you did.'

'I know it was wrong. It's just a bit of a culture shock, this new way of living.'

'Hmm.'

'I don't mean to be a bitch. Everything's so different from what I'm used to. You can understand why that takes a bit of adjusting to, can't you?'

'You used to be happy with life around here. Before St Mary's turned you posh.'

'Yes,' Rhianna said with a sigh. 'I've been away too long. I was angry earlier, about Max and the tattoo, and I was on my worst behaviour. Sorry.'

'All right,' Brooke said, her frown lifting a little. 'Well, I suppose we should both be trying harder.'

Rhianna smiled. 'So when did you give Hayden Bailey a job? I'd forgotten all about the time I pushed him to get him back for pranking you.'

'He worked his first shift the night you turned up with the kids. Mum's bright idea.'

'You and him seem friendly.'

Brooke shrugged, trying not give anything away, although she could still feel his kiss tingling on her lips. 'He's all right. Pours a good pint, now I've trained him up.'

'I get the feeling you see that as the ultimate compliment,' Rhianna said, laughing.

Brooke let herself laugh too. 'I suppose that is pretty sad.'

'Here, I made you supper. I guessed you'd be hungry after your shift.' Rhianna went to get something from the kitchen.

Brooke smiled as Rhianna handed her a steaming Pot Noodle. It wasn't much, but it showed her sister was trying not to turn her nose up at every single bit of food in their cupboards.

'Thanks,' she said. 'And I won't give the kids meals they're not supposed to have, if you just let me know what's allowed. I'm working from what we used to eat when we were their age, which probably wasn't the most nutritious fare.'

'With Mum's cooking, I think we did well to make it to adulthood. Has she managed to poison anyone in the village yet?'

Brooke laughed. 'Not yet. Still, I can't see us becoming the leading gastropub in the Calder Valley any time soon.'

'Why did you decide to start doing food?'

'We thought it might bring in more people. It's only a little menu: just toasties, chips and burgers, plus a couple of pub meal favourites and some of Mum's stodge puddings. I'm not sure it's made much difference in terms of pulling in customers but it's a bit of extra income.'

'Oh.'

An awkward silence fell. To give herself something to do, Brooke swallowed a forkful of Pot Noodle.

'What's in there?' she asked, pointing to the A4 notebook on Rhianna's chair arm.

'That?' Rhianna looked slightly guilty. 'Nothing. Nothing important.'

'It must be something.'

'Just some figures I wanted to take a look at.'

Brooke frowned. 'Is that… Rhia, that's my accounts book!'

'It's *our* accounts book,' Rhianna corrected her. 'As I seem to keep having to remind you, I own a share in this place too.'

Brooke laughed. 'I don't bloody believe you! You know, I actually fell for that apology. You were looking to see how far the profits had fallen, weren't you?'

'I was looking to see if there was any way we could make savings,' Rhianna said, lifting her chin. 'Now I'm getting more involved, I thought I could be a little more use than serving drinks. What's wrong with that?'

'Bullshit, Rhia! You were thinking about Nick sodding Weyborough and his million quid.' Brooke shook her head. 'I can't believe you're still going behind my back on this. I suppose that little performance earlier was all part of your plan to ruin the business as fast as you can before Willowtree Taverns withdraw their offer, was it?'

'You see, this is what makes you such hard work,' Rhianna snapped. 'You find it impossible to believe I might actually want to help, don't you?'

'What reason have you given me to believe it? All you've done is try to undermine me and alienate the customers. That's unlikely to fill me with confidence in your loyalty to the pub.'

There was silence while they looked daggers at each other.

'I can't see why you're so stubborn about the idea of selling,' Rhianna finally burst out. 'We're losing money hand over fist, I can see that from the accounts. We won't get a better offer than the one from Willowtree if we wait fifty years. Are you allergic to making life comfortable for yourself?'

'I knew it! I bloody knew that's why you had the accounts out. You two-faced cow!'

'Mum wants to sell. Did you know that?'

'Bollocks she does.' Brooke paused. 'Did she say that?'

'She as good as said it.'

'So no, in other words.'

'What about Dad? What about what he'd want?' Rhianna demanded. 'Mum told me he left me my share to provide for me if James ever left me up the creek. Well, that time has come, Brooke.'

'Don't you even dare bring Dad into this,' Brooke said in a low voice. 'You don't know a *thing* about what he'd want. You weren't here when he... when he...'

'When he died,' Rhianna said quietly. 'I know I wasn't.'

'I was the one who had to watch it. It was me who held his hand while he slipped away.'

'I came as soon as I could. I regret every day that I was too late. That doesn't mean I don't care.'

'You care about yourself. That's all,' Brooke whispered, blinking back tears. 'Always number one, right, Rhianna?'

'No, Brooke, my children are number one. And right now, they're facing a very uncertain future with no home and no money.'

'I said I'd do what I could to help you, but I need this place.' Brooke sighed. 'Look, I love you. I love the kids. But giving up The Highwayman's? That's too big an ask, I'm sorry.'

—

Janey was in her room, trying to read, but all she could focus on was the hum of angry voices coming from the living room. Again.

Her plan had failed, then. She'd been hoping that forcing the girls to work in the pub together would help Rhianna understand what made Brooke tick, but all it seemed to have achieved was to spark off another row.

She pushed her book to one side, sighing. Always it was one step forward and two steps back with that pair.

What could she do about it? Gone were the days when she could force her girls to shake hands and say sorry, then they'd be firm friends again. In the pre–St Mary's days, their fights had been hot but brief, and quickly forgotten.

Brooke was the one with the fiery temper. Rhianna was quieter, but nevertheless capable of flaring up when roused. Brooke yelled, Rhianna sulked. Brooke called names, Rhianna was quietly cutting. But they loved each other, and when they were children Janey had always known how to get them to remember that fact. She used to keep a supply of things in a special box for after a big row: colouring books, jigsaws, craft kits, Lego. Things they could play with as a pair; a shared project that would remind them what a brilliant team they could make when they worked together.

An image of two little heads bending over a jigsaw in deep concentration popped up in her head. Side by side, like it was them against the world.

Could the same technique work now they were adults? It was an idea. She certainly needed help, and if they were both involved...

The angry bumblebee buzz was louder now. Making up her mind, Janey swung her legs over the bed and marched to the living room.

'All right, what is it tonight?' she demanded when she walked in on her daughters glaring at each other. 'The children are trying to sleep. It's a big day for them tomorrow.'

'Don't ask me,' Rhianna said sullenly. 'I was being nice. I made her one of those disgusting MSG things she loves and everything. It's not my fault she can't accept an apology.'

'She's been going through our accounts!' Brooke told her mum.

'Why shouldn't I go through the accounts?' Rhianna demanded. 'It's partly my pub, Brooke.'

'Because you just want to make us sell it, that's why!'

'Stop,' Janey said, holding up her hand. 'Family court. Brooke, get the hammer.'

'Oh God, do we have to?' Brooke said.

Rhianna shook her head. 'You two still do family court?'

'In emergencies,' Janey said. 'And this involves my love life, which means it's very much an emergency. Brooke, hammer.'

Groaning, Brooke went to fetch the hammer. She presented it to her mum, who banged it on the coffee table like a gavel.

'OK, court in session. On the agenda today, your mother's lack of a sex life.'

Rhianna raised her hand.

'Yes?' Janey nodded to let her know she was permitted to speak.

'I'm not sure I want to hear about your sex life, Mum.'

'Well, you're in luck, because I haven't got one. That's what we're here to discuss.'

'What, you mean you—' Brooke began, but her mum banged the hammer on the table, raising an eyebrow.

'Sorry.' Brooke raised her hand, and Janey nodded to her. 'You mean you want to start seeing people again?'

'I think it's time. Does that get your blessing, daughters?'

'Aren't you a bit old for that sort of thing?' Rhianna said.

'Of course she isn't,' Brooke said, glaring at her sister. 'You can't be too old for love. Or sex either, not that I'm especially keen on thinking about it.' She nodded to her mum. 'Fine by me, Janey. You don't need my blessing, but if you want it, it's yours.'

'Why are you asking us?' Rhianna asked. 'You're well over the age of consent, Mum.'

'Because I need your help. Both of you.'

'Us? Why?'

'Well, it's all on the internet now, isn't it? You have to get yourself downloaded onto Grindr or whatever to meet people these days.'

Brooke shot her sister an amused glance. 'Er, I don't think you want a profile on Grindr, Mum.'

'Why not?'

'It's just… not for you. Tinder's what you need. That'll be where all the silver foxes are hiding out.'

'Oh. All right, well, I'm sure you know best.' Janey fumbled down the side of the armchair for her mobile phone, which had a dead battery from neglect as usual. 'Can I get Tinder on here?'

'On that?' Rhianna laughed. 'I doubt you could get Snake on that.'

'So what do I do then?'

'You can do it on the computer if your phone hasn't got internet.'

'She can't, you know,' Brooke told Rhianna. 'Last week she sent me an email typed entirely in the subject line. All in caps. It said "LOOK BROOKE I FINALLY LEARNT HOW TO DO MY EMAIL".'

Janey banged the table with her hammer. 'All right, no taking the piss out of your mother. Now, are you two going to help me get on this Tinder or what? I'm not going to meet hubby number two without assistance.'

Rhianna looked at Brooke. 'What do you think? Can we work together?'

'Well, if we let her do it on her own, she'll have sent her bank details to a Nigerian prince within the week.'

'True.' Rhianna held out her hand. 'Truce then?'

Brooke hesitated before shaking it. 'All right. For Mum's sake.'

Rhianna gave her parent a benevolent nod. 'OK, Mum, we're on board for some stepdad-hunting. We'll help you set a profile up tomorrow night after Livvy and Max are in bed.'

Chapter Eleven

Rhianna poked her head out of her room when she heard her sister moving about in the hallway the next afternoon.

'Are you going to work?' she asked.

'Yes, why?'

'I want to help.'

Brooke blinked. 'You're offering to help in the pub?'

'That's right.' Rhianna flashed her a strained smile. 'I'm going to make more effort from now on, Brooke, I promise.'

Brooke narrowed one eye. 'Mum put you up to this, didn't she?'

'She didn't, honestly. I just want to show I support the place. I wasn't lying when I said I was looking through the accounts to see if I could help.'

'See if you could force us to sell, you mean.'

'I can't force you if you don't want to, can I? All I said was I wished you'd consider it.'

'Well, I won't.'

'I'd picked up on that,' Rhianna said drily. 'So, do you want a hand?'

'It's fine,' Brooke said, turning away. 'Hayden's working today. I was supposed to have the afternoon off actually, but I fancied going down for an hour or two. It's calming, pulling pints.'

Rhianna wondered if her sister often felt like working an unnecessary shift when Hayden Bailey was behind the bar.

'Please, I want to,' she said. 'Mum's in the kitchen, you're behind the bar: it's only right I should be doing something useful too. You and Hayden can give me a bit more training.'

'Well… all right. But get changed first – something presentable this time.'

'Thanks, I will.' Rhianna disappeared back into her bedroom to pick an outfit from the limited range she'd brought from home.

Or, not home; not any more. The six-bedroom house she'd occupied for the last eleven years was James's home, not hers. Rhianna didn't know where home was, now. Certainly not this place, with the five of them crammed in like pickled onions and Brooke giving her the evil eye every time they bumped into one another. Rhianna sensed even her mum felt uncomfortable having her here, although she often repeated that Rhianna should consider The Highwayman's Drop her home. Which in one sense it was – one-third of the bricks and mortar belonged to her – but that didn't stop Rhianna feeling like a stranger. She was too much an outsider to fit in with her family now. If she'd visited more often then perhaps it wouldn't be such a culture shock, but James had hated her and the children to be away too long. Not enough to come with them, of course, but enough to ensure their brief visits happened no more than once a year.

The worst thing was the guilt she felt over how little time she and the children had spent with her dad in the years leading up to his death. When Rhianna had broken the news to Max and Livvy that Grandad had passed away, they'd been more puzzled than sad. Yes, she could blame James, but she should have insisted on more visits. That the children had barely grieved for their grandfather, that Rhianna had spent only a handful of weekends with her dad in the decade before he died, was her fault – no one else's.

Rhianna caught sight of her cracked nails as she opened the wardrobe and grimaced. Dominique, her manicurist, would have a swooning fit if she could see them.

But what did nails matter, in the general scheme of things? What did anything matter, except making sure the children were going to be OK? Rhianna would be lying if she said she didn't miss the luxury and comfort of her life with James, but there were worse things in life than chipped nails.

She rifled through her wardrobe, trying to guess what outfit Brooke would choose. Rhianna wasn't sure she'd brought anything loud enough for bar work. There was only the black top she'd bought at Selfridges last month – that was tight-fitting, at least, and it had sequins on it. Anyway, it was going to have to do.

Today had been... difficult. The children had looked so lost and small when she'd left them at their new school, so frightened, that as soon as Rhianna had got back to the flat she'd just sobbed her heart out. After what Brooke had said last night, she was haunted by the idea that Livvy and Max might find themselves bullied for the way they spoke or acted. Children could be so intolerant of others' differences. Her poor babies, alone among all those strangers!

She'd never forgive James for what he'd done to her – never. Ugh, it made her want to swear, to scream out some profanity, where everyone could hear her. That would shock them. It would shock James, who'd never seen her as anything but the perfect, passive housewife. What would he think if he heard her yelling out a really good, meaty 'fuck!' with all of her lungs? God, that would feel satisfying. And why shouldn't she? Because she was Rhianna and not Brooke?

All her life, everyone had expected her to be the good one. Brooke got to spend her teens partying, screwing whoever she felt like and going out whenever she wanted, while Rhianna spent her nights studying alone. The pressure to achieve, to live up to her potential, had become almost unbearable. And for what? To keep house and raise kids for a man who for all she knew had been sleeping around on her the whole time?

For a minute, she almost did swear. Then… she didn't. She just took off her blouse and started pulling on the sequinned top.

A hundred times that day, and on every day since she'd taken the children and run, Rhianna had asked herself if she was doing the right thing. The rage that filled her every time she thought about James Garrett – her husband, his parents' golden boy, whiz kid marketing director, golf club captain and cheating scumbag – dissipated when she pictured him with the children. He hadn't spent lots of time with them – he worked too much – but when he did make time for play, he was so good with them. They asked about Daddy every day, and he texted no less often demanding to know when they could set up some access visits so he could see his children. Rhianna was plagued with guilt that she'd taken Max and Livvy from the father they loved, the luxurious home he'd provided them with and the first-rate private education he paid for, to squat in a flat above a pub.

He'd texted her again this morning. Every day, new messages. *It's over with Shari now, I swear. Flops, I love you – please come home. I just want to talk. You owe it to the children. We can get help. For God's sake, Rhianna, just see me!* And every day Rhianna had looked at her children – sleep-deprived, pale and afraid – and now weakened just a little more as she tapped back, *Not yet. Not yet. Not yet.*

If only Brooke would sell! The Highwayman's was a lame duck; that much was clear from the accounts. If they sold now then Rhianna, her mum and sister would have over £300,000 each. As Janey had observed, a third of a million was a drop in the ocean compared to the wealth Rhianna had enjoyed as James's wife, but you quickly remembered the value of money when you were flat broke. That kind of cash meant independence. A home of her own. A new start.

Rhianna could start afresh, guilt-free, and give her children a decent quality of life. Janey could enjoy her retirement – see the world, in all the luxury she deserved. And Brooke would have more than enough to get her started in another pub. Whereas if they held out now, they'd never get another offer like this. The Highwayman's Drop would continue to flounder, and in a few years it'd be worth peanuts – if it didn't plunge them all into bankruptcy.

But Brooke was too stubborn to even consider it. Despite what Rhianna wanted; what she needed, for her children. Despite what she could tell their mum wanted, although Janey refused to admit it. It was just so selfish!

That was Brooke all over, assuming that because her voice was the loudest, it must be the most important. When Rhianna had been young, she'd thought that brains were what mattered – that as long as you had those, you could get anywhere you wanted in life. Now she was an adult, she realised confidence would always get you further than any other quality, and that was one thing she'd never have. Brooke, of course, had the stuff in spades. It must have been a big joke to Mother Nature, doling out both their shares to just one sister.

So Brooke's unquenchable hubris was going to run the business into the ground, and their mum was going to stand by and watch it happen. Rhianna knew, of course, that Brooke was Janey's favourite child – the one who'd stayed; the one who most resembled her. So Rhianna would have to watch her hope of independence go up in smoke because her sister was too wilfully blind to see what was right in front of her.

She took a deep breath, counting to ten, before she got angry again and dashed her resolution to make more of an effort with Brooke.

Cuddling a flushed, sleeping Livvy in bed last night, Rhianna had promised herself that she was going to make life easier for them all by being more cooperative. Perhaps the pub was doomed, but it still had the potential to bring in more money – she'd seen a dozen ways they could be making savings when she'd gone through the accounts last night. So, when she'd heard Brooke emerge from her room, Rhianna had screwed her toes into her Louboutin flatties and gone out to offer some help.

Maybe it wouldn't be so bad. She'd never admit it to Brooke, but in some ways she'd quite enjoyed working behind the bar last night. That boy Hayden was fun to chat to, and she'd got to know some of the customers a little, too. Far from her home and friends, with only Brooke's glare for company, it had been refreshing to see friendly faces. No one had judged her for working behind the bar, as she'd feared, and people from all walks of life seemed to come through the door. Besides, working would keep her mind off her worries about the children until it was time to pick them up from school.

After a cursory glance in the mirror, Rhianna went down to the bar.

'Didn't you say Hayden was working today?' she asked Brooke, looking around for him.

'Yeah, he's due in soon.' Brooke frowned. 'Why, what's it to you?'

Rhianna laughed. 'Oh my gosh.'

'Oh your gosh what?'

'You're jealous.'

'Don't talk daft.'

'You are! You like him, don't you?'

'Course I don't. We're friends, that's all.'

'Well, I promise you've got nothing to worry about,' Rhianna said. 'Your boyfriend's quite safe from me.'

'He's not my boyfriend.' Brooke lowered her voice as a rotund old gentleman headed their way. 'And keep your voice down. Here's Martin Brady. I'll let you serve him.'

'Um, hello,' Rhianna said to Martin, flinching slightly. This was the bit she found difficult: the easy chat Brooke was such a natural at.

'Afternoon, young ladies,' Martin boomed. 'Well, we are spoilt. All we need is your mam and we'd have a hat trick of beauties to gaze at. I suppose she's in the kitchen, is she?'

'That's right.' Brooke took down a glass and put it under the Boltmaker pump. 'This is Martin's drink, Rhia. Let's see what you learned last night.'

Rhianna tried to remember what Hayden had taught her as she guided the pump towards her. She did her best, but she wasn't sure she got it quite right. The beer she put down in front of Martin looked a bit foamy on top to her inexperienced eye.

'Got a Flake to go in that?' he asked her jovially.

'Um, I'm not sure.' She glanced at Brooke. 'Have we?'

Brooke laughed. 'It's a joke, Rhia. He wants a top-up. Here, let me do it.'

She elbowed her sister aside so she could top Martin's pint up for him.

'That's the stuff,' he said, eyeing it appreciatively. 'You pour nearly as good a pint as your mother, Brooke. She's wasted in that kitchen.'

'Oh, so you've tasted her cooking,' Rhianna said with a smile. Martin gave a big belly laugh.

'A looker like her should be out front where us lads can admire her,' he said, picking up his drink. 'Well, tell her I said hello. See you, girls.'

'That was good,' Brooke said, nodding approvingly. 'You did banter, Rhia. I never knew you had it in you.'

'Seems to me there's a fine line between customer banter and sexual harassment.'

'Sometimes. Martin's harmless, though. He's just from the past, when telling women they look fit was what passed for chivalry.'

They watched Martin pick up a *Daily Mirror* from the rack where today's papers were kept and sit down.

'He seems very interested in Mum,' Rhianna observed.

'Well, they're old friends.'

'Do you think he's *interested* interested?'

'I shouldn't think so. I told you, that's just the way his generation learned to talk to women.'

Rhianna watched Martin sipping his pint as he read the paper. 'It's early to be drinking on his own, isn't it?'

'Oh, he'll probably be joined by the rest of the merry widowers in a bit,' Brooke said.

Rhianna blinked. 'The what?'

'His mates. There's four of them, they come in most days – sometimes on their own, sometimes together. They like to pop in for a chinwag with the staff and to enjoy a quiet pint over the paper. It beats being lonely at home, missing their other halves.' Brooke nodded to a gaggle of people chatting animatedly. 'And that's the decorating committee for the 1940s festival, having a planning meeting over a drink. Over there are the leaders of the Explorer Scout group just back from their Queen's Scout expedition, winding down with a pint. And old Billy Cromwell from Ryecroft Farm with his sons, and their sons, celebrating the fact they've just found out the next generation's on the way. See, we provide a public service, Rhia.'

Rhianna looked around the various groups – their relaxed, happy faces – and for the first time had an inkling of what it was about The Highwayman's her sister thought was special.

'If everyone in Leyholme loves this place, why has business fallen off so much?' she asked.

'All right, don't shout about it to everyone,' Brooke said in a low voice. 'I don't know, do I? All the regulars come in same as always, but casual trade – walkers, holidaymakers – we're not seeing so much of. And the regulars thin out a bit every year too.'

'Why?'

Brooke smiled sadly. 'Same reason you're behind the bar and not Dad. No one lives forever.'

'Ah. I see.'

'There's a different sort of new blood taking the place of the old. The days when everyone knew everyone round here are gone, Rhia. Commuters love living in Leyholme, in the clean air with the moors all around them, but they do their socialising in the towns where they work. To them The Highwayman's is just another boring country boozer. An old man's pub, I've heard they call us.'

'Really? That's sort of sad.'

'I know. But that just makes this place all the more invaluable as a social hub for those who do see it as the heart of the village.'

'I can understand that.' Rhianna nodded to the door. 'Here's your boyfriend.'

'Oh, shut your face,' Brooke muttered. But Rhianna saw her lips flicker.

'Hello again,' Hayden said to Rhianna when he joined them. 'I wasn't expecting you.'

She shrugged. 'I was at a loose end with the children at school so I thought I'd make myself useful.'

'Demon possession, I think,' Brooke said in response to his enquiring eyebrow. 'I'm hoping I can get her to change a barrel or two before a passing priest exorcises it.'

'You still need me though, right?' Hayden said, and Rhianna detected a certain appeal in his tone.

'Of course I— *we* need you,' Brooke said, quickly correcting herself. 'I told you last night you were here to stay.'

One of the Explorer Scout leaders approached to get another round in.

'I'll get it,' Hayden said, reaching for the Guinness tap at exactly the same time as Brooke. Their hands met, and he flushed as he snatched his away again. 'Sorry.'

'No problem,' Brooke said, looking flustered herself, and Rhianna suppressed a smile. There was definitely something going on between those two. Brooke had taken an awfully long time to lock up last night…

When the customer had taken his drinks, Hayden turned to them with his eyes sparkling.

'OK, Brooke, so tell me to shut up if this is completely off the wall, but I had an idea,' he said.

'An idea about what?'

'This place. What you said about—' He cast a wary glance at Rhianna. 'I mean, a way we can increase business. Possibly. Unless it's stupid.'

Rhianna straightened up. 'That sounds good. What is it?'

Hayden cast an enquiring look at Brooke, as if asking for her permission to speak.

'It's all right,' Brooke said. 'You might as well say it in front of her.'

Rhianna frowned. 'And it's my pub, thank you, Brooke.'

'It's a bit your pub.' She nodded to Hayden. 'Go on, what's this amazing idea?'

He grimaced. 'I'm worried I've built it up too much now. I wasn't expecting an audience.'

'Hayd, just tell us already. We've got lives to lead here.'

'Well, um…' He took a crumpled leaflet from his jeans. 'I picked this up in the post office. It's a map you can follow to learn about the village. The Leyholme History Walk.'

'Yeah, I know it. You amble around and see such amazing sights as the blue plaque for some obscure poet who once had a piss behind a tree here and the site of the village stocks before someone nicked them for firewood. What about it?'

'Well, this place is on it.' He put it down on the bar and smoothed it out. 'See? "*The Highwayman's Drop, Leyholme's village pub, dates back to the 1600s. Once known as The Brown Boar Inn, it owes its current name to the local legend that Dick Turpin stayed there on his famous ride from London to York.*"'

'Let me have a look.' Rhianna slid the leaflet towards her and read the section on the pub with interest. She'd heard the legend before, of course, but it had been a long time since she'd had cause to think about it.

'I don't get it,' Brooke said to Hayden. 'Everyone in Leyholme knows that. It's just an old fairytale. The real Dick Turpin never even rode from London to York.'

'All right, no need to piss on my bonfire quite so thoroughly,' Hayden said, looking deflated. 'I'd never heard it before. I just thought it was a good marketing angle.'

'Sorry. I didn't mean to be down on the idea.' Brooke gave his arm a consoling pat. 'It was a good suggestion, but it's too old hat to help us much.'

Rhianna looked up from the leaflet. 'No, Hayden's right! We could use this, Brooke.'

'Eh? How?'

'What did you tell me before? Your regulars are loyal, but you're struggling to bring in walkers and holidaymakers? Well, what do tourists love?'

'You're going to have to help me out with this punchline, Rhia,' Brooke said. 'I don't know, what do tourists love?'

'A story! If it's a story with a bit of actual history in it then so much the better, but as the wife of a marketing director, I picked up a thing or two. One was that you should never let the truth get in the way of a good story.'

'All right,' Brooke said cautiously. 'How do we use it, though? Get the staff kitted out in tricorne hats and masks?'

'I wouldn't go that far. Still, there must be a way to make more of it. Some chalkboard artwork outside; theme up the food menu.' She pulled one towards her. 'OK, liver and onions. What could we do with liver and onions?'

'Yuck,' Hayden said, pulling a face. 'Dunno, burn them with fire?'

Brooke frowned at him. 'Hey. That's our top seller, that is. It's the only thing my mum can cook.'

'What about…' Rhianna thought for a moment. '…Stand and De-liver and Onions?'

Brooke snorted. 'That's the cheesiest thing I've ever heard.'

'People like cheesy, though. Everyone secretly enjoys a good groaner.'

'People *love* cheesy.' Hayden grabbed the menu from Rhianna. 'All right, let me play. How about, um… Spotted Dick Turpin?'

'Oooh, yes!' Rhianna said. 'Hey, this is fun. What about Black Bess Pudding?'

'That sounds like it's made from an actual horse, Rhia,' Brooke said. 'Rumours we're feeding people horsemeat are the last thing our reputation needs on top of Mum's cooking.'

'There's a brewery in York does a beer called Black Bess,' Hayden said. 'A stout. Why don't we try that as a guest ale?'

'And we could print some history leaflets for people to take,' Rhianna said. 'Maybe put a few in the local shops, see who we can lure in.'

'But it's not true,' Brooke protested. 'We're going to get in trouble, putting fibs on our marketing materials.'

'Brooke, that *is* marketing.' A lightbulb dinged over Rhianna's head. 'Ooh! What about our own ghost?'

'There's no such thing as ghosts.'

'A lot of people think there are. Come on, haven't you ever noticed anything ghostly round here?'

Brooke shrugged. 'Mum lost her reading glasses last week. She swore she left them in the living room, but they turned up down here in the kitchen.'

'There you go then. Conclusive proof.'

'Whose ghost is it?' Hayden asked. 'Turpin's?'

'Of course,' Rhianna said. 'You need a celebrity, unless you've got some extra-spooky happenings involving mysteriously rocking cradles or twins in knee socks. There's nothing worse than a Z-list ghost.'

'I've got some twins I could loan you for a reasonable fee.'

'Are they identical?'

'No, sorry.'

'No good then. It'll have to be Dick.'

'But they hanged him in York,' Brooke said. 'What would he be doing haunting this place?'

'Maybe he really enjoyed the beer.' Rhianna took out her phone to note down their ideas. 'Anyway, that's what we're going to say on the leaflets.'

Brooke still looked doubtful.

'I don't know, you guys,' she said. 'We're getting dangerously close to theme pub territory here. If it ain't broke, don't fix it, our dad used to say.'

'Except it is broke,' Hayden reminded her.

'You know what I mean. It's no good pandering to the occasional trade if it alienates our regulars. No matter how bad things might be, it's the villagers who are our bread and butter.'

'We won't alienate anyone if we do it right,' Rhianna said.

'Hmm. I'm trying hard to keep this place out of the hands of a chain who I'm convinced want to suck out its soul. I don't want to do that only to take it in the same direction myself. We're not a novelty act for tourists.'

'I'm not talking about making it a theme pub,' Rhianna reassured her. 'I'm just talking about changing the narrative.'

Brooke narrowed one eye. 'Is that marketing speak?'

'Yep. We take a story, we claim it, and we weave it into this place.' Rhianna met her sister's gaze. 'Brooke, those people you pointed out to me earlier – this will still be a sanctuary for them. It'll just have something unique to offer people from out of town. Serve a man a beer and he'll drink it, enjoy it and go. Tell him a story and he'll remember it all his life.'

'We can give it a go, at least,' Hayden said. 'What have we got to lose?'

'Well…' Brooke hesitated, looking from one eager face to another. 'All right. I guess we can try it out.'

Chapter Twelve

At quarter past three, Rhianna went to collect Max and Livvy from school. She found them in the playground, waiting among the other children. Livvy was surrounded by a little group of fellow Year Two pupils, all listening rapt as she – there was no other way to describe it – held court. Max, on the other hand, was lurking by the fence alone.

It felt strange, coming back to the school she'd attended herself for so many years. It was still the same stubby Victorian building topped by a belltower, but everything now seemed so... small. Rhianna smiled slightly as she looked around, remembering fun times in this same playground with her friends.

She'd been happy here. In some ways it felt like this was the last place she had truly been happy, before St Mary's and the pressure to achieve had taken over her life. She hoped her own children would be happy here likewise.

Rhianna kept at a little distance so she could hear what Livvy was saying.

'...and where we used to live, the last Saturday of each month is always French Day,' she was announcing to her crowd of admirers.

'Did you go to France on French Day?' one wide-eyed little chap asked breathlessly.

'No, silly. That's too far away to go all the time,' Livvy told him with a patronising benevolence. 'But we have all French food and French music, and Avril only talks French to help us learn. She's our old pear.'

'What's an old pear?' a little girl asked.

'It's like someone who helps your mummy and does jigsaws with you.'

'Why is she called an old pear?'

Livvy looked stumped for a moment.

'Um… that's French,' she declared confidently. 'Old pear is French for Grandpa.'

'But isn't the old pear a lady?'

'Yes. That's because in England sometimes French words get changed. So's English people can understand them.'

'All right, Olivia Garrett, come along,' Rhianna said with a laugh. 'That's enough about old pears for today.'

'Mummy!' Livvy shrieked and barrelled into her. Smiling, Rhianna bent to kiss her head.

'Max!' she called to her son from across the playground. 'Come on, sweetie. Home time.'

Max cast a wary look at the children around him before going to join his mum and sister. Rhianna held out her free hand to him, the other having been claimed by Livvy, but he hesitated to take it.

'What's wrong, my love?' she asked him gently.

'I don't want the others to see,' he whispered.

'Oh. No, of course not.'

They started walking home, Livvy swinging her schoolbag and humming to herself. Max, however, continued quiet.

'Well, darlings, how was your first day?' Rhianna said. 'I suppose the new school was a bit different from what you're used to.'

'It was sick!' Livvy announced.

Rhianna blinked. 'It was what?'

'Sick. I made a friend called Taylor and she told me sick was what you say here when something's really good. Not like *being* sick. A good sort of sick.'

'I'm not sure I like that very much, Livvy.'

'No, but it's OK because everyone in my class says it,' Livvy informed her. 'When I go back to Ferndene, I can teach everyone there to say it too.'

Rhianna cast her a worried look. 'Sweetie… would you miss Ferndene very much if you had to move schools for good?'

Livvy blinked. 'But you said I only had to leave for a little bit.'

'Well, yes, I did, but… things might change for us in the next few months.'

Livvy's top lip started to wobble. 'But then I wouldn't see Ella or Lottie or Tammy or any of my Ferndene friends.'

'We can still go and see your friends,' Rhianna hastened to reassure her. 'Leyholme Primary isn't such a horrid place, is it? It looks like you've got lots of nice friends there already, and it's a sweet little school. Your mummy went there too when she was small.'

Livvy looked up at her with damp eyes. 'Did Brooke go as well?'

'That's right.'

'Was she in a bigger class than you?'

Rhianna smiled. 'No, I was in the bigger class. Brooke is two years younger than me. I had to look after her when the naughty children were mean to her.'

'Why?'

'Well, because that's what big sisters do.'

'Did you have the same teacher as me when you went there?'

'I rather doubt it, unless she's very ancient indeed,' Rhianna said, laughing. The threat of tears averted, she turned her attention to her silent, thoughtful son. 'What about you, Maxie? Did you make any new friends?'

'I talked to some boys,' he said, before falling back into pensive silence. Rhianna waited for him to speak again, but he stayed quiet.

'Did you like them?' she asked.

'They were OK. But...' He looked up at her. 'Mummy, they said I was wrong and they wouldn't listen when I told them I wasn't.'

Rhianna frowned. 'What did they say you were wrong about?'

'Zach Ackroyd said that at dinnertime he'd be sat at the end table so I could go sit there with him and his friends if I wanted, because I didn't know anyone. I said I would but that he ought to say *sitting* at the table, not sat, because that was wrong. And he said *I* was wrong, even though I wasn't, and then I thought he wouldn't like me any more so I just sat on my own.'

Rhianna felt a stab of guilt. This was what Brooke had meant. A boy had tried to befriend Max and her son had alienated this potential friend because of lessons she and James had taught him about speaking up when he heard something incorrect.

'I was right, wasn't I, Mummy?' he said.

'You were right,' she said slowly. 'Sitting is correct and sat isn't. But… Max, sometimes the polite thing to do is *not* to point out someone's mistakes.'

He blinked. 'But if they're wrong, they'll want to know so they can get it right next time, won't they? That's being kind, because it's helping someone do better.'

'Not always, sweetie. People might think that you're looking down on them for not knowing the same things you do. It's not kind to make people feel bad about themselves.'

'But you said—'

'I know what I said. Things are… different here. I think we all need to learn a few new lessons.'

They were approaching the pub now. Rhianna's gaze fixed on a man who was standing outside, looking as if he was waiting for someone.

He was the sort of man you noticed. He wouldn't have stood out if she had spotted him on the leafy row in Nantwich where she'd lived with James – there he'd fit right in. But here in Leyholme, his tailored suit, silk tie and immaculately groomed hair stuck out like a sore thumb.

'Mummy, what's for tea?' Max was asking. He really seemed to have embraced this new addition to his vocabulary since Brooke had taught it to him.

'Dinner,' Rhianna corrected automatically. The well-dressed man had caught her eye now and was smiling a welcome, as if it was her he'd been waiting for. Was he someone from James? A lawyer?

Her stomach lurched. Oh God, he wasn't here about the children? James would be able to afford the very best legal representation if he chose to fight her for custody, but he wouldn't be so cruel, surely, as to try to take her babies.

'I'm… not sure what's for dinner yet, sweetie,' she said absently to Max, her worried gaze still on the stranger. 'Why don't you run inside and up to the flat? I'll be there in a moment.'

Max stared at her. 'Go in the pub?'

Rhianna never normally allowed them to walk through the pub when it was open, always taking them up the back way.

'Just this once,' she said. 'Take your sister, and don't talk to anyone except Brooke and Nana. Be your mum's little helper like you always are, all right, Maxie?'

She had been reflecting on what Brooke said last night, about the mummy thing. It hadn't sounded odd among their Nantwich circle, where it was what most people said. Even James, a man approaching forty years old, called his parents Mummy and Daddy. People from his background just did, like characters in an Evelyn Waugh novel. But here… Brooke was right; it was only going to get Max teased by his peers. In this world, it didn't sound high-brow; it sounded infantile. Better to teach him a new habit now, before he alienated the other children entirely.

'In you go now,' she said to Max and Livvy, squeezing their hands. 'I won't be long, loves.'

Looking puzzled, Max took his sister's hand and they ran ahead to the pub.

'Mrs Garrett,' the man said when she reached him, nodding. He certainly didn't look hostile – not that that meant much, if he really was a lawyer.

'Actually it's Ms Padgett,' Rhianna told him, keeping a cautious distance. 'I'm using my maiden name again now. You can tell your client that when you see him.'

He raised an eyebrow. 'I wasn't aware that I had one.'

She frowned. 'Weren't you sent here to wait for me?'

'I'm certainly waiting for you. No one sent me but my own desire to put a face to a voice – and perhaps to have a little talk.' He smiled pleasantly as he slipped a business card into her hand. 'This ought to clear things up.'

'Nick Weyborough.' She glanced up from the card. 'You're from Willowtree Taverns.'

'That's right. Might I be permitted to shake your hand, that being the case?'

'Oh. Yes, of course.' Rhianna summoned a smile as she took the hand he offered. 'I'm so sorry, I thought you must represent my husband. My estranged husband, I should say.'

'Well, since you're smiling at me now then I'm very grateful I don't,' he said, laughing. 'Could we talk? Perhaps I can take you somewhere we can chat over a drink.'

'I can't, I'm sorry. My children are waiting inside for me.'

'All right, then I'll make this quick. I take it you received our final offer?'

'Yes, but I'm afraid, um, that we're not interested,' Rhianna said, shooting a quick look through the window to make sure they weren't visible to Brooke.

Nick, seeing where her gaze was directed, took her elbow and guided her out of sight.

'I haven't spoken to your sister about this, Ms Padgett, since I can tell I'm banging my head against a brick wall with her,' he said in a low voice.

You don't know the half of it, Rhianna thought, but she managed to bite her tongue.

'I'm also picking up that your mother is likely to follow where her daughters lead, business-wise. You, I sense, are more willing to listen than Brooke.'

'Just say what you've got to say,' Rhianna told him, trying not to let her face give anything away.

'I've spoken to my superiors and such is their wish to add The Highwayman's Drop to their stable of pubs, they've agreed on another final offer.'

'So, a *final* final offer.'

Nick laughed. 'Exactly so. £1.2 million.'

'Bloody hell.' Rhianna's hands flew to her mouth. 'Oh gosh, I'm so sorry. I don't know where that came from. I hardly ever swear normally.'

'I think under the circumstances it can be justified,' Nick said, smiling warmly.

Rhianna had no idea why Brooke had described Nick as slimy. To her he seemed a perfect gentleman: charming, polite and well-dressed, with a sense of humour too.

'I mean, it's… a generous offer,' she said. 'More than generous. But I'm sorry, Mr Weyborough—'

'Nick, please.'

'I'm sorry, Nick, but I suspect my sister's views will remain the same no matter how high your company goes. The pub means more to her than any sum of money.'

'I'd picked up on that,' Nick said with a dry smile. 'Why is that, do you think? At the end of the day, it's just a building.'

Rhianna hesitated. What would Brooke's answer be? She thought back to what her sister had shown her today: the grieving widowers, finding comfort and consolation away from their lonely homes. The groups planning events for the community, the families meeting across the gener-ations…

'I think she feels it's important to the village,' she said slowly. 'People rely on it, as a sort of hub for the community. And it's been the family business for a long time.'

'I wonder, in that case, why she didn't accept my offer to run the place as our tenant.'

Rhianna frowned. 'What?'

'I offered Brooke the option to remain as manager. That would seem the ideal solution: she could have her pub, and the money too. She turned me down flat.'

'But… why would she do that?'

Nick shrugged. 'You know her far better than I do. As you say, it's been a family business for a long time – several generations, I understand. Perhaps she hopes to keep it in the family for her own children.'

'She hasn't got any,' Rhianna murmured, half to herself. 'She doesn't want children. They make her uncomfortable.'

'Well, then for your little boy and girl.'

Rhianna laughed. 'Max and Livvy? Oh, no. Not in a million years.'

'Then I couldn't say what her reason was. All I know is her answer.'

'But I don't understand. That makes no sense.'

He fixed her with an earnest look. 'Ms Padgett – Rhianna. My superiors have been quite clear that this will be absolutely the final offer they're going to make on The Highwayman's Drop. Already, they feel this is beyond generous. They've given me three months to make their case to your family, after which the offer will be withdrawn.'

'Why are you telling me? If Brooke won't sell, I can't make her.'

'Oh, I don't know,' Nick said, smiling. 'I imagine you can be quite persuasive.'

Rhianna felt a little dizzy. Were they still talking business? He almost sounded like he was flirting with her.

'Not when it comes to my sister,' she said, smiling a little uncertainly back.

'But your mother. If she could be persuaded, then your sister would be outvoted.'

'That isn't how it works, Nick. We aren't a board of directors. We're a family.'

'Just think what £400,000 could get you, Rhianna. Independence for you and your children, with no need to worry that every person you see lurking around is a spy for your ex-husband—'

'Estranged husband,' Rhianna corrected him. 'Look, I'm grateful for the offer but I really can't go against my family. I wish I could, but they don't want to sell and I have to accept that. I'm sorry, really.'

'As am I, for both our sakes,' Nick said with a sigh.

'I need to go to my children. Thanks again for the offer.'

'Wait,' Nick said as she turned to go. 'Might I call you sometime so we can discuss it further? Maybe we could go out for that drink, when your children can spare you.'

'I don't think my sister would like that very much.'

'But you would,' Nick said, smiling his charming smile. 'Wouldn't you?'

Rhianna couldn't help smiling back. 'Perhaps I would. That doesn't make it a good idea, does it? Goodbye, Nick.'

Chapter Thirteen

When she'd finished locking up the pub, Brooke trudged upstairs to the flat. She felt unutterably weary.

Hayden hadn't said anything today about what had happened between them last night. Still, things had been a little awkward once Rhianna had left. Brooke couldn't look at him without thinking of the kiss they'd shared; how good it had felt. God, it was such a long time since she'd been kissed! Actually, she wasn't sure she'd ever been kissed like Hayden had kissed her. Not passionate or urgent, like her boyfriends in the past, but sort of sweet and uncertain. She'd felt like she hadn't wanted it to end – partly because she knew that once it did, she'd have to confront the fact that it wasn't a good idea to ever repeat it.

It was no use dwelling on it, though. Hayden was a dad, and Brooke really wasn't the mothering kind. Apparently she'd already half-poisoned her niece and nephew with evil processed food and possibly indoctrinated Max into a biker gang, and that was when she'd been doing her best impersonation of a responsible adult. There were so many fuck-ups waiting to happen if someone like her started dating a single dad.

And yet, here she was thinking about him again. His lips, soft and enquiring; his fingers in her hair...

Sex deprivation. That was what it was. Perhaps it wasn't only her mum who needed to get back out dating. Brooke might resurrect her old Tinder profile, see if she could meet someone who shared her fun, no-strings agenda. The problem was, men like that became harder to find the older you got. And then there was work. The pub needed so much of her time, it was difficult to fit even a casual boyfriend around it.

Brooke glanced over the bannister at the empty pub, dimly lit by the Fire Exit sign above the front door, before unlocking the flat. A pub without people seemed an eerie thing, like a marionette hanging on a peg.

All she wanted was to slide into bed without talking to another living soul. But she couldn't, because she and Rhianna had promised to get their mum set up on Tinder tonight.

She found Janey and Rhianna in the living room, watching the news.

'Evening all,' she said. 'Are the kids in bed?'

'Yes, fast asleep,' Rhianna said.

OK, why was her sister looking at her like that? Sort of… cold, as if she was sitting on some suppressed irritation. They'd got on all right today in the pub, for the first time in a long time. When Rhia had teased her about Hayden and they'd joked about their mum's cooking, it had felt for a moment like they'd recaptured a little of the relationship they'd had as kids.

But now Rhianna looked like she was pissed off about something. What had changed?

'So, er, how was their first day at Leyholme Primary?' Brooke asked.

'Livvy had a whale of a time, but Max is struggling. He's very shy.'

'Hopefully things'll get better when he's settled in.' Brooke glanced at her mum. 'So, are we getting this Tinder profile sorted out?'

'Yes please,' Janey said, flicking off the TV. 'I'm not getting any younger here, daughters.'

'Turn the main light on,' Rhianna said to Brooke. 'We'll need it to get a good profile selfie.'

Janey frowned. 'Do I need to have my photo taken then?'

'You won't get any interest if you don't,' Brooke said, pressing the light switch. 'People will just assume you're hideous.'

Janey laughed. 'So why not include a photo and confirm it beyond all doubt?'

'Oh, give up. You look great, Mother.'

'Ta.' Janey glanced down at her top. 'Still, I'd better run a brush through my hair and put a nice blouse on. There's a gravy stain on this. Give me a minute, girls.'

When she'd gone to change, Brooke smiled awkwardly at Rhianna.

'So… how shall we do this?' she asked. 'I suppose download the app to one of our phones?'

'We can both download it,' Rhianna said. 'Then either of us will be able to log in and check who she's chatting to.'

'That feels a bit like spying on her.'

'We won't read her messages. I just want to make sure she isn't getting targeted by creeps.'

Brooke smiled. 'Bit of a role reversal, eh? It doesn't seem so long ago that she was giving us dire warnings of what to be wary of in potential boyfriends.'

'No.'

Silence fell. Brooke couldn't help feeling there was still a coolness in her sister's manner that hadn't been there earlier.

'Um, hey,' Brooke said. 'Look, I wanted to say thanks for this afternoon. It was good of you to help out.'

'No problem.'

'And I hope I didn't come across as too down on that idea of yours and Hayden's. You're right, we've got nothing to lose by trying new things. I was impressed by how well you were able to flesh out his suggestion.'

Rhianna shrugged, not making eye contact. 'Just trying to do my bit.'

Brooke frowned. 'Look, are you pissed off with me? I kept my tattoos covered around the kids. I didn't feed them anything non-approved. I'm trying too, Rhia.'

Rhianna scowled at the blank TV screen.

'Brooke, did you tell Nick Weyborough you wouldn't consider staying on here as a Willowtree Taverns tenant?' she demanded.

Brooke blinked. 'Well, I… yes. How do you know about it?'

'Why, Brooke? That's a win-win. You could keep your beloved pub, and you and I and Mum could have £400,000 each to do what we like with. Money that as you know, I badly need.'

'£400,000?'

'That's right, Willowtree upped their offer again. £1.2 million. They were adamant this was the last one, though. In three months' time, they'll withdraw it and that will be that.'

'Why would Nick go to you with a new offer and not me?'

'He said talking to you was like banging his head against a brick wall. I was half tempted to say I knew what he meant,' Rhianna snapped. 'Anyway, why shouldn't he come to me? Who do you think you are in this family, Vito Corleone?'

'Yeah well, it doesn't make any difference. I can't sell this place, Rhia. I'm sorry, but that's the way it is.'

'Why not? You could keep your pub and I could have the money I need for me and my children – the money that'll save me having to crawl back to my cheating bastard of a husband out of sheer desperation if I find I'm unable to provide for us. What are you trying to save this place for? The children you've sworn a hundred times you're never going to have? Because I sure as hell don't want to pass it on to the next generation on my side of the family.'

Brooke glared at her. 'Well, obviously. You couldn't have your precious darlings getting their hands dirty in a common place like this, right?'

'I just think their talents could be better employed elsewhere,' Rhianna said, sticking out her chin. 'Max was top of his form for English. Do you think I want to see him waste his brain pulling pints?'

'Like I do, you mean.'

'You do you, Brooke, as the saying goes. I'm not going to apologise for wanting more for Max and Livvy, just like Mum and Dad wanted more for me when they encouraged me to take the entrance exam for St Mary's.'

'You promised you were going to drop this, Rhianna.'

'Yes, well, that was before I got new information.'

'I can't give this place up,' Brooke said for what felt like the hundredth time. God, why couldn't her sister get that one simple fact into her thick skull? 'It's Dad's, isn't it? It's a piece of him – and a piece of me. The Highwayman's shaped me in a way it never did you.'

'Then why won't you consider running it as a tenant? It'd still be Dad's legacy – still belong to the village. Things would be no different than they are now.'

'They bloody would. You think I could watch those bastards at Willowtree suck all the life out of the place while I stand by powerless? Sign away the home I grew up in for City Boy wankers like Nick Weyborough to mutilate?'

Rhianna shook her head. 'You are quite unbelievably selfish.'

'*I'm* selfish?' Brooke snapped, every hair on the back of her neck standing on end. 'You'd really make me sell? Even though you know this place means as much to me as your kids do to you?'

Rhianna laughed. 'Do you realise how pathetic that sounds? It's just a building, Brooke. If it's taking the place of a husband and children in your life, you really need to take a look at your priorities.'

'It's not my fault you were so blinded by James's looks and money you couldn't see what a sleaze he was,' Brooke shot back. 'You landed yourself in this mess, Rhianna. Why should I give up the things I love to dig you out?'

Rhianna's face crumpled, and Brooke winced with shame.

'Oh God, Rhia, I'm sorry,' she said in a softer voice. 'That was uncalled for.'

Rhianna was silent for a moment, staring down at her knees.

'Well, I guess I shouldn't have called you pathetic for not wanting kids either.' She summoned a watery smile. 'So much for trying harder, eh?'

Brooke sighed. 'It'd be nice to make it through twenty-four hours without falling out. It was nice in the pub today when we weren't fighting.'

'I'm sure we can behave like civilised human beings while we help Mum out, can't we? This means a lot to her.'

'You're damn right it does,' Janey said from the doorway.

Brooke turned to look at her. 'You heard all that?'

'I heard. I don't think you two realise how far the sound of your arguments carries. Why don't you stay off the subject of the pub? It's clear you're never going to agree on it.'

'It's a bit hard when we're both living in it,' Rhianna said.

'Mum, if I ask you a question, will you give me an honest answer?' Brooke asked.

Janey took a seat in the armchair. 'Is it about my love life? Because you might decide an honest answer is the last thing you want.'

'No, it's about this place. Tell me truthfully: do you want to sell?'

Janey sighed. 'I don't know. When your father was alive, it would never have occurred to me. Now he's gone... everything feels different.'

'So you do want to.'

'No. What I really want is to see it restored to its glory days. I always planned to sign my share of The Highwayman's over to the two of you when I retired so we could keep it in the family. £400,000 would be unimagined wealth, yes, but I can't take it with me when I go. I'd far rather see my grandchildren running this place, like four generations of your father's family before them. However, since it seems increasingly likely that my youngest daughter isn't going to procreate, and since I sense my eldest has more elevated plans for her little ones, that feels like a pipe dream these days.'

'What do you want, then?'

'I don't really know,' she said with a wistful smile. 'All I know is, if you don't want to sell, Brooke, you'll never find me pressuring you.'

Brooke fell silent, thoughtfully chewing her thumb-nail.

'What about me?' Rhianna asked. 'I want to sell. Why do you always take her side, Mum?'

'I do no such thing,' Janey said. 'I'll do whatever I can for you through this crisis in your life, Rhianna, but I think you know in your heart that it isn't right to ask your sister to make a sacrifice like that.'

'Huh. You'd pressure me to sell fast enough if Brooke needed money.'

'You're wrong about that. I'd never pressure you to part with something you loved.' Janey summoned a smile. 'Now, are we going to find me a man or what? I can feel my wrinkles deepening every second we waste.'

'Right.' Brooke shot her sister an uneasy glance as they settled into another wobbly truce. 'Rhia, do you want to get an account set up? I'll sort a photo.'

Rhianna nodded and took out her iPhone.

'Well, how do people pose for these things?' Janey put one hand behind her head and pouted provocatively. 'Like this?'

Rhianna glanced up and laughed. 'Mum, you look like you've had a dodgy batch of lip fillers.'

'Oi,' Janey said, glaring at her. 'This is my sexy waif pose, I'll have you know. People used to say I looked like Twiggy when I did that.'

'I think your waif days are over, Mum.' Brooke positioned her mum's head so she was looking at the camera, but tilted slightly upwards. 'There you go. Now smile.'

'Like this?' Janey slapped on a self-conscious Cheshire Cat grin.

'God, no, that's terrifying. Just... try to look natural. Pretend someone's come up to order a pint off you.'

'Right.' Janey rearranged her face into something a bit less toothy. 'There.'

Brooke nodded. 'Much better. Rhia, what do you think?'

Rhianna looked up from her phone. 'Good. But smile with your eyes too, Mum.'

'What, and show my crow's feet off?'

'No one's going to care about those. They make you look fun.'

'I suppose.' Janey tried again, smiling with her whole face this time, and Brooke snapped a couple of photos.

'Perfect,' she said. 'Rhia, I'll WhatsApp you the best one.'

'OK, done,' Rhianna said when she'd added the photo to her mum's profile. 'Now the bio. What shall we put?'

'Oh, I know how to write these,' Janey said, brightening. 'I used to read the lonely hearts ads in the paper for a laugh. Put, um... right. "Mature but well-preserved widowed lady, GSOH, WLTM handsome older gentleman..." er, no, take out handsome: it makes me sound shallow. "WLTM distinguished older gentleman, sixty-plus, for friendship and companionship, maybe more. Interests include walking, music and *The Crown*.

Solvent with own transport. Sensitive F, sixty-two." How does that sound?'

Brooke rolled her eyes at Rhianna. 'Oh my God.'

Rhianna nodded in sympathy. 'This is going to be harder than we thought.'

'What?' Janey said, looking from one daughter to the other. 'What did I do wrong?'

'For a start, you're not paying by the word,' Rhianna said. 'You can write in full sentences. And GSOH and WLTM went out sometime in the Cretaceous period.'

'What the hell is "solvent with own transport" about?' Brooke asked.

Her mum blinked. 'Well, so he'll know I'm not a gold-digger.'

'Jesus,' Brooke muttered. 'All right, Rhia, take this down. "Silver single dying to mingle. If you're looking for someone to carpe some diems with, I'm your girl! Sixty-something young at heart, looking for fun-loving male, fifty-five-plus, for friendship and much more." Stick a winky emoji in, for the really obtuse ones who don't know a euphemism when they see it. Then add this: "Interests include long walks, cool tunes and *very* hot nights. I also own my own pub, boys, so try not to fight over me." Another winky emoji, but this time the cheeky one with the tongue sticking out.'

'Coming across a bit full-on,' Rhianna said as she tapped away. 'Let's add a quote. That shows she's got brains as well.'

'Right. Any suggestions?'

'How about… "Live as if you were to die tomorrow. Learn as if you were to live forever."'

'That's John Lennon, isn't it?' Janey said.

Rhianna shook her head pityingly. 'It's Ghandi, Mum.'

'Right. That's who I meant. Ghandi, the fifth Beatle.' She looked at Brooke. 'Do you really think I ought to have all that? I sound a bit… bouncy.'

'It's internet dating, Janey. Bouncy's the name of the game,' Brooke told her. 'People love confidence in an older woman. You'll be fighting them off.'

'You've made me sound like a right randy old goat.'

Brooke shrugged. 'If the cap fits…'

'I agree with Mum, it is a bit much,' Rhianna said. 'She'll be deluged with perverts if we make her sound too frisky. Let's tone down some of the language, swap "very hot nights" for "cosy evenings in front of the TV" and take out the winky emojis.' She made the changes and passed the phone to her mum to approve.

Brooke pulled a face. 'Too far the other way. Now she'll get nothing but accountants in milk-bottle specs.'

'No, I like that,' Janey said, handing the phone back. 'Just the right amount of bounce.'

Brooke shrugged. 'It's your funeral.'

'OK, here I go. Hitting publish.' Rhianna tapped at the screen, and everyone fell silent. It felt momentous, somehow.

'Well, now what happens?' Janey asked. 'Do I just sit here and wait for my dream man to turn up?'

'You can wait for someone to contact you, or you can start looking for yourself,' Brooke said. 'I recommend the latter. Rhia, pass me the phone.'

Rhianna gave it to her and Brooke flicked through a few profiles.

'Look,' she said, showing one to her mum. 'Here's Gerald, fifty-eight. He's got a daughter and two grand-children, and a teacup Yorkshire terrier called Mr Jeffries.'

Janey frowned. 'Called what?'

'Mr Jeffries.'

'Sounds like an oddball.' She peered at the screen. 'Fifty-eight my arse. He's sixty-five if he's a day. Maybe I should've shaved a few years off too if that's how it works.'

'All right, so it's a no to Gerald. In that case, all you do is swipe his profile card left off the screen.' Brooke demonstrated. 'Whereas if you like someone, you swipe right. If someone you've right-swiped on right-swipes you back, you can message each other. Oh, and if you super-like them you can swipe up, but I'd be a bit coy about that if I were you.'

Janey looked interested. 'That's a novel way of doing it. Can I have a look?'

'All right, here.' Brooke passed her the phone, and Janey started looking through some profiles while Brooke went to sit by Rhianna.

'What is Mum's type?' Rhianna asked Brooke. 'Apart from Dad, obviously.'

Brooke laughed. 'David Essex in skintight trousers.'

'Oh!' Janey said, staring wide-eyed at the phone.

'What?' Rhianna said.

'I think I just swiped on someone. I didn't mean to.'

'Which way?'

'Up, I think.'

Rhianna stood up. 'Let me see.'

She took the phone and tapped the icon for matches. Her eyes widened. 'Oooh. Oh dear.'

'Who is it?' Brooke asked.

'Someone called Chad. He's got a shaven head made of pure muscle and a neck tattoo.' She glanced at her sister's arms. 'No offence.'

Brooke scoffed. 'Chad. That is so not his real name. He's just trying to sound cool and American. What does his bio say?'

'It's only short.' Rhianna grimaced. 'It says "U n me baybee ain't nuffin but mammalz. Jus wanna make u scream laydeeeez". With four Es and a Z.'

Brooke pulled a face. 'Yikes.'

Janey took the phone back.

'What does that mean?' she asked, pointing to a dot that had appeared next to the speech bubble icon.

'It means you've got a message,' Rhianna told her.

Janey tapped the icon. 'Oh. It's from Chad. He says "send nudes". Is that how it works nowadays, then?'

'No it bloody isn't.' Brooke snatched the phone and quickly blocked Chad before he decided to send any nudes of his own. 'You need to be careful, Mum. There's some real creeps out there. You have to learn what the red flags are before you end up with an inbox full of dick pics.'

Janey blinked. 'Red flags?'

'Yeah, you know, warning signs that a bloke might be a bit of a perve. Like a bio saying he wants to make you scream, for example. Huge red flag right there.'

'It's very different to how things were in my day, this modern dating,' Janey murmured, looking rather warily at Rhianna's phone. 'It seems like there's dodgy men all over the shop.'

'There always were. This is just a convenient way to find them all in one place,' Brooke said. 'The worst are the ones who manage to pass for nice guys. That's why you need to look out for the subtle red flags as well as the obvious ones.'

'How do I spot them then, these red flags?'

'You need to learn to read between the lines,' Rhianna said. 'Like for example, if his bio says something like "proud to be British" then he's almost certainly a far-right bigot. Also, it's a massive no to anyone in either army uniform or medical scrubs.'

'Even if he's a doctor?'

'Doctors don't pose for their dating profiles straight from the operating theatre, Mum.'

'Oh. No, I suppose not.'

'Those profiles are all catfish.' She glanced at her mum's blank expression. 'They're not who they say they are, I mean. Fraudsters out to scam you.'

'That reminds me. Look out for the ones holding a big fish in their profile pic as well,' Brooke said. 'They are definitely over-compensating for something.'

Janey blinked. 'Are there ones holding big fish?'

'Always, Mum. Always.' She took the phone and scrolled through a few profiles. 'I remember some of the flags I came across back when I was still Tindering. Men whose profiles were just a list of demands, with nothing about themselves. Topless gym selfies. Bios that were basically rants about everything they thought was wrong with society. There are a million of them.'

Janey rubbed her temples. 'My head hurts.'

Rhianna patted her mum's shoulder. 'Well, don't worry, there'll be plenty of nice guys to discover too. We'll be here to help you spot the weirdos.'

She smiled gratefully. 'Thanks, girls. I don't know what I'd do without you.'

Brooke arched an eyebrow. 'So now all we need to do is find you your first date, don't we?'

Chapter Fourteen

'Mum, can you mind Livvy and Max for an hour?' Rhianna asked just over two weeks later, in the second week of the children's Easter holidays.

Janey was in the kitchen with a piece of toast sticking out of her mouth, rummaging through drawers.

'I'm a bit busy, Rhia,' she mumbled, the toast waggling up and down as she spoke.

'Please. I'll be as quick as I can, but...' Rhianna cast a glance at the children, who'd thrown themselves down in front of the television as soon as they'd come home from their trip to the playground – a habit she knew she ought to crack down on, but that right now was doing a lot towards making her chaotic, *sans*-au pair life easier. '...um, it's sort of urgent.'

'Ask your sister,' Janey said, removing the toast from her mouth as she pulled open another drawer. 'She isn't working.'

'I'd rather not.'

'Why? It'll do her good to spend some time with them.'

'Because it scares her to death. And because... I just don't care to.'

'I thought you two were getting along today.'

Rhianna couldn't help reflecting that the fact their mother measured her and Brooke's relationship in twenty-four-hour segments was rather telling.

'We are,' she said. 'I'd just prefer you to watch them.'

'Too much to do,' Janey muttered. She opened another drawer and slammed it shut again. 'Where the *hell* is my vape? Sorry, sorry, sorry, I didn't mean to use bad words in front of the kiddies. Nicotine cravings are murdering my nerves.'

'I know where it is.' Rhianna stood on tiptoes to fetch it from the top of a cupboard. 'I put it up here, out of reach of the children. Sorry.'

'Thank God,' Janey said as she practically snatched the thing from her daughter's hand. She put it in her mouth, and Rhianna cast a worried look at Livvy and Max.

'Mum, I don't want to be a nag, but you did promise you wouldn't use that thing where the children could see,' she said in a low voice.

Janey closed the kitchen door.

'It's not switched on,' she said. 'Having it there calms me down, that's all. Psychological. I'll go outside for a proper fix in a minute.'

'What're you so on edge for?'

Janey laughed. 'You're seriously asking? You and Brooke were the ones who persuaded me I ought to meet this serial killer tonight.'

'He's not going to be a serial killer,' Rhianna said, smiling. 'The odds are at least ten to one against.'

'Mmm. Very reassuring.'

'You wanted to get out husband-hunting. You have to pop your dating cherry with someone, don't you?'

Janey smiled. 'You're starting to sound like your sister, you know.'

'Oh God, don't say that,' Rhianna said, laughing. 'Mum, you'll be fine. You'll have your phone on you in case of emergencies.'

'I just hope I haven't forgotten how to do it.'

'For my own sanity, I'm going to assume the "it" in that sentence means dating,' Rhianna said. 'Can you keep an eye on Max and Livvy? Please.'

'Why, where is it you're going?'

Rhianna lowered her voice. 'I got a text from James. He's here, Mum.'

'Here!'

'Not *here* here, but nearby. He says he's had enough of me putting him off and he wants to talk about access to the children. I had to agree to meet him; he was threatening to come to the pub otherwise and I didn't want a scene. That's why I don't want to ask Brooke to look after the kids. She'd only make a fuss about me seeing him.'

Janey looked worried. 'You definitely feel up to facing him?'

'I'll be OK.' Rhianna threw back her shoulders. 'It's time. I've been putting him off for over a month now. No matter what he's done, he's Livvy and Max's father and he's got a right to see them.'

'Huh. It's him seeing *you* I'm worried about.' Janey put a hand on her arm. 'Rhianna...'

'What?'

'Just... stay strong, all right, chickie?'

'How do you mean?'

'Rhia, I know what goes through that head of yours better than you think. I'm a mum too – what's more I'm *your* mum, and that comes with a special kind of intuition. I know you beat yourself up about taking the kids away from their dad, their friends, their posh schools and big house. I know you wonder constantly about whether you did the right thing. I know you're struggling in these cramped quarters without your home comforts, and I

147

know a little voice tells you every hour, on the hour, how much simpler life could be if you just gave up the fight and went back to him. Doesn't it?'

Rhianna blinked. 'You knew all that?'

'Course I did. I'd be exactly the same in your place.' Janey pulled her into a tight hug. 'But for my sake, stay strong, eh?' she whispered. 'For eleven years you raised that man's children and kept his home. Supported his career at the expense of your own, despite having more brains in your little finger than James has in his whole body. And how did he repay you? If he cheated once, he'll do it again – and again and again, until he's broken you completely. And don't you believe a word if he tries to convince you otherwise.'

'But the children…'

'The children are better off as they are,' Janey said firmly. 'If you took them back there, what would they grow up seeing? Parents who can't love each other; their mum sacrificing her self-respect for their sake. An upbringing like that, they'll be riddled with all kinds of guilt by the time they leave home. They can still have a healthy relationship with their father if you two separate.'

'But I can't give them what James can give them. I'll be lucky if I can earn enough to support the three of us, with a CV that's been empty for over a decade.'

'Oh, we'll work something out,' Janey said, although Rhianna couldn't help thinking that was rather too vague to be comforting. 'You're a Cambridge graduate, aren't you? Anyway, this could be the making of Max and Livvy. Better than coasting through life on their parents' money, the way their father always has.'

'What will I say to him, Mum?'

'You'll know when the time comes. Just don't let him wheedle his way back into your good graces. Hold on to your anger; you're going to need it.'

Rhianna gave a wet laugh. 'You know what's really pathetic? I still love the bastard. I keep waking from this recurring dream where things have been magically reset and we can go back to how we were.'

'That's only natural. But you can't, Rhia.'

'I know.' Rhianna gave her mum a kiss on the cheek. 'I won't be long. I'll tell the children I'm going shopping.'

'Don't forget what I said,' Janey called after her as she went to kiss Max and Livvy goodbye. 'Don't let... the shopping get round you. It's only thinking about itself.'

As Rhianna drove to the coffee shop in Halifax where she'd reluctantly agreed to meet her husband, she tried to settle her thoughts. The last time she'd seen him, she'd been consumed by a white-hot anger that she'd been forced to hide while she executed her escape plan. Now, more than a month after his betrayal and her flight, she wasn't sure how she ought to feel. When she pictured his face, everything was a jumble.

She was angry with him still, of course. It wasn't the consuming rage she'd felt immediately after her discovery of the affair, which had given her the adrenaline rush she needed to temporarily develop a backbone, take her kids and get out. This was more of a simmering resentment, touched with disbelief that the man who'd slept beside her all these years could do something so utterly devastating. But she loved him still, too. How could she not? Love couldn't just be switched off, even in the wake of such a thorough and life-shattering betrayal. His features were etched indelibly on her brain; he was there in the faces of her children when she kissed them goodnight. She hated him, and she loved him, and she knew that one way or another, she could never, ever be free of him.

She'd given everything to that man. Sacrificed so much, from her never-realised career to the muscles of her pelvic floor. Why would he throw away everything they had for something so damn… *trivial?* Did he love her, this twenty-five-year-old he couldn't control himself around? If there was one question Rhianna wanted an answer to, it was that – just, *why?*

When she arrived at the coffee shop, James was waiting. He jumped to his feet when she came in, awkwardly clutching a bouquet of lavender roses.

That was a novelty, anyway. James never did anything awkwardly. He was the most confident person Rhianna had ever known. She fixed her face into an expression of stern civility as she approached him. She felt like crying, but she wouldn't. It was time to show James just how strong she could be.

'Good afternoon,' she said briskly, helping herself to a seat. 'Shall we get on with it, then?'

James stared, taken aback by her business-like attitude.

'Um… yes.' He stood still for a moment before sitting down. 'You look well, Flops.'

'Don't call me that, James. Let's just get this over with.'

'Right.' He hesitated, then, as if remembering the flowers, he held them out. 'I brought these for you.'

'I don't think that's particularly appropriate, do you?'

'Please. They're a peace offering,' he said, his eyes entreating. 'Lavender roses, you see? The same flowers I brought you on our first date.'

She snorted. 'A peace offering? A dozen roses for fucking someone else, is that really the going rate?'

James's eyes bulged. 'Rhianna, good God!'

Rhianna couldn't help smiling. She'd been right; that had felt satisfying.

'Oh come on, James, we're both adults,' she observed coolly. 'There are no children here for me to have to watch my language around, are there?'

'Yes, but it sounds so brutal when you say it. It's hardly ladylike.'

'And sleeping with co-workers behind your wife's back is hardly gentlemanly. I only said it, James. You were the one who did it.'

He shook his head. 'Why are you talking like this?'

'Because I can. Because I'm free now from having to be your ideal, which means I can talk however the… shit I like.'

Bloody hell, where was this coming from? Was she channelling her sister? James was totally on the back foot with this all-new, straight-talking, hard-cursing Rhianna, his usual unflappable confidence nowhere to be seen. She ought to take up poker.

Still, she found it hard to meet his eyes. She knew if she looked into them long enough, she'd start to weaken.

'I take it this is for me?' she said, nodding to the steaming mug in front of her.

James stared at her.

'Um, yes,' he said, finally putting the flowers down. 'Chai latte. I know you like those.'

'Thank you.' She sipped it calmly. 'Well, let's discuss what we've got to discuss, shall we? I don't want to be away from the children for too long.'

James looked like he was in more familiar territory now. He sat up straight.

'You've got no right to keep them from me.'

'I'm not. I just felt it would be a good idea to let them get used to a new routine before we set up some visits.'

'It's been a month, Rhianna! They're my children. I want to see them.'

She felt herself soften slightly at the earnestness in his tone, but forced herself to stay strong.

'All right,' she said evenly. 'That's reasonable. Now they're settled into their new school, we'll make a plan for access.'

James gazed down into his coffee.

'Do they ask about me?' he said quietly.

'Not as much as they ask about Avril. Even the paid help spent more time with them than you did, so naturally they mete out their affection accordingly.'

'Oh.'

Rhianna relented when she saw him press his eyes closed, as if fighting back tears.

'All right, that isn't true,' she said in a gentler voice. 'They ask about you every day. And James, I want you to know that I wouldn't ever try to keep them from you. You'll always be their father.'

'Thank you.'

'I thought perhaps every third weekend they could go to you. If you wanted them that often.'

'Well, with work that might be…' He stopped. 'I mean, yes. I'd like that.'

'And we could set up some playdates in the summer hols if you like. Day trips and things, the four of us. There's no reason we can't act like civil adults around one another, for Max and Livvy's sake.'

'No.' He swallowed hard, then leaned across the table to take her hands. 'Rhianna, please. Just… come home, please. The place is in a complete stew without you. I'm in a stew. I need you so, so much, darling.'

Gently she drew her hands away. 'I'm sorry, James.'

'I swear it's over with Shari. She's not even with the company any more. I promise that if you come back, it'll be all about you and the children. I'll stop working late so often; it could be like it was when we were first married. We were happy, weren't we?'

'Very.' Rhianna sighed as she thought back to those early, joyous days when they were so utterly in love. He'd been so tender, spoiling her with expensive gifts, showering her with affection, treating her like a queen...

'And we can be again,' he said, a glimmer of hope appearing in his eyes. 'Just give me one more chance. I'll never do anything like that to you again, I swear it.'

Rhianna could still hear her mum's voice. *Stay strong. If he cheated once, he'll do it again.* But it was hard to stay strong when he looked at her like that, eyes big and blue and appealing. The Janey voice had faded to a dull buzz now. God, how much had she loved him? How much did she still, in spite of everything...

'Once is enough,' she managed to say.

'You really can't find it in your heart to give me one more chance?'

'No, I... I can't.'

'Rhianna, come on, don't be that way,' he said, his voice soft and crooning, as if he was comforting one of the children. 'We'll go away together, have a second honeymoon at Mummy's place in Tuscany. Don't you think you owe it to Max and Livvy to give me a second chance? I'm their father.'

He'd seized her hands again. Rhianna laughed and pulled them away. 'Me? Don't you think you owed it to them to keep it in your underpants in the first place?'

'I suppose I deserved that,' he murmured, casting a look around the almost empty coffee house. 'I don't know what I can say except that I'm sorry. It was the biggest mistake I've ever made and I spend every day hating myself for it.'

'Then why did you do it?' Rhianna said in a softer voice.

He sighed. 'You're young still, Rhianna. Perhaps when you get to my age… well, I suppose it happens differently for women. The fact is, I saw my fortieth birthday hurtling towards me and it brought on a sort of panic. I was weak and I gave in to a need to feel young and virile again.'

She laughed. 'You're blaming your affair with a younger woman on a midlife crisis? I thought you despised vulgar cliché, James.'

'I suppose I am. I never expected…'

'To get caught?' Rhianna said, arching an eyebrow.

'Well, yes,' he mumbled. 'I thought I could get it out of my system, exorcise whatever demons were driving it, and there'd be no need for anyone to get hurt.' He glanced up at her. 'How did you know anyway?'

'Never mind how I knew. I did, that's all.'

'I knew it was wrong, and yet it made me feel… alive. Can you understand that?'

She snorted. 'Having sex with a woman fourteen years your junior made you feel alive, did it? That's convenient.'

He flushed, dropping eye contact. 'You make it sound tawdry.'

'Well, wasn't it?'

'It was… complicated. But it's over now,' he said, meeting her gaze again with a pleading expression. 'I'm ready to swear on the lives of our children that it's over. I know I've got a lot of work to do before you can trust me again, but I'll do it. If it takes me years, I'll do it. I love you, Rhianna.'

She hesitated. Seeing she was weakening, James lifted one of her hands and pressed it to his lips.

'Come home,' he whispered. 'We can collect Livvy and Max from your mother's and we can go right now. Tonight I can have you back in my arms and things can be just like they were before – better.'

God, yes. To go back, to reset things and make this whole nightmare go away. To feel safe and protected again, and know the children had all that they needed. It was so hard to resist that soft croon, lulling her, silencing the voice of resistance in her head...

'Come home, Flops,' James said again, still in that same soft voice. 'You were never meant for this life.'

Rhianna looked up, frowning, as the dream fled. 'What does that mean?'

'This life, this world: it's all wrong for you. You've only been here four weeks and already it's poisoning you.'

Rhianna pulled her hands away from his. 'I'm sorry? Poisoning me?'

'Now, don't be offended,' he said soothingly. 'You're able to hear yourself, aren't you? How different you sound from your real self? You never used to be crude. Even your accent has started to change.'

She laughed. 'Crude? What, cruder than shagging the accounts girl over your desk with your trousers round your ankles?'

James flinched. 'You see, this is exactly what I mean. Your language has tumbled right into the gutter, just like that awful sister of yours. Goodness knows what the children have been learning from her. Not to mention the twenty-a-day cigarette habit they've probably picked up from your mother.'

'She doesn't smoke any more. She vapes now.'

'That's hardly a vast improvement.' He looked at her nails, the polish chipped and callouses on her fingers after nights spent pulling pints and changing barrels. 'You've been working with them in that blasted pub. Haven't you?'

'Yes I have. Why shouldn't I work in the family business? Thanks to your bloody prenup, James, a share in The Highwayman's Drop is all I have in the world now.'

'I can't bear seeing you like this, Rhianna,' he said, softening his voice. 'That place is turning you into something you're not and it's painful to watch.'

'Or you turned me into something I'm not.' Rhianna got to her feet. 'James, I spent eleven years having your children, looking after your house, being polite to your boring, pompous work contacts and generally trying to anticipate your every whim. Despite that, and despite sacrificing any chance of my own career, and most significantly, despite your middle-aged, frantically wandering, and, I might add, pretty underwhelming penis, I'm not entitled to the dirt under my feet in a divorce. But you know what? I bloody well want one, all the same.'

James blinked. 'What?'

'You heard me. I want a divorce, James. I'll never try to keep your children from seeing you, but as for you and me – that's over. And absolutely nothing you say is going to change my mind.'

She marched out, leaving her now cold coffee on the table in front of a gaping James. She managed to make it to her car before she finally gave in, dropped her head onto her arms and sobbed.

Chapter Fifteen

Brooke was reading in her room, enjoying a rare day off, when her mum poked her head around the door.

Brooke sniffed. 'You stink of synthetic blueberries, Mother.'

'I'm trying to steady my nerves, aren't I? You know, in readiness for my inevitable hacking to bits later.'

'Oh, give up. I've set up one-press emergency call on your phone if he turns out to be a weirdo.'

'Huh. I bet he can disable that with some sort of hidden zappy thing. Serial killers are very tech-savvy these days.'

'Well, that'll make one of you.' Brooke put her book down. 'Stop worrying, Mum. He's a retired gardener, not James Bond.'

'Exactly. Good at digging and wielding sharp objects. I bet loads of gardeners are serial killers on the side, all those transferable skills.'

'This was what you wanted, wasn't it?'

Janey pushed her fingers through her hair. 'That was before you and Rhianna turned me into a nervous wreck with your red flags. Look, can you do me a favour?'

'What is it?'

'Can you keep an eye on Max and Livvy for ten minutes or so? Your sister's popped out and I want to give Hayden a hand on the bar.'

'I thought me and you were experimenting with these things called days off today. Hayden can cope.'

'I know, but I need something to take my mind off things.'

Brooke hesitated. 'Mind the kids on my own?'

'They don't bite, Brooke.'

'I always seem to get it wrong when I'm left in charge of them, though. I don't want another row with Rhianna.'

'It won't be for long. Rhia said she'd be back in an hour.'

'When was that?'

'An hour and a half ago,' Janey said, smiling. But her eyes looked worried.

'She's OK, isn't she?' Brooke asked, frowning.

'She's fine. She's just gone to the shops.'

'You're a terrible liar, Mum. Where's she really gone?'

Janey turned away. 'You'll have to speak to her about that. I'll see you in a little while, eh?'

She disappeared. Sighing, Brooke folded over the page of her book and went into the living room. Livvy was puzzling over the old family Monopoly set while her brother did some homework.

Max beamed at her. 'Hiya, Brooke.'

'Um, hiya,' she said, smiling uncertainly back. He'd never greeted her like that before. That must be the new school's influence – unless it was hers, in which case she'd probably be in for a bollocking from Rhianna because the correct form of greeting was something like 'good day, my fine fellow'.

'What are you two up to then?' she asked. 'Enjoying your holidays?'

'Excuse me but I can't make this game work,' Livvy told her, glaring at the top hat she was holding. 'It's a stupid game. There's lots of money and a little dog and a boat, and I don't know how they go together.'

'Oh. Well, maybe I can help,' Brooke said, falling to her knees. Rhianna surely couldn't object to her teaching the kids to play Monopoly, could she? It taught valuable skills to prepare them for middle-class life, like obsession with property prices and what to do when you were jailed for tax evasion.

'Right, so first we need the board,' she said, unfolding it. 'And then… it's ages since I played but I think someone has to be the banker. Max, would you like to do that?'

'OK.' The little boy put his work to one side with alacrity and knelt beside her.

Brooke tugged at her sleeve, making sure her tattoos weren't visible, before she passed him the tray of money.

'So, first you have to give us all £1500,' she said.

Livvy's eyes widened. 'Wow! That's lots!'

She laughed. 'I know. Shame it's not real, eh?'

'If I had £1500, do you know what I'd buy, Brooke?'

Brooke suppressed a smile. Livvy's forthright way of talking always made her laugh.

'What would you buy, Livvy?' she asked soberly.

'I'd buy a bigger house for us. Bigger even than my daddy's house. But it'd still be a pub, because you like pubs. Only with a swimming pool and a waterslide.'

Brooke raised her eyebrows. 'A pub with a swimming pool! That sounds fun.'

Max giggled. 'Livvy, you're silly. You can't have swimming pools in pubs, in case people drink too much beer and drown.'

Livvy looked put out by this quenching of her idea. 'Can so,' she muttered.

'If there were lifeguards, maybe you could,' Brooke said, playing peacemaker. 'So are we all going to live in this new pub then?'

Livvy nodded enthusiastically. 'Yep. Me and you and Max and Mummy and Nana, and Daddy and Avril too. I want all of us to live there together. That'll be so sick.'

'That sounds… lovely, sweetheart.'

'Brooke, why are Mummy – I mean, Mum and Dad fighting?' Max asked.

Ugh. And it had been going so well…

'Hey, you want to be the boot?' Brooke asked brightly. 'Me and your mum always used to argue about who got to be the boot when we were kids.'

Max just stared at her, his brown eyes unblinking, and she sighed.

'I can't really answer that question, Max,' she said softly.

'Don't you know?'

'I… do, but it's not up to me to explain it to you. You need to talk to your mum.'

'She won't tell us,' Livvy said as she arranged her Monopoly money into piles. 'She just says Daddy did something bad, but it's OK because he still loves us. If he still loves us, we should get to go home, shouldn't we?'

'I don't want to go home,' Max announced. 'I like it better here.'

Brooke blinked. 'Do you?'

He nodded. 'We play more here. Mummy – I mean, Mum plays with us more. And she lets us do stuff we're not allowed at home. At home there were loads of rules about when to watch TV and things.'

'I miss Avril though, and my Ferndene friends,' Livvy said.

'I don't miss my Abbotleigh friends much,' Max said. 'Maybe Archie. But Zach borrowed me his Thanos Jet Lego kit so I probably like it here best.'

How fickle was childhood…

'*Lent* you his wotchamacallit Lego, Max, not borrowed,' Brooke corrected him, wondering when exactly she'd morphed into her sister.

'I know. But Zach says borrowed and Mum says I oughtn't to make him feel bad for saying it wrong, so now I say it too.'

'Oh. Well, that's… very considerate of you.'

'You miss Daddy, don't you?' Livvy asked her brother.

'Ye-es,' Max said slowly. 'But he did something bad, though. That's why we had to come here.'

'I don't believe he did anything bad,' Livvy said, folding her arms. 'Daddy doesn't do bad things.'

'He did. Mummy said.'

Brooke sent up a prayer of thanks to the god of lucky breaks as her sister walked in, halting a conversation that was taking her well out of her comfort zone.

'Mummy!' Livvy yelled. 'Are you going to play with us? We're playing Ponopmoly.'

Brooke examined her sister with concern. Rhianna's face was flushed, and her eyes looked swollen. That must've been one hell of a traumatic shopping trip…

'Yes, you're just in time,' Brooke said, summoning a jovial tone in the hope the children wouldn't notice anything amiss. 'We're just about to have a jaunt around London putting up hotels. Max has already bagsied the boot, I'm afraid.'

'Brooke, can you come into the kitchen a moment?' Rhianna said in a shaky voice.

Livvy frowned. 'But we're playing the game, Mummy.'

'You can play in a minute. I just... need a moment with Aunty Brooke.'

Brooke blinked. 'All right.'

She stood up and followed her sister into the kitchen. As soon as the door closed behind them, Rhianna burst out crying, heaving with silent sobs as the tears streamed.

'Oh my God!' Brooke pulled her into a hug. 'Rhia, what's up?'

'I... saw James,' she gasped.

'James! That bastard was here?'

Rhianna nodded. 'I met him in Halifax. To talk about... about access to the children. Except he didn't really want to talk about access.'

'What did he want to talk about?'

'Me going back to him, of course.'

Brooke held her back so she could look into her face. 'Rhia...'

Rhianna laughed through her tears. 'Oh, don't worry, I haven't just come back to grab the kids. I know you think I'm wetter than a month-old lettuce, Brooke, but I have got at least a couple of vertebrae.'

'Well, what happened?'

'I'd be lying if I said I wasn't tempted,' Rhianna admitted, taking a piece of kitchen roll to dab her eyes. 'When he offered me the chance to get my old life back – God, I wanted it so badly. But then he made the mistake of sneering at the pub, and at you and Mum. That woke me up.'

'What did you say?'

'You'd have been proud of me. Honestly, I think I must've been possessed. In all our years of marriage, I've never said boo to that man. Suddenly I was swearing like a docker, telling him exactly where he could get off.'

'Seriously?'

Rhianna cast a look at the door and lowered her voice. 'I told him he had an underwhelming middle-aged penis.'

Brooke laughed. 'You never did!'

Rhianna nodded shyly. 'I asked for a divorce too. And it felt so good, Brooke, letting all the anger out. There's no therapy like giving your cheating ex a telling-off.'

Brooke stared thoughtfully at her reflection in the copper jug on the windowsill. 'You told James off because he insulted the pub?'

'No, I told him off because I caught him going at it with another woman. But that was the trigger I needed to snap me out of any daydream about going back to him, yes.' She rested a hand on Brooke's arm. 'I know you think I hate this place. That's not true, Brooke. For all that I think selling would've been a wise decision, it's still ours. And no bastard gets to insult The Highwayman's but us, right?'

Brooke smiled. 'Right. Excellent use of the past tense in "*would've* been a wise decision", by the way.'

She shrugged. 'I know when to give up.'

Brooke gave her sister another hug.

'You're right, I am proud of you,' she whispered. 'Rhia, I need you to know that however much we might argue, I don't want you going anywhere until you're ready. And I certainly don't want you feeling pressured into going back to that bastard. No matter how much I snap, I want you here, OK?'

'Thanks, sis.' Rhianna wiped her eyes and summoned a smile. 'So. We're playing Monopoly, are we? There's one way to guarantee a family row.'

'You remember when we argued so much that Dad threw the tray of money out the window? The beer garden looked like a scene from *Scarface*.'

'How could I forget?' Rhianna patted her sister's arm. 'It's nice to see you spending time with the kids.'

'Mum forced me into it. Still, for underdeveloped humans they're not so bad.'

Rhianna smiled. 'Generally we refer to those as "children", Brooke.'

She shrugged. 'Whatever. They're funny, though. Max is such a serious little thing, and Livvy cracks me up when she tries to talk all grown up.'

'I know, she has an old soul,' Rhianna said, laughing. She glanced at her sister's long sleeves. 'And thanks for making an effort to be a good influence. I know it's a lot to ask when we've come crashing in to disrupt your life.'

Brooke flushed. 'Oh. No problem.'

'Well, shall we go play Monopoly?'

'Wait.' Brooke put a hand on her sister's arm. 'What is happening with their dad, Rhia? Did you get anything sorted?'

'I suggested they spend every third weekend with him. James seemed happy with that. That's almost as much as he saw them at home, with his busy work, golf and extramarital sex schedule.' She caught her sister's expression. 'It's no good looking like that, Brooke. He's their father. I can't cut off access, no matter how I feel about him.'

'I know. That wasn't what the look was in aid of. I just think you need to have a conversation with them.'

'About what?'

'When you came in, Max was asking what this bad thing James had done was. I said that was something he needed to talk about with you.'

Rhianna looked worried. 'Max asked that?'

'I think it's been preying on his mind. I know he's only ten, but that's old enough to know a bit about what can make or break a marriage.'

'But what will I say?'

'I just think they need some context. Right now all they know is that they've been taken away from home because of something Daddy did and they're puzzled as hell about it.'

'Right.' Rhianna paused with her hand on the door handle. 'Right.'

'I mean, not necessarily now,' Brooke said. 'When you're ready.'

'No, you're right. They need to be told, sooner rather than later.' Rhianna glanced back at her. 'Will you, um… help me?'

Brooke blinked. 'Me? I don't know how to talk to kids.'

'Oh, you do really. You three looked as thick as thieves when I came in.'

'When you came in, I was floundering like a grounded halibut because Max wanted answers about his dad and I had no idea what to tell him.'

'Please, Brooke.' Rhianna fixed a look on her with eyes dry and sore from too much crying. 'Just stay for moral support. You don't have to say anything. I've noticed Max has become attached to you.'

Brooke couldn't help relenting when she saw the appeal in her sister's eyes.

'Well, all right. For you.'

She followed Rhianna into the living room. Her sister sat down on the sofa, and Brooke, feeling very much like she shouldn't be here for this deeply personal conversation between a mother and her children, took a seat beside her.

'Can we play now, Mummy?' Livvy asked. 'Max found the 'structions and he knows how you do it. But there's a jail if you steal from the bank so don't cheat.'

'In a moment.' Rhianna glanced at Brooke. 'So, um, guess who I've just been to see?'

'Who?' Max asked.

'Daddy. I met him to talk about what we're going to do.'

Livvy squealed, clamping both hands to her mouth like she'd just won an Oscar. 'Is Daddy here now? Are we going home?'

'Are Nana and Brooke coming too? Can we come back for when school starts again?' Max asked.

Rhianna held up her hand for silence. 'One question at a time, please. Livvy, I'm sorry, but we're not going ho— we're not going to Daddy's house, and he isn't here now. He just drove over so he and I could talk about some things.'

Livvy's lip wobbled. 'He drove here and didn't come to see us?'

'He wanted to,' Rhianna said gently. 'But I said… that is, we agreed it would be better if you went to visit him next month instead, and had a proper sleepover rather than just a quick visit. You'll like that better, won't you?'

Max had fixed his earnest little eyes on Brooke.

'What's up, love?' his aunt asked him gently.

'If Daddy— if Dad did something bad, I don't want to go,' he said. 'I'd rather stay with you and Nana please, Brooke.'

Brooke shot a worried look at Rhianna.

'Don't you want to see your dad, Maxie?' Rhianna asked him.

'Not if he does bad things.'

'Well, the bad thing he did wasn't anything to do with you and Livvy. He still loves you very much. The… problems are between me and Dad, nobody else.'

'Did he do a bad thing to you?' Max asked, blinking up at her.

'He didn't hurt me or anything awful,' Rhianna reassured him. 'This… this is the sort of bad thing that's hard to explain. It's really a very grown-up, married-people thing.'

'We understand grown-up things,' Livvy said. 'Don't we, Max?'

Max nodded, his eyes still fixed on his mum. Rhianna slid to the floor so she could draw her children into her arms.

'I don't think you'll understand this very well until you're older,' she said gently. 'But I know you're intelligent children, and this concerns you as well as me. I'll do my best to explain it.'

She looked up at Brooke, who nodded encouragingly.

'When you get married, it's a very special thing,' Rhianna told the children. 'It's different to having boyfriends and girlfriends, because you have to make promises to the other person. These are promises that you swear solemnly never, ever to break.'

'Did Daddy break a promise?' Livvy asked.

'Yes, my love. He broke a very important promise, that he'd only love one person all his life. I'm talking about romantic love, like adults have for their husbands or wives. It hurt me a great deal when I found out he'd done that.'

'That was the bad thing?' Max asked.

'Yes,' Rhianna said, closing her eyes for a moment. 'That's why we came here. I couldn't stay once I… after

I found out. It was painful for me – the sort of pain you feel inside when someone hurts your feelings very badly.'

'If Daddy says sorry though, we could go home then, couldn't we?' Livvy asked hopefully.

Rhianna shook her head. 'When you're bigger, Livvy, you'll understand that there are some bad things even a sorry doesn't fix.' She summoned a smile. 'But that doesn't mean Daddy loves you and Max any less. He hasn't broken any promises he made to the two of you, and he misses you very, very much.'

Livvy looked sceptical.

'I don't know why we can't go home, if Daddy's sorry,' she whispered to Max. But Max, with his four additional years' experience of life and love, looked like he partly understood.

'Well, I said it was hard to understand,' Rhianna said. 'You'll both know what I mean one day. Now give me a hug and let's play our game, shall we?'

She smiled sadly as two little heads burrowed under her arms. From the sofa, Brooke mouthed a 'well done'.

Chapter Sixteen

'Shouldn't you be getting ready for your date?' Hayden asked Janey as she poured a pint for Martin Brady. 'I've got things covered here.'

'Now then, who's been gossiping?' Janey said. 'That's supposed to be top secret, that is.'

'Brooke. And Rhianna. And Brooke again. You didn't bring your daughters up to be able to keep a secret, did you?'

'Huh. I blame their father.'

'Aren't you going up? This was supposed to be your day off and you've done nothing but pull pints.'

'Well, it's good for the girls to spend time with the kiddies. They'll fetch me when they want me.' She put Martin's beer on the bar. 'There you go, Marty. Just the way you like it.'

'You're a wonderful woman, Janey Padgett,' he said with a smile. 'Don't let anyone tell you different.'

She smiled back. 'You old sweet-talker.'

'So, um…' He looked awkward, as if on unfamiliar ground. 'What's this about a date?'

'Oh, it's this mad idea of the girls'. They think I ought to be seeing people again now it's nearly two years since Eddie passed. I told them I was too old for that sort of thing but they wouldn't have it.'

'Brooke told me it was your idea,' Hayden said.

Janey shot him a look. 'Yes, thank you, Hayden. You know, considering I'm the boss and you're only a humble employee, you've got a right bloody lip on you.'

He grinned. 'And I don't even charge you extra.'

'Nice, is he, this man you're going out with?' Martin asked.

Janey shrugged. 'He's from one of these online dating sites. He looks pleasant enough.'

'You want to be careful with those internet things, love. I saw this documentary about a serial killer who—'

Janey groaned. 'Oh God, please don't. I've been worrying about that all day.'

'Well, you'll likely be OK,' Martin reassured her. 'If you get into any trouble, you've got my number. Let's see how he fancies an ex-copper to tangle with.'

'My knight in shining armour, eh?'

'Always.' He winked before taking his pint back to his table.

'You've got an admirer there,' Hayden observed. 'He asks after you every time he comes in.'

'Martin?' She laughed. 'Don't be daft. We've been friends since we were swimming round the primordial soup together; me, him, Eddie and Mave – that was his missus.'

'Just calling it how I see it,' he said, shrugging.

Janey squinted at him. 'You all right, love? You look shattered.'

'Yeah, I am a bit. It gets on top of me sometimes, the two jobs and then making sure I'm spending a decent chunk of time with the girls. One bad night's sleep can throw me for the week.'

'Hmm.' She regarded him with maternal concern. 'Maybe we ought to cut your shifts. Our Rhianna could take on a bit more while she's here.'

'No! Please don't do that. I can take it, honestly.'

'Well, we won't if you don't want us to. Still, Hayden, you ought to watch you don't burn out. You're no good to your daughters in a hospital bed.'

'It's only for a little while. Just until I've got a bit put away for whatever might crop up in future.'

Janey smiled. 'And then we lose you, I suppose.'

'I suppose so.' He glanced around the pub. 'I'll be sorry to go. I've got fond of this place.'

'Well, for your sake I hope you can leave us sooner rather than later,' Janey said. 'You'll be missed though, Hayden. Brooke was saying this morning how glad she was you'd proved her wrong in her original assessment of your bartending abilities. That's high praise from her. She thinks the world revolves around this bloody pub.'

Hayden looked pleased. 'Did she really say that?'

'She did.' Janey nodded to a table of thirty-something women drinking wine. 'I'm crediting the Hayden Effect for this lot too. Jolene Hancock and her pals have been coming in a lot more often since you started. Nice to see a younger crowd in.'

He laughed. 'Flirting with me right before a date? Janey Padgett, you hussy.'

'I need the practice, love.' She examined his face again. 'You really should look after yourself. We all need to sleep.'

He sighed. 'Yeah, I could do with a few more hours in the day lately. I wish everything for St Mary's didn't cost so damn much.'

Janey nodded sympathetically. 'Tell me about it.'

'Oh, right. I keep forgetting you were a St Mary's parent too.'

'You've applied to Di Kershaw, I suppose?'

He blinked. 'To who?'

'It's a what, not a who – the Lady Diana Kershaw Hardship Fund. Do they still do that at St Mary's?'

'If they do I've never heard of it. What is it?'

'A fund for parents struggling with non-fee-related costs. We got a grant of a couple of hundred a year towards what Rhianna needed. We still had a lot to cover, but it was a huge help.'

'I think they must've stopped it. Otherwise I'd have been told, surely.'

'Not necessarily. Schools like St Mary's are used to the sort of pushy parents who ask for things rather than waiting to be told. Worth an enquiry.'

'Yeah, thanks, that's really helpful. I'll email Darcie's form tutor about it when I get in.' He nodded to the stairs. 'Here's Brooke for you.'

Janey grimaced. 'Oh God. Well, lad, it's been nice knowing you.'

Brooke smiled at Hayden across the bar – a little bash-fully, Janey thought, although Lord knew Brooke had precious little of embarrassment in her nature.

'Sorry, Hayd, I'm going to have to pinch my mum,' she said. 'It's time for her pre-date beautification. Naturally, me and Rhia are expecting that to take a while.'

'Oi.' Janey folded her arms. 'No cheek or I'm backing out.'

'You can't back out. I made us a makeover playlist.'

Janey groaned.

'What dating site is he off, this bloke?' Hayden asked Brooke.

'Tinder. Still, he looks relatively normal.'

'No giant fish?'

'Nope, he's entirely piscine-free.'

Janey shook her head. 'What is the thing with the fish?'

'I reckon some blokes think it looks macho,' Hayden told her. 'Sort of like "me big hunter-gatherer. Me provide sexy fishy sustenance for ladyfolk". Or just the classic overcompensating.'

'That's what I told her,' Brooke said, and they both laughed.

Their eyes met over the bar, and Janey suppressed a smile. She'd been noticing the not-so-subtle signs of an attraction between these two for a while, and she was waiting for the opportunity to give them a nudge. It was about time Brooke stopped messing around with casual flings and found someone who really got what was special about her.

When they arrived upstairs, Rhianna was waiting for them.

'I put *Moana* on for the kids so they won't bother us while we're working,' she said.

'Is getting me ready work?' Janey asked.

Rhianna looked her up and down, taking in her beer-sloshed top and frizzy hair. 'Yes.'

'Come on.' Brooke grabbed her mum's arm and pulled her into her bedroom.

'So, where should we start?' Rhianna asked. 'Clothes, hair, make-up or coaching?'

Janey blinked. 'Coaching?'

'You don't think we're going to send you out without some prep, do you?' Brooke said. 'The seventies are over, Janey. Gone are the days when you could pop your bra off in a man's face and call it foreplay.'

She laughed. 'The *Carry On*s aren't a documentary about life in the 1970s. There was actually very little bra-popping in real life.'

'I thought if you remembered the seventies you weren't there,' Rhianna said.

'That was the sixties.' Janey shook her head. 'Why does any conversation with you two leave me feeling ancient?'

Brooke glanced at her sister. 'I don't think she wants us to answer that, do you?'

Rhianna nodded soberly. 'The truth can hurt.' She flung open the cupboard. 'Let's start with clothes. I'm thinking for an Italian restaurant we want classy but not too dressy, smart-casual…'

'Wait.' Brooke took out her phone. 'Music first. I made a special playlist to get us in the mood.'

'Sweet Baby Jesus,' Janey muttered.

'I've got songs from every film that features a makeover on here,' Brooke said, turning the volume up high. '*She's All That*, *Miss Congeniality*, *Grease*, *The Breakfast Club*…'

Janey raised an eyebrow as the first tune started. '"I'm Getting Married in the Morning"?'

'Well, *My Fair Lady*'s about a makeover, isn't it? Besides, we are ultimately husband-hunting here.'

'You're lucky my date can't see us doing bridal makeovers. He'd be running for the hills.'

'Let's sort out your hair.' Brooke grabbed a hairbrush. 'There's no time to wash it so you'll have to have it up. You've got pub frizz.'

'Here.' Rhianna chucked Janey a blouse and a pair of bootcut jeans while Brooke ran the brush through her tangles. 'Put these on.'

Janey was starting to feel dizzy.

'Can't I have my hair done first?' she asked. 'I can't try clothes on while Brooke's yanking this thing through my knots. And ow, by the way.'

'Sweet revenge,' Brooke muttered.

'I suppose,' Rhianna said. 'All right, hair then clothes.'

'Rhia, there's makeover refreshment in the fridge,' Brooke said. 'Do you want to fetch us all a glass?'

Rhianna nodded and went to get it.

'How was minding the kids?' Janey asked while Rhianna was out of the room.

'Good. Rhia came home and we all played Monopoly. Without falling out, which is a mini miracle in itself.' Brooke stopped brushing for a moment. 'They're good kids really.'

'Course they are. They're ours.'

'Max seems happier now. I'm glad he managed to make some friends.'

Janey smiled. 'He thinks you're God's gift, that boy. He always asks where you are first thing when he comes home from school.'

'I know, it's weird. Why? Usually kids pick up on how nervous I feel around them and they can't get away from me fast enough.'

'I think he remembers how you were kind to him when they first arrived. The day you made them fish finger sandwiches.'

'That? But that was nothing. They were hungry so I made them tea – and got bollocked for it by Rhianna because fish fingers aren't on the approved meal list.'

Janey shrugged. 'Little things can mean a lot to a shy, frightened child in a strange place.'

Rhianna came back in carrying three glasses of prosecco.

176

'Here you go, ladies.' She handed them one each. 'Cheers, eh?'

'Cheers.' Janey tried to take a sip while Brooke did strange things to her hair, sticking pins in it here, there and everywhere. 'I was half worried you and the littlies wouldn't be here when I came up from the bar, Rhianna.'

Rhianna flushed. 'To be honest, there was a brief period this afternoon when I was thinking the same thing.'

'She did us proud though,' Brooke said. 'She told James to shove his reconciliation, demanded a divorce, insulted his willy and stormed out.'

'I insulted more than that,' Rhianna said, smiling. 'No one bad-mouths my family but me.'

'That's my girl,' Janey said. 'I doubt he'll give up though. Just remember—'

'Stay strong, I know. Oh!' Rhianna flashed a delighted look at her sister as 'Kiss Me' by Sixpence None the Richer started playing. 'Brooke! It's our favourite.'

Brooke smiled. 'God, that was some awful karaoke we insulted everyone's eardrums with at that family wedding, wasn't it?'

'They just didn't appreciate musical genius when they heard it.' Rhianna leaned over her and sang a snatch into Brooke's hairbrush, and Brooke, laughing, joined in.

Watching them in the mirror, Janey smiled to herself. All right, she was potentially about to be murdered by a complete stranger – or at the very least, bored to death by him – but seeing Brooke and Rhianna laughing together, she still felt that recruiting her daughters to help her get out dating was the best idea she'd ever had.

–

An hour later, Janey had been brushed, dressed and painted and was admiring her reflection in the mirror.

'Mum, I don't say this very often but you are a stone-cold stunner,' Brooke said. 'You're going to knock this Mike guy off his feet.'

Rhianna nodded. 'You look lovely, Mum. Class on legs.'

'Well, Janey, shall I drive you over?' Brooke asked. 'It's half-seven.'

'Yes.' Janey's gaze was still fixed on her reflection. 'In a minute, love. Just give me a moment to calm my nerves.'

They nodded and left her alone.

When they'd gone, Janey reached out to touch the image in the mirror.

An hour ago, when she'd come up from the bar, it had shown her a tired, harassed old woman. Now... well, she was still old, there was no getting around that. Everyone has to get old. But with her hair pinned up in a stylish chignon by Brooke, and clad in the smart blue top and black wrap Rhianna had picked out for her, she looked... genteel. That was the word people used to describe ladies 'of a certain age' who still managed to give an impression of beauty and sophistication. And yes, Janey felt that she did look beautiful. That wasn't a very modest thing to think about yourself, she supposed, but modesty could sod off this once. It wasn't often she felt beautiful, and for a little while she was going to bask in it.

God, but she was nervous, though. The girls' quick course in modern dating hadn't helped: her head was spinning with the various suggested conversation topics and 'red flags' to be on the lookout for. And yet, she was excited, too. Janey felt all of a twitter, the tummy butterflies she hadn't experienced for so long awake and in flight once more. She remembered that same feeling the night she'd prepared for her first date with Eddie; every part of her anatomy feeling like it was fluttering.

'Wish me luck, old man,' she said to her husband's photograph, holding up crossed fingers, and Eddie smiled back. Then, screwing up her courage, she strode out to go and meet her date.

Chapter Seventeen

Twenty-five minutes later, Brooke dropped her mum off at Sorrento's Italian restaurant in Halifax.

'Good luck.' Brooke held up crossed fingers, just as Janey had to Eddie's photo. Her mum tried not to look anxious as she waved her off.

'Hi,' she said to the waiter on the restaurant front desk. 'My, um… that is to say, there's a table for two booked under the name Mike Weaver.'

The man nodded. 'Yes, the gentleman is here already. Follow me please.'

She followed him across the restaurant, trying to calm the flutterings in her belly. It wasn't really so scary, was it? Perhaps the mechanics of dating had changed since her day, but people didn't change. Mike was the same generation as her. Why should it be any more awkward now than it would've been in their teens?

According to his profile, Mike Weaver was a retired gardener of sixty-five: not handsome, but tall, broad-shouldered and with a full head of grey hair, which at their age was a fair substitute for good looks. The girls had selected him from the profiles Janey had swiped right on because he looked 'safe'. Not that they thought the others looked dangerous, they'd reassured her. They meant 'safe' as in solid; reliable. Not the sexiest qualities, but admirable in a potential mate, certainly.

Anyway, it wasn't like Janey expected to meet husband number two her first time out. Brooke had advised her to treat this date as a practice, just to get her arm in. She should focus on having a nice time and working on her conversation skills, without worrying about whether it was love at first sight. And if she liked the man, well, so much the better.

The waiter showed her to their table – a little booth for two – and Mike stood up to greet her. Janey was pleased to see that his photo hadn't done him justice. He actually was rather handsome. And big! He must be six foot tall, and practically the same across. Must be all that gardening. She flushed when she noticed him looking her over at the same time, his smile suggesting he approved of her as much as she did of him.

'Well, this is cosy,' she said to break the ice, gesturing to the booth.

'Yes, I suppose it is a bit,' Mike said. 'Um, is that OK?'

'Oh, yes. I prefer it that way.' Janey winced, remembering the injunctions from the girls to play at least a little coy. 'I mean, it's nice to have some privacy so we can get to know each other.'

'I couldn't agree more.' He indicated for her to take a seat.

'Can I get you some drinks while you decide what to order?' the waiter asked.

'White wine spritzer please. Plenty of soda,' Janey said. She wanted to keep a clear head, and she'd had two glasses of prosecco while the girls had been making her up.

'A merlot for me,' Mike said. The waiter nodded and disappeared.

Well, now they were alone. Janey twisted her ankles together.

'So,' she said. 'A red wine drinker.'

'Yes. I'm something of a connoisseur.' Mike grimaced. 'No I'm not. I just said that to impress you. I don't know one red from another and I picked that one at random from the wine list.'

'Well, I appreciate your honesty.'

'So my pretence at sophistication is over before it's begun,' he said, smiling awkwardly. 'The only thing I can really claim to be a connoisseur of is real ale.'

'If you wanted to impress me, I would've led with that,' Janey said, laughing. 'As a pub landlady, I take a professional interest in beer.'

Mike laughed too, visibly relaxing. It felt comforting to know he was as nervous as she was.

The waiter came back with their drinks. Janey's phone pinged as he put down her wine, and she took it from her pocket to read the message.

'Sorry,' she said to Mike. 'It's my youngest daughter, checking up on me. She does make a fuss.'

That was probably largely because her mother had spent the day expressing her fear that she might be murdered on this date, but Janey thought it best not to mention that. Mike didn't seem too murdery, thank goodness. And if he was, well, best not to put ideas into his head.

'You don't have to tell me,' Mike said. 'I've got an adult son of my own. I keep fit and active, but the way Chris talks you'd think I was a doddering old man with one foot in the grave.'

'Same,' Janey said, smiling. 'How old is your boy?'

'He'll be forty this year. Two children, one about to take his GCSEs, which makes me feel about as ancient as the pyramids. How about you?'

'Two daughters, Brooke and Rhianna. Brooke's thirty, Rhianna's coming up to thirty-three.'

'Grandkids?'

'Yes, Rhianna's children, Max and Livvy. Ten and six.'

He gestured to the phone. 'What does your daughter say then?'

Janey laughed, blushing slightly. 'She wants to know if you're more of a David Essex or a Les McKeown.'

Mike laughed too. 'She knows who Les McKeown is? I can picture Chris's blank expression if I mentioned the name to him.'

'Does she heck. She's looked it up on Google because I made the mistake of telling her I liked the Bay City Rollers.'

Mike raised an eyebrow. 'You admitted that? Out loud?'

She smiled as she sipped her wine. 'You boys were just jealous because all us girls were mad about them.'

'So, what will you tell her? Can I compare with Les?'

'I was actually an Eric girl myself.' Janey cocked her head to appraise him. 'But I think I'll tell her… you're more of an older David Bowie.'

He laughed. 'That's the nicest thing anyone's ever said to me.'

There was silence for a moment, but not an awkward silence. More just a temporary absence of words as they waited for another conversation topic to present itself.

'So you were a gardener then,' Janey said, remembering the quick course in dating small talk she'd had from the girls.

'Forty years, man and boy. I used to work in the grounds at Cavendish Hall.'

'Oh, what a lovely place to work! Me and my late husband loved visiting Cavendish Hall. Please, tell me more.'

–

Brooke's phone buzzed and she picked it up to look at the screen.

'What does she say?' Rhianna asked.

'"Older, musclier David Bowie."'

'I could go for an older David Bowie.' Rhianna headed to the kitchen to open a fresh bottle of prosecco. 'Is that Mum's type, do you think?'

'It's Bowie, Rhia. You don't need to have lived through the seventies to know he was everyone's type.' Brooke held up her glass for a top-up. 'Thanks.'

'Mummy?' a little voice whispered from the doorway. Max had appeared in his pyjamas, rubbing his eyes.

'What's up, my love?' Rhianna asked softly. 'Did you have a nightmare?'

'No but I'm too thirsty to fall asleep. Can I have juice?'

'Of course.'

He looked at Brooke. 'Can you get it for me?'

She blinked. 'Me?'

'Yes please.'

'Um, OK.' She went into the kitchen to make him a glass of squash.

'Here you go, Maxie,' she said when she came back in, presenting it to him. 'Go to sleep now, eh? It's pretty late, even for school holidays.'

'Can I read my book until I'm sleepy again?'

Brooke glanced at Rhianna, who nodded.

'Just for a little while,' she said. 'I'll be coming in in half an hour to check you're asleep.'

'OK.' He hesitated, then threw his arms around Brooke's middle. 'Night night, Brooke. Night night, Mummy.' He gave Rhianna a hug too, then went back to bed.

'What just happened?' Brooke said, blinking dazedly. 'I feel like I've been run over by a tiny steamroller.'

Rhianna smiled. 'It's called a hug. I'm not sure why, but with no effort on your part whatsoever he's decided you're the best aunty since sliced… aunties.'

Brooke tried not to look too pleased. 'He's still disoriented, I suppose. He's a good little lad, though.'

'Still determined you don't want your own?'

Brooke sat back down and claimed her drink. 'I don't think that's a very good idea, do you? I'd only break them.'

'Come on. I know you like kids really.'

'Yeah, I like them – some of them. I like butternut squash too, but I've never felt the need to eject one from my vagina.'

'You're always so flippant about it. Be serious for once.'

Brooke shrugged. 'Kids are OK – other people's kids. I'm just not parent material, Rhia. I couldn't do what you do, or what Mum and Dad did for us. I'd just fuck it up, and ruin more lives than mine in the process. You have to be a proper grown-up to be a mum.'

'That's how we all feel before we have kids. The idea of parenthood's terrifying, because… well, parenthood's terrifying. But it's pretty wonderful too.'

'For some people. Not for me.'

'Well, that's your prerogative. Just keep an open mind about it.'

Rhianna dropped to her knees by the box of toys Brooke had given Livvy.

'I remember these.' She smiled as she took out an old jack-in-the-box. 'Dad bought us this from a charity shop not long after I'd started primary school. I thought it was great, but you just wouldn't stop screaming.'

'I stand by Toddler Me on that,' Brooke said, laughing. 'That thing's horrifying.'

Rhianna pressed the button and the jack popped out with a muffled screech, making Brooke shudder.

'All right, you may have a point.' Rhianna turned it over to look on the base. '1976. I suppose a lot of our toys were from the seventies and eighties. Dad got nearly all our birthday and Christmas presents second-hand – typical Yorkshireman, couldn't resist a bargain.'

Brooke bristled. 'He didn't have a choice. Money was tight. It was nice stuff, wasn't it? You never had a problem with it until—'

'—until I went to St Mary's. All right, Brooke, don't be so touchy. I wasn't criticising.'

She relaxed a little. 'No. Sorry.'

Rhianna took out a strange construction. It was three thick cardboard tubes stuck to a base, painted red and decorated with sequins. Underneath, the words *BESTIST SISTUR RIANNAH FORM BROOKE* had been felt-tipped.

'My pencil pot you made me on Beaver camp,' Rhianna said. 'I thought it'd been thrown away.'

Brooke felt a lump rise in her throat. She remembered making that, all the care she'd put into painting it, back when she still thought her big sister was the best thing ever.

'Take it,' she said. 'When you go. To remember us by.'

Rhianna laughed. 'I'm not emigrating to Mars, Brooke.'

Wasn't she? If it was anything like the last time she'd left home, she might as well be. But Brooke bit her tongue.

'Have you considered where you're going to go?' she asked instead. 'Not that I'm rushing you away. I was just wondering if you'd thought about jobs.'

'I was looking this afternoon. After I saw James, I knew I had to stop stagnating and do something positive for mine and the kids' future.'

'Did you find anything?'

Rhianna shook her head glumly. 'Not a single solitary sausage.'

'Really? I'd have thought with a Cambridge degree, you could walk into whatever you wanted.'

'Not in the real world, Brooke. With further work, yes, I've got options. I could do the training that'll enable me to qualify as a barrister, like I'd been planning to when I met James. I could consider teacher training. But that stuff takes years and costs money, and what I need right now is cash to live on. All a Cambridge degree does is make me look overqualified for the sort of work that's available right away.' She reached for her drink and took a gloomy sip. 'Let's face it. I've got no experience, no training and an empty CV. I don't know what I can do.'

'It's just so unfair,' Brooke said, scowling at the carpet. 'You put all that work into your life with James, and some stupid bit of paper says you get nothing in a divorce when he's the one who's been playing away? These prenup things ought to be banned.'

'Certainly if I'd known then what I know now, I'd have thought twice about signing it – without an infidelity clause anyway. But I was twenty-one, in love for the first time…' Rhianna smiled sadly. 'James was so apologetic. He told me his brother had had a bad experience with some gold–digger and so to keep his parents happy he'd said he'd speak to me about it. Well, I couldn't grab a pen fast enough. I was glad to have the opportunity to prove I loved him for himself, not his money. At that age, a future where James was unfaithful and I was left broke with two kids wasn't one I even considered.'

'Course you didn't. God, what a prick! I wish you'd told us before you signed it. Dad was horrified when he found out.'

'What would you have done? You couldn't have advised me.'

'We didn't need to understand all the legal aspects to know that it's morally dodgy for a husband to deny his wife anything in the event of a divorce.'

There was silence for a moment.

'Well, it's done now,' Rhianna said with a resigned sigh.

'I was impressed, you know,' Brooke said. 'When you walked out on him without a penny like that. That showed gumption I never gave you credit for.'

'Thanks.' Rhianna gazed thoughtfully at her pencil pot before summoning a smile. 'What about your love life, then? If you think I haven't noticed those looks that pass between you and Hayden Bailey, you're very wrong.'

Brooke felt her cheeks heat. 'Don't be daft. What looks?'

'The smouldering ones. The ones that say "ooh, Hayden, hold me in your manly arms and clasp me to your manly chest. Manlyly".'

Brooke couldn't help laughing. 'Get lost. He's a mate, that's all. A manly-shaped mate.'

'He doesn't want to be a mate, though. He wants to be a date. Doesn't he?'

'No.'

'Come on. You have to tell me, I'm your sister. I've got the pencil pot to prove it.' Rhianna reached for the prosecco bottle to top them up again. 'There's something going on with you and him, isn't there?'

'Well, if you're going to ply me with booze,' Brooke said, smiling. 'All right, I'll tell. But don't tell Mum, OK?'

Rhianna crossed herself solemnly.

'He did ask me out. There was a kiss as well – a pretty damn good one. I had to say no though, didn't I?'

'Why? You never used to say no to boys you liked. Especially the good kissers.'

'This boy's different.' Brooke watched the bubbles rise and pop on the surface of her drink. 'Hayden's a dad, Rhia. That comes with responsibilities. It couldn't be like it's been with boys before: a date every once in a while when we were free, the odd shag, then move on to the next one.'

'Why not?'

'Because… Hayden's better than that. You know he's working all these hours to put his kid through St Mary's?'

'Yeah, Mum told me.'

'He's a good guy. He needs a proper girlfriend, not a roll in the hay. Someone who's potential stepmum material if it ends up getting serious.'

'Well, you can be that person.'

Brooke snorted. 'You've had too much prosecco.'

'You like him, don't you? He obviously thinks you're amazing, I mean, God knows why but he does. Go out with him.'

'Yeah, and what about his kids?'

Rhianna shrugged. 'I'm sure he can get a babysitter.'

'I meant in the long term. I can't be a mum to them. Let's face it, I can barely look after myself.'

'Why are you rushing ahead to that? I'd start with a date, personally.'

Brooke shook her head. 'No, I like Hayd too much as a friend to mess him about. And I like him too much in the other way to risk getting closer only to find out it's destined not to work.'

They were interrupted by Rhianna's mobile ringing.

'Who is it?' Brooke said, peering at the screen.

'No one.' Rhianna hit the End Call button. 'Just a sales call.'

Brooke frowned. 'Is it? I thought it said Taryn.'

'Right.' Rhianna looked awkward. 'Yes. Taryn's a friend from ho— from Nantwich. I said, um, we could arrange to meet up.'

Brooke regarded her curiously. Rhianna's cheeks had flushed, and she was avoiding eye contact.

'Don't mind me,' Brooke said. 'You can answer if you like.'

'No, I'll ring her back later.'

'Well, any time you want to have her over, let me know. I can take Max and Livvy to the park or something, get them out of your way.'

'Oh no, that's OK. I'll meet her in town somewhere. I don't want to get under your feet.'

Brooke shook her head slowly. 'I don't believe it.'

'What?'

'You're still bloody ashamed of us, aren't you?' She laughed, resting her forehead on her palm. 'You know, Rhia, I was actually starting to think you might be turning back into a human being. That somewhere inside that tangle of snobbery and middle-class neuroses was my sister. But you just can't bear the idea of your posh

Cheshire friends finding out this is where you came from, can you?'

Rhianna's cheeks were bright red now.

'It isn't like that,' she mumbled. 'I'm not ashamed.'

'Right.' Brooke nodded to the phone. 'Well go on then. Call this Taryn back and invite her round. I'll make you a buffet of Pot Noodles and fish finger sandwiches, we'll make a party of it. Oh, and I will be sure to have my awful rough tattoos on display for your friend to admire.'

'Now you're being ridiculous.'

'Or I was being ridiculous when I thought you'd changed. You'll never change, will you, Rhianna? It's too bloody late.'

–

In the restaurant, Janey and Mike had finished their main courses.

'…of course, it's a huge mistake to prune your shrubs right after winter, especially if you're aggressive with the clippers,' Mike was saying. Janey nodded along. She'd had a nice time overall, but her date certainly liked to talk about plants!

He was a lovely man, though. She'd been on the lookout for what the girls called red flags and hadn't spotted any, unless you counted his divorce ten years ago, but she didn't think that was a flag unless he'd locked his ex-wife in the attic or something. She wasn't sure Mike was the one for her, but he was charming, good company, and he'd made her feel young and attractive for the first time since Eddie had died. She fixed him with a benevolent smile.

'It's better to wait until your shrubs flower, and old wood is best for that,' Mike went on. 'So if you can just hold off until…' He trailed off, smiling sheepishly. 'But I'm boring you, aren't I? I forget that not everyone's as fascinated by shrubs and bedding plants as I am.'

'No, no, it's very interesting,' Janey said politely.

Mike perked up. 'Is it?'

'Oh, yes. I love green spaces.'

'You did say you had a garden?'

'Yes. Well, it's a beer garden so I wouldn't say I'm that green-fingered, but if I ever retire then I'd love a little plot.'

Mike was looking at her eagerly, as if waiting for her to ask a question.

'Um, I assume you've got a patch at home?' Janey asked, and Mike beamed.

'Yes indeed.' He took out his wallet. 'I've got some photographs here if you'd like to see it. I've been doing a lot of work in it since I retired.'

That was very Mike. Other people their age carried photos of their grandchildren in purses and wallets. For him, it was rockeries.

'Lovely,' Janey said as he put a photograph under her nose.

'Isn't it? My own slice of heaven.'

The waiter materialised to take their plates.

'No pudding for me, thanks,' Janey said in response to his enquiry. 'I couldn't eat another thing.'

'Nor me.' Mike glanced at her. 'I fancy a nightcap though. How about you, Janey?'

She smiled. 'I could be tempted.'

'What do you think to having it at my place? I've got a bottle of sherry open, and I'd love to show you the work I've been doing on the garden. The photos don't do it justice.'

Janey hesitated, and Mike laughed.

'Oh, don't worry, I'll be a perfect gentleman. One little drink, a tour of the garden, then I'll kiss your hand and put you into a taxi.' He clasped one hand to his heart. 'You have my word.'

Chapter Eighteen

Back at the flat, Brooke and Rhianna were trapped in another blazing row.

'Brooke, come on!' Rhianna said. 'It's not any kind of snub to you and Mum, OK? I just can't have Taryn here. She… she wouldn't understand.'

'Understand what? That not everyone lives in a home with multiple wings? That au pairs aren't an essential part of every household? That there's more to life for some of us than endless rounds of colonics and facials?'

'She just inhabits a different world. I don't want her…'

'Don't want her to what? Find out about us?'

'I don't want her to tell the people I know back in Nantwich that I've fallen on hard times, all right?' Rhianna snapped, finally making eye contact. 'I don't want her to blame me for taking the kids from their home to live in… well, a place like this. I don't want her to say anything that's going to make me feel guilty for…' She lowered her voice. '…for not going back to James.'

Brooke's frown lifted slightly.

'That's what this is all about?'

'Yes, Brooke, that's what it's about. I've got enough voices in my own head whispering that I'm a terrible mother for taking them away. I don't need to add one more.' Rhianna choked on a sob. 'I'm not strong enough for one more.'

They were interrupted by the sound of the landline phone in the hall.

Brooke blinked. 'Who's ringing at this time?'

'Mum?'

'She'd ring us on our mobiles, surely.' Brooke stood up, and Rhianna followed her out into the hall.

'Hello?' Brooke said, picking up the phone. Her eyes widened. 'She's what? Oh my God, what happened? Is she OK?'

'Shit, Brooke, what is it?' Rhianna said.

Brooke covered the mouthpiece. 'It's Mum. She's at the bloody police station!'

'Oh my God!'

'Yes, I understand you can't give us certain information over the… look, can you just tell us if she's OK?' Brooke demanded of the officer on the phone. She let out a sigh of relief. 'All right, thank you. Yes, we'll pick her up right away. Goodbye.'

'What is it? What's happened?' Rhianna asked.

'He wouldn't tell me why she was there but she's not hurt. He wants us to fetch her home.'

'Do you think she… that this Mike guy…'

'I'm sure it's all OK,' Brooke said, but she couldn't help feeling worried.

'What do we do?' Rhianna's tone was edged with panic. 'We've been drinking, we can't drive. Shall I phone a taxi?'

'I'm sure Hayden would offer a lift. He'll be closing up now, I'll run down and ask. You stay here with the kids and I'll be back as soon as I can.'

-

In the pub, Hayden was putting the chairs up on the tables.

'Evening.' He frowned as he caught Brooke's expression. 'You OK, love? You look – oof!'

Hayden staggered backwards as Brooke's body collided with his, his arms instinctively wrapping around her.

She wasn't sure what had made her fling herself at him. All she knew was that she was worried, and Hayden's arms looked big and warm and comforting, and she'd probably had far too much prosecco.

'Um, OK,' he said, patting her back dazedly. 'Not what I was expecting. What's up, boss?'

'It's my mum,' Brooke said, her voice muffled by his chest. 'Hayd, have you got your car?'

'Yeah, it's in the car park. Why?'

'Then can you drive me to the police station? I'm over the limit and I need to get her home, ASAP.'

'The police station! What the hell's happened? Is Janey OK?'

'I don't know, they wouldn't tell me. All they said was that she's not hurt.'

'Well yes, if you need me to then of course I can. The girls… but never mind about that, I'll text my mum in the car. Come on.'

Brooke summoned a weak smile. 'Thanks, Bailey. You're a good mate.'

She locked up the pub before following him to his car. Hayden tapped out a quick text to his mum to let her know he'd be late home.

'What do you think's happened?' he asked.

'I don't know but I'm worried,' Brooke said in a low voice. 'God, she's been fretting all day about this guy being some dangerous pervert and me and Rhia just laughed it off. What if she was right, Hayd? What if he's… you know, done something to her?'

'I'm sure it's nothing. Your mum's a tough old broad. If he tried anything, it'll be him who came off worse.' Hayden unlocked the car and Brooke slid into the passenger seat.

'Thanks for this,' she said as they set off. 'I'll never forgive myself if anything bad's happened. I shouldn't have let her go on her own. We should've arranged for her to meet him in the pub, where we could keep an eye on her.'

'You did everything that could've been expected of you. Your mum's sixty-two, Brooke. If she wants to get out dating, you can't hold her hand through it.'

'No.' Brooke fell silent, staring at her knees. 'She's so naive, though. I mean, about how things are nowadays: all these online predators. I can't help worrying about her.'

'I know. I'd be just the same.' He glanced at her. 'So what've you been up to on your night off other than getting smashed?'

She smiled. 'I'm not smashed. Just… tired.'

'Mmm, I can tell. That hug was a dead giveaway that you'd had a pretty "tiring" evening. Don't tell me you and your sister have actually been getting along?'

'Yes. And no.' She grimaced. 'We were doing really well, until another row broke out.'

'What about this time?'

'Oh, it was my fault. She got this call and… I was too quick to get offended, I think. I felt like she didn't want her Cheshire friends to find out where she was living so I flew off the handle. I hadn't considered that maternal guilt about taking the kids away from their dad might be at the root of it.'

'Sounds like you ought to talk about it.'

'We were about to. Then the police rang.' She flashed him a wobbly smile. 'You talking to me to keep my mind off worrying?'

'Yeah, is it working?'

'Not really, but I appreciate the effort.'

He took his hand from the gearstick to squeeze her fingers. 'I'm sure your mum's OK, Brooke. Here if you need me, eh?'

'I don't deserve you.'

'No. But anyway, here I am.'

'Hayd, you're not, um... you don't mind, do you?' she said, meeting his eyes in the rearview mirror.

'Mind what?'

'You know.'

He flushed slightly. 'Just being friends, you mean? I don't mind. I always did think you were a pretty cool girl to be mates with.'

'You're sure?'

'Honestly?' He sighed. 'I'd be lying if I said I wouldn't like to be more. I know you want different things in your life than the things I've got in mine, but I can't help... liking you, I guess. I've told myself there's no point, but there you go, I still do. But if this is what you want, well, you're the boss. I mean, you are literally my boss.'

'Hayden, I wish...'

'What?'

'I'd like to. If you'd asked me out when we were teenagers, I'd have said yes like a shot. But we're grown up now, and I can see all too clearly where it'll end.'

'Me too.'

She blinked. 'Can you?'

'Yeah, I think so. With a nice dinner, followed by some energetic sex and a cuddle. Then maybe a bit more sex for a nightcap.' He glanced over at her. 'Why, where were you thinking it'd end?'

'I didn't mean where the date would end. I meant where we would. You and me.'

'I didn't know you were into astrology.'

'Come on, don't pretend you haven't thought about it. There are three possible ways this can go. We'll have a date, discover we don't gel after all and decide to just stay friends. That's outcome one, and definitely the best of the three.'

'Christ,' Hayden muttered. 'She's only gone and done a bloody flowchart.'

'Outcome two,' Brooke went on. 'We go on a date, it goes great, much sex ensues, then I meet your kids, they hate me and that's the end of that.'

'What's outcome three then?'

'Three is the ultimate nightmare scenario. We go on a date, it goes great, much sex yada yada, and... we fall for each other,' Brooke said, looking away. 'And *then* I meet your kids, they hate me, you realise I'm never going to be stepmum material and we both get our hearts broken, plus we can't even stay friends because it'll be too painful.'

'All right,' Hayden said evenly. 'Can I add an outcome to the list?'

'If you want.'

'How about we have a date, we gel like crazy jelly people, much sex yada yada, then you meet my kids, they think you're as awesome as I do and we all live happily ever after?'

Brooke shook her head. 'Not going to happen.'

'Why not? I know they'd love you. I'm not sure why you think different.'

'Because kids don't like me, Hayden. They can smell the fear on me.'

'What about your niece and nephew? They must like you.'

Brooke thought about Max, and the hug he'd given her earlier.

'Well, they're family so they have to. I still feel awkward as hell around them though, even then. I couldn't take on any sort of parental role, whether it was my own kids or someone else's. I'm just not cut out for it.'

Hayden slowed down as they approached the police station. 'I was hoping you could start in a more my-girlfriend type role and we could discuss what comes next when we've practised that a bit.'

'No, Hayd, I'm sorry. I'm just not what you and your family need. Honestly, you'll thank me one day, when you and the girls are happily settled with the person you were meant to be with.' She patted his hand. 'I do like having you around, though.'

He smiled. 'I'm glad I made the grade. I well remember those far-off days of four weeks ago when you were convinced I wasn't barman material and bit my head off every time I tried to charm you.'

'Well, I'm not too proud to admit I was wrong. Don't go anywhere, will you?'

'I won't. Not just yet.' He opened the car door, then glanced back at her. 'Sure you won't reconsider?'

She shook her head. 'I'm the wrong fit for you, Hayden. One day you'll see it too.'

He sighed. 'I was afraid you might say that. Let's go get your mum then.'

They entered the station and Brooke approached the front desk.

'Um, hi,' she said to the officer on duty. 'I'm here to pick up my mum, Jane Padgett.'

'Oh. So you're here, are you?' a voice said. Brooke turned to find her mum behind her with her arms folded, looking rather dishevelled. One arm was blue with a blossoming bruise, and there was bracken poking out of her hair.

'Oh my God, Mum!' Brooke pulled her into a hug. 'Are you OK?'

'This is her, Officer,' Janey said to the woman on the front desk, pointing to her daughter's back. 'I think a twelve-year stretch in Wormwood Scrubs is a fair sentence for wasting police time, don't you?'

The woman laughed. 'Well, just this once we'll let her off. But try not to let it happen again, eh, Janey? We would technically be within our rights to charge you with wasting our time if you started making a habit of it.'

Brooke stepped back. 'I don't get it. What're you doing here, Mum? Mike didn't… I mean, nothing happened to you, did it?'

'Well, I learned some interesting facts about hydrangeas and got pretty tipsy. Actually I had a rather nice evening, apart from getting nicked by the Filth at the end.' She nodded chummily to the woman on the desk. 'No offence, Paula.'

'None taken,' the woman said, smiling.

'Evening, sunbeam,' Janey said to Hayden. 'What're you doing here?'

'Giving Brooke a lift. She was over the limit,' Hayden said. 'How about you?'

Janey glared at her daughter. 'Some young idiot thought it was a good idea to set up an SOS function on my phone, so it automatically calls emergency services when you press and hold the menu button. Well, two sherries and a few wines at the restaurant and I don't mind admitting I wasn't quite as steady on my feet as I might otherwise have been. I tripped and fell into Mike's rockery. The phone was in my back pocket and my bum landed right on the emergency button.'

Brooke laughed. 'Oh my God. That's all?'

'It's no laughing matter, young lady,' Janey told her sternly. 'What with the state of me, I couldn't convince the two coppers who turned up that I wasn't covering for a "domestic incident" so they hauled us both in. Mike went home in a taxi a quarter of an hour ago after we finally persuaded the police it was all a misunderstanding. Then I realised I'd left my handbag, phone and purse at his house and I didn't have the fare to get home, so one of the nice constables said they'd give you a call for me.'

'Thank God! I thought you might've been assaulted or something awful.' Brooke pulled her into another hug. 'Let's get you home, eh? Rhianna's worried sick.'

Chapter Nineteen

Rhianna was waiting for them in the hall. Brooke had texted her a brief account of what had happened while Hayden was driving them back, but she still looked anxious.

'Mum.' She let out a sigh of relief. 'Thank God you're home. I've worn a hole in the carpet.'

'Oh, Rhianna. You and Brooke make such a song and dance. I'm a big girl, you know.' Nevertheless, Janey looked rather pleased as she submitted to a hug from her eldest daughter.

'I don't think it's unreasonable to worry when the police call to say your mum's in their custody and won't tell you why,' she said, letting Janey go. 'Pardon my language, Mum, but I'm bloody glad you're safe. Did the police give you a grilling?'

'No, they were nice. I think they just wanted to make sure I wasn't covering up any abuse. It's a sad world we live in, girls.' She glanced at Hayden. 'Thank God for the good men. Cheers for helping us out tonight, love. You feel like one of the family these days.'

'My pleasure, Mrs P,' Hayden said. 'I'd better get home myself, before I give my own mum something to worry about. Goodnight, Padgetts all.'

He walked to the door that led onto the fire escape. Brooke went after him.

'Er, hey,' she said as she followed him onto the metal platform. 'You were great tonight, Hayd. Honestly, I don't know what I'd have done without you.'

'No worries. I get time and a half for that, right?' He smiled at her expression. 'Kidding, Brooke.'

'Sorry.' She laughed, rubbing a hand over her forehead. 'Sorry. I'm too zonked to have a sense of humour tonight.' She gave him a hug. 'See you Friday, eh? Thanks again.'

'Anything for you, boss.' He gave her a kiss on the cheek – soft, slightly lingering; something between a friendly peck and a lover's goodbye. 'Night, Brooke.'

Brooke watched him descend the fire escape steps, then went back inside. Her mum and Rhianna were still in the hall, both grinning at her.

'What?' she said to them.

'Nothing,' Janey said. 'Nothing at all.'

'Nice hug?' Rhianna asked nonchalantly.

'Yeah, it was nice. That's the point of hugs, isn't it? Their general sort of niceness?' Brooke glared at them as they continued grinning. 'Can you two stop smirking? I was just thanking a friend for doing me and my family a big favour. That's what people do. Everyone does that.'

'We didn't say a word!' Janey protested.

'You didn't need to. I'm fluent in eyebrow.' Brooke's tone softened. 'You're sure you're OK, Mum? Getting hauled to the cop shop and questioned on whether you're an abuse victim must shake you up a bit.'

Janey sighed. 'It wasn't exactly an interrogation, but I can't deny I'm a bit on the trembly side. Not to mention having a rather bruised backside from the rockery, and a rather bruised ego from the rest of it. Shall we get the kettle on?'

'Let me,' Rhianna said.

Brooke followed her mum and sister into the living room. Rhianna disappeared into the kitchen.

'She's coming on, isn't she?' Brooke said to Janey. 'When she got here, I didn't think she knew how to use a kettle.'

'I heard that!' Rhianna called. She flicked the kettle on and came back in, sitting down next to Brooke. 'Well then, Mum?'

'Well then what?'

'How was Mike? That's what we really want to know.'

'You agreed to go back to his place so I'm assuming things were going well,' Brooke said, smirking.

Janey smiled. 'He was… nice. Really nice.'

Rhianna clapped her hands. 'Mum, that's great! When are you going out again?'

'Well, I'm going to have to pop over tomorrow and pick up my bag and phone. Then we thought we'd meet up at the Harrogate Flower Festival in a couple of weeks.' She smiled at her daughters' eager expressions. 'Now, don't look like that. I hate to burst your romance bubble, but it's not a date.'

Brooke blinked. 'Isn't it?'

'I'm afraid not. We got on well, chatting about the old days, and it was lovely to feel young and sexy again – he's certainly a very competent flirt. But in the end, we both agreed we were more suited to being friends.'

'Well, that's disappointing.' The kettle clicked off and Rhianna stood to go make the tea. 'Why did you decide that?' she asked as she headed to the kitchen.

Janey shrugged. 'Different interests. Mike's seriously garden-mad. I mean I like plants, but if things went much further there'd end up being three of us in the marriage:

me, him and the wisteria.' She smiled. 'But I had a lovely time. It was nice to make a new friend.'

'That's positive, anyway,' Brooke said as Rhianna came back in with their tea. 'It sounds like a good date to ease yourself back into the swing of things. I mean, apart from your subsequent arrest, obviously.'

Rhianna sat down again next to Brooke. 'We need to get looking for the next potential Mr Right then, don't we? Who else is on your Tinder right-swipe list, Mum?'

'I'd prefer to leave it a little while before diving back in. I don't think my nerves could cope with another full day of worrying my date might be a potential murderer so soon after the last one.' Janey sipped her tea thoughtfully. 'I can't help fretting about it, this internet dating lark. I struck it lucky with Mike tonight, but it feels like such a lottery. You know, four men have sent me photos of their todgers so far.'

Rhianna grimaced. 'Sorry, Mum. We've been trying to vet them but there are bound to be a couple of weirdos who slip through the net.'

'Oh, don't apologise,' Janey said, flicking a hand. 'Your mother is a woman of the world, you know. Me and the girls in the Knit and Natter group have been having a good old giggle over them.' She sighed. 'Still, I do miss the old days. You know, when you could meet someone in a bar and chat to them for a bit before you agreed to a date. It's not the same, trying to work out what someone's going to be like from their photo and a bit of text their kids probably wrote for them.'

'Can't you do it that way?' Brooke asked.

'Who's going to chat up an old lady like me?'

'Well, other old people like you.'

'Other old people assume folk their age are spoken for. I mean, unless either of you know of any uptown fleshpots catering specifically for the sixty-plus singles market.'

Brooke shook her head. 'Sorry.'

'I didn't think so.' Janey gazed pensively into her tea. 'I think I'll finish this in bed. It tires you out, a life of crime. Thanks for looking after me, girls.'

When she'd left them, Brooke flashed an awkward smile at her sister.

'So. Nice to end the night with a spot of drama.'

'God, I'm glad she's OK,' Rhianna said. 'I was imagining all sorts of awful scenarios.'

'I know. Me too.'

Rhianna smiled. 'Accidentally called the police with her own bum. How Mum is that? Dad'll be laughing like a drain.'

'Won't he just?' Brooke glanced at her. 'You miss him?'

'Every day.'

'Same.'

They were silent for a moment, alone with their thoughts.

'It's great she had a good night, even if Mike wasn't the one,' Rhianna said after a while. 'She doesn't take nearly enough time off from this place.'

'Her and me both.' Brooke put her tea down. 'Look, Rhianna, about before—'

Rhianna held up a hand. 'No, let me go first.'

'All right.'

'Brooke, I know you think I turn my nose up at everything to do with the pub but I'm genuinely not ashamed of you or Mum, or of this place. Taryn called and… like I said, I didn't want her to imply I'd done the wrong thing in bringing the kids here – not when I was already riddled with guilt. You're just so quick to get angry when you get it into your head that I'm embarrassed by you, I decided not to say anything. I knew you'd jump straight to that conclusion.'

'Well, you were right. I did.' Brooke's gaze fell on the pencil pot she'd made for Rhianna twenty-odd years ago. 'That's not entirely surprising, is it? All those years at St Mary's, hiding where you lived from your friends. Then you married James and it felt like we hardly saw you any more. I did resent it. What I resented most was losing the girl who for the first nine years of my life was my best friend.'

'I wasn't ashamed, you know,' Rhianna murmured. 'Back then, I mean. I know that was how it looked.'

'Come on. You know you were.'

'Maybe a little, after the peer pressure started,' she admitted. 'Embarrassed rather than ashamed, that my life was so different from the other girls'. But mainly I was just… weak. I wanted to fit into that new world, and I didn't think about who I'd hurt trying to do it.' Rhianna looked up, her eyes not sheltered as they so often were but wide and guileless. 'I never wanted it to be you, Brooke. You were my sister and I loved you. That's the honest truth.'

'You could've talked to me, you know,' Brooke said quietly.

'You wouldn't have understood. You were a child, and… there were things I couldn't have explained.' Rhianna glanced at a compass inked onto her sister's left forearm. 'Why have you got so many tattoos? No judgements. I just want to know how it feels.'

Brooke lifted her arm, patterned from wrist to shoulder with pictures in black ink. 'I suppose… it's a way of feeling in control. So many things are out of my control, like getting older or my health, but this is one thing that belongs totally to me. It's kind of about defiance. A way of telling the world – and some of the men I've met in particular – that this is my body and I make the rules.'

'I can understand that.'

Brooke tensed her arm so the pictures shifted on her skin. 'How do they make me look? How would people from your world think I look?'

'I think they make you look... broken.' Rhianna met her eyes. 'Are you?'

Brooke shrugged. 'Isn't everyone?'

There was a long silence.

'Brooke, can I show you something?' Rhianna spoke suddenly and quickly, as if she needed to hurry out the words.

'I guess.'

'You can't tell Mum, OK?'

'OK,' Brooke said, blinking. 'What is it?'

Rhianna rolled up her sleeve and presented her left arm, turning her face away so she didn't have to look at it. Brooke took hold of it and stared.

'Rhia,' she whispered. 'You didn't do this?'

Rhianna nodded, her eyes closed. 'A long time ago.'

Brooke traced one of the thick white scars with her finger. 'But why did you... why would you...'

'The same reason you get your tattoos. To stay in control. It felt like a way to focus all the mental pain and anxiety into one physical sensation before my brain exploded with it. Maybe that sounds crazy, but... that's how it felt.'

Brooke couldn't speak for a moment.

'When?' she finally managed to ask.

'At St Mary's. I was fourteen when I started, with one of Dad's razor blades. It was all that got me through.' Her face collapsed as emotion took over. 'Brooke, it was so hard,' she whispered. 'I never said a word to Mum and Dad – I knew how hard they worked to get me everything I needed, and I didn't want to seem ungrateful, but… it was so hard.'

'What happened that made you feel you needed to do this to yourself?'

'The bullying was unbearable. All seven years I was there. That's why I was so worried when you said it might happen to Max. God, I never felt so much like cutting myself again, just to deal with that whirl of anxiety about James and the kids and… everything.' She caught her sister's worried look. 'Don't worry, I didn't. I've been clean twelve years now. I don't do that any more.'

'Who bullied you?'

'This group of girls in my year. Honestly, they made my life a misery.'

'Because of where you came from?'

'I thought so, then,' Rhianna murmured. 'I wondered, when I was older, if maybe they were envious too. That I'd got in on merit rather than my parents' money. They targeted the other scholarship girls as well.'

Brooke scowled. 'I bet they were jealous of you. Cruel, spoilt, nasty little brats who probably came from cruel, spoilt, nasty little parents. God, if I'd known, I'd have—'

'I know you would've,' Rhianna said with a sad smile. 'That's why I never told you. That's why I asked Mum and Dad for expensive things; so I wouldn't stand out and make myself a target. That's why I got off the bus three stops early. That's why I never brought any of the girls I knew from school home. The bullies tried to make me feel ashamed, and perhaps they succeeded. But mostly I just wanted to keep my head above water, Brooke. I came so close to being sucked under, and the only thing I could do to stop myself sinking was…' She finally looked at her arm. 'This.'

Brooke took her hand.

'You should've told me,' she said gently.

'Sweetie, you were just a kid. What could you have done?' Rhianna lifted her arm to examine the scars, wincing as if it hurt her to look at them. 'James hated to see these. They didn't fit with the image: the good little girl, the perfect wife. He was forever on at me to have cosmetic surgery, but I wouldn't. I felt like I needed them, as a reminder of what I'd survived. Battle scars that told me I was stronger than James made me feel.'

'That bastard,' Brooke muttered. 'I can't think about him without wanting to slap something. Preferably his cheating fucking face.'

Rhianna gave a grim laugh. 'Those girls at St Mary's did him a big favour. They broke my nerve, so I was ready to be a passive little wifey for the first man who made me feel safe and protected.' She looked at her sister. 'Do you know how jealous I was of you? Of how confident and strong you were? I bet you'd have shoved that prenup right up James's bum, wouldn't you?'

Brooke blinked. 'You were jealous of me?'

'Of course. A million times I wished I had the ovaries to say exactly what I thought like you always did. The older I got, the more I felt intimidated just being around you. I felt so weak and pathetic beside you.'

'You? Who survived years of those nasty little bullies without letting them break you? Who took your kids and walked out on your cheating prick of a husband with nothing but your self-respect?' Brooke pressed her sister's hand. 'Rhia, I wish I had half the iron in my soul you do. I never realised how strong you were until recently.'

Rhianna gave a wet laugh. 'Give up.'

'I'm not kidding,' Brooke said. 'Do you know how jealous I was of *you*? My big sister, who had all the looks and all the brains? I wanted to be you for so long.'

'Ah, but you got all the boys.'

'Only because you were studying hard, like I ought to have been. I was just the runner-up prize.'

'Rubbish. It was because you had all the charm.'

'You mean I was a terrible flirt,' Brooke said, laughing. 'And then I was jealous because I knew you were Mum and Dad's favourite.'

Rhianna blinked. 'What? No I wasn't. You were their favourite.'

'Don't be daft. I couldn't compete with you, could I? The scholarship girl with her Oxbridge degree, and me with more ex-boyfriends than GCSEs by the time I left school.'

'But you were the one who took after them. The one they trusted their business to.'

Brooke smiled. 'Shall we wake Mum up and ask which of us they loved best?'

'I think we can guess the answer,' Rhianna said, smiling too. 'She'll tell us they loved us both the same.'

'Then I suppose we'll have to take her word for it.' Brooke looked again at the thick white scars standing out against Rhianna's skin. 'God, Rhia,' she whispered. 'I thought your life was so perfect. I thought you had everything. These must've been deep, were they?'

'They... could be. If I needed them to be.'

No wonder Rhianna had always kept her arms covered, even in the depths of summer. No wonder she'd refused to wear bikinis or revealing strappy tops when they went on family holidays…

'My own sister and I never knew,' Brooke murmured. 'You know, for years I resented that school for stealing you from me. You were my total hero when we were kids, and then you started at St Mary's and it felt like you became this complete stranger. And all that time…'

'I'm sorry,' Rhianna whispered. 'I never stopped caring about you, you know. Life just got complicated, and I was too young to know how to deal with it.'

'Come here.' Brooke pulled her into a hug.

'No more fights, all right?' she whispered. 'From now on, we're a team. I promise to stop being so touchy if you promise not to turn your nose up at anything around here that's different.'

'Deal,' Rhianna said. 'And Brooke… I want you to know that if you're set on keeping the pub, I'm behind you. I won't say another word about selling. I'd like to be more involved too, if you and Mum will have me. Formally, not just the odd shift behind the bar.'

Brooke held her back to look into her face. 'Are you sure?'

'I'm sure. Well, it's like you said, isn't it? We're a team.' She glanced at the pencil pot Brooke had made her. 'More than that. We're sisters.'

Chapter Twenty

When Brooke awoke the next morning, she could hear Rhianna moving around in the kitchen and got up to seek her out.

'Um, hi,' Brooke said, smiling sheepishly. She nodded to a sizzling pan on the hob. 'What's cooking, Rhia?'

'Morning.' Rhianna's smile, too, looked a little self-conscious after their heart-to-heart of the night before. 'I'm doing crêpes for Max and Livvy. Well, pancakes, but I promised Livvy a French Day so I've rebranded them. Would you like some? I got fresh strawberries.'

Brooke was about to automatically decline when she stopped herself.

'I would, thanks,' she said. 'Have you and the kids got plans today?'

'It's going to be sunny so I told them we could have a game over at the recreation ground.' Rhianna glanced at her. 'You're welcome to come along.'

Again, Brooke was about to say no when she stopped.

'I'd like that,' she said instead.

'And later, um, I thought I could help in the pub. Start as I mean to go on.' Rhianna looked up from the pancake she was frying to meet her sister's eye. 'I meant it, Brooke. I want to help. Actually, I was thinking—'

They were interrupted by a squeal of 'Mummy!' as Livvy bounced into the kitchen in her pyjamas. Max and Janey soon joined them, and the chaos that belongs exclusively to the school holidays settled on the household.

They shared a noisy breakfast together in the living room. Max sat between Brooke and his mum on the sofa, while Janey and Livvy had a competition to throw a strawberry into each other's mouths.

The flat was certainly a different place these days. If anyone had told Brooke prior to four weeks ago that her home would soon be alive with the sound of children – and what's more, that she'd have come to prefer it that way – she'd never have believed them. And yet, here they were.

Things had changed over the last month too. Janey and Livvy's strawberry-chucking game would once have earned them a stern lecture from Rhianna about playing with food. Now, she laughed and cheered them on. The children looked a hundred times happier than the pale little waifs they'd been when they arrived.

'Brooke, watch this.' Max tilted his head up and balanced a strawberry on his top lip. 'Ta-da!'

'Oh my gosh! Max, you've grown a moustache that looks like a strawberry! That's amazing.'

He giggled and popped the fruit in his mouth.

'What's your best way to have strawberries?' he asked, snuggling comfortably against her. 'Mine is with whipped cream.'

'Yeah, that's a good way. But the really *best* best way is dipped in melted chocolate fondue.'

'Yum!' Max smacked his lips. 'I've never had that.'

'You're missing out.' Brooke nudged him. 'Tell you what. We'll get some for your birthday, shall we? A chocolate fountain with strawberries to dip in it.'

'Ooh, yes! Can we have a party too? I can invite Zach and my friends from school.'

'That's a good idea, Maxie,' his mum said. 'We could use the pub's function room. Perhaps you could invite some of your old Abbotleigh friends as well.'

She glanced at Brooke, as if she wanted her sister to see she was making a real effort to show she wasn't ashamed of them or the pub. Brooke smiled back.

'Consider it done, Max,' she said. 'Eleven's a pretty big deal, we ought to celebrate it.'

'Hooray!' His face fell. 'But it's not for three months though. I hope we won't have to go home by then.'

'I'm sure wherever we are, Nana and Brooke will let us have your party here,' Rhianna told him tactfully.

Max continued to chatter as he ate, and Brooke noticed she found it surprisingly easy to chatter back. The ramblings of children had always put her on edge; it felt like such unpredictable nonsense, it was hard to know how to respond. But Max's flights of fancy were so much fun, they struck just the right chord with her own sense of humour. He had a whole fantasy world in his head that it was a pleasure to be invited to share. Max had seemed so serious when he'd arrived, but freed from worry, he was a happy little soul.

After breakfast, Brooke, Rhianna and the children walked to the village recreation ground with the girls' old rounders bat and a tennis ball. Janey cried off, claiming a headache, although Brooke suspected she was just making an excuse to give the sisters some time together.

When they reached the field, another young family were already there, playing with a football.

'Oh great,' Brooke muttered as she watched Hayden take the ball from the darker-haired girl and dribble it down the field. 'It had to be them.'

'Why do you say that?' Rhianna asked. 'You two looked pretty close last night, making with the just-good-friends cuddles.'

'It just feels weird bumping into him outside work.' Brooke shot a wary look at the two girls, dressed in matching Leeds United tops with their names, Darcie and Cara, on the back. 'And, um… you know, when he's with his kids.'

Rhianna examined them with interest. 'His girls aren't much older than Max, are they? Hey, we ought to join up with them. We can get a better game going with seven.' She looked at Max and Livvy. 'What do you think, kids? Shall we ask if Brooke's friend and his daughters want to play with us?'

'OK!' Livvy said eagerly. An eleven-year-old girl was a glamorous creature to a six-year-old of the same gender. Max looked shy, but he nodded.

Rhianna started to approach the other family, but Brooke hung back.

'What's up?' Rhianna asked. 'You don't mind, do you?'

'No. It's fine.' Brooke summoned a smile. 'I'm being daft. Let's go, then.'

The idea of being introduced to Hayden's daughters made her uncomfortable. Perhaps it was because she could sense his eagerness for her to like them, and them her, whenever she tried to convince him she wasn't cut out for being around kids. But they were here now, and there was no getting around it that wouldn't seem weird.

She could wish Hayden wasn't wearing those shorts if they all had to play together, though. The way his thigh muscles shifted as he dribbled, the mud that plastered his face, his sweat-sodden curls… well, she was going to find it difficult to keep her eye on the ball.

'He shoots, he scores!' Hayden was saying when they approached, weaving nimbly around one of his daughters to kick the football between a couple of rocks. 'Yes! In your face, Cara Bailey.'

He clasped his hands above his head and shook them triumphantly as he jogged a slow-motion victory lap around his daughter, blasting out 'We Are the Champions'. Brooke's lips curved in a reluctant smile.

'Pfft.' Cara folded her arms. 'Lucky shot.'

'Yeah? Best of three?' Hayden pushed his damp curls out of his eyes when he noticed the other family. 'Oh. Hi, Padgetts.'

'Morning.' Rhianna nodded to the girls. 'These must be the famous Bailey twins. They look just like you, Hayden.'

'I know, poor unfortunate souls.' Hayden drew them forward proudly. 'This is Cara, my eldest by eight minutes, and her baby sister Darcie.'

'Huh,' Darcie muttered. 'She's the real baby.' Cara elbowed her in the ribs.

'Hi girls,' Rhianna said with a pleasant smile. 'I'm Rhianna, a friend of your dad's from work.'

'Hello,' Darcie said politely.

'Rhianna was a St Mary's girl too,' Hayden told her.

'Really?' Darcie looked at Rhianna with more interest. 'Did Miss Fairfax teach there when you went?'

Rhianna blinked. 'She did actually. Wow. She must be a million years old by now.'

Darcie laughed. 'More like a *billion*. She's my form tutor.'

Cara was getting a good look at Max, who flushed under her scrutiny.

'What's your name then?' she asked him in the superior tone of one who'd detected she was some months his senior.

'Maxwell James Thomas Garrett,' he told her shyly.

'That's a lot of names. Do I have to call you all of them?'

'No. You can just call me Max if you want.'

'Hey kid, you know how to play football?' Cara enquired with indulgent condescension.

Max nodded, and Cara looked at her father. 'Can they play with us, Dad? We can make a proper game instead of just doing dribbling practice.'

'If they don't have plans,' Hayden said, glancing at the rounders bat Rhianna was carrying.

Rhianna laughed. 'Actually, our coming to talk to you was a calculated act of desperation. We were hoping you'd ask us.'

Darcie looked at Brooke, who was lurking silently behind Rhianna, feeling awkward. 'What are you called?'

'Me?' Brooke shot a helpless look at her sister. 'Brooke. I'm called Brooke.'

Darcie considered this.

'That's pretty,' she said. 'Like a stream. Do you know my dad?'

'Er, yes. A little bit.'

Hayden laughed. 'That's nice, isn't it? And after you launched yourself at me last night too.'

Brooke flushed. What did he have to mention that for?

'I didn't launch. I just… stumbled.'

'Stumbled right onto me.'

'You were conveniently there to break my fall, yes.'

'What's launch?' Cara asked.

'It's what rockets do. And sometimes people who want a friend to give them a hug.' Hayden chucked the football to her. 'Well, are we playing? Kids against grown-ups, what do you say?'

'There's more kids though,' Darcie said.

'Yeah, but we're bigger than you.' He smiled warmly at Livvy, who'd edged up to Darcie and was regarding the older girl with a reverent look. 'Besides, I think this little person really only counts as a half.'

'That's bad, being bigger,' Darcie told him. 'You lot are too huge and lumbering to dribble properly.'

'I kicked both your bottoms just now, didn't I?'

'That was luck. Me and Cara were about to kick your bottom loads more.'

'I'm captain of my team at school,' Cara informed Max. He looked suitably impressed.

'Well, let's see how us big lumbering dinosaurs get along, shall we?' Hayden said. 'Take your places, guys.'

'We're supposed to let them win, right?' Brooke muttered to Hayden as they lined up opposite the children. 'I mean, with them being all small and helpless.'

'Helpless? Wow. You really don't know much about kids.' He nodded to Cara. 'Watch that one. She's a dirty tackler.'

'So we don't let them win?'

'Bloody right we don't. I like to beat them now and again, remind them that their dad's not quite as old and washed up as they think.' He glanced at her. 'At football, that is. I don't literally beat my children.'

She laughed. 'I promise not to call social services.'

Hayden looked at Rhianna, who was helping Livvy put her hair into a ponytail. 'You two are hanging out today, are you? I take it that means you made up after your row.'

220

'Yeah,' Brooke said, smiling. 'Actually, I think we made a proper breakthrough. Before, when we've fallen out and made up it's always felt like just papering over the cracks, but this time we really hauled through some stuff. We understand each other better now.'

'As a dad of sisters, I'm glad to hear it.' He glanced at Darcie and Cara, who were showing off their passing skills to an awed-looking Max. 'This is the last place I'd have expected to run into you, though. I thought you avoided kids like the plague.'

'It's hard to avoid them when they're family.'

'They're really not so bad, you know. Once you get to know them.'

Rhianna finished getting Livvy ready and she trotted over to the other kids. Cara kicked the ball to Max to start the game, and to Brooke's relief her conversation with Hayden was halted.

For Brooke, who wasn't used to running-around games with groups of children, it was a dreamlike afternoon, full of mud and noise and joyous, laughing chaos. Everything she'd loved about football when she was a kid herself came flooding back, and she threw herself into the game with vigour.

It was weird seeing Hayden in family-man mode, though. Of course Brooke knew he was a dad, but she'd never thought about him *being* a dad. He was just Hayden Bailey, a sexy grown-up version of the boy who'd put frogspawn in her pumps. Witnessing this warm, protective, responsible adult-type person he became around his girls, Brooke found herself seeing him in a whole new light.

She watched him let Livvy pretend to tackle him, pulling a frustrated face as the little girl gleefully tottered away with the ball.

'You got hay fever or something?' he asked Brooke as he jogged up to her.

'Oh. No.' She wiped her eyes. 'The wind's making my eyes sting.'

She didn't know what she was getting emotional for. Watching Hayden with his girls couldn't help but bring back memories of her own dad. It hardly seemed like any time ago that it had been him, her and Rhianna having family kickabouts in the park. And now… now their dad was gone. To Livvy, Grandad was probably no more than a foggy cloud in her memory, and even Max, Brooke suspected, was starting to forget.

But his gift to the family wasn't gone. The Highwayman's was still there. Brooke found herself thinking about what Rhianna had told her: that their dad had left her a share in the pub so she'd never have to depend on James. Dad had known James was a wrong 'un the minute he'd found out about the prenuptial agreement his daughter had been pressured into signing. It was typical of their father, wanting to protect his daughters from the big bads of the world when he wasn't around to do it himself.

Yes, they still had the pub. Dad's legacy, to his family and to the village. And Brooke was certain that somehow, there was a way to make the place provide for them all.

Chapter Twenty-One

It was two days later when Brooke saw Hayden again. He was looking very different from the last time she'd seen him, well-groomed in a smart shirt and skinny jeans ready for his shift. Brooke got a waft of his aftershave as he joined her behind the bar. She inhaled deeply, trying not to look too obviously like she was smelling him.

'Hi,' he said, smiling warmly. 'Miss me?'

She smiled back. 'I'm not answering that. Did the girls have fun the other day?'

'Yeah, they've not stopped talking about it. Cara and your nephew seem to have hit it off. She loves anyone who lets her boss them about.' He helped himself to a bag of peanuts. 'I'll pay for these. Rushed here straight from a job so I haven't had any tea.'

'Do you ever not rush here straight from a job?'

'Not these days.' He sighed as he ripped open the peanut packet and threw a handful down his throat. 'It feels like the girls are growing up before my eyes, Brooke, and I'm hardly there to see it. That day we bumped into you on the rec was the first time we'd spent any significant time together for weeks. As much as I hate turning work down when every penny counts, I do need to start making more time for my kids before they stop being kids any more.'

'You should. They obviously think you're the mutt's nuts right now. That won't last forever.' She smiled uncertainly. 'You're not thinking of leaving us though, are you?'

'Course not.' His gaze drifted to the pumps. 'Not just yet.'

'Still struggling for money?'

'Well, I've got enough put aside to tide us over for a little while. Still, you never know what's going to be around the corner.'

Brooke hesitated. The fact was, with Rhianna committing herself to becoming an active partner in the business, from The Highwayman's point of view Hayden was kind of dispensable. From Brooke Padgett's point of view... well, she'd miss him like hell.

But he had two kids at home he was devoted to, and who needed him far more than the pub did. And God knew, getting over this... whatever this thing was that had Brooke staring at this thighs and surreptitiously sniffing him wasn't getting any easier. He said he wasn't as desperate for money as he had been. The unselfish thing would be to let him go.

'Um, because if you did want to leave, we could probably manage,' she said. 'You wouldn't have to feel guilty on our account.'

He blinked at her. 'You want me to leave?'

'No. I just thought, if you're struggling... well, Rhianna's here now. You probably want to be at home with your girls in the evenings, don't you?'

'Yes, I do, obviously, but...' He reached up to rub the back of his neck. '...um, do *you* want me to go?'

'Absolutely not.'

'You're sure?'

'Course I'm sure.' She met his eyes. 'But I know we can't keep you forever.'

'No.' He fell silent, staring at his feet, before summoning a smile. 'No Rhianna today?'

'She's gone to meet some friend from Nantwich for a coffee. She ought to be here soon.'

Sure enough, Rhianna appeared at the bar within half an hour, a laptop under her arm.

'All right, you two,' she said. 'Team meeting.'

Brooke blinked. 'What?'

'Team meeting. Mum says she's delegating everything to us and we can fill her in on what we decide later.'

Hayden shot a bewildered look at Brooke. 'Delegating what to us?'

'No idea,' Brooke said. 'Rhia, what's going on?'

'I'll answer that in the form of a PowerPoint. Come on. We'll sit where we can see the bar, then we can pop back if anyone needs a drink.'

Rhianna's eyes were shining with enthusiasm. Exchanging another puzzled look with Hayden, Brooke followed her to an empty table.

'So what was that about a PowerPoint presentation?' Hayden said.

'That's right, you lucky people. And...' Rhianna opened her laptop and the sound of Adam and the Ants singing 'Stand and Deliver' started up. '...it has themed background music! Never say I don't spoil you.'

The presentation had a title slide with the words *Get SMART* over a photo of the pub.

'I'm confused,' Hayden said to Brooke.

She nodded. 'I'm also confused.'

'James was obsessed with SMART goals for his projects,' Rhianna said. 'Targets that are specific, measurable, achievable, romantic and… telepathic. That might not be what the last two stand for. Anyway, it's the specific and achievable we want to focus on.'

'Right,' Brooke said dazedly. 'Do we?'

Rhianna nodded. 'These are my ideas for improving the business. When I said I wanted to be more involved, Brooke, I wasn't just talking about pulling pints.'

'Well, I'm glad you're thinking about how we can improve things. Let's not get carried away, though.'

Rhianna laughed. 'I know that look. Don't worry, OK? I know you're cautious about trying new things but I'm not going to force anything on you. Besides, we've got Hayden here as a neutral casting vote.'

Hayden shook his head. 'Don't go dragging me into it. It's your business.'

'Sorry, Hayd. Like it or not, you're part of the team now.'

'Er, thanks. That's both flattering and terrifying.'

Rhianna clicked to the next slide, which was titled *Problems*.

'So. Our issues.' A bullet point slid into position. 'Falling trade, and consequently falling profits. For over a year now, custom's been dropping. Why?'

'Dad died,' Brooke said quietly. 'The atmosphere seemed to change after that.'

'I'm not sure I buy that, Brooke. You said the old regulars come in, same as always. It's the younger villagers and the occasional trade we aren't getting through the door, right?'

'Well, yes, that is true,' Brooke conceded.

'So the groups we're not seeing are…' Rhianna clicked to bring up some sub-bullets. 'Occasional trade – walkers, campers, holidaymakers – and new villagers, largely commuters, who ought to be joining the ranks of our regulars but aren't. Am I right?'

'Yes, that's a fair summary.'

'Why do you think the walkers aren't coming in as much as they used to? Is there more competition locally now?'

'Definitely. Willowtree have bought up three pubs in the surrounding area, including the White Bull in Morton. Had the places totally refurbed, revamped the menus, brought in new chefs. That's where our occasional trade's been drifting off to, I'm sure. We can't compete with that sort of investment.'

'Let's move on.' The next slide appeared, titled *What We've Tried*. 'So far, we've introduced Knit and Natter mornings, a monthly bonus ball draw, book group, live music nights and a food menu. Has anything worked in terms of increasing custom?'

'Not really,' Brooke said. 'Mum's Knit and Natter group brings in decent numbers, but it's first thing in the morning so obviously they're not drinking. A dozen old ladies paying £2.50 for a cup of tea and a biscuit is barely worth us opening early for. The book group, similar problem. They meet in the evenings, but they're busy talking literature so they'll buy maybe one drink each over two hours. The live music we put on just pissed off the regulars who like this place because they can have a quiet conversation, and the food menu... well, we all know Mum isn't the greatest chef. It feels like we've tried everything and profit-wise, it's mostly been a flop.'

'Live music aside, I can't see any of that doing much to change the perception of this place as an old man's pub,' Hayden said. 'What music did you put on?'

'We had a folk group in a couple of times, then this rock covers band, Deff Buzard. We thought they'd go down well with the younger villagers, but we didn't get much of a showing.'

'I don't think you should give up on the idea. Try a different band, or a different night. Get one that does stuff from different eras: Arctic Monkeys, Kaiser Chiefs, Red Hot Chilis and so on mixed in with your Stones and your Quo.'

'What we need is more things like the quiz night,' Rhianna said. 'It's far and away our most successful night of the week – even more so than Fridays and Saturdays. They're busier, but the quizzers drink more.'

'What else can we do, though?' Brooke asked.

'Well, we could try another band, like Hayden said. Open-mic nights could be popular with the younger folk, and karaoke. And...' Rhianna clicked to her next slide, *Solutions*. 'What about monthly theme nights?'

'Theme nights? Such as what?'

'Well, we're getting the new chalkboard art next week, and the leaflets with the Dick Turpin connection emphasised. We could do a highwayman fancy dress night, couldn't we? I bet there's some anniversary we could exploit, Turpin's birthday or something. If nothing else, the photos would look good on the pub Facebook page.'

'We haven't got a pub Facebook page.'

'You're kidding!' Rhianna scribbled that down. 'Right, well we'll get that sorted out. That's a huge missed opportunity.'

'You're sure we shouldn't be running this stuff past Mum?'

'I told you, she's delegated it. She says fresh young eyes are exactly what this place needs.' Rhianna smiled. 'She did have one suggestion, but I didn't think it was worth adding to the slides.'

Brooke laughed. 'Let me guess. It involved Hayden's trousers.'

'Spot on.'

'What about my trousers?' Hayden asked.

Brooke patted his bottom. 'Don't you worry about it, cupcake. Just stay pretty.'

'I feel objectified.'

'I know, you lucky man.' Brooke turned back to her sister. 'What other theme nights could we do?'

'I've got loads of ideas.' Rhianna clicked through her bullet points. 'Highwayman night, Christmas quiz and carols, Fright Night for Halloween, something to tie in with the Bunny Hop race they do over at the school, like a family Easter egg hunt in the beer garden... oh, and my favourite. This was inspired by what Mum was saying last night.'

'Speed dating?' Hayden read, as the next bullet point slid onto the screen.

Rhianna nodded. 'Our mum was bewailing the fact that dating was all online now and there was no way for her generation to meet people socially, like they used to when they were young. But there is, isn't there? A silver speed dating night would be perfect.'

'I don't know, Rhia,' Brooke said. 'I wouldn't even know where to begin organising something like that.'

'You can leave it all to me. It's a great idea, isn't it? There must be lots of older single people who'd love to meet someone but feel intimidated by online dating. Like those men you pointed out, the four widowers.'

While she was always cautious about anything that might alienate the regulars, Brooke couldn't help being infected by a little of her sister's enthusiasm.

'What do you think?' she asked Hayden.

'It's not up to me, is it?'

'Yes it is. We told you, you're part of the team.'

He shrugged. 'All right, then I think it's a class idea. I bet we'd pull people in from the neighbouring villages too, and even further afield if we set up a Facebook page to plug it on.'

'Then if you're both keen, let's go for it.'

Rhianna beamed at her. 'Thanks, Brooke.'

'Is that it then? The end of the presentation?' Hayden asked.

'Nearly.' Rhianna clicked to bring up the last point. 'This is a big one, because it takes some thinking about. But Brooke, I've been through all the figures and I really don't think we can justify locking Mum up in the kitchen every day, given how little we bring in from food.'

'But if we stop doing meals, we're the only pub in a ten-mile radius that doesn't have a food menu,' Brooke said. 'That's a big disadvantage, especially when it comes to the walkers. If they can't get a meal here they'll just go to The Blue Parrot instead, or walk down to the Bull.'

'What have we got to tempt them through the door in the first place, though? We've got a menu of, what, six meals and a couple of puddings?'

'We're still very much a wet-led pub, yes – I mean, we have to be, without a proper kitchen staff. I just think we need something other than bar snacks on offer.'

'I agree we need some sort of food offering, but I wonder if we could approach it differently,' Rhianna said.

'Let's face it, we're never going to be serious competition for the gastropubs with Mum's cooking.'

'Hire a chef, you mean? We can't afford anyone who could compete with the Bull's guy. He used to work at some Michelin-starred place before Willowtree headhunted him.'

'I was thinking of a partnership with an existing village business. There's no point being in competition if we can work together.'

'What, you mean The Blue Parrot?'

'Why not?' Rhianna said. 'You're on good terms with them, aren't you? It's worth a chat.'

'You know, that's not bad,' Brooke said slowly. She blinked. 'Bloody hell. That's actually a really great idea.'

Rhianna smiled. 'Not as useless as I look, am I?'

'We've run the refreshment tent with them at the 1940s event for the past two years. We could definitely extend that to a more permanent business relationship, if Theo and Lexie were keen.'

'Theo is. I popped into the cafe earlier and spoke to him. With the baby due any day, I think he liked the idea of teaming up. He's going to talk to Lexie about it tonight.'

Brooke was lost for words for a moment.

'When she loses the power of speech, that's usually a good sign,' Hayden said to Rhianna.

'I'm just... surprised,' Brooke said. 'Surprised and impressed. I didn't know you were so business-savvy, Rhia.'

'Neither did I. I enjoyed it though, putting a plan in place. I'm looking forward to getting cracking.'

'Well, I, um... I appreciate your commitment.' After all the times Brooke had accused her sister of conspiring to force her to sell the pub, she felt a bit guilty at the effort Rhianna was now putting in to save the place.

Rhianna glanced at the bar, where a couple of people were waiting to be served. 'We'd better go back to work. I'll start sketching out the details for the speed dating night later. Once we've fixed a date, I can get some posters printed.'

The three of them headed back to the bar. However, no sooner had they reached it than the background music from the pub's hi-fi system stopped, the fruit machine fell silent and all the lights went out, leaving the place steeped in afternoon gloom.

'For God's sake, not again,' Brooke murmured as a worried buzz broke out among the customers.

'What is it?' Hayden asked.

'The electrics must've tripped. It happens every once in a while. I'll go down to the cellar and sort it while you two serve these guys.' She raised her voice for the benefit of the customers. 'Sorry about this, folks. Just a temporary power cut; we'll be all lit up again in five minutes or so.'

She grabbed the torch she kept under the bar and headed to the cellar.

Chapter Twenty-Two

'Hey, that was good work with the presentation,' Hayden said to Rhianna when they'd served the two men waiting for drinks. 'How did you think of all that stuff?'

Rhianna shrugged. 'My husband works in marketing. I must've picked up more from listening to him drone on than I realised.'

'Don't go giving him the credit. They're your ideas. I think you ought to be proper proud of yourself.'

She smiled. 'It did feel good. I've let my brain stagnate for too long. Working through the pub's issues reminded me how much I used to enjoy problem-solving.'

'How come you never did anything like that before? You've obviously got a knack for brainstorming or mindgasming or whatever they call it now. You could've had your own little business.'

'James hated the idea of me working,' Rhianna said, talking half to herself. 'I wouldn't have had the confidence anyway, when I was with him. Over the years we were together, I came to believe I didn't have a worthwhile thought in my head. Max was born before we'd been married a year, and I told James I wanted to do my barrister training once he started school. But by the time that happened I was pregnant with Livvy and… I suppose by then, James had me believing that keeping house was all I was fit for.'

Hayden scoffed. 'Your husband was one of those, was he? Threatened by a more intelligent partner so he has to put them down to feel like a man? Pathetic.'

'Yes,' Rhianna said dreamily. 'I suppose it was that. I always made excuses for him. Told myself that coming from old money, his values just reflected the more traditional way he'd been raised. Now I'm back in Leyholme, it seems ridiculous I could have deluded myself so easily.'

'Whatever you had, Rhianna – your education, your degree – you earned. No one had to buy it for you. Obviously that made this guy feel insecure when he should've been proud of you. You're well out of it, love.'

'You're right.' She sighed. 'I just wish I knew what the future held. I can't hide in my parents' pub forever.'

'What would you like to do? If you could.'

'I'd really like to finish what I started all those years ago and do the course I'd need to go on to pupillage and ultimately practise as a barrister.' She smiled sadly. 'But that's just a castle in the air right now. I've got two children depending on me, and until I can provide for them, doing something just for myself is a luxury I can ill afford.'

'Sounds familiar,' Hayden said quietly. 'Rhianna, can I ask you a question?'

'All right.'

'When you went to St Mary's – was that rough on you?'

Rhianna frowned. 'Has Brooke been talking to you?'

'No. I was thinking about Darcie, that's all. I know it's an amazing opportunity, but I can't help worrying about her. Her relationship with her sister, in particular.'

'Oh. I see.' Rhianna rubbed her arm. 'Well… things have probably changed a lot since I was there.'

'Which means yes. Doesn't it?'

'It was a struggle,' Rhianna admitted. 'It felt like such a different world from Leyholme Primary. People spoke differently, behaved differently, expected different things of me; talked about stuff I'd never heard of like they were the most everyday things in the world. And yes, it did ultimately drive me and Brooke apart. When one group of girls started to bully me, I didn't know who I could talk to so I just... closed myself up. Kept it all inside.' She looked at him. 'But it doesn't follow that that'll be Darcie's experience. From what I've seen of her, she's a pretty no-nonsense young lady. When I was her age I was scared of my own shadow – I mean, apart from that time I pushed the boy who'd been playing tricks on my sister into a puddle, obviously.'

Hayden laughed. 'Well, Brooke was right. I did have it coming.'

'Is it something you could talk to her about? Or her mum, if you think Darcie would be more likely to open up to her?'

'She doesn't have a relationship with her mum. Carol-Ann... well, she's got her own life. She hasn't seen the girls since they were six months old.'

Rhianna looked at him with sympathy in her eyes. 'That must be hard for you.'

'I can cope,' Hayden said. 'It's the girls I worry about. They've got their nan, but I do sometimes sense they wish they had someone younger to talk to about their girl stuff. They're getting to that age, you know?'

'Well, I'd be happy to talk to Darcie if you ever feel she's pining for an understanding ear. Knowing she's got someone in her circle who went through the St Mary's scholarship experience too might be a comfort for her.'

'You'd do that?'

'Of course. We're friends, aren't we?'

Hayden smiled. 'You know, I made completely the wrong call about you that first night you worked here.'

'Thought I was a stuck-up cow, right?' Rhianna said, smiling. 'You weren't the only one.'

'Not quite, but I did think you were the chalk to Brooke's cheese. You and your sister are a lot more alike than I realised.'

She laughed. 'Oh well, if you're going to insult me...'

'Oi!' Martin Brady called. 'Any chance of some light today, Hayden? I'm having to hold this paper so close to my face you can read today's cricket scores off my nose.'

'Brooke is taking an awfully long time,' Rhianna said to Hayden. 'I'd better go see if she needs any help.'

'Let me. If she's struggling, I might be able to put my sparky skills to good use.'

Hayden made his way carefully down the uneven cellar steps in the darkness. A hoppy smell of old beer filled the dank air. He found Brooke examining the fuse box by the light of her torch, swearing profusely at it.

'Bastard bastarding twatty arsehole wanker bellend bloody... oh.' She broke off when she spotted him. 'Um, hi.'

'You know, if you call it names it's just going to sulk even more.'

'It deserves it,' she said, glaring at the box. 'Normally I just need to flick the master switch a couple of times, but today it's having none of it. And it just electric-shocked me, the little dickhead.'

Hayden went to stand behind her, leaning in close so he could see inside the box.

'Bloody hell, how old is this?' he asked.

'I don't know. When did they hang Dick Turpin?'

'I bet this thing was an antique even then.' He took her hand so he could guide the torch beam. 'It's blown a fuse, I should think. Have you got any fuse wire? If not, I've got some in the car.'

'Um… Hayden?'

'What?'

'You, er… nothing. Sorry, what did you just ask me for?'

He couldn't see her face but her voice sounded strange; sort of husky. Suddenly Hayden found himself very aware of how close they were; his body against her back as he peered over her shoulder, the smell of her perfume, his fingers on her hip. He was still holding her hand.

'Some… fuse wire,' he said, noticing his voice had gone husky too. Guided by an instinct, he moved his left hand over her hip and down to her thigh.

'There's a reel taped to the underside of the box,' she whispered. Her breathing had become ragged.

'Right. Well I can sort it out for you if… you know, if…'

She turned to face him, and the words died in his mouth. Her torch dropped to the floor.

'Jesus, Brooke,' he whispered, his lips dropping to her neck as her arms snaked around him.

'You just had to come down, didn't you?' Already her trembling hands were untucking his shirt so she could trail her fingertips over the skin of his stomach. 'I only barely made it past those bloody football shorts.'

He swallowed a groan as he buried his face in her hair. 'I haven't had sex in nine months.'

'I haven't had sex in a year.'

'I'm not sure I remember how to do it.' He laughed hoarsely as she teased his earlobe with her tongue. 'Ah, right. It's all coming back to me.'

Hayden lifted her up and hoisted her on top of one of the beer kegs. He eased himself between her thighs, his hands sliding under her top and inside her bra.

'Hayden, we have to stop,' she whispered.

'I know.' He massaged one nipple until he felt it peak below his thumb.

'There's… the pub.' Her hand found its way to the waistband of his jeans and she ran one finger under it longingly. 'Everyone's waiting for us to go back up.'

'Right. We should fix that fuse.'

'We should definitely fix that fuse.' She moaned slightly, biting her lip, as he kissed along her shoulder.

'I know,' he mumbled against her skin. 'I know, I know, I know. Fucking fuse.'

He pulled away. In the dim light of the torch on the floor, her brown eyes looked huge and cloudy.

'Oh, sod it,' he muttered, pulling her back towards him.

Brooke's fingers wove into his hair as they kissed, her tongue exploring his mouth. Perched on top of the barrel, she tangled her legs around his body. And God, that kiss was everything he'd thought it would be; everything he'd been dreaming it would be. He was aroused like he hadn't been since he couldn't remember when. But the last brain cell still resident in his actual head and not some other part of his anatomy kept yelling at him… they really did have to stop.

'Mmm… no.' Reluctantly he pulled away, panting. 'If we don't pack it in now, in a minute I'm going to rip every stitch of clothing off you and in another two your sister's going to walk in on us shagging against the Timmy Taylor's barrels.'

'We could always turn the torch off and pretend to be mice.'

He let out a hoarse laugh, resting his forehead against hers. 'God, you're amazing.'

She laughed too. 'Who knew fuse wire could be so erotic?'

'I bet there's a fetish website for it somewhere.' He lifted his head to look at her, thrusting his hands into his pockets to avoid the temptation of that open, panting mouth and heaving chest. His body was begging him to touch her again and it was all he could do to try and ignore it. 'Brooke… I know I said I wouldn't ask again, but I have to do something to kill the time until my erection goes down so what the hell. Won't you think about it? We go great together, don't we?'

She looked wary. 'I don't know, Hayd. The outcomes, remember?'

'Oh, bugger the outcomes. I like you. I fancy you. I want to see more of you, and I want to hear a lot more of you making those noises you were making just now. Why can't it be that simple?'

'You know why.'

He groaned, pressing his eyes closed. 'Yes, I know why. But that's not something to worry about now. It's something to worry about when we get to a point where it's something to worry about.'

Brooke hopped down from the beer keg and retrieved her torch.

'We'd do better to worry about it now,' she said in a low voice. 'Before anyone gets hurt.'

He took her free hand and pressed it to his lips. 'No one has to get hurt. I know kids make you nervous, Brooke. They did me until I had a couple. That's normal, and it's fixable. You've got a good relationship with your niece and nephew now, right?'

'It's still true that if I go out with you, I don't just get you. You and your girls are a package deal. That's some commitment, Hayden.'

'Yeah, but if you just got to know them—' He stopped, seeing her nervous expression. 'I mean, if you got to know them in the future. After you've got to know me a lot better in the present. I'd really, really like you to do that.'

'Hayd, you're a great dad,' Brooke said softly. 'Your kids are so lucky to have you. And I'm... not someone who's ever going to be able to complement that. Trust me, I'm not what your life needs.'

'That's for me to decide, isn't it? I was talking about a drink, not an elopement. Don't you think we're worth one drink?'

She closed her eyes, looking as if there was a battle going on inside her.

'All right,' she said at last.

He blinked. 'All right? As in, yes, you'll go out with me?'

'Well, I'm still pretty turned on so this is probably the oestrogen talking. But... I guess we can give it a try. One date, then we'll take it from there.'

He laughed, pulling her into his arms. 'Oh my God.'

'Don't start that again,' she said, laughing too as she extricated herself. 'We don't want to get carried away just when we'd managed to get our raging hormones under control.'

'Raging hormones are the least of my worries. It's all very well for you.'

They blinked as the cellar was suddenly bathed in light.

'Oh,' Brooke said. 'We're fixed. I guess it wasn't the fuses then.'

'Must've been a power cut,' Hayden said, squinting as his eyes readjusted. 'Cupid must be playing games, forcing us alone together in all that sexy darkness.'

Brooke nodded. 'He's a tricksy bugger.'

'So when do you want to go out?'

'We can plan that later,' she said, turning to go. 'We ought to get out of here before the blindfolded little bastard hits us with another arrow each to the genitals.'

Hayden put a hand on her shoulder.

'We can plan it now,' he said firmly. 'It'll be a good few minutes till I'm fit to go upstairs.'

She smiled. 'Ah. Well, it'll have to be daytime. One or the other of us is due on the bar every night.'

'I can't do weekdays. I'm booked solid with work for the next month.'

'How about next Saturday?'

'I always spend Saturday mornings with the girls then try to squeeze in a couple of jobs before I'm needed here. I earn extra for taking emergency call-outs at weekends.'

'Next Sunday then, before the quiz,' Brooke suggested. 'I'm supposed to have a shift in the afternoon, but I'm sure Rhia would cover for me.'

He grimaced. 'Cara plays football on Sunday afternoons. I mean, you're welcome to come along?'

'When I suggested a date, watching kiddies' five-a-side together wasn't really what I had in mind.' Brooke sighed. 'It's a lost cause, isn't it? Between your kids, your job and my pub, we'll never manage to make it work.'

'No!' He took her hand and pressed it. 'I'm not giving up. You said yes, I heard you. That means that by law you can't back out.'

'Well, what are we going to do?'

'Just… leave it with me.' He drew her to him so he could kiss the top of her head. 'I'll make it happen, Brooke.'

Chapter Twenty-Three

It was nearly midnight when Hayden got home. He tiptoed past the girls' room, trying not to wake them.

'Dad?'

The whispered voice of one or other of his daughters was becoming a sound all too familiar when he came home late from a shift. Sighing, he pushed open their bedroom door and went in. Darcie was sleeping but Cara was sitting up in bed, scribbling in her sketchbook by the light of her bedside lamp.

'You are in so much trouble,' he whispered. 'Do you know what time it is, Car?'

Cara shrugged. 'I wanted to hug you before you went to bed.'

She lifted her arms up, and he leant over her so she could throw them around his neck.

'Well, I suppose it's hard to stay mad at you when hugs are on offer,' he said, cuddling her back.

Darcie was waking up now, rubbing her eyes.

'I waited up for you as well, Dad.'

Cara snorted. 'No you didn't. You've been snoring like a big fat pig for ages.'

'I'm glad one of you has been getting some sleep.' Hayden went over to the other bed to give Darcie a hug too. 'Hello, sweetheart.'

'Dad, can we have a midnight feast?' Darcie asked, yawning.

Hayden let her go and tried his best to look like a firm, stern father from the 1950s.

'No, you can't have a midnight feast. You can go back to sleep right now – you too, Car. It's far too late for you to be awake.'

'Pleeeease! It's not a school night,' Darcie said. 'Anyway, we missed you. You should stay and hang out with us.'

Hayden couldn't help relenting. Brooke was right; his daughters wouldn't be this keen to share his company forever. There were worse things for them than messed-up sleep patterns.

'Well, all right. But we can't make a habit of it.' He reached into his coat pockets for the two bags of crisps he'd brought back from work. 'Here, you can have what should've been your Saturday dinnertime treat. It's not exactly a feast but it's the best I can do.'

'Yes!' Darcie ripped hers open while Cara carefully closed her notebook.

'I've got cheese and onion,' Cara told her sister.

'I've got prawn cocktail.'

'Halvsies?'

'Yeah, cool.'

They each exchanged a handful of crisps, not without a liberal distribution of crumbs, and Hayden smiled. It pleased him to see that his girls were the same best mates they always had been, even now they were at different schools. He couldn't help worrying when he thought about how St Mary's had driven the two Padgett sisters apart. For all the advantages a private education could bring to Darcie, if he thought it was going to drive a wedge between her and her sister then he'd pull her out tomorrow.

He sat down on the edge of Cara's bed, letting this moment with his daughters wash over him; freezing a snapshot of it in his memory to keep forever. There weren't enough moments like this in his life any more.

'Here.' Cara thrust her crisps under his nose. 'You have to have one too.'

'That's all right. I'm going to get a sandwich in a minute.'

'You have to, Dad,' Darcie told him sternly. 'Or you can't be in Midnight Feast Club.'

He smiled and took one. 'Well, OK. If it's going to stop me getting kicked out of the club.'

'Was work good?' Cara asked him.

'It was… as good as it ever is. Nothing interesting to report, apart from everyone having to sit in the dark for ten minutes when the power cut out.'

'Nan says you can leave soon. Now we're getting money from the Kermit thing.'

'The Kershaw Fund,' he said. 'Well, we haven't got it yet. Darcie's teacher says we're certain to be approved though, which'll be a big help. Still, I'd like to stay at the pub a while longer. There are lots of other things we have to pay for.'

'Like what?' Darcie asked.

'There's this house, for a start.'

'I thought Great-Nana left the house to you and Nan.'

Hayden hesitated, wondering how to explain the concept of mortgages to an eleven-year-old.

'She left… part of it to me and Nan,' he said. 'The rest of it has to be paid for, every month. You see, Great-Nana had to sell a bit of it to pay for the care home she went to live in so not all of the house was hers when she died. And I'm still hoping to get enough cash together to have the loft converted. I don't think you guys are going to want to share a bedroom forever, are you?'

Cara shrugged. 'That's OK. We like sharing.'

He smiled. 'I'm glad about that. Still, I think we'd all appreciate a bit more space.' He nodded to Cara's sketchbook. 'What're you drawing, Car?'

'A portrait.' She opened it to show him. 'It's good, isn't it?'

'All right, Miss Modesty.' He frowned. 'Is that the lady we met at the rec on Wednesday?'

'Yeah, it's Brooke.'

'It is good. You've got her eyes just right,' Hayden said, his gaze skimming over the sketch. 'What made you want to draw Brooke?'

'She had an interesting face. The other lady was prettier, but I thought Brooke had a better drawing face.'

Darcie nodded. 'I thought she looked interesting as well. I kept trying to talk to her but she seemed sort of shy.'

'Is she shy at work?' Cara asked her dad.

Hayden ran a finger under his collar. 'Shy' was probably not the word he would've used for Brooke when she was wrapping her legs around his thighs in the beer cellar earlier.

'Er, no,' he said. 'No, she's not shy at work. I think she's just a bit nervous around children.'

'Why, what's scary about children?'

He shrugged. 'Dunno, their snotty noses and weird hair?'

'Shut up!' Cara said gleefully. 'That's better than having snotty *hair* and a weird *nose*, like you.' She held up a palm to her sister, who high-fived it.

Hayden laughed, putting a finger to his lips. 'All right. Not so loud with the father abuse, please.'

'Dad, I made up a plan,' Darcie said, brushing crisp crumbs off her duvet.

'What plan is this?'

'A plan to make more money, so you wouldn't have to work all the time. And it's dead easy, too.'

'Does this plan involve lottery tickets at all?'

'No. I thought of that but you only have a one in forty-five million chance of winning, I checked online. My plan's loads better.' She folded her arms with an air of satisfaction. 'All you have to do is get married! Then your wife would have a job too, so it wouldn't be so hard to pay for things. And if Nan got married as well, then that's another person, so we'd have even more money.'

'OK,' Hayden said, his mouth quirking. 'And who are these poor suckers— I mean, these lucky people who me and Nan are going to get married to?'

'There's loads of people you could marry,' Darcie said dismissively. 'Like Bianca Smith-Howson's mum. She's got loads of money, and Molly Sollis said she heard Bianca's mum say to her mum at the parents' night that she wouldn't mind a bit of rough if it's got an arse like that. I don't know what the first bit means but I think she was saying she likes your bum.'

Hayden raised an eyebrow. 'Was she now? Well, I'd thank Bianca's mum to watch her mouth around my kids. Sorry, Darce, that's a definite no.'

'You could marry one of those ladies from your work,' Cara said. 'I don't mind if Max and Livvy come to live with us. It'd be cool to have a new brother and sister.'

'We're packing plenty of us into this three-bedroom bungalow. Any preference as to which one I marry, or shall I just flip a coin?'

Cara shrugged. 'Brooke maybe, so I can draw her. I bet she's not really scared of children. Max told me she's funny when she stops being shy. He thinks she's dead cool.'

'Well, I think that's enough trying to marry your dad off to every eligible spinster in a ten-mile radius.' Hayden stood up and kissed each of them on the forehead. 'Good-night, loves. Get some sleep now, eh?'

'Dad?' Darcie said as he prepared to leave.

'What?'

'Me and Cara don't mind, you know. If you get a girlfriend.'

He smiled. 'Especially if she's rich, right?'

'No. Just… one you like. Someone nice who's fun to have around.'

'Yeah, you haven't had one for ages,' Cara said. 'Not since Year Seven.'

'Oh, I'm sure I've had one or two since then,' Hayden said. 'I distinctly remember getting dumped by Joanna Summerfield in Year Eleven the morning of my first GCSE exam, for one.'

'She means since *we* were in Year Seven,' Darcie said, rolling her eyes. The idea of their parent ever having been young enough to be in Year Seven himself was clearly too far-fetched to be entertained.

Cara nodded. 'Not since Kirsty or whatever her name was. And you only dated her for, like, two months. It's a bit sad really.'

Hayden nodded. 'So I'm a big loser. I'll remember to include that in my dating profile.'

'It's not your fault,' Darcie told him indulgently. 'You ought to get one soon, though. Otherwise you'll be too old and all the best people will be married.'

He laughed. 'I'll see what I can do. Night, girls. I love you.'

'Love you too, Dad,' Cara mumbled as she snuggled under her duvet.

Darcie yawned. 'I'm glad we stayed awake.'

Hayden closed the door gently and went to the kitchenette to make himself a supper of a ham sandwich and cup of tea. Pam was in the open-plan living room, reading a book.

'Hiya Mum,' he said. 'You're up late.'

'Mmm. It's a real page-turner, this,' Pam said, waggling her thriller at him. 'I only planned to read a chapter. Four hours later, I'm nearly finished. If you ask me, the ex-husband's masseuse did it.' She inserted a bookmark. 'Girls are still awake, then?'

'Heard us chuntering, did you?' He flicked on the kettle. 'Yeah, they waited up for me again. They need to stop doing that.'

She shrugged. 'They miss spending time with you.'

'I know. I try to be cross with them, but it's sweet they still want a hug from their dad before they go to sleep. You having a cuppa before bed?'

'Go on.'

He brewed a couple of cups of tea, handed one to his mum and sat down.

'Why don't you quit the pub now, love?' Pam asked him. 'The Diana Kershaw grant's certain to be approved, you've got a bit in the bank, Carol-Ann's paying her child support again. Things aren't as desperate as they were.'

'Yeah, Carol-Ann's payments are going to be a big help. I'm glad she found a job.' He sipped his tea thoughtfully. 'Do you think it's odd that the girls never ask about her?'

'Why should they? She never asks about them.'

'Don't get defensive, Mum. It's a normal, healthy thing for them to want to know about their mother. They used to ask about her all the time, but now they never seem to mention her.'

'I suppose it goes through stages,' Pam said. 'It's natural that curiosity should give way to resentment or indifference now they're growing up. There'll be more questions one day.'

'Watching them with those Padgett girls made me realise how much they miss out on, not having a mum-aged person around.' He glanced at her. 'I mean, they've got you, thank God. I don't know how I'd have coped bringing them up totally alone. But the way they latched on to Brooke and Rhianna, it did make me think they could do with a younger female presence in their lives now they're getting older; someone they could see as a role model.'

'Yes. It's a shame they've got no aunt, really.' She fixed him with a piercing look. 'But you didn't answer my question. Why don't you quit the pub? You could afford to.'

'I'd just… like to stay on for a bit, that's all.'

'And I know why. It's that girl you're stuck on, isn't it? The child-hater.'

'She's not really a child-hater. It's just lack of experience that puts her on edge. Once she got used to them, I bet she'd be great with kids.'

'Well, do you deny that's why you want to stay?'

He pressed his eyes closed. 'No. You're right, Brooke is a big part of it. But it isn't just her. It's the pub.'

Pam frowned. 'What about the pub?'

'I suppose… I've got invested in the place. Brooke and Rhianna have come up with all these ideas for giving it a boost, and they told me I was part of the team, and I really feel like I am now, you know? That I can't go without seeing it through.'

'But mainly it's the girl.'

'Well, yes, mainly it's the girl,' he admitted. 'She's part of a package, though. The pub, her sister, her mum… as much as I'm desperate to spend more time with my children, I just want to hang on a bit longer and see how things work out.'

Chapter Twenty-Four

Hayden was helping Brooke behind the bar a fortnight later when Theo Blake, joint manager of The Blue Parrot 1940s cafe, walked in, looking abnormally pleased with himself.

'Here he is,' Brooke said, smiling. 'The proud father. Hayd, get this man a free pint.'

Theo laughed. 'I should've brought you all cigars really, shouldn't I?'

'Girl or boy?' Hayden asked as he pulled a pint of Golden Best.

'Girl. Hazel. Seven pounds nine.'

'How's Lexie?' Brooke asked.

'Absolutely beautiful.'

She smiled. 'Correct answer, well done. What about Connor? Is he enjoying being a big brother?'

'Are you kidding? He's already designing the baby's costume for CalderCon.'

Rhianna appeared from the kitchen, looking flustered.

'Theo. Thank God,' she said, looking like she was ready to hug him. 'You're just the man I need to talk to.'

'What's wrong, Rhia?' Hayden asked, putting Theo's pint down in front of him. 'Your mum driving you round the twist?'

'I'll say. For someone who thinks the beige lumps in her mashed potato are just "the goodness in it", she's a right bloody pastry Nazi.' She turned back to Theo. 'Have you thought any more about how we're going to make this partnership between the pub and the Parrot work? I liked Lexie's idea of a commission model.'

'Come on, sis, give the man a break,' Brooke said. 'He's just had a baby.'

'Well, not me personally,' Theo said. 'Lexie ought to get at least… sixty-eight per cent of the credit.' He took a sip of his beer. 'Although actually, that was what I popped in for, to talk partnerships. That and the enticing prospect of a free pint.'

'Good,' Rhianna said fervently. 'The sooner we can get my mum out of that kitchen, the better.'

'Me and Lexie were thinking we'd expand our menu to include some classic pub grub alongside the ration book stuff,' Theo said. 'We've never bothered with things like fish and chips because we didn't want to tread on your toes, but if we're working together then that's not an issue. You can put some menus out and we'll run it as a takeaway service, with you guys phoning the orders over to us. You provide the crockery, cutlery and drinks, we'll supply the food. All for, say, twelve per cent commission for The Highwayman's?'

'Twenty,' Brooke said.

Theo shook his head. 'Come on, Brooke. We'll have to hire another part-time chef, not to mention ferrying the food over. All you lot have to do is set the tables.'

'Yeah, I know,' she said, smiling. 'Sorry, I'm one of nature's hagglers. You guys are doing us a massive favour, really. Twelve per cent it is.'

'Well, Lexie actually gave me permission to let you talk me up to fifteen per cent, so let's call it that, eh?' He offered her his hand.

'Done,' she said, shaking it firmly. 'When can we start?'

'Within the fortnight, if you want. I can email over a suggested menu tonight. It's not like I'm going to be getting any sleep.'

'Thanks so much for this, Theo,' Rhianna said. 'Mum's going to be thrilled. She hates being stuck in the kitchen. The customers are going to be pretty thrilled too, I should think.'

'I'm kind of excited about it as well. I think it'll work well for both our businesses.' Theo took a leaflet from the bar. 'What's this about?'

'It's a history of The Highwayman's Drop,' Hayden said, trying not to look too proud of his one contribution to the business.

'Oh, right. Good idea.' Theo skimmed the leaflet, which featured a drawing of the pub from sometime in the dim and distant past. 'Does Dick Turpin really haunt your beer cellar?'

'Absolutely,' Rhianna said. 'And his horse as well.'

'How do you know?'

'Mum keeps hearing hooves when she goes down to change a barrel. She's very spiritually attuned.'

'You sure she's not sampling the beer while she's down there?'

'Honestly, it's a bona fide highwayman ghost,' Hayden said. 'We could be on *Britain's Most Haunted* if we wanted.'

'Why aren't you?'

He shrugged. 'The ghost thought it was tacky.'

Brooke handed Theo another leaflet. 'Here, take this one as well.'

'Silver Singles' Night?' Theo read. 'How old do you think I am, Brooke?'

'I thought you might like to spread the word among your older customers. It's next month. Speed dating, party games, dancing and a Bay City Rollers tribute act. Anyone aged fifty-five to seventy is welcome. Retro fancy dress optional.'

'Right.' He tucked it into his pocket. 'I can think of a few who might be interested. Cheers again for the pint.' He took his drink to finish at one of the tables.

The door to the kitchen swung open and Janey marched out.

'Where'd you disappear to?' she demanded of Rhianna. 'I thought you were helping me make apple pies.'

'I had to pop out and have a brief nervous breakdown.'

'Well you can just finish having it in the kitchen. That butter and flour isn't going to start resembling fine bread-crumbs on its own.'

Rhianna groaned.

'You see what I mean?' she whispered to Hayden and Brooke. 'She's a real perfectionist for someone whose pastry has the texture of grit on damp cardboard.'

Janey glared at her. 'I heard that. Come on, young lady, back to work.'

'Never again,' Rhianna muttered as she followed her mum to the kitchen.

Hayden watched them go.

'Er, back in a sec,' he said to Brooke. 'I just need to… I won't be long.'

He jogged after them, walking into a kitchen that looked like a lightly floured bombsite.

'Something up, love?' Janey asked him.

'Um, I had a favour to ask you both.'

'OK, ask away.'

'Well, I wondered if you'd mind letting me lock up tonight.'

'You're certainly welcome to,' Rhianna said. 'That's not really what I'd call a favour, Hayden.'

'I mean, I wondered if you'd mind letting me lock up on my own. With Brooke.'

Janey smiled. 'Ah, I see. What're you planning?'

'A date, of sorts. I can't tell you more than that, it's a surprise.'

'And, er, should we expect my sister back late from this date?' Rhianna asked, raising an eyebrow.

He laughed. 'I certainly hope so.'

'It's about bloody time, that's all I can say,' Janey said. 'All right, lad, we'll keep out of your way. Good luck.'

'Thanks, Mrs P. I'll need it.'

'No you won't,' Rhianna said. 'Brooke's mad about you. Don't let her try to deny it, it's obvious.'

Hayden gazed thoughtfully at the cooker. 'I hope you're right. I'm kind of mad about her too.'

'We know,' Janey said. 'That's obvious as well. Have fun, eh?'

—

Brooke yawned as she, Rhianna and Hayden watched the last customers leave.

'Well, ladies and gentlemen, time at the bar,' she said, rousing herself. 'Let's get everything shut down.'

Hayden shot a significant look at Rhianna.

'Oh. Right.' She glanced at Brooke. 'Um, I think I'd better head upstairs, make sure Mum didn't have any trouble getting the kids off to bed.'

Brooke frowned. 'The kids'll have gone to bed hours ago, won't they?'

'Still, I feel like I ought to check on them. My maternal Spidey sense is tingling. I'll see you in a bit.'

'Let's get tidied up then,' Brooke said to Hayden when her sister had gone. 'I'm sure you're dying to get to bed.'

'Yes.' He hesitated. He'd been planning this for days, but now it came to it, he felt a bit awkward. 'Um, Brooke?'

'Mm?'

'Could you come down to the cellar?'

She frowned. 'The cellar? What for?'

'There's just, er… something I need to show you.'

'Like what, the ghost of Dick Turpin?'

'I feel like there's a really obvious innuendo opportunity there that I just can't bring myself to take advantage of.' He nudged her. 'Come on. You'll like it, I promise.'

He opened the cellar door, and Brooke, looking puzzled, followed him down the steps.

'What's flickering?' She sniffed. 'What smells? Oh my God, is there a fire?'

'Er, kind of.' They reached the bottom step, and Hayden gestured around the room. 'Ta–da. Um.'

Brooke stared at the picnic blanket on the floor. A bottle of wine was chilling in a cooler beside it and pillar candles had been dotted around to illuminate the room.

'Bloody hell,' she whispered, running her finger over an old-fashioned wicker picnic basket. 'Hayd, did you do this?'

'Yeah.' He smiled bashfully. 'It's a date, see? I told you I'd make it happen.'

'So this is what you were doing when you sneaked down here earlier.' She kissed his cheek. 'I love it. Where the hell did you get the picnic basket?'

'In my younger days, I was a member of the Famous Five.' He sat down on the blanket and gestured for her to join him.

'Is that what we're having?' she said as she sat beside him. 'Ham sandwiches, cream buns and lashings of ginger beer?'

'This picnic's a bit more Mediterranean. I've packed olives, carrot sticks and houmous as starters. What would you like first?'

She smiled. 'None of those. Sorry.'

'Oh.' He blinked. 'All right. Well, um… I've got some quiche.'

'Nope. Not quiche either.'

'Boiled egg?'

'My God, you're slow.' She grabbed his collar. 'Just bloody well come here.'

-

'Well, if I was going to end my long run of celibacy with anyone, I'm glad it was you,' Hayden said breathlessly as they lay on the blanket together afterwards, naked and tangled.

'I'm just glad you remembered how to do it.'

'It's like riding a bike. Once you get your arse in the saddle, you soon remember how to work the pedals.'

'Did you just compare my vagina to a bike?'

'Metaphors really aren't my strong suit.' He trailed a finger over the pattern of briars on her forearm. 'We gave Mr Turpin quite a show, eh?'

'It's the only fun he gets these days.' Brooke leaned over him to rummage in the picnic basket, extracting a tub of olives. She opened it and popped one in Hayden's mouth.

'Thanks.' Hayden swallowed his olive and pulled her on top of him. 'You're pretty great, you know that?'

'You're pretty great yourself.' She kissed his nose. 'I'm glad you didn't hoist me up on a cask again, though. I didn't want to say anything last time because we were in the moment, but the bung was getting right up my bum.'

He slid his hands down to her buttocks. 'I feel like I ought to apologise to it personally. Sorry, Brooke's bum. I swear I'll make it up to you.'

She stroked her thumb over his cheek. 'What happens now, Hayd?'

He shrugged. 'I'm ready to go again.'

She smiled. 'I mean, what happens with us?'

'Well, as first dates go, I reckon that went pretty well. The earth certainly moved for me.'

'And me. Twice.'

'I noticed.' He rolled her off him so he could sit up and pour the wine. 'Anyway, I thought we could make it a regular thing.'

She sat up too and started kissing his shoulder. 'It's not going to be easy, love.'

'If you start talking about your bloody outcomes again, I swear I'm going to burst out crying.'

'I'm not going to use the o-word,' Brooke said, sipping the wine he'd handed her. 'I just meant that it's rare to find a window where we're both free, with work and your family commitments.'

Hayden was optimistic there'd come a time when his family commitments and his love-life commitments could be made to cross over to an extent, but he stayed silent on that point. He didn't want to scare Brooke off, just when she was finally opening up to him and encouraging him

259

to tear all her clothes off. One picnic and a pretty amazing shag was a good start, but it wasn't a relationship. Not yet.

'I think we just play it by ear, don't we?' he said, putting his wine down so he could lean over to nibble her earlobe. It was hard to concentrate on picnics when Brooke Padgett was next to him stark naked.

'Take our opportunities as they arise, you mean?'

'You said that on purpose, didn't you?' he mumbled as he kissed her neck.

She smiled. 'Maybe.'

'Well?' he whispered. 'Is it a yes to more dates? To shamefully misquote Humphrey Bogart: we'll always have the beer cellar.'

'It's a yes to more dates.'

'Which makes you my girlfriend. Which means I can let you ravish me again without worrying you'll think I'm easy for going all the way on our first date.' He pulled her on top of him. 'Now bloody well come here.'

Chapter Twenty-Five

Janey nudged Rhianna as Brooke came up from the pub three weeks later, humming to herself.

'Here she comes, love's young dream,' she said. 'Look at her, Rhia. She looks like she's floating on her own fluffy-wuffy little cloud, doesn't she?'

'What're you humming, Brooke?' Rhianna asked.

'Nothing.' Brooke stopped immediately. 'I'm not humming. I don't hum.'

'You've certainly been doing plenty of mooning lately, that's for sure,' Janey said, smirking.

'What? I've been doing no such thing!' If they were referring to what went on between her and Hayden in the beer cellar after hours, well, that was their own fault for looking.

'I didn't mean getting-your-bum-out mooning,' Janey said. 'I meant the other sort. Wandering about with that glazed, blissful face on you like you've just been given a chemical lobotomy.'

'Shut your pieholes.' But Brooke smiled as she sat down next to her sister.

Livvy was on the carpet in her pyjamas, colouring in, while her brother watched YouTube videos on his tablet.

'Why is Brooke mooning, Nana?' she asked.

'Because she's in love, sweetheart.'

'With Cara and Darcie's daddy?'

'Mum, stop filling their heads with that rubbish.' Brooke turned to Livvy. 'Pay no attention, Liv. Nana's just teasing me.'

'Is Hayden your boyfriend, Brooke?' Max asked.

She hesitated. 'Well, sort of.'

'She means yes, Maxie,' Rhianna said.

Brooke shook her head. 'Families. Who'd have 'em?'

Janey stood up. 'Right. Do you want to see something secret, small people?'

'Ooh, yes!' Livvy said, clapping her hands. 'I love secrets. What is it?'

'It's a top-secret secret that has to be seen to be believed. Come into my bedroom and I'll show you.'

Livvy and Max jumped to their feet and followed her out.

'What is it?' Brooke asked Rhianna.

Rhianna laughed. 'I think it's her costume for the speed dating tomorrow.'

'What, is she going in fancy dress?'

'Yeah. I hope it's not too traumatic.' She raised an eyebrow. 'So, will you be seeing your gentleman friend tonight?'

Brooke shook her head. 'Seriously, what do you lot talk about when my love life isn't available?'

'Hey, I was only asking.'

'I am, as it happens,' Brooke said, smiling.

'He's not on the bar, is he?'

'No, he's got a parents' evening so he swapped a shift with Mark. He's going to sneak out later though, when the girls are in bed. Hopefully we can squeeze in half an hour together.'

'Still going well?'

'It's going great. It's just going great in twenty- to thirty-minute chunks.' Brooke sighed. 'I wish we could see a bit more of each other. Go out on a proper date.'

'Can't you? I'm happy to cover for you one night.'

'I guess we could. He just gets so little time with the girls, he feels guilty if he's not spending his free hours with them. Then we have to fit whatever our thing is into times when they're in bed or at school. A quick drink in the pub after hours, catching our death in the beer cellar...' She lowered her voice. 'We did it on the back seat of his bloody Kia the other day. I haven't done that since I was seventeen.'

'Why don't you go over to his place?'

'I can't, can I? His kids are there.'

'Well?'

'I just want to keep separate from that part of his life. At least until I know where this is going.' She met Rhianna's eyes. 'Rhia, you're a mum. You think I'm right to be cautious, don't you?'

'Well, yes, to an extent,' Rhianna said slowly. 'Taking on someone else's kids is a big commitment. They're at a difficult age too, with the nightmare of puberty just around the corner.'

Brooke shuddered. 'God, I hadn't even thought that far ahead. My main worry is that they'll hate me, which'll kill whatever me and Hayd have got going on.'

'I know. And I do think you're right to be cautious.' Rhianna patted her knee. 'I also think you're falling hard for Hayden Bailey, and in the end you're going to decide he's worth it. And I think that ultimately, his kids are going to love you.'

Brooke smiled. 'Then we'll all live happily ever after, I suppose.'

'I don't see why not. They're nice girls, and I could sense when we played with them that they're starved for younger adult female company. It must be tough not having their mum around, especially the age they are now.'

'Hayden keeps dropping hints that he wants to introduce me to them properly – as his girlfriend, I mean. But I never signed up to be a stepmum, Rhia, or any kind of mum. I just don't think I'd be any good at it.'

'None of us do,' Rhianna said, giving her a squeeze. 'For what it's worth though, I think you'd be brilliant. My two have come to love you, and that was when you weren't even trying.'

'I always had this policy of never dating single dads. I'm not sure how Hayden Bailey managed to worm his way into my affections in spite of my better judgement.' She smiled. 'He is worth it, though. I do want to take it slow, but this is the first time I've had something like this.'

'You're lucky, Brooke. Not all men are like Hayden.'

'How are you feeling about the kids going to James tomorrow?'

'Absolutely awful,' Rhianna murmured. 'I realise he's got to see them, but I've just got this horrible sick sensation in my stomach. Like… they might not come back.'

'The first visit was always going to be rough on you,' Brooke said, resting a hand on her shoulder. 'Eventually it'll become part of your routine, then it'll get easier.'

'He's got his awful mother staying. He had to let Avril go, obviously, so he's drafted Nicole in to help. Livvy looked appalled when I told her.' She sighed. 'Maybe I should go with them. I doubt James would object. I know he'd spend the weekend badgering me about going back to him, though.'

'Has he still not got the message?'

Rhianna shook her head. 'He texts or emails every day. Long messages, outlining point by point why it makes social, moral and financial sense for us to reconcile.' She snorted. 'I think "getting wife back by autumn" is one of those bloody SMART goals he loves so much.'

'It's better to let Max and Livvy go on their own. He'll spend some proper time with them then, being an actual parent rather than expecting you to do the donkey work.' Brooke squeezed her shoulder. 'And me, you and Mum can have some fun while they're away, eh? How about a girls' night Saturday?'

'I can't on Saturday. I've got a thing.'

'What thing?'

'I'm meeting someone.' Rhianna's cheeks pinkened. 'Sort of a date, actually.'

'A date! Is it not a bit soon for that?'

'There's nothing really… romantic. We've met a few times for coffee, me and this guy, but it's just been friendly. Once James and I are legally separated though… well, we'll see what happens.'

'Who is he? Someone from the village?'

'I met him through a friend. It's all innocent right now, but I do enjoy his company. He makes me laugh.'

'I'm glad you're over James enough to think about moving on anyway.'

'Me too.'

Brooke smiled. 'So if Mum meets someone at the speed dating tomorrow, that's all three of us paired off.'

'Do you think she will?'

'You never know.' Brooke laughed. 'She might even meet husbands two, three and four.'

Livvy came back in, giggling.

'Mummy, it's SO FUNNY!' she yelled.

Rhianna smiled. 'What is, sweetheart?'

'I am, apparently,' Janey said as she followed with Max. 'We've been having a little fashion parade. It seems my outfit for tomorrow is the ultimate in hilarity.'

'What's Nana going to be wearing, Max?' Brooke asked.

'Can't tell you,' Max said, zipping his lips. 'Nana says it has to be kept super, super secret so you'll be surprised. I wish we could stay and see how surprised you are instead of going to Dad's.'

'What's speed dating please?' Livvy asked her mum.

Rhianna pulled her up onto her knee. 'Well, it's like ordinary dating but really, really fast.'

Max squeezed himself onto the sofa between his mum and aunt. 'Is that what Nana's going to do?'

'That's right. It's a bit like Musical Chairs. When the music stops you sit down, and whoever sits opposite you is your date for the next two minutes. Then you have to ask as many questions as you can to decide if you like each other.'

Max looked at Brooke. 'Then what happens? Do you have to get married to the last person left?'

Brooke laughed. 'I hope not, for Nana's sake.'

'If he's dishy I wouldn't mind,' Janey said. 'He couldn't be any worse than the oddballs on Tinder.'

'You only met one oddball off Tinder, Mum. And he wasn't even that much of an oddball, other than the weird plant obsession.'

'Yes, but I saw enough dodgy profiles to put me off internet dating for a good long while. No, this is a far better idea. How many tickets have we sold so far, girls?'

Rhianna pulled a face. 'Only about ten, and apart from your friend Mike they were all to women. We did say people could pay on the door though, so hopefully there'll be more than that there on the night.'

'Ooh, I am looking forward to it!' Janey said, glowing at the thought. 'Rhianna, you're a genius.'

'Brooke should get the credit, really. She was the one who fleshed it out by adding a fancy dress theme and a band.'

'Rubbish. You did all the legwork,' Brooke said. 'I just chucked a few ideas in the pot.'

Janey smiled. 'Look at you two, arguing about something positive for a change. Three months ago I could never have imagined it.'

'Me neither,' Brooke said, smiling at her sister.

'Well, chickens, time for bed,' Janey said to the children. 'Max, you can read for a bit but lights out by nine, please. Livvy, we'll read another chapter of your book before sleep. Mummy will come in to kiss you goodnight in a little while.'

Livvy looked at Brooke. 'Can you put me to bed?'

Brooke blinked. 'Me?'

Livvy nodded. 'Nana or Mummy always put me to bed but you never do. I want to see what it's like when you put me to bed.'

Brooke turned a panicked look on her sister.

'Go on,' Rhianna said, smiling.

'But I don't know...'

'There's no art to it, Brooke. You just read the story, tuck her in and give her a kiss. She's not reading *The Shining*, you don't need to look so terrified.'

'Pleeease, Brooke,' Livvy said, pushing out her lip.

'Um...' Brooke hesitated, but no convenient excuse presented itself. 'Well, all right.'

'Yay!' Livvy hopped down from Rhianna's lap and ran to the bedroom she shared with her mum. Brooke followed, wondering what she'd just let herself in for.

When she entered, Livvy was already under the covers with the duvet pulled up to her chin, her favourite plush rabbit on the pillow next to her.

'That's my book,' she said, pointing.

Brooke sat on the bed and picked up the book. It was actually one of her own from childhood that Livvy must have found somewhere, *The Owl Who Was Afraid of the Dark*.

'Oh, I love this story,' Brooke said.

'Oh my gosh, I love it too!' Livvy sounded delighted they had this in common. 'This is my second time reading it.'

'Your mum and me used to ask for it all the time when we were little,' Brooke said, gazing dreamily at the cover. 'Dad— I mean, your grandad used to read it to us. What's your favourite part?'

'I like when the boy thinks Plop's a Catherine wheel and then they watch the fireworks.'

'Really? That's my favourite part too.'

'I knew it would be,' Livvy said in a satisfied tone, as if this just cemented her view that her aunt was a pretty all-round cool and impressive person. Brooke was starting to feel that having a kid or two around could do wonders for your self-esteem.

'Read it please,' Livvy commanded, and Brooke obediently started reading the next chapter.

'No, that's not right,' Livvy said before she was two sentences in. 'You have to make the voices all different. Like, Plop's voice should be like this.' She made a high-pitched little *squee-squee-squee* sound.

'Sorry,' Brooke said penitently. 'Let me take another crack at it.'

She started again, making sure Plop's voice was as squeaky as a baby owl's ought to be, and Livvy gave her a benign smile of approval.

Brooke soon found these characters who'd once been such a big part of her life easing themselves back into her mind: old friends long forgotten, brought to life again through Livvy's eager, shining eyes.

'So, how did I do?' Brooke asked when she reached the end.

Livvy thought about this for a moment.

'You did the voices better than Nana,' she said at last. 'You should read it a bit slower next time, though.'

'Marks out of ten?'

'Um… eight.'

'Oh, well. That's not bad for my first go.' Brooke stood up to tuck the covers tight around Livvy's little body. 'Goodnight, Liv.'

'Night night,' Livvy said, yawning. 'Can we read some more tomorrow, please?'

'You'll be sleeping at Daddy's tomorrow, sweetie.'

'Oh yeah. I wish we could stay here.'

'Don't you want to see your dad?'

'I want to. I just wish he could come here instead. Then I wouldn't have to miss you and Mummy and Nana while we're gone.' Livvy pulled a face. 'And Granny is at our old house now instead of Avril. If I put my elbows on the table, she sends me to the naughty step. Just for putting my elbows on the table! That's not fair, is it, Brooke?'

Brooke almost laughed at the little girl's indignant tone, but she managed to control herself.

'No, it's rubbish.' She leaned over to kiss Livvy's forehead. 'But I'm sure your grandma's missed you both, just like your dad has. Try to be good for them, eh?'

'OK,' Livvy said sleepily as she burrowed under the covers. 'Brooke?'

'Yes?'

'Why don't you like us to call you aunty? We always call Aunt Lily it. She's Daddy's sister. And I don't even like her as much as you – but that's a secret though, so don't tell.'

Brooke hesitated.

'Well, I suppose I never felt all that much like an aunty before,' she said.

'What does being an aunty feel like?'

'Like… you have to take care of people, I guess. Your nieces and nephews.'

'You do that, though. You help my mummy look after us. Why didn't you feel like an aunty?'

'I don't think I felt grown up enough to be one.'

Livvy blinked. 'But you're *really* grown up.'

'I certainly ought to be by now.' Brooke stroked her niece's soft hair. 'I was scared I wouldn't be any good at it, Liv. That I'd get it all wrong and you wouldn't like me.'

'We think you're good at it. Me and Max do.'

Brooke smiled. 'Thank you.'

'Do you feel like an aunty now?'

'Yes,' she said after a moment's pause. 'Yes, I do.'

'Can I call you aunty then?'

'Would you like to?'

Livvy nodded vigorously. 'Yes please. Then everyone will know you're my aunty. I want everyone to know that. Max wants to call you it as well but he's too shy to ask if he's allowed.'

Was that really how they felt? Were they so proud of her?

'All right, if it's important to you then you can call me aunty,' Brooke said softly. 'Sleep tight, Liv.'

–

'Well, it's definitely comfier than the beer cellar,' Hayden said later as he and Brooke lay cuddling under a blanket on the back seat of his car.

'Only marginally.' She shuffled to try and get comfortable, throwing one bare leg over the back of the driver's seat. 'My bum's gone numb. Do you ever wonder what it would feel like to do it in a bed?'

'Is that a thing some people do?'

'So I'm told. Sounds a bit kinky but I'm nothing if not adventurous.' Brooke's head shot up. 'What was that?'

'What?'

'I heard a noise.'

Hayden sighed. 'Not this again.' He shuffled up to look out at the dark, empty moors stretching around their little parking spot. 'There's no one there, Brooke. It's midnight.'

'Are you sure?'

'Well no, it's pitch black, but if it was a pervert or a copper then I suspect they'd carry a torch. It was probably a grouse or something.' He lay back down and started kissing her shoulder. 'Stop being so jumpy. I thought you were a sexually liberated wild child once upon a time. This ought to be exciting for you, moorland romps on the back seat.'

She smiled and flexed her neck to give him better access. 'I know. I must be getting old.'

'I suppose we should think about going home,' he mumbled against her skin. 'It's late.'

'In a minute. I don't want to let you go just yet.'

'All right.' He snuggled against her. 'So, how was your night?'

'A bit scary. Livvy insisted I read her a bedtime story.'

He laughed. 'God, what? You're right, that sounds terrifying.'

'It wasn't so bad in the end. We bonded over our favourite book.' Brooke flushed. 'She asked if she could call me aunty.'

'What did you say?'

'I said I'd like that. She was mad keen to be allowed to do it. I never realised I meant so much to them.'

'Course you do. You're brilliant.'

She smiled and kissed his nose. 'How was Cara's parents' night?'

'Well, we're going to have to dedicate some time to her maths. She's in danger of dropping a set. Her art teacher thinks she's God's gift, though. Oh, which reminds me.' He nodded to a rucksack tucked under the driver's seat. 'Can you reach that?'

She leaned over to pass it to him. 'What's in it?'

'Cara wanted me to give you something.' He took out a sheet of paper in a plastic wallet.

Brooke shuffled into a sitting position so she could take it from him. 'What's this?'

'It's you. She drew it. Hang on.' He leaned over the front seats to flick the light on. 'There. Good, isn't it?'

Brooke examined the pencil sketch. 'It is good. Talented little soul, isn't she?'

'I know. I'm glad she's got her own thing so there's no need to feel jealous of her sister. Handily, Darcie might do well in nearly every other subject but she can't draw for toffee.'

'What made Cara want to draw me?'

'She started it after we met you on the rec.' He smiled. 'Apparently you've got an interesting face.'

'Have I?'

'Cara thinks so.' He trailed a finger over her cheek. 'So do I.'

'Do they know about us then, your girls?'

'Well, yeah. There didn't seem to be any reason to hide it. Besides, I'm proud of you.'

She smiled. 'That's sweet.'

He brushed her hair over her shoulder so he could kiss her neck. 'You know, we could be discovering the joys of doing it in a bed,' he whispered. 'You only have to say the word.'

'Not at my place we couldn't, the walls are too thin. Max would be traumatised for life.'

'You know I meant my place.'

She shook her head, frowning. 'Hayden, please, don't start that again.'

'I just think it's time, that's all. Sneaking around shagging in cars and cellars is fun for a bit, but eventually we're going to have to take the next step before one of us gets lumbago.'

'Yeah, eventually we'll take the next step. It's been three weeks, Hayd.'

'It feels right though, doesn't it? Why wait if we're sure about our feelings?'

She raised an eyebrow. 'Our *feelings*? Do we talk about those now? Bloody hell, we're racing ahead.'

'I mean, we know we'll be in this for the long term.' He leaned round to look into her face. 'We do, don't we?'

'I… yes. I mean, I hope so. That doesn't mean we have to rush. At the rate you're going, you'll be proposing in another fortnight.'

He took her hand and squeezed it. 'Brooke, I like you. More than anyone I've met in… well, ever. But at the moment it feels like all we do is have sex and as great as it is, I'd kind of like to do other stuff together too. I hate that I have to choose between spending my free time with the girls or with you when I could be doing both. I mean, you've met them once already.'

Brooke felt a cold shiver down her spine.

'Accidentally bumping into them when we were still just mates is very different from being introduced to them officially as your girlfriend, Hayden,' she said.

'OK, I get that, but it's going to happen eventually. It might as well be now as later.'

'After three weeks, though? What's the hurry?'

'I guess I'm just excited about this. Us. I want to share it with the girls too.'

'Hayden, it's too soon. Obviously ultimately I know I'm going to have to meet them – I want to meet them. But me getting to know your kids: that's a huge step forward for us. You can't pretend it isn't a big deal.'

'I'm not pretending that. I just thought that with things going so well, and the bond you've got with Max and Livvy now—'

She frowned. 'Why are you still pressing me on this?'

'I'm sorry.' He dropped her hand, blinking. 'I didn't mean to put pressure on you. If that's how it sounded then I'm sorry.'

'Well, it is how it sounded.' She fished her knickers from down the back of the seat. 'We'd better get home.'

'Come on, don't be angry. Maybe I am going a bit fast, but that's only because I love being with you. I'd like to spend more time with you and I'd like you to meet the other important people in my life.'

'Yes, well, it's too soon. I'm not ready.'

'I'm starting to worry you might never be ready,' he muttered.

'I'm sorry?'

'I don't want a fuck-buddy, Brooke, I want a girlfriend.' He looked up to meet her eye. 'Can you honestly tell me that's what you want too? Do you mean it, when you say you'll take that next step when the time's right? Or is this just about sex for you?'

She scoffed. 'What, those are my two choices? I can either be using you for sex or committing to being a substitute parent for your kids? You know, Hayden, there is a middle ground.'

'Who mentioned being a substitute parent for my kids?'

'Well, isn't that what it comes down to, ultimately?'

'No, it bloody well isn't,' he snapped. 'What it comes down to is me and you, and the fact I like you a hell of a lot and I want to share the other parts of my life with you. Because that's never happened to me before, Brooke. So, you know, I've been feeling pretty excited about it.' He looked hurt now as well as angry, pulling his jeans back on. 'Is that really how you see it? That all I want from you is a mum for the girls?'

'I… no. No, of course I don't. I just know this is major and I don't appreciate being rushed into it this early in a new relationship. I don't get why that's hard for you to understand.'

'I'm not trying to rush you. I'll wait as long as you like, if you can promise me that's where this is going. I've had enough of casual flings, Brooke, so if that's what this is to you then I'd rather call it a day now, before…'

'Before what?'

'Never mind.' He didn't make eye contact as he struggled into his T-shirt and squeezed through to the driver's seat. 'Come on. Let's get out of here.'

Chapter Twenty-Six

Rhianna finished attaching the foil *Let's Boogie!* sign to the wall and stepped back.

'Perfect finishing touch,' she said to Brooke. 'I think we're all ready.'

Psychedelic bunting decked the pub and a disco ball span overhead. A line of tables and chairs had been placed down the middle of the room, ready for the speed dating. The Bay City Rollers tribute band they'd booked, Shangri-La, were currently setting up under Janey's watchful eye, with an area cleared to serve as a dance floor.

'It looks like a whole new place,' Brooke said. 'Very "Disco Inferno". We'll have them necking like teenagers by the end of the night.'

'I hope we get more people than the dozen who bought advance tickets,' Rhianna said. 'And only two of them men. This could be a complete washout if no one comes, Brooke.'

'It won't,' Brooke said, with more confidence than she felt. She glanced at her sister's face, which was haunted by a barely suppressed anxiety. 'How are the kiddywinks?'

'They were full of bounce when I phoned. James had taken them out to this restaurant we used to go to on their birthdays. They get to wear chefs' hats and help cook their own meals… you know, the sort of place I could never afford to take them.' She sighed. 'They love it there.'

'Well, that's OK,' Brooke said gently. 'It's a good thing if their dad's spending quality time with them – that's what they're there for, right? It's not going to make them want to go live with him, just because he takes them to some fancy restaurant. You're their mum.'

'I know. It just feels like they've finally settled here, they're happy, they've got new friends and routines. And now they're being plunged back into their old lives for a few days and they're going to come home dissatisfied, because they're kids and things like nice restaurants and expensive toys matter to them.'

'Not as much as their mum does.'

'Even so. I worry James has got some plan to… I guess to weaponise them against me. Weaken me so I'll ultimately go back to him.' Rhianna scowled. 'You know, all this week he's been sending me links to articles outlining the many terrible outcomes for kids raised in single-parent families. If I divorce him it's tantamount to passing them a dirty syringe and inviting them to start shooting up, apparently.'

'I'm sure he'll send whatever suits his agenda. It's bollocks though, Rhia, obviously – you only need to look at Hayden's kids to see that. This is exactly what James wants, to get you beating yourself up over nothing.'

'Yeah, you're right. I just can't help feeling stressed while the children are away from me.' Rhianna twisted the wedding ring that from habit she still wore, turning it round and round on her finger. The skin underneath had become red and sore, and Brooke wondered if, like the legacy of the white scars on her sister's arm, the pain was a way for Rhianna to keep control of her whirling emotions. 'Brooke, I can count the nights I haven't been there to kiss them at bedtime on the fingers of one hand. I'll be a bag of nerves until I get them back.'

Brooke gave her a swift hug. 'I know, love. Here for you, eh?'

Janey approached them.

'Right, I need to go change into my pulling gear,' she said. 'You two can babysit the band. They just need supplying with cups of tea.'

Rhianna glanced at the five-man band, all dressed in tartan shirts open to the waist, huge denim flares and shoulder-length wigs. 'They certainly made boy bands differently in the bad old days. Why are they called Shangri-La? I don't get the connection.'

'I asked the lead singer that,' Janey said. 'Apparently they used to be called Shang-A-Lang, you know, after the Rollers hit, but it turned out there was already a tribute band called that so they changed it to something similar to save money on rebranding.'

Rhianna squinted at the band logo on the drumkit. 'Oh yeah, you can see where they peeled the letters off. No wonder they were so cheap.'

'No Hayden?' Janey asked. 'I thought he'd be here by now.'

Brooke flushed. 'No, not yet.'

Rhianna frowned. 'Something up, Brooke?'

'Oh, we… it's nothing. We had a bit of a row yesterday, that's all.'

'What about?'

'He started going on about introducing me to his kids again and I snapped at him. Then he got in a strop about something I said and… we haven't spoken since.'

'I don't know why you're so against the idea of meeting his girls,' Janey said. 'You might as well do it now as later, since it's obvious you're nuts about each other. Then you wouldn't have to juggle your schedules so much.'

'Oh right, take his side.' Brooke scowled at the carpet. 'I'm not ready yet, all right? Kids weren't something I ever expected to have in my future, and now... I just want to know we're not rushing into it. It needs some serious mental preparation on my part before we take that leap.'

'I suppose that's fair enough,' Janey said soothingly. 'Talk to him about it, chick. I'm sure he'll understand if you explain.'

Rhianna nodded to the door as a Hayden-shaped silhouette loomed behind the frosted glass. 'Here he is.'

'Right.' Janey glanced at Rhianna. 'Well, I'm going to get changed. Rhianna, didn't you say you had something to do in the kitchen?'

'Me? No.'

'Yes you did. You specifically told me you had to be in the kitchen right at this very moment.'

Rhianna followed Janey's glance to Hayden approaching. 'Ah. Right. So I did.'

They disappeared, leaving Brooke and Hayden to talk.

'Um, hi,' he said, rubbing his neck.

'Hi.'

There was silence as they both looked anywhere but at each other.

'Look, Hayd—' she began.

'Brooke, I wanted to—' he said at the same time. They both stopped, laughing.

'All right, me first,' he said. 'Brooke, I'm sorry. You were right and I was wrong. I'm an idiot and you're amazing.'

She smiled. 'I'm liking this apology so far. Go on.'

'I shouldn't have pressured you. The last thing I want is for you to feel on edge when you meet the girls, and you're right, it is very soon. I was excited about how things were going and I guess I got carried away. I'll wait for as long as you want, OK?'

'Thanks, Hayden. And I'm sorry I upset you when I suggested you expected me to be a substitute for their mum. I know what a huge honour it is that you want me to get to know them.' She beckoned to him. 'Come here then.'

He took her in his arms and kissed her forehead. 'Friends again?'

'Friends again. It's just a big deal, you know? Your kids are the most important people in the world to you, naturally, and I've got ten million things to worry about when it comes time for me to be introduced to them as your girlfriend.'

'You honestly haven't. I told you, they're going to love you.'

'Hayden, please. I know you're trying to be reassuring, but what I need you to do right now is understand. This is terrifying for me.'

'Sorry,' he said softly. 'Go on. Tell me what you're afraid of.'

'Well, I'm afraid your kids won't like me, because kids generally don't, and then *you* won't like me, and I'll lose the thing that's currently making me the happiest I've ever been. I'm afraid of saying or doing the wrong thing around them, and being a poor role model. I'm afraid they'll look to me for advice about things and I won't know what advice to give. I'm afraid they'll expect me to take their mum's place, and I'm not adult enough or mumsy enough to do a good job. And I'm afraid, just a little bit, that something will go wrong between me and you and then I'll lose three people I've come to care about instead of just one.'

He blinked. 'Wow. That is a scary list.'

'I know.'

'I liked that bit about you being the happiest you've ever been, though. Birth of my children aside, that's how I feel too.' He lowered his voice to a whisper. 'As a father I'm morally obligated to say that. Actually I was a nervous wreck the day my children were born.'

'So you get it, then?'

'I get it.' He kissed her softly. 'And I know I can't say anything to stop you worrying about those things, but I can promise to be right there next to you, holding your hand. When you're ready let me know, OK?'

'Thanks, love.' She lowered her voice. 'Hey. Max and Livvy are away at their dad's tonight. Do you want to sleep over?'

'What, you mean have sex in a bed?'

'Yep. Make-up sex, the best kind.'

'Glory hallelujah.' He kissed her forehead and let her go. 'I'll have to run out on you early though, so I can be home before the girls get up.'

'That's OK.'

'Oi!' one of the band called. 'Any chance of a cuppa when you two have finished snogging?'

Brooke rolled her eyes. 'These tribute bands are real divas. You know, I bet we could've got the actual Bay City Rollers for the same money.'

'I'll sort them out. You'd better set up a table by the door to take cash. Shouldn't be long until people start turning up.'

'I just hope some of them are men, or this speed dating idea could be the biggest flop we've had yet.'

-

The first person to arrive was Colin Ackroyd, one of the four widowers who came in for a drink most days.

'Oh,' he said when he spotted Brooke sitting just inside the door with a money tub and a stack of question sheets. He took a look around the pub and its retro decorations. 'Something special going on tonight, Brooke love?'

'That's right, it's our Silver Singles' Night for over-fifty-fives. You're welcome to join us, Colin. We've got speed dating, a band and some games for later. It's a fiver in though, sorry about that.'

'Oh, no. I'm too old and knackered for all that nonsense.' He paused. 'Your, er… your mam coming, is she?'

'She is.'

'Well, I might stay for a drink now I'm here.' He took out his wallet and chucked a fiver in her tub, then glanced at the question lists. 'What's all this?'

'It's for the speed dating. You'll be matched to someone for a two-minute date and this is a list of suggested conversation-starters. You don't have to take part if you don't want to though.'

'Right. Well, may as well get my money's worth.' He picked one up. 'See you later.'

Next through the door was Martin Brady.

'What's all this then?' he asked Brooke, blinking at the flashing disco lights.

'It's our over-fifty-fives singles' night,' Brooke said again. 'We've had posters up for weeks, Marty. Haven't you noticed them?'

'No. Must've passed me by.' He tugged at his too-tight shirt collar. 'Janey joining in?'

'Yes, she's been looking forward to it. Still on the hunt for her perfect man.'

'Ah well, I suppose I can stay for a pint. May as well, eh?' He fished out a fiver – apparently he knew the entry price, despite not having noticed a single poster – then grabbed a list of questions and went to sit down.

Next was divorcé Nigel Horsforth, one of the village's parish councillors, wearing his best shirt and tie.

'Oh,' he said when he walked in, his face a mask of surprise. Brooke sighed.

'Yes, it's a special night. Yes, my mum's taking part. Here's your list of speed dating questions and you can chuck a fiver in the tub.' She thrust a question sheet at him and he took it, blinking, before paying his entry fee and going to sit down.

Five minutes later, Rhianna joined her.

'How's it going?' she asked. 'Seems to be filling up.'

'I'm spotting a trend,' Brooke said, smiling wryly. 'Apparently the mature menfolk of Leyholme are all very surprised, having turned up here in their Sunday best for no reason, to discover we're holding a singles' night. Despite the stack of flyers on the bar, the ten or so posters around the pub, the twenty or so stuck to lampposts all over the village and the one in the post office window, it's a complete shock to them. But they've all graciously decided they'll stay for a drink now they're here.'

Rhianna laughed. 'What is it, do you think? Some sort of macho thing?'

'Embarrassment, I suppose. The men are shyer about admitting they're here on the pull than the women. Their pride demands they pretend it was all an accident.' Brooke glanced at Martin Brady and his mates. 'What's really worrying is that most of them are here for Mum.'

'You're kidding!'

'Nope. About half the men in here specifically asked if she was joining in.'

Rhianna looked over at the stairs. 'Well, here she comes, ready for her admirers to start throwing themselves at her feet.'

Brooke laughed. 'Bloody hell. Where'd she get those clothes?'

Janey was wearing a pair of hip-hugging denim dungarees decorated with crocheted flower patches over a rainbow-striped top. A pair of huge platform heels added a couple of inches to her height, and her chestnut hair was brushed and sprayed into a Farrah Fawcett–esque feathered style. Nearly every male eye turned to look as she descended, sweeping the stairs with her massive flares.

'Oof. That is painfully seventies,' Rhianna said, shielding her eyes.

'It suits her though,' Brooke said. 'Hey, those bellend dungarees are quite flattering, aren't they?'

'Bell-*bottom*, you turnip.'

'I stand by what I said.'

Janey grinned as she came to join them.

'So, daughters, how embarrassed are you on a scale of one to ten?'

'I'd say a solid eight for me,' Brooke said. 'The dungarees do wonders for your bum, though.'

'You think I don't know that?' Janey took a disappointed look around the busy pub. 'Not many out-of-towners, are there? I was hoping to see at least a few faces I didn't recognise.'

'Mum, don't be so ungrateful,' Rhianna said. 'They only came for you.'

Janey blinked. 'Me?'

'That's right,' Brooke said. 'We've barely had a man through the door who didn't ask if you were taking part before he agreed to part with a fiver. I'm starting to see why business has been bad, when we've been hiding our star attraction in the kitchen.'

Janey blushed. 'Give over.'

'I'm not kidding. Apparently there isn't a man over fifty-five in this village who doesn't fancy you.' Brooke handed her a question list. 'Here. I'm going to get things started.'

Chapter Twenty-Seven

Janey had been buzzing about this night ever since her girls had first suggested it, but as she sat opposite Colin Ackroyd on their micro-date, listening to him drone on about his assorted ailments while the Rollers' 'Saturday Night' played, she was beginning to wonder why.

She'd known Colin for years; he was an old drinking buddy of her Eddie's. But honestly, he could complain for England these days. Yes, they all had aches and pains now they were getting on a bit, and trips to the GP were more frequent, but there were surely other topics of conversation than which bits of them were in danger of dropping off. The perpetually glum expression on Colin's face made him look like Droopy.

'…anyway, our Sal suggested going to one of those homopathics to help with the old *waterworks*' – he mouthed the word as if it was something terribly shocking, pointing to his groin in case she didn't get it – 'but Ted says the medicine they give you is just tap water and it's all a scam. You ever tried it, Janey?'

'Er, no,' Janey said, wondering how they'd drifted onto the subject of Colin's waterworks in the first place when the question she'd asked as a conversation-starter had been 'what colour best describes your personality?'.

'Well, I probably won't bother. Ted's likely right. Everyone's out to fleece you these days.'

The buzzer went for them to move on, and Janey held on to her sigh of relief. Colin looked disappointed, though. He'd obviously been having a whale of a time telling her which parts of him were falling to pieces.

'Well, Janey, we must do this again,' he said, and for a moment she was worried he was going to try kissing her hand, but thankfully he thought better of it. 'You look smashing tonight. Brings back my youth to see you all dolled up. Would you be free for a drink sometime?'

She smiled her best barmaid smile. 'You always know where to find me for that,' she said, nodding to the bar. 'I'll see you soon, Colin. It's been a pleasure.'

She shuffled on a seat and stifled a groan when she found herself opposite Nigel from the parish council. Between his obsession with planning permission and his hobby of collecting wartime memorabilia, she wasn't sure she was going to manage to stay awake for this one.

Eventually Brooke announced a five-minute break so everyone could replenish their drinks. When the other speed-daters had gone to the bar, Brooke sidled up to her mum.

'How's it going, Janey?' she whispered.

'Well, a greater bunch of tedious old coots than the men in this village I've never had the misfortune to sit opposite,' Janey muttered back. 'All they want to talk about is their illnesses, the state of the country today and the shortcomings of the younger generations. They've turned into the same boring, uptight old folk we used to roll our eyes at when we were teens. Did we really have to get so old?'

'Sorry, Mum,' Brooke said, patting her shoulder. 'I was hoping the band might put everyone in a young-at-heart sort of mood. No such luck, eh?'

'Maybe this is all there is for me now. These are the eligible bachelors available and I'm going to have to make do and mend.' She glanced at Mike chatting animatedly to Carmel from the post office. 'I shouldn't have been so quick to dismiss Mike, should I? He might be obsessed with plants, but at least he doesn't make small talk about his urinary tract over dinner.'

'Don't give up yet. There's still plenty of dates to go. And if some of them are dull, well, at least it's only two minutes.'

'Yes, I suppose that's one advantage.'

Brooke squeezed her elbow. 'I'm sorry it's not been fun for you, Mum. I know you were looking forward to this.'

'Well. Like you say, it's not over yet.' Janey glanced around the room at groups of people chatting while the band played. 'From the point of view of the pub, it's certainly a success. Everyone looks to be having a great time.'

'I know. Plus, they're all buying plenty of drinks. Rhia was right: the odd theme night to keep things fresh could be just what we need.'

'I suppose it's time to get back into the meat market,' Janey said with a sigh. 'You'd better honk your buzzer, chick. I've got Martin next so at least we can have a good catch-up. The next man who starts telling me about his colon problems or something, I'm going straight to the bar for a treble gin.'

'Good luck.' Brooke gave her shoulder another pat before pressing her buzzer to get things going again. Janey sat down opposite Martin Brady, smiling warmly.

'Um, hiya,' he said, colouring as he ran his finger under his shirt collar.

'Evening, Marty.' She reached out to squeeze his hand by way of a hello. Well, they were old friends. No need to stand on ceremony this time.

He looked bashful as she withdrew her fingers. 'So I suppose we should talk about these questions, should we?'

Janey laughed. 'What've you gone shy for? I thought I was at least going to have one decent chat tonight when I saw you in the line-up.'

His mouth flickered. 'Well. It's all new to me, this, you know.'

'What, Martin Brady, Yorkshire's answer to Casanova?' she said, smiling. 'I remember when you had a line for every pretty girl around here. They worked as well which was more than most of the lads could say.'

He laughed, relaxing a little. 'That was a long time ago.'

'I know it was.' She smiled sadly as the band launched into a cover of David Essex's 'Hold Me Close'. 'We got old, didn't we, Marty?'

He looked into her eyes, and she noticed an earnest look on his face that she'd never seen there before.

'I don't mind the getting old so much,' he said. 'I mean it's no picnic, but it's losing people that's the hard part.'

'Yes.' She reached over to pat his arm. 'I miss Mave too.'

'I often think about how I used to share a pint and a game of pool with your Eddie. He was a good lad.' He glanced along the row of tables. 'What would they make of this daftness, do you reckon?'

'Eddie would still be laughing at my dungarees.'

Martin cast an appreciative glance over them. 'I think he'd find it hard to keep his eyes off your backside.'

She laughed. 'You old flirt.'

'Is that what you think this is?'

He looked suddenly serious. Then the buzzer sounded, letting them know it was time to move down the line.

'It was nice to chat, Marty,' Janey said, meaning it this time. 'Let's catch up later.'

'I'm not sure at my age that I want to wait until later.'

'What?'

'Here.' He pressed a bit of paper into her hand before standing up. Rather than moving down the line, however, he excused himself to Carmel in the seat next to Janey's and disappeared.

Blinking, Janey opened the note. Martin had scribbled it on the back of a corner torn off his question list.

> *Fancy playing truant? Meet me in the beer garden*
> *in five minutes.*

Janey hesitated, taking a look at who was going to be opposite her next. It was Ted King, a retired accountant who ran the village's drystone wall repair group. Since she knew his favourite conversation topic was his hobby of taxidermy, Janey wasn't anticipating an enthralling conversation.

'Um, excuse me,' she said to him. 'The little girls' room calls. Carry on without me, please, and I'll slot back in when I can.'

She slipped out into the beer garden. Martin was sitting on one of the tables, swinging his legs.

'All right, what's this all about?' she said, smiling as she held up the note.

He shrugged. 'I didn't want to spend the rest of the night listening to tales of people's hip operations.'

'You too, eh?'

'Well. None of us can help getting old. They're a good bunch of girls.' He smiled. 'But not the one I came for.'

'You're not talking about me?'

He laughed. 'Who do you think I'm talking about, Olivia Newton-John? Get your bum up here.'

She hesitated before kicking off her platforms and climbing up next to him.

'Still off the fags, lass?' he asked her.

'Yep, I'm on to vaping now. How about you?'

'Not had one since I had that heart murmur eight year ago.' He sighed. 'Remember when we were going to live forever?'

'Vividly.' Janey lowered her voice. 'Hang on and I'll show you something my kids don't know about. Top secret, mind.'

She jumped down and went to lift an upturned plant pot in the pub's back porch. Underneath was a single cigarette and a lighter.

'I've been saving this for a special occasion,' she said as she hopped back up on the table.

'Is this a special occasion?'

'It might be. Come on, I'll split it with you.'

He laughed as she lit it. 'Now this reminds me of being young, sharing fags we'd cadged off our parents because we were too poor to buy a pack.'

'Mmm.' She took a drag and passed it to him, a ring of fuchsia lipstick around the filter. 'Wasn't always just a fag either, was it? Not when we rolled our own.'

'Better keep your voice down,' he said, passing it back to her. 'My kids refuse to give any clout to the idea I might've been young once.'

'Thank God they don't know about those leather trousers you had, eh?'

'Heh, you're not wrong.' He glanced down at his beer belly. 'Those were the days.'

Janey exhaled a cloud of smoke appreciatively. 'I used to fancy you rotten when we were teenagers.'

'I had that effect on a lot of girls.' He slipped an arm around her. 'Like a sexier Marc Bolan, they used to say.'

'Impossible,' Janey said, laughing. She passed him the last of the cigarette. 'Here, you finish it. And for God's sake, don't tell my kids.'

He inhaled deeply before putting it out in the ashtray. 'That's the ultimate marker of old age, I reckon. When you're young, you try to get away with as much as you can without your mam and dad finding out. When you're older, your kids try to get away with as much as they can without you finding out. Then once you reach sixty or so, you try to get away with as much as you can without your kids finding out. The three ages of man.'

'Brooke and Rhianna make such a fuss, you'd think I was a newborn baby. They've got no idea what we used to get up to.' Janey smiled fondly. 'Still, they're good girls.'

'Mine too.' He shuffled closer to her. 'Will they mind, do you think?'

'Mind what?'

He didn't answer. Just smiled, picking at a thread on his trousers.

'Do you know what I've been doing for days, Janey?' he asked.

'Should I?'

'I've been wearing a hole in my carpet, wondering if this was going to be the night I'd finally get my nerve up and tell you how I feel about you. I came so close to chickening out.' He nodded to the pub. 'As soon as I saw them all waiting to try their luck with you, I knew it was man or mouse time. Hence the note. I think the last time

I passed some bird a note to meet me behind the bike sheds, I was sixteen.'

She smiled uncertainly. 'Come on, Marty. You're teasing me, are you?'

'I'm bloody not.' He put one finger under her chin. 'Janey, I've been trying to tell you for ages. Did you not notice all the hints I dropped whenever I came in the pub?'

'Those were hints? I thought you were just messing about.'

He sighed. 'Well, happen I'm not as good as I once was at this flirting lark.'

Janey felt a bit fuzzy.

'Marty, I'm confused,' she whispered. 'You can't really mean you…'

In answer, he pressed a soft kiss to her lips.

'There,' he said quietly. 'Is that any clearer?'

'But… we've been friends for years.'

'Well? I've always thought friends made the best lovers. I don't think Mave or Eddie would begrudge us, do you?'

'Well, no.' She shook her head to try and clear it. 'I'm just… surprised, that's all.'

'What do you want to do with the rest of your life, Janey?'

'I don't know really,' she said dreamily. 'I suppose I hoped I'd meet someone I could share it with, take a step back from the pub. The girls are practically running the place between them now; they don't need their mum any more. And then I thought I'd like to travel. I've done so little of it in my life – barely set foot out of Yorkshire, really. I want to buy one of those little campervans and just go wherever the mood takes me, in this country and Europe and…' She trailed off, laughing self-consciously. 'That sounds silly, I suppose.'

'It sounds wonderful.' Martin rubbed his grey hair. 'You know, I've got a bit put away. Not a king's ransom, but enough to enjoy my twilight years.'

'Why are you telling me?'

'I just... thought you might be interested. I always thought I might use it to see the world, when I found someone who wanted to see it with me.'

'You mean me?'

He looked up to smile at her. 'Are you not getting it yet? Yes, I mean you, you daft cow.'

She laughed. 'Martin Brady, are you asking me out?'

'No I'm not. I'm sixty-four years old. I haven't got time to go around asking girls out.' He took her hand and pressed it to his lips. 'I'm asking you to marry me.'

She stared at him. 'You what?'

'Well, we're not getting any younger, are we? If I'm going to be travelling about in a campervan, I'd like to do it with a wife. Not least because at my age, it sounds daft to introduce you to people as my girlfriend.'

'But... Marty, it's so sudden. We've never even... I had no idea you...'

'I know,' he said softly. 'But if I didn't do it tonight, when I've got a couple of pints inside me and the Rollers setting the mood, I knew I'd never get my nerve up again. Do you want to think about it? I can wait.' He looked at his hands: wrinkled, now, and gnarled. 'But not too long, eh?'

Janey trailed a finger over his cheek. He looked... different. Her old friend was still there, but in his eyes she could see the boy he'd been – the one who'd got her heart racing when she was a teenager – peeping out. He was really very handsome, she thought as she perused his features. Eyes clear and blue, crinkled with humour...

His confession that he saw her as more than just a friend didn't feel so strange, now her initial surprise had worn off. Had she known already, somewhere inside? Perhaps her loyalty to Eddie, and to her old schoolfriend, Martin's late wife Mave, had made her hide something from herself that was all too obvious. That it was always supposed to be Marty she was meant to spend her autumn years with; no one else.

'Well?' Martin said, looking anxious as he watched her thoughts flicker in her face. 'Do you want to take some time? Or can you give me an answer now?'

'I don't need any time,' she said quietly.

'Come on then, lass, put me out of my misery. I'm tying myself in knots here.'

She smiled. 'It's a yes, Marty. A great big yes.'

Martin laughed as he took her in his arms and kissed her again. 'Thank God for that. I don't think I've taken a bigger risk in my life than I did tonight. You won't regret it, Janey.'

Chapter Twenty-Eight

Rhianna stared at the novel she was trying to read. She'd read the same sentence fourteen times now, and it still hadn't made it from her eyes to her brain. A car rolled by outside, and she jerked in her seat on the sofa.

'Are you going to do that every time a car passes?' Brooke said, looking up from her own book. 'James only texted you an hour ago. It'll be at least half an hour yet until he drops the kids off.'

'Sorry. I can't help it.'

'You want a cuppa to steady your nerves?'

'No, it won't help.' She put her book down. 'I might as well give up on reading, though. It's not going in.'

Rhianna's phone buzzed and she took it out, fumbling a little in her anxiousness.

It wasn't her husband. It was just another notification from her banking app to tell her she was at the limit of her overdraft. She and James had never had a joint bank account, but he'd transferred a regular sum to her for what he quaintly called the 'housekeeping'. He hadn't stopped the direct debit when she'd left him, and the money still appeared there week after week. He probably thought he was being generous. But that and the small amount she earned from her shifts in the pub wasn't enough to support two children who needed to be fed, clothed and educated, not to mention the credit card that had already been close

to maxed out when she'd left him and whose communic-
ations, too, were becoming increasingly urgent. Rhianna
knew, though, that if she asked James for more financial
help, he'd just use her desperation as leverage to try to get
her back again.

She had to do something though, and soon. She was
living on the edge of her funds, and every week brought
her closer to financial disaster.

What she really needed was a job: something part-
time that she could fit around the pub and her children's
schooling. She flicked to the Indeed app and scrolled
down the list of vacancies that had appeared since last time
she'd checked.

Nothing. Nothing she had the experience for; nothing
even worth applying for. She sighed and put the phone
away again.

They heard the front door open, and Rhianna jerked.

'Ugh. Sorry,' she said to Brooke. 'That'll be Mum back
from Martin's, won't it? I'm a bag of nerves today.'

Janey came in, her cheeks glowing from the warm
summer sunshine – and perhaps from something else as
well.

'Well, look what the cat dragged in,' Brooke said,
putting down her book. 'Had fun with your fancy man,
have you?'

'I have, not that it's any of your nosy business,' Janey
said, smiling. 'I wanted to be here to welcome the kiddies
home, though. I've missed them to bits.'

'When will you be bringing your new boyfriend round
to see us then?' Rhianna asked.

'Oh, you've met him a million times.'

'Yeah, but that was before he was having it away with
our mum,' Brooke said. 'That puts a different complexion

on things. We're going to have to ask him about his intentions.'

Janey's cheeks coloured. 'Actually, I wanted to talk to you on that subject. I was hoping we could have a word before the little ones got back.'

Brooke frowned. 'How do you mean?'

'Well… you'd better sit down.'

'We are sitting down.'

'Oh. Yes. Well, then I'd better sit down.'

She took a seat in the armchair.

'Now, I know this is going to sound strange to you two young people,' she said. 'But when you get to the age me and Marty are, and when you've lost people before, things are… different. You value every moment when you're aware you don't know how many you've got left.'

'You're OK, aren't you?' Rhianna said, her brow creasing.

Janey laughed. 'Oh God, I didn't mean anything like that. No, don't worry, I'm in rude health as ever. What I'm trying to tell you is that Marty and me… well, there's no point beating around the bush. We're engaged.'

Brooke's eyes bulged. 'You're *what*?'

'We're engaged, Brooke. He asked me on Friday at the speed dating, and today…' Janey blushed as she took a diamond ring from her pocket. '…today he gave me this. It's beautiful, isn't it? It was his grandmother's.'

Rhianna felt dizzy. 'But… you can't be engaged. Not just like that.'

'Why not, love?'

'Well, it's so… sudden.'

'Is it?' Janey said, smiling at her ring. 'We've known each other for half a century, Rhianna. We were at school together. Perhaps it was a surprise when he told me his feelings weren't as purely friendly as I'd always believed, but once that wore off, I knew it was the right thing for us.'

'But…' Brooke shook her head. 'Bloody hell, Mum. You can't be in love with him, surely?'

Janey shrugged. 'Love is an abstract concept, isn't it? When you get older, you feel it differently than you did as a young thing. In your teens, love is this whooshing, heart-stopping, many-splendoured thing that carries you off with it in spite of yourself. In your sixties, it's more like a warming glow. It might not be rushing tides and throbbing hearts, but it's just as real.'

'So you do love him?'

'I always did. But it was only on Friday that I realised the love I had for a friend could quite easily become something more, if I wanted it to,' Janey said. 'I'm sorry that doesn't sound as romantic as you two would probably like.'

'Well, I guess… I mean, congratulations.' Still feeling dazed, Rhianna went to give her mum a hug. 'I can't say I'm not reeling with the suddenness of it, but I'm happy for you, Mum.'

'Thanks, sweetheart.' Janey gave her a squeeze, then glanced at Brooke. 'Well? Do I get your blessing too?'

'I just… can't get my head around it.' Brooke blinked a couple of times. 'I'm not asleep, am I?'

'I'm afraid not.'

'And you really love him? He makes you happy?'

'He does. Very much so.' Janey met her eye. 'It isn't like what I had with your father, Brooke, but it's just as meaningful in its own different way. Just know that it doesn't mean I love your dad any less, or that I'll ever forget him. OK?'

'I know.' Brooke looked thoughtful for a moment, then summoned a smile. 'Well, if Martin makes you happy, Mum, that's good enough for me. I've always liked him.'

Janey smiled as Brooke stood up to embrace her. 'You're a good girl.'

'Tell you what. I'll grab a bottle of the good bubbly from the pub, shall I?' Brooke said, letting her go. 'This is definitely something we ought to be celebrating, even if it has knocked me for six.'

'That sounds like an excellent idea.'

Brooke went down to the bar to fetch a bottle of champagne from the wine fridge. When she got back, she poured them each a glass.

'Well, cheers,' Rhianna said when they were all furnished with a drink. 'Here's to… the future, I suppose.'

'The future,' they chorused, clinking glasses.

'So what happens now, Mum?' Brooke asked.

'We – that is, Marty and me – thought it might be nice to have a little engagement party in a few weeks, down in the pub.'

Brooke smiled at Rhianna. '"Marty and me." Hark at her.'

'It'll be nice to celebrate with friends from the village,' Janey went on. 'As for the wedding, we want a quiet do somewhere abroad. Of course you girls are invited, and the littlies, and Martin's son and daughter with their partners and kids, but we don't want anyone else.'

Rhianna blinked. 'Abroad?'

'That's right. We're planning to cash up our little pots of savings and go travelling. Marty's scouring campervan websites this afternoon looking for one that'll suit us.'

'But… you're not moving out, are you?' Brooke asked.

Janey laughed. 'Brooke, come on. You don't think we're going to squeeze Marty in here on top of the five of us, surely? I'm going to move in with him in the bungalow. Although our plan is to spend as little time there as possible while we satisfy our mutual wanderlust.'

'But what about The Highwayman's?'

'I've been thinking for a while that it was time for me to step back. You two are doing such a cracking job here, you don't need your mum any more. I've been impressed watching you rejuvenate it with all your fresh ideas. I think that was all the place needed, in the end: the two of you, working together.' She smiled softly at them. 'I've never been prouder of you both.'

'But it's your pub,' Brooke said. 'Yours and Dad's. I can't do it without you, Mum.'

'Yes you can, Brooke.' Janey leaned across to press her hand. 'You've got your sister to help you now, and young Hayden. It's time for me to walk away.'

'But...' Brooke swallowed. 'I don't want to do it without you.'

'You will, though. And you'll do it brilliantly,' Janey said. 'I've given decades of my life to The Highwayman's, and now... well, there are other things I want to do while I've still got a life to do them in. It's time to pass the torch on to the next generation. I'm going to speak to a lawyer about signing my share of the pub over to you two next week.'

A knock sounded at the fire escape door, and Rhianna jumped, sloshing champagne all over her top.

'That's them!' she whispered. 'James must have brought them up the back way.'

'You want us to come with you to answer it?' Brooke asked.

302

'No.' Rhianna threw back her shoulders. 'No. I need to do it.'

When she answered the door, James was smiling self-consciously, one arm around each of the children. Max was wearing his paper chef's hat from the restaurant they'd been to, clutching a paper bag with the Lego logo on it, and Livvy was in a pink tutu and ballet pumps. When she saw her mum, she barrelled into her legs with her usual shriek of 'Mummy!'. Max wasn't far behind, trying to elbow his sister aside as he burrowed into Rhianna's stomach.

Rhianna had promised herself she wasn't going to get emotional in front of James, but as she gathered her children to her, she found her eyes were full.

'Oh, my babies,' she whispered, crouching down to hug them both tight. 'I've missed you so, so much.'

'We missed you too, Mummy,' Max said in a muffled voice, his face buried in her stomach.

'Did you both have fun at Daddy's?'

Livvy nodded enthusiastically. 'Mummy, we had a party! A garden party! And all my Ferndene friends came, even Tammy, and Avril came to visit too, and we had a bouncy castle and pony rides and a paddling pool and jelly. Only I wished you and Aunty Brooke and Nana could have come, because it was really the best party ever. Oh, and guess what? Daddy's going to buy us a pony! Not just to ride but our very own to keep. It's going to live in the field behind our house – I mean our old house, not this one, and its name's going to be Plop like the owl from my book, we decided. Isn't that the sickest?'

'It certainly is,' Rhianna said, forcing herself to smile.

Max extracted his face from her stomach to hold up his Lego bag. 'Mummy, look! Daddy got me the Avengers

Tower kit. I'm going to ask Zach if he wants to come and make it with me.'

'That's brilliant, Maxie.' She glanced up at James. 'Daddy's certainly feeling generous.'

James rubbed his cheek, looking embarrassed.

'Darlings, why don't you run inside with your bags?' he said to the children. 'I'd like to talk to Mummy for a moment.'

'OK!' Max said. 'I want to show Nana and Aunty Brooke my Lego kit.'

'And I want to tell them about our pony,' Livvy said.

Rhianna gave them a last squeeze, inhaling the smell of their baby-soft hair, before releasing them. 'Nana and Aunty Brooke are in the living room. Give Daddy a kiss goodbye, then you can go tell them all your news.'

They gave their father a hug and a kiss before scampering inside. Rhianna stepped out onto the fire escape, closing the door slightly to give them some privacy.

'I thought I'd better bring them up this way,' James said. 'I didn't think you'd want them walking through the bar.'

'Thank you.' She forced a smile. 'Were they well-behaved for you?'

'Well, they seem to have picked up a few bad habits. They looked at the dining table as if they'd forgotten how to use it. Mummy wasn't impressed at the state their table manners had got into.'

'Wasn't she? I'd say that was none of your mother's business,' Rhianna snapped, politeness quickly giving way to irritation. 'What the hell is this about buying them a pony, James?'

He flushed. 'I'm sorry. I know I shouldn't have agreed to any such thing without speaking with you. I've missed them, that's all. It's hard to deny them anything when they've been away from me for so long.'

'James, you can't *do* things like that! If they spend every third weekend having garden parties and riding ponies and being treated to expensive meals and gifts, it's just going to make them dissatisfied with their life here. I want them to have a relationship with you, but I don't want you using them as a bloody… bargaining chip.'

'That's not what this is, Flops. I told you, I missed them. What's the point in working hard if a man can't spend the money he earns on his children?'

Rhianna folded her arms. 'You ought to discuss it with me first.'

'I know. It won't happen again.' He sniffed. 'Why do I smell cheap wine?'

'That's me. I spilled a glass of champagne on myself.'

'You're drinking at this time?'

'It's a special occasion,' she said, bristling. 'If you must know, my mum just got engaged. We were toasting to her future. Is that all right by you?'

'I'm sorry, I didn't mean to sound judgemental.' He paused. 'Did you see my email?'

Rhianna snorted. 'What, the one with the statistics on how many children from broken homes end up in prison?'

'No. The one with the link to the couples' counselling website.' He met her eyes. 'Won't you, Rhianna?'

She turned away. 'I'm sorry.'

'The children want you to. I could tell this weekend that as glad as they were to be back, if their mummy wasn't there too then they could never be fully happy.' He reached out to take her hand. 'Neither can I,' he said softly.

'This is their home now.' She drew her hand away. 'It's no good, James. I… I don't love you any more. I'm sorry to say things that will hurt you, but you've got no one to blame except yourself.'

He scowled. 'It's him, isn't it?'

Rhianna blinked. 'Him who?'

'This man. The one Livvy was talking about.'

'What man?'

'Livvy let it slip you'd been seeing someone new. I'd have thought you'd have the delicacy to conceal it from the children, at least. We've not been separated three months.'

Rhianna flushed. 'It isn't like that. He's a friend, that's all.'

'Are you sleeping with him?'

'That's none of your business.' She glared at him. 'Anyway, who are you to lecture me on sexual morality?'

'You are still my wife, Rhianna. The mother of my children.'

'And you're my husband. It didn't stop you getting your bits out for Shari on a regular basis, did it?'

He looked down at his expensive shoes, polished to such a high shine he could admire his reflection in them. 'Is a man not allowed to make one single mistake in his life?'

'Yeah, if that mistake is accidentally defrosting the freezer or forgetting to bring in the washing. Shagging someone else is a whole other level, wouldn't you say?'

'I realise that,' he murmured. 'But for the children, Rhianna. You should have seen how happy they were this weekend. All it wanted was you and it would've been perfect.' He curled his lip at the building behind her; old, uneven, blackened by a century of soot from the local

306

weaving mills. 'I can't believe you'd rather raise them in this unhealthy place than try to work things out. Not to mention how their education is suffering. Their vocabularies and diction have become quite shocking.'

'Yes, well. If the last few months have taught me anything, it's that there are things in life that matter a hell of a lot more than sodding diction.'

'I can tell,' he muttered. 'Have you managed to get a job yet?'

'I've got a job here.'

He snorted. 'A pub barmaid. You, with a double first from Cambridge. You, who could've been anything you wanted.'

'And why aren't I? Whose fault is it?'

He flushed. 'It wasn't like that. We didn't need two incomes so it made sense for one of us to be at home with the children.'

'And that one of us was me.'

'Well, yes. You're their mother. Besides, my career was established before we ever met. Yours had yet to begin. Obviously it made more sense for me to be at work.'

'It was never about the money, James! It was about me. When you got me to sign that prenup and persuaded me not to pursue a career, you robbed me of any chance of independence. And like the fool I was, I loved you enough to think I'd never need it.'

'I'm sorry,' he murmured. 'Would it make a difference if I could change that?'

'What?'

'If I paid for you to join an Inn and take the Bar course. Then would you consider working things out?'

She blinked. 'You'd do that?'

'Well, yes. If it was important to you.'

'I couldn't take the Bar course just like that, though. There's an aptitude test I'd have to pass first, and it's nearly twelve years since I finished my degree so all my legal knowledge is out of date. I'd need to do a postgrad conversion course to even be considered.'

'I could pay for that too. I can engage a new au pair to replace Avril, and hire a cleaning lady who can come every day. Then you'd have all the free time you needed for study.'

She narrowed one eye. 'What for? Like you said, we don't need two incomes.'

'Because it means a lot to you. Because I love you.'

'I'm sorry, James. It's a generous offer, but it's still no. I'll call you in a few weeks about their next visit.'

'Flops, please.' He took her hand again. 'Please, just think about it. Will you at least promise to do that? Just put your anger to one side and think about it, properly? I only want what's best for you and the children, I swear to you.'

'Yes, well, you should've thought about that before, shouldn't you?' She pulled her hand away. 'Bye, James.'

Chapter Twenty-Nine

The pub was in festive mood as the Padgett family welcomed the residents of Leyholme for Janey and Martin's engagement party one Saturday the following month.

It was a family event, spilling out into the beer garden where a bouncy castle had been put on for the kiddies. Max and Livvy had been allowed into the pub for a rare visit and were dressed in their best clothes, casting awestruck looks around them as they hung on to their nana's skirt. Brooke was minding the bar while Rhianna finished setting up the buffet their new business partners at The Blue Parrot had provided.

Brooke felt a little emotional as she gazed at the banner over the door proclaiming *Congratulations Jane and Martin*, with the requisite clipart of horseshoes and champagne glasses. While officially they were celebrating her mum's engagement, to Brooke it felt more like a goodbye party. For Janey it marked the beginning of a new phase in her life, but for her youngest daughter it seemed like the end of something.

There was a drawer under the bar. Brooke slid it open. In it was the sign that for most of her life had been nailed above the pub's front door.

Edward and Jane Padgett. Licensed to sell beers, wines, spirits and tobacco for consumption on or off these premises.

Brooke blinked back a tear as she looked at the ageing plaque. She'd never believed there'd come a time when that sign wasn't there to welcome visitors to the pub.

The current plaque over the door bore Janey's name and her own. That would have to be changed, she supposed. Whose name would be on it now? Hers and Rhianna's? Never in a thousand years could Brooke have predicted she'd one day be running this place with her sister, but it did feel right. Rhianna was part of the place too, now. If there wasn't a Padgett or two on the sign above the door, was this even still The Highwayman's?

'End of an era, eh?' Rhianna said softly.

Brooke jumped. 'How did you creep up on me?'

'It wasn't hard. You were miles away.' She smiled at the old sign. 'We've got big shoes to fill, sis.'

'I know.' Brooke looked at her mum with Martin. Her future stepfather had his arm around Janey's waist while they chatted to a gang of well-wishers, including a couple of rather jealous-looking men. The pair of them looked blissfully happy. 'I'm pleased for her, Rhia, obviously, but she'll be missed around here. Not least by me.'

'I'm sorry. I know you two are close. Closer than she and I are.'

'That's not true. It was just a different sort of relation-ship we had.' Brooke sighed. 'But I've always had her here. Whenever I needed her, she was there for me.' She choked on a sob. 'Mum taught me everything I know, about pubs and about life. How will we manage without her, Rhia?'

'She's not dying, Brooke. You're talking like we'll never see her again.'

'I know. I shouldn't let myself get maudlin about it.' Brooke slid the drawer shut again. 'Do you think we will get by without her, though? I mean, in terms of running this place.'

'We've got you, haven't we?' Rhianna said, smiling. 'The queen of barmaids.'

Brooke laughed. 'And you, the brains of the operation.'

'And Hayden to bring the sex appeal. How can we fail?' Rhianna nudged her sister. 'Come on, cheer up. We're supposed to be celebrating.'

'Yeah, I know. I'll snap myself out of it.'

'You'll have to.' Rhianna nodded at the red-headed woman approaching the bar. 'Customer.'

Brooke forced herself to smile. 'Hiya Nell.'

'Hiya,' the Reception class teacher said. 'The usual for my mum, Deb and Xander, please, Brooke, plus a white wine for me and a Fruit Shoot for our Milly.'

'Anything for Florrie?'

Nell laughed. 'She's good with her bottle for now, but I'm sure she'll be hitting the hard stuff later.'

'Would you and Stevie rather have prosecco?' Brooke asked. 'Fizz is on the house today, courtesy of the prospective bride and groom.'

'Ooh, on the house, my favourite words. Yes please, love.'

'Coming up.'

'Happy day, eh?' Nell said as she watched Brooke pour her drinks.

'Very.' Brooke glanced at her mum and Martin. 'And a little sad. My mum's been a licensee here for decades. It'll be strange not seeing her name over the door.'

'Is she leaving then?'

'Yes, she's going travelling with Martin,' Rhianna said. She shot a fond look at her sister. 'But don't worry, she's leaving the place in good hands.'

Brooke blinked as Hayden strode into the pub with an anxious look on his face. He caught sight of her behind the bar and grimaced.

'I didn't think he'd be coming,' she said to Rhianna. 'He's normally booked up with either jobs or his kids on Saturdays.'

'I suppose he wanted to drop in and offer his congratulations.' Rhianna nudged her. 'Go on, go have a canoodle then. I'll finish getting Nell's drinks.'

Brooke smiled. 'Thanks, Rhia.'

She nipped out from behind the bar and hurried over to Hayden. Her emotions had been reeling all day and she badly needed to be held, even if everyone in the pub could see.

'Hayd,' she said, smiling. 'I'm bloody glad you're here.'

She threw herself at him for a hug, and he patted her back.

'Brooke, what's up?' he asked. 'You know there are people watching, right?'

'Oh, just… nothing really. I'm having a funny sort of day. Sorry for the unprecedented public display of affection.' She looked up and frowned at the expression on his face. 'What's up? You look worried about something.'

'Look, I jogged on ahead so I could give you a heads-up. I know I said I'd wait, but your mum sent an invitation to the household and they were so desperate to see you that I didn't know how to—'

Brooke's eyes widened as the front door opened and Hayden's mum Pam appeared, shepherding two curly-headed figures in their direction.

'You brought your *kids* here to meet me?' she hissed.

'I'm sorry.' He rubbed his neck. 'It was an accident.'

'Hayden, I can't! I'm not—' She forced a smile as the little group joined them. 'Um, hello, Pam.'

Pam beamed at her. 'Hiya, Brooke, love. I'm sorry to spring this pair on you, but they were desperate to meet the person who's been putting the smile on their dad's face this past month.'

'Hi Brooke!' Cara said eagerly. 'Remember us?'

'Er, yes. Hi girls.' She cast a panicked look towards the bar. 'Look, sorry, but I'm actually at work right now. I'd better, um… my sister probably needs help.'

'Brooke,' Hayden said in an undertone. 'Please.'

She turned a helpless look on him that clearly tele-graphed *I can't*. God, she had to get away! She hadn't prepared for this. She could feel the sweat beading on her temples as her body urged her to make an escape.

Cara's face had fallen. 'Didn't you like my picture I drew you? Dad said you'd want to tell me.'

'Yes.' Brooke tried to force herself to calm down. 'Of course, it was a lovely picture. You're very good, Cara.'

The little girl beamed. 'I knew you'd like it. That's why I wanted you to have it.'

'Yes. Thank you.'

'Cara and me think your face is dead interesting,' Darcie said, beaming too. 'We were super happy when Dad told us you were his new girlfriend. We wanted him to have one.'

'Max says you're loads of fun,' Cara said. 'And you're good at football too, so we knew already we were going to like you.'

Hayden smiled at Brooke. 'Relief to know you've made the grade, eh?'

'Yes,' Brooke said from behind a clenched smile. 'That's, um… important. I'm sorry, you guys. I don't mean to be rude, but I really do have to go back to work.'

The twins looked disappointed.

'Will you come and talk to us later, Brooke?' Darcie asked.

'Er… I'll do my best. I'm going to be quite busy while the party's on.' She started to leave, then turned back. 'It was… lovely to see you both. I hope you have a nice time.'

'OK, bye!' Cara waved as Brooke hurried back behind the bar.

'Why don't you go out to the beer garden?' she heard Hayden say to his family. 'I'll meet you there.'

She turned her face away as he appeared at the bar.

'All right, what the hell was that about?' he demanded in an undertone.

Rhianna cast him a surprised glance. 'Is there something wrong?'

'I don't know, Brooke, is there?' he asked, still frowning at her sister.

She turned full eyes to him. 'You promised, Hayd. You said as long as I needed, that was OK.'

'And I meant it. I told you, it was an accident. They saw the invitation addressed to the whole family and I didn't have the heart to tell them they couldn't come.' He sighed. 'I'm sorry. But you didn't have to be rude, did you? They've been so excited about it, you'd think they were waiting for Christmas morning. They're going to be gutted you weren't pleased to see them.'

'I wasn't being rude, Hayden, I was having a bloody panic attack! You knew how anxious I was about this; how much psychological preparation I needed to feel I was ready for it. How could you just spring it on me like this?'

'Brooke, the guests can hear,' Rhianna murmured. 'Can you two discuss this somewhere private?'

'Right.' She ran her fingers through her hair. 'Yes. I don't want to ruin Mum's party.' She jerked her head to the door that led down into the cellar. 'Hayden, come on.'

He followed her down the steps. Brooke couldn't help thinking of all the happy times they'd spent in this place as she flicked the light on. They'd had their first date here, and their first sexual encounter. And today, it was going to be the scene of their first big fight.

'Well?' she demanded, folding her arms. 'What have you got to say for yourself?'

'Brooke, I don't want to argue. Let's just talk it through calmly, OK?'

He tried to hold her, but she stepped back.

'No, Hayden. There's no kissing and making up happening here. This is serious.' She swallowed hard. 'How could you do that?' she whispered. 'You promised you'd wait. You said you understood.'

'I... do.' He rubbed his cheek. 'I never meant it to happen like this. What are you supposed to say to two madly excited eleven-year-olds who've been invited to a party and are thrilled about meeting your new girlfriend?'

'You didn't even warn me, Hayden! Not a text, not a call; nothing.'

'I didn't have a chance. I came home from a job and they were dressed up ready to go.'

She narrowed her eyes. 'You did this on purpose. Didn't you?'

'What? No!'

'You did.' She laughed, shaking her head. 'I don't believe you! I said I wanted to wait and you… you tricked me into moving faster than I was comfortable with. Why would you do that?'

'I admit I was keen for you to meet them but this was genuinely sprung on me, Brooke. I wasn't trying to trick you.' He reached for her hand, softening his voice. 'Is it really so bad? You can see they think you're the best thing ever. Isn't that what you were afraid of, them not liking you?'

'It wasn't just that. I told you I never expected kids to be a part of my life. Being introduced to your daughters as your girlfriend was… huge for me. Something I needed to feel properly ready for.' She pulled her hand away. 'You told me you'd wait as long as I needed, Hayden. That you understood why I was afraid. And then…' She lowered her head, blinking back tears. 'Then you steamed ahead and did just exactly what you wanted, didn't you?'

'That wasn't what happened. It was a genuine accident. Why are you so determined to believe the worst of me?'

'You've been pressing for this ever since that first night you asked me out.' She looked up to meet his eyes. 'Can you swear to me this wasn't a deliberate attempt to push me into taking the next step?'

'I can't deny that's what I want. I love being with you, Brooke. I'd like to see a lot more of you and I'd like you to start being a part of my family. But I never meant to push you.'

'Then why did you?'

'Why are you so against the idea of getting to know my kids?' he demanded. 'I see you with your niece and nephew, how good you are with them, how much they love you. I hear you rave all the time about what great

316

kids they are. All I want is the chance for you to be that person to my children too.'

'Livvy and Max are family. It's not the same.'

'Well, I'd like my kids to feel like they're family.'

'There's a big difference between being an aunt and being… whatever it is I'd be to Darcie and Cara. You know there is.'

'It's been seven weeks, Brooke,' he said quietly. 'Can you honestly say you're going to be ready in another seven, or another, or another? The more time I spend with you, the more I wonder if you're ever going to feel like it's time for that next step.'

'That's my prerogative, isn't it? If you really cared about me, you'd wait.'

'If you cared about me, you'd see why I'm sick of juggling my two jobs, my kids and my girlfriend. You'd notice that it's taking a hell of a toll on me and I don't know how much longer I can manage before something has to give,' he said. 'I'm tired, Brooke; I'm so, so tired. And I believe that me and you, what we have, is worth more than a series of beer cellar quickies and back-seat shags.'

'Then wait for me.'

'For how long?'

She turned away from him. 'I don't know how long. Human beings aren't predictable like that.'

'I can't wait forever.'

'And I'm not going to be recruited to fill in for your kids' real mum just because I happen to be convenient.'

He shook his head. 'Not this again. You know that isn't fair, Brooke.'

'Isn't that what I'd be though, ultimately? That's where this has always been heading, right?'

'I didn't want a mum for them, I wanted *you*. I'm starting to wonder if you ever really wanted me the same way.' He glanced at the stairs. 'I need to go back to my family.'

'You should.'

He started to leave, then turned back. His eyes were filled with hurt.

'You know I don't need to be here any more, right?'

She blinked. 'What?'

'I don't need this job. I could've quit a while ago, when I got a grant for Darcie's school things and my ex started paying child support again. But I didn't.'

'Why not?'

'For you. Because even though I was desperate for more time with my kids, I couldn't bear not to see you regularly any more. Because I cared about this pub that I know means so bloody much to you and I wanted to help get it out of its slump.' He glanced upwards at the busy party going on overhead. 'And now it's out. Business is booming thanks to you and your sister. Which means you don't need me any more, right?'

'Hayden, what are you…'

'I think it's best if I leave now. Leave my job, and… I mean, it's clear we're never going to want the same things.'

'Are you… you're not breaking up with me?' she whispered.

'I'm always going to be a dad first, Brooke. I don't think that's something you can ever accept, no matter how much I want you to.' He turned to the stairs, laughing softly to himself. 'The funny thing is, I'd actually managed to fall for you. What was that one, Outcome Three?'

'Hayden…' She put a hand on his arm, but he drew it away.

'Brooke, I'm sorry.' He glanced back at her over his shoulder. 'I'll miss you like crazy.'

'Hayden, please don't go. I don't want you to go.'

'I have to. My kids are waiting for me. And like I said, my kids come first.'

Chapter Thirty

'Brooke!' Rhianna said when her sister trudged up from the beer cellar. 'What the hell is going on? Hayden stormed up with a face like thunder and marched out without saying a word.'

Brooke swallowed. 'We… we broke up. We had a big row and then he said he wanted to break up.'

Rhianna sighed. 'Oh sweetie, I'm so sorry. What happened?'

'He said he'd fallen for me but that I could never accept his kids were the biggest part of his life, then he… he quit his job and walked out.'

'He'll change his mind though, when he's had time to calm down. Won't he?'

'I honestly don't know, Rhia. He sounded so… hurt.' Brooke grabbed a cocktail napkin to dab her eyes. 'Do you think you can manage the bar on your own if I go upstairs? My head feels like it's being pounded with a sledgehammer and I'm only barely holding back a crying fit.'

'Of course. Whatever you need.'

'Thanks. If Mum asks, just tell her I wasn't feeling well.'

Rhianna gave her a hug. 'I'll be up as soon as I can, all right? Once the party's over, I'll put the kids to bed and we can get into our PJs and talk it all through. Mum's staying over at Martin's so we'll have the flat to ourselves.'

'That sounds like just what I need.' She choked back a sob. 'Oh God, Rhia, I think I just made the biggest mistake of my life. What's wrong with me?'

'There'll be time for "what's wrong with me?" and "how do I make it right?" later. You go have a good cry and then we'll get everything fixed, OK?' Rhianna squeezed her arm. 'I love you, stinkosaurus.'

Brooke smiled. 'I can't remember the last time you called me that.'

'Worth reviving, I thought.'

'Thank God I've got you.' Brooke patted the hand on her arm. 'I'll see you in a bit. Love you too, by the way.'

Brooke dragged her weary, heavy body upstairs. As soon as she reached her room, she threw herself down on the bed and sobbed.

What had Hayden told her? He'd fallen for her? And of course she had for him, not that she'd ever officially admitted that to herself. That was a big part of what had got her panicking to an almost unbearable degree about how her first official meeting with his kids was going to go. Because in her heart she knew that the stakes were far higher than she was prepared to admit.

And then he'd sprung it on her and she'd gone and fucked it all up. His daughters probably hated her now. And as for Hayden... how could he do that to her, even when he knew how afraid she was?

He hadn't walked away from her for good though, surely. She couldn't lose him like that... not just like that.

She was still weeping softly when she heard the fire escape door open an hour later and children's voices ringing out. She dried her eyes; tried to compose herself. After a few seconds, her mum's head popped round the bedroom door.

'Brooke, Marty and me were just going to...' She trailed off when she saw her daughter's puffy eyes. 'Sweetheart, what's wrong?'

'Oh... nothing.' Brooke finished dabbing her eyes and lobbed the damp tissue at her bin. 'It's nothing, Mum.'

'I know what nothing looks like, and this is definitely a something. What's happened?'

'I had a row with Hayden, that's all.'

Martin's head popped round the door next to her mum's.

'Everything all right, Brooke love?' he asked.

'Yeah, I'm OK. Just... girl stuff.' She forced a smile. 'So how come you left your party?'

'It's petering out now,' Janey said. 'We just brought Max and Livvy up. Carmel invited me, Marty and Mike over for a few drinks so we were going to ask if you could mind the kiddies until Rhianna's finished serving the last of the guests, but if you're not feeling up to it...'

'I'm honestly fine, Mum. You two enjoy your special day.'

'Right.' She hesitated. 'Are you sure, though?'

'I'm absolutely sure. Go have fun, please, or I'll feel guilty forever. Rhianna's waterproofed her shoulder ready for me to have a cry on later.'

'Right,' Janey said again, but still she didn't go. 'Is it serious? The, er...' She cast a look at Martin. 'The thing you're upset about?'

'Nothing that can't be fixed, I'm sure,' Brooke lied. 'Now go on, go.'

'OK.' Janey came in to give her a hug. 'If you need me, ring me. Take care of yourself, chick.'

'I will. Thanks, Mum.'

'The kids are watching TV. You know the drill: just glance in occasionally to make sure they aren't running with scissors or juggling lighted matches.'

'No problem.'

When her mum and Martin had gone, Brooke blew her nose and went into the bathroom.

'Ugh,' she muttered when she saw her reflection. She looked like a blobfish with a banging hangover. She swilled her face with water a few times until she looked slightly less undead, then went into the living room.

'Hiya guys,' she said to the kids, forcing a brightness she didn't feel. 'How's tricks? Did you enjoy the party?'

That was the sort of thing she should've said to Cara and Darcie, wasn't it? And instead she'd panicked, and screwed the whole thing up. Poor lambs. They'd been so excited, so thrilled their dad was seeing her, just like she'd hoped they would be. God, what was *wrong* with her?

Livvy nodded emphatically. 'I like grown-up parties. I had lemonade and did a giant burp on the bouncy castle.'

Brooke laughed. 'Impressive. How about you, Max? Have any adventures?'

'Me, Zach and Cara climbed the big tree in the beer garden and I got highest even though I'm youngest,' he said, puffing himself up. 'But then Nana came and told us off.'

'I should think she did, shinning up trees in your best clothes,' Brooke said, trying not to flinch at the sound of Cara's name. 'I'm glad you enjoyed it, monkeys.'

Livvy turned to look at her. 'Where've you been, Aunty Brooke? You weren't at the party.'

'I felt a bit poorly so I came to lie down.'

'Are you better now?'

'A little bit better,' she lied. 'I've got a headache, that's all.'

A mobile phone ringtone emerged from somewhere in the vicinity of the sofa.

'Where's that coming from?' Brooke asked.

Max shrugged. 'Dunno.'

She rummaged down the side of the cushions until she found Rhianna's iPhone. Her sister must've left it when she went down to work.

'That's Mummy's,' Livvy said. 'Shall we get her?'

'No,' Brooke said absently. She was staring at the screen, which was still flashing with an incoming call. A photo of the caller had come up. He was in casual clothes and smiling warmly, as if the person taking the photograph was an old friend, but she still recognised him. Besides, his name was over the picture.

Nick Weyborough...

'That's my mummy's friend,' Livvy said, peering at it.

'Friend?' Brooke said dazedly.

Livvy nodded. 'The one she goes to the cafe with.'

'Liv,' Max whispered. 'It's secret, remember?'

Brooke's gaze was still fixed on the screen, which was now showing a missed call. Her head was spinning dangerously, and she felt nauseous. She gripped the sofa for support.

'This is who your mum goes out to meet sometimes?' she asked the kids.

Livvy looked wary now Max had reminded her of the promise they must've been cajoled into making, but she nodded.

'Only sometimes. Not loads,' she said, as if aware from Brooke's expression that something was wrong.

Brooke pressed the phone's menu button to unlock it. There was a six-digit passcode to get in, which was as predictable as you'd expect from a mum: Max's birthday worked when Livvy's didn't. She flicked to the missed calls list.

Nick Weyborough. James. Mum. Her. Nick Weyborough. Taryn. James. Nick Weyborough. Her again. Mum. Nick Weyborough. Nick Weyborough. Nick sodding Weyborough…

There were text messages from the bastard too, interspersed with overdue payment notices from Rhianna's credit card company and notifications about her overdraft. *Free this afternoon? Been thinking about you ;-p*, one said. *Can't wait to meet up again x*, read another. Who knew Nick was an emoji and kisses sort of a guy? Brooke couldn't help snorting as she read them.

And the most recent – that was the most damning of all.

> I've been pondering what you told me, your mum signing over her share of the pub to you and your sister. Could be an interesting development as far as you and I are concerned. Ring when you can and we'll have a chat x

'You oughtn't to look at people's phones without asking,' Max told her. Brooke ignored him. She threw the iPhone down on the sofa and ran into the kitchen to rifle through the drawer where she kept her important correspondence.

The letter she was looking for was near the top. She snatched it out and took it from the envelope.

It was the final offer from Willowtree Taverns, the one Nick had made in person to Rhianna. There'd been a follow-up letter to confirm formally what they were offering – £1.2 million – and the time period of three months in which they had to make a decision. The deadline was printed there on the letter. 26th July – five days from now.

'She wouldn't,' Brooke muttered. 'Surely she wouldn't.'

She jumped as she heard the front door opening. A moment later, Rhianna appeared in the kitchen.

'Hiya,' she said with a warm smile. 'How are you feeling? I thought you'd be in your room, lying down.'

'Mum asked me to mind the kids,' Brooke murmured. She was still in a daze as she tried to process what she'd just seen.

'Mum, your phone was ringing,' Max called from the living room. 'Aunty Brooke was looking at it. I told her she should ask first.'

'Don't tell tales, Max,' Rhianna said automatically. She frowned as the words registered. 'What do you mean, looking at it?'

'He's right,' Brooke said. 'You've got a missed call from Nick Weyborough. One of many, it looks like.'

She watched her sister's face fill with horrified realisation, and if Brooke had been holding on to a hope that it might all have been some sort of misunderstanding, it was dashed when she saw the guilt in Rhianna's eyes.

'Brooke—'

'You'd better send the children away, don't you think?'

Rhianna stood stock still for a moment, staring at her helplessly, like an animal caught in a trap. Then she turned to face Max and Livvy.

'Kids, would you mind going to your bedrooms?'

'But Mummy, we're watching our programme,' Livvy protested.

'Livvy, please!' Rhianna took a deep breath. 'Please. I need you to leave us alone for a moment.'

Max looked frightened when he heard the panicked tone in his mum's voice.

'Liv, come on,' he said. 'You can come in my bedroom. I've got a jigsaw app to show you on my tablet.'

'Oooh, OK!' Livvy was too small to be sensitive to any sort of atmosphere. Happily oblivious, she jumped up and followed her brother out.

'It's not what it looks like,' Rhianna said quietly when she and Brooke were alone.

'Really? Because what it looks like, Rhia, is my sister conspiring with Nick fucking Weyborough and those twats at Willowtree Taverns to do me out of my pub!'

'It isn't what you think, Brooke. I swear to you it isn't.'

'So you haven't been seeing him, then? And those kissy-kissy messages I saw on your phone were from… who? Another Nick Weyborough identical to the one we know?'

'You had no right to look at those.'

'Yeah, well I did.' Brooke shook her head, laughing. 'All these months, I really believed you were in my corner. After you bared your innermost that night, I thought we'd made a breakthrough – that we were properly sisters again. And this whole time you've been plotting with that fucker to screw me over. I know you need money, Rhia, but I never believed you'd stoop to stabbing your family in the back to get it.'

'Brooke, you're getting this all wrong,' Rhianna whispered.

'Right. So you're saying you haven't been seeing Nick behind my back.'

She flushed. 'I… yes. I mean, I've seen him a few times.'

'I knew it,' Brooke muttered. 'So all these ideas of yours for improving the business: that was just to lull me into a false sense of security, was it, while you and that greasy City Boy plotted to get my pub?'

'It was nothing to do with the pub, Brooke!'

'Well, then what was it to do with?'

Rhianna's cheeks turned an even deeper shade of crimson. 'It was to do with… with me. I liked him, OK? I liked him and he complimented me and made me laugh, at a time when I wondered if I was ever going to be able to laugh again.'

Brooke snorted. 'Your excellent taste in men strikes again. Surely even you couldn't be that naive.'

'Naive enough to think he might like me for myself? Yes, Brooke, I was. I was vulnerable and afraid for my future, my little sister was looking at me like she wished she could jettison me into space, and there was Nick Weyborough, flirting with me and joking and making me feel like an actual human being again; an attractive one that some people, at least, might enjoy being with. So yes, I was that naive.'

'Come on. He's got slimeball written all over him.'

'I didn't think so. I thought he was charming. When I met him, he seemed like…'

'Like what?'

Rhianna flushed. 'Like someone from my world. The sort of person I could relate to in a place where I felt like a complete alien.'

'Christ,' Brooke muttered. 'So all this time, for fucking *months*, you've been sleeping with the enemy. I trusted you, Rhianna!'

'I haven't slept with him. I haven't even kissed him. All we do is meet up for coffee sometimes and talk. That's all.'

'And that's when you let him schmooze compromising business information out of you, is it? Like the fact you're about to own half this business instead of a third.'

'I didn't mean to tell him that,' Rhianna said, looking pained. 'I was talking about the engagement and it slipped out. I don't always remember who he works for when we're chatting.'

'Yeah, the hell you don't! Did you talk to him about this place – about me? Did you tell him how desperate you were to sell, and how your evil sister was blocking you at every turn?'

Rhianna was silent, her eyes averted. Brooke laughed.

'You fucking did! You two-faced… what about his latest message, then? Why's he so interested in Mum signing over her share of the business?'

'I haven't replied to that.'

'Well you better had, don't you think? After all, there's only five days left until Willowtree's offer expires. I imagine your boyfriend could get you an extension though, if you need a bit more time to really give the knife in my back a good twist.'

Brooke pushed past her to go to her room.

'Brooke, wait,' Rhianna said, putting a hand on her sister's arm. 'I promise this isn't what you think. Everything that's happened, trying to save the pub, me and you getting closer: that was real. I'll swear on my kids' lives if that's what it takes to make you believe me.'

Brooke's face worked feverishly as she struggled with tears.

'The worst thing isn't even that you've been seeing him,' she said in a choked voice. 'It's that you hid it from me; lied to me when I really believed we were on the same side. Why, Rhia?'

Rhianna turned her eyes away. 'I suppose... I didn't want you to think badly of me. I know you don't trust him.'

'No,' Brooke whispered. 'But I did trust *you*. I had a hell of a time learning to trust you again and then... this.' She gave a damp laugh. 'I guess there's a lesson in that.'

'Brooke, please! I don't want to leave things like this.'

'You hurt me, Rhia. Hurt me like I didn't think you could be capable of.' Brooke closed her eyes. 'You're not my sister,' she whispered.

'Please don't say that.'

'I just did.'

She walked out, leaving Rhianna staring after her.

–

Brooke felt like she barely slept that night for crying. First the break-up with Hayden, then her sister's betrayal. She'd never wanted her mum so badly – the only person in the world she felt was still on her side. But Janey was with Martin, planning their new life together, and Brooke just couldn't bring herself to take the shine off her mum's happy day.

She must eventually have drifted off. She was woken by the sound of the front door banging closed as someone entered the flat. Her phone told her it was late morning; nearly half past ten.

She got up and sat on the edge of her bed, wondering what to do. She didn't want to go out and face Rhianna, with the pain of her betrayal still burning. She especially didn't want to see the kids, and have to look at their little faces full of innocent enquiry. So she just sat, staring at her own ghost-like reflection in the mirror.

Five minutes later, a knock sounded at her bedroom door.

'Go away, Rhia!' she called. 'I don't want to talk to you.'

'It's not your sister,' a soft voice said. 'It's me, love. It's Mum.'

'Mum.' She jumped up, opened the door and threw herself at Janey for a hug. 'Thank God you're here.'

Her mum shushed her softly, just as she used to do when Brooke was upset as a child. Brooke found the tears starting to fall again, dampening her mum's cardigan, and wondered that she should still have any left to shed.

'Is Martin here?' she mumbled from the depths of the hug.

'No, it's just me. I had an attack of mum intuition telling me I was needed.'

'You are needed. God, Mum, everything's such a mess.' She sniffed. 'Is Rhianna up? Did she tell you what happened?'

Her mum held her back to look into her face. It was only then that Brooke noticed the worry etched on her brow.

'Mum, what is it? What's wrong?'

'It's your sister,' she said quietly. 'She's gone, Brooke.'

Chapter Thirty-One

Brooke blinked. 'Gone?'

'That's right,' Janey said. 'And the children too.'

'She can't have gone. Where would she go?'

'There's a letter in the living room that tells you all about it. It's addressed to you but it's open. I hope you don't mind me reading it.'

'But... she can't be gone.'

Brooke ran out of her bedroom and flung open the door to her sister's. Sure enough, the cupboard was hanging open; empty. Rhianna's clothes and Livvy's little things were gone – just a few of the less portable items had been left. When she ran into Max's room, she found the same there: his clothes, his favourite books and toys, all gone.

'Mum, what's happening?' she asked.

'They must've snuck out early this morning while you were sleeping.'

'But... why?'

'Here.' Janey put an arm around Brooke and guided her into the living room, onto the sofa. She picked up a letter from the coffee table and pressed it into her hand.

'Read this,' she said. 'I'll make tea.'

The ink swam before Brooke's eyes until it eventually formed into her sister's familiar handwriting.

Dear Brooke,

Apologies for the cliché, but by the time you read this, we'll be gone. It's clear you don't trust me any more, and I can't blame you. Nevertheless, I'd like you to know the whole story.

Nick Weyborough asked me to go out with him by telephone shortly after he approached me with the final offer for the pub. It was weak of me to say yes, and even weaker not to tell you what I'd done, but I was flattered by his attention and found him to be a charming man: funny, and good company. Fresh from my life in Nantwich, Nick felt like 'my kind of people' – sorry if that sounds snobbish, but that was how it felt. Perhaps it was my ego urging me on, or perhaps a need for someone who seemed to understand me, but I can promise it was never an attempt to undermine you or force you to sell the pub.

Nick and I met for coffee approximately five times, as well as sharing numerous phone calls and texts. As I told you, we never slept together. We never even held hands. We just talked. However, it was all over by the time you saw him trying to contact me yesterday. I'd realised that Nick had always been more interested in the pub than in me. You were right, I was naive, but not so naive as not to realise he was pressing me more and more on the future of the pub as the Willowtree deadline drew near. He gets a performance-related bonus on top of his salary, did you know that? Although I think in the end, it was as much about not wanting to admit he'd lost as it was about acquiring the pub.

333

His sort can't bear that. It upsets them to think there's anything money can't buy.

Anyway, his elation when I let slip that Mum would be signing her share over to us, making me an equal partner, was the final straw. I told him I knew that his interest was in the pub, not in me, and that I wouldn't see him again. As you saw from my phone, he's continued to badger me with calls. If you'd looked a little closer, you'd see that none of them have been answered or returned since the date a week ago when I ended things between us — if you can say there ever was anything between us. I'm not sure that you can.

I'm sorry that I destroyed the trust you had in me, and the bond we'd built as sisters. I was a fool to let myself be manipulated by Nick for so long, but as you pointed out, I do have my track record against me. Anyway, it's done now and I can't take it back.

I spent many sleepless hours thinking last night, and I finally concluded that I had to take positive action for my and the children's future. I know you don't want to sell the pub, and despite what you might believe, I'd never expect or want you to — not any more. The Highwayman's ought to have a Padgett over the door. But I do desperately need security, and money to provide for my family. Every month it gets harder to keep treading water. There are no jobs for someone like me, and no way for me to easily become financially independent. For this reason and others, I've decided to take Max and Livvy home. Back to their father.

334

Brooke looked up in horror as her mum handed her a cup of tea. 'James! She's gone back to that bastard?'

Janey nodded to the note. 'Read on.'

Brooke put her tea down and carried on reading.

James has apologised over and over for his 'mistake', as he calls it. He wants us to go to marriage counselling, and he's sworn to me nothing like that will ever happen again. For my sake and the children's, I choose to believe him. He's also offered to pay for my barrister training, which ought to guarantee my future financial security: something that I would never be able to afford for myself. Brooke, I know you'll think this is a terrible idea, but I've spent a lot of time thinking about this and I genuinely believe it's for the best. I hope you can forgive me now you've read this, and that you'll be willing to call me your sister again, but please don't try to talk me out of it. It's what's best — for me, for the children, and for you too. We've been a burden on you and Mum for too long. You both have your own lives to lead — Mum with Martin, you with Hayden and your pub. Max, Livvy and I will be fine, and what's more, we'll be provided for. Please, please don't worry about us.

I love you. Please believe I mean that, and I never meant to hurt you. And please, if you can bring yourself to forgive me, do me a favour and make things up with Hayden. You two are made for each other.

Your sister,

Rhianna

'Oh God, Mum,' Brooke whispered. 'What the hell did I go and do?'

—

Three days later, Rhianna was sitting in James's conservatory while the children played in the garden, staring at her iPhone.

Her thumb hovered over the Fitbit icon. She scrunched her eyes closed for a moment, then slipped it back into her pocket.

'Oh. Here you are,' James said as he came in. 'Darling, you're going to catch a chill sitting in the draught.'

'I'm all right.' She roused herself. 'I like to sit where I can see the children. I'll go into the living room in a little while.'

'You mean the sitting room.'

She frowned. 'James, must you keep correcting me?'

'Sorry.' He sat down beside her and rubbed her shoulder. 'I didn't mean to offend you. Would you like me to fetch a blanket for your legs?'

'No, that's OK. But thank you.'

He leaned over to kiss her neck. 'You know, Flops, you don't have to watch the children,' he said in a whisper. 'Ursula's with them. They'd be quite safe if you and I were to sneak upstairs.'

James was currently making overtures to the children's old au pair, Avril, trying to lure her back from her new employers with generous offers of a pay increase and additional holiday, but for now Max and Livvy were being cared for by a stern Swiss lady he'd recruited: Ursula. Rhianna's reassurances that it was fine, she could care for them herself without any additional help, had fallen on deaf ears.

She tried not to flinch as James nibbled her ear.

She'd managed to avoid it so far, but Rhianna knew she would have to have sex with her husband at some point. This was the choice she'd made, and whether she loved him or not, she was going to have to lie in the bed she'd made for herself and think of England.

But right now, his affair was still too raw. When she pictured him with Shari, it turned her stomach.

Gently she extricated herself from his embraces.

'Not today,' she said, forcing a smile. 'I've got terrible cramps. Maybe tomorrow.'

He looked put out. 'Three days' worth of cramps?'

'It happens, James.' She shuffled to face him. 'I did want to show you some of the graduate diploma courses I've been looking at though. There are some distance-learning options that would be perfect for fitting around the children, and I could easily—'

'You don't need to rush into that, do you?'

She blinked. 'But the new academic term starts soon. If I hurry, I might be able to get a last-minute place.'

'Why scrabble to get in this term?' He lifted her hand to kiss it. 'There's plenty of time, Rhianna. The rest of our lives. For now, why not just enjoy being home?'

'Oh,' she said, deflated. 'Um, all right. If that's what you think is best.'

He glanced at her arm. 'Have you thought any more about what I was talking about last night?'

'Yes.' She bowed her head. 'Yes, I… I suppose you're right. If you want me to have the surgery, James, then… I will.'

He beamed. 'That's my good girl. Then you can be as beautiful as God meant you to be.' He planted a soft kiss on her lips. 'I'm going to toddle over to the office for a while. Then I'm going to come back here and whisk you away for a romantic meal at that Thai place you like, just the two of us. How does that sound?'

'You're going into the office again?'

'There are a few little jobs I'd like to get finished.' He raised an eyebrow. 'You're not still worried, are you?'

'No. I just… didn't think you'd be going in today. You said you wouldn't need to if you worked yesterday evening.'

'Would you like to come with me? Check there isn't anything untoward going on?'

She flushed. 'Don't be silly.'

'I can get you signed witness statements from Jeremy and the other staff if you like. That's if you still don't trust me.'

'I trust you, all right?' she said, failing to keep the irritation out of her voice. 'I was only surprised you were going in. Nothing else.'

'Good. Because there is nothing else.' He leaned down to kiss the top of her head. 'I'll be back in a little while. I love you.'

'Goodbye.' She suppressed a grimace as he waited expectantly. 'I… I love you too.'

–

Seventy miles away in Yorkshire, Brooke was leaning on her fists behind the bar when Martin Brady appeared.

'Smile, love,' he said with his usual jollity. 'It might never happen.'

'It already did happen, Marty. And do you know how bloody annoying that is, some bloke telling you to smile when you're not in the mood?'

'All right,' he said, blinking. 'Just trying to cheer you up. Not like you to snap.'

'Yeah, well, that was when you were a customer. Now you're family.'

He smiled. 'I suppose that's an honour of sorts.'

'It is, actually.' She sighed. 'God, I'm sorry, Marty. I didn't mean to have a pop at you. Let me get you your drink.'

'No word from your sister?' he asked as she pulled his pint.

Yes, there'd been word. Rhianna had eventually picked up the phone after Brooke's repeated attempts to contact her – not that it had done any good. She'd only repeated in a soft, dreamlike voice exactly what she'd said in the letter: that she'd thought it through, and it had nothing to do with Brooke or with anything else. She just genuinely believed going back to James was in the best interests of both her and her children. She hadn't sounded resentful at all. She'd sounded... defeated. And no amount of entreaty or apology on Brooke's side had been enough to make her change her mind.

She had at least answered the phone though, which was more than Hayden was doing. He was currently ignoring Brooke's calls altogether. God, she was desperate to talk this through with him; to feel his comforting arms around her and know he was on her side...

'Brooke?' Martin said.

She forced herself out of her reverie as she put his pint in front of him.

'No. No word from Rhia,' she said in answer to his question. 'At least, not the words I wanted to hear. I couldn't change her mind. Same response as Mum got when she tried to convince her to come home.'

'Ah well. Happen she'll see sense in the end.'

Brooke sighed. 'I think it might be too late for that, Marty. She seemed determined to make a go of it with James for the children's sake. And he's just such a… you-know-what.'

'Aye, we all know what he is,' Martin said with a grim smile. His face glowed as Janey appeared behind the bar with a tray of dirty glasses. 'Heyup. What's this vision I see before me? Could it be Aphrodite, the goddess of love, come to earth to steal men's hearts?'

Janey laughed, pushing an escaping tendril of hair away from her hot forehead. 'I don't know. Does the goddess Aphrodite smell of stale beer?'

'She does in my version of heaven.'

'Well, then I suppose it must be.'

He leaned over the bar to steal a kiss.

'I'd better get back to the boys,' he said. 'I have to enjoy this bachelor lifestyle while I can, don't I? See you later, ladies.'

'How're you doing, love?' Janey said softly to Brooke when they were alone.

'I'm scaring the customers with my miserable face. Everything's such an almighty mess, Mum.'

'I know. But we'll fix it.'

'How?'

'Well, I don't know that yet,' Janey admitted. 'But we will. We've come too far together for it to end like this.'

'Hayden didn't turn up for his shift.'

Janey lowered her head. 'I noticed.'

'I guess he really meant it. About quitting and… and the rest of it.'

'Well, we'll see about him too.'

Silence fell. Brooke gazed at her left arm.

'I might book another tattoo,' she said.

'Why?'

She shrugged. 'Something to do.'

'What will you get this time?'

'Dunno. I thought maybe a little owl.'

'Like Plop, you mean.'

Brooke frowned. 'What?'

'Plop,' Janey said. 'From that book you liked when you were little. The one you and Livvy were reading.'

Brooke swallowed when she pictured Livvy, her eyes bright with adventure by proxy as her aunt read the story to her – being careful, of course, to do all the voices just as instructed. Brooke had quickly become the first choice to do story time, and had been looking forward to introducing her niece to some of her other favourites from childhood. She just knew Liv was going to love *Mrs Pepperpot*, and *The Worst Witch*, and *My Naughty Little Sister* and…

Was that what had made her think of an owl? Had she subconsciously been thinking of Plop, and of Livvy? Brooke Padgett, long convinced that she and children were better off out of each other's way, hadn't believed she was capable of missing a pair of kids as much as she missed her niece and nephew. The flat felt so miserably dead and quiet without them.

But she had what she wanted, didn't she? She cast a resentful look around the pub. Yes, she had The Highwayman's Drop, the thing that had filled her life ever since her dad had died. The thing that had taken the place of meaningful human relationships and kept her frozen in a sort of half-life, unable to fully move on from her grief. Until Rhianna and the children and Hayden had come into her world to show her what really mattered.

And now she'd driven them away. Her sister, her niece and nephew, the man she loved – even her mum, her life's one constant, was about to leave her. Yes, she had her pub, but it was all she bloody had.

God, how had she been so selfish – and so blind? She'd called her sister selfish for wanting her to sell the pub, never acknowledging how her own refusal to grant Rhianna the value of her share was ultimately going to force her back to the husband who cheated on her, infantilised and belittled her. It was the exact opposite of what their dad had surely intended when he chose to leave part of the pub to Rhianna to keep her out of James's power.

Brooke winced with shame when she thought of Hayden too. She'd treated him appallingly, accusing him of trying to use her as a substitute mother for his kids when all he'd wanted was to make her a part of the family he adored. And now she was left with no family at all, neither his nor her own; just this. Just a building; a building where every day she was expected to screw on a smile for strangers after she'd pushed all her own loved ones away.

Well, she wasn't sure what to do about Hayden, but there was still a chance to make things right with Rhianna. There was one sure-fire way to set her sister free, so she'd never have to depend on James again. A way to show her she mattered more to Brooke than any mere thing. And yes, there was still just time…

'Mum?' she said.

'Yes, love?'

'I've got an idea. To get Rhianna home again.'

Janey blinked. 'Have you? When did you have that?'

'About thirty seconds ago. I'm going to need your help, though.'

'What've you got in mind?'

'The nuclear option.' She closed her eyes. 'I need to call Nick Weyborough.'

Chapter Thirty-Two

'Brooke, are you sure about this?' Janey whispered as they sat in the lobby of the Willowtree Taverns headquarters. Everything about the office block – its height, the pristine white walls, the sheer volume of glass and marble used in its construction – seemed designed to impress and intimidate. If Nick Weyborough was a building, he'd be this one.

'What choice do we have?' Brooke murmured back.

'But The Highwayman's!' She sighed. 'I hoped I'd never see it leave the family.'

'This is for the family's own good. Dad left shares to me and Rhianna so that whatever happened, we'd have our independence.'

'You love that place, though.'

'Not as much as I love my sister.' Brooke squared her shoulders. 'It's a sacrifice I have to make, Mum. Not just for the money, although if that's what it takes to get Rhia away from that bastard before he breaks her completely then that's no small part of it. But… to prove something.'

'What?'

'That Rhia, Max and Livvy matter more to me than The Highwayman's. Yes, I love it, but it's just a building. Just a thing. It can't take the place of the people I care about, and I'd rather lose it forever than see them suffer.'

Janey reached over to press her hand.

'You're a good girl, Brooke,' she said softly. 'Or a good woman, I should say. I'm ever so proud of you, sweetheart. So's your dad.'

Brooke smiled. 'You think so?'

'He always was. But never more so than today, I think.' She looked at the rings from her first marriage, which she'd moved to the third finger of her right hand while her engagement ring from Martin occupied the left. 'I do wish Hayden knew what we were doing, though.'

'It's nothing to do with Hayden. It's our pub.'

'But he's become a part of it. It feels like this concerns him.' She looked at her daughter. 'Do I take it the black look means he still isn't returning your calls?'

'Yeah. I've phoned, I've texted...' Brooke blinked at her hands. 'He means it, Mum. He really means it.'

'I can't believe that. Once he's had time to start missing you, he'll be in touch.' Janey sighed. 'I dreamed I might see the two of you running The Highwayman's one day. He's perfect pub landlord material. I suppose not.'

There was silence for a moment.

'Mum?' Brooke said. 'Rhianna will leave James again when we tell her, won't she?'

'I honestly don't know. She must've felt she'd reached rock bottom the night you two argued, if she was desperate enough to go crawling back to him.'

Brooke flinched. 'I know, I know. It was all my fault and I hate myself for it.'

'Now, I wasn't trying to point fingers. I'm just as much to blame as you: too wrapped up in my own affairs to realise how badly she was worrying about money,' Janey said. 'The problem is, your sister made a big commitment when she decided her future lay with James. Even with her financial independence guaranteed, she might not want to create more instability for the kiddies by yanking them away from their father a second time.'

'How did she sound when you spoke to her?'

'She sounded… resigned,' Janey said quietly. 'Like a woman dissatisfied with her lot but determined to accept it.'

'I thought so too. Subdued, like she'd had her spirit broken.'

'Does this Nick bloke know she's not coming today?'

'Yes. I told him it'd be just us and he said that was fine, she could fill in the paperwork later. He was desperate to get us to sign on the dotted line before we changed our minds, I think – he knows Rhianna always wanted to sell; it's us he's worried about.'

'Wouldn't it be better for us all to have come together?'

'I'd rather do it this way. I want to be able to tell Rhia we did our part, so she knows I really mean it.'

They looked up at the sound of a throat clearing. Nick Weyborough had appeared in the lobby to fetch them, and was smiling far too smugly for Brooke's liking. They stood up.

'Well,' Nick said. 'Thanks for your call, Brooke. That was unexpected. Still, I did tell you everyone had their price.'

'And I told you The Highwayman's was my price,' Brooke said. 'I was wrong about that, though. My family's my price. I know that now.'

'I appreciate your sense of showmanship, waiting until the day the offer expires.'

She smiled tightly. 'I'm thrilled you find it entertaining.'

He presented his hand. Brooke curled her lip at it and Nick, seeing that no handshake was going to be forthcoming, drew it away again.

'Let's just get this over with, shall we?' Janey said.

'Please. This way.' He gestured for them to follow him.

They stepped into the lobby's brushed chrome elevator then followed Nick down a hallway to a minimalist but expensive-looking office with a plaque on the door that bore his name and job title: Nicholas Weyborough, Business Development Manager.

'Take a seat,' he said, indicating two chairs on one side of his desk.

Janey eyed her chair as if it was an object of great disgust before sitting down.

'We don't want to be here any longer than we have to,' she told him. 'I make it my policy never to socialise with the sort of men who manipulate women to get what they want. Especially if one of them is my daughter.'

'Rhianna needed a friend and I was there for her,' he said, shrugging. 'Yes, there was a business agenda, but I believe I provided her with an emotional service.'

Brooke shook her head. 'Christ. You talk about her as if she's another bloody business deal.' She nodded to his computer. 'Have you got a spreadsheet dedicated to her on that thing? Did you claim for those coffees you had together on expenses?'

'I gave Rhianna something she needed, and I hoped she might help me to get something I needed. Believe me, sometimes mixing business and pleasure is the best way to achieve results.' He shot her one of his shrewd glances. 'What she really wanted from me was an understanding ear, Brooke. When we met, she seemed to feel that wasn't something she could expect from anyone else.'

'Can we just sign this sodding contract and get out of here?' Janey asked. 'I don't want to know any more about your relations with my daughter, thank you. Her track record with men isn't the best, and we've got another arsehole we need to help her deal with.'

He raised an eyebrow. 'Oh?'

'None of your business,' Brooke said. 'Where's the contract, then?'

He passed some papers to them. 'Four copies, one for each of the parties concerned. All I need are the signatures of the three owners, and mine as a representative of Willowtree Taverns, to indicate we're all in agreement about proceeding with the sale of the premises. Rhianna can sign as soon as she's able to make it to my offices, and then we can move to the next stage.'

'That's it? We don't need witnesses or anything like that?'

'Just the four of us. You're welcome to take the paperwork away and seek legal advice first if you like.'

'No,' Janey said. 'We want to get this done now. Today.'

'As you wish. Feel free to take your time reading through.'

Brooke skimmed through the various sections. They didn't make much sense to her, but she assumed it was the usual terminology you'd find in one of these agreements.

'You ready?' she said in an undertone to her mum. Janey nodded.

'OK. Here I go.' Brooke took a deep breath, picked up the biro and signed. Janey signed too, then they passed around the other three copies for signatures to be added.

'Well, that's it,' Nick said, gathering them all back to him. 'All I need is Rhianna to add her signature and we can proceed to the sale, after which you ladies will have netted yourselves a tidy £400,000 each. I can make the arrangements with her by telephone if you like, unless one of you would prefer to do it. She seems to be avoiding my calls.'

'I wonder why,' Janey muttered.

'I'll get in touch with her, if it's all the same to you,' Brooke said. She paused. 'Actually, could you pass me one of those contracts a second?'

He handed her one, and she flicked to the signature page and took a photo on her phone.

'Don't worry,' she said in answer to his look. 'I'll keep it confidential. I just want to show it to my sister.'

Brooke and Janey stood up. Nick followed suit, extending his hand again.

'Thank you,' he said. 'I must say, I think you've made the right decision. And if the pair of you did want to stay on as managers under Willowtree, then of course that offer's still on the table.'

Janey looked at his hand as if willing it to wither and drop off.

'Huh,' she said, then spun on her heel and walked out.

Brooke shrugged. 'You heard the lady. Huh.' She turned and left the office.

Chapter Thirty-Three

When Rhianna walked into the kitchen to make lunch for the children, Ursula was in there already, chopping spring onions.

'Oh,' Rhianna said. 'Um, sorry.' There was something about the stern au pair that left her feeling she needed to apologise for being in her own house. 'I was just going to make the children some sandwiches to eat out on the lawn.'

'Don't you worry about that,' Ursula said. 'I'm preparing something for them now, Mrs Garrett. I'll call you all in when the table's set.'

Ursula intimidated Rhianna. She wasn't warm and friendly like Avril had been. The steady, fun-loving twenty-year-old had been almost like a big sister to Max and Livvy. But there was no warmth in Ursula, although she worked hard. She reminded Rhianna of one of the strict, scary nannies from the beginning of *Mary Poppins*, and she often found herself wishing a stray gust of wind would come and blow Ursula away.

Such was Ursula's effect on her, Rhianna was about to turn and walk out. Then she stopped herself.

'It's just, um, I thought it might be nice to eat in the garden,' she said humbly. 'I mean, with the sun shining and everything.'

'Oh, no. We don't want to encourage bad habits, do we? Mr Garrett asked me to be especially attentive to the children's table manners.' Ursula shot her a look. 'He feels there's been a slide recently.'

'Right. Well, I suppose he knows best.'

Defeated, Rhianna went out to the garden, where the children were playing a subdued game of Monopoly on a blanket. James had bought them their own set after hearing Livvy rave about this new game she'd discovered. He was still in generous mood, denying the children nothing in his excitement at having got them back. He was denying his wife nothing either, showering her with little presents, taking her out for meals, being more affectionate towards her even than when they were first married. She knew she ought to be ecstatic. And yet…

Rhianna sat down on one of the lawn chairs. It was a gorgeous day, balmy and warm: just what a late July afternoon ought to be. The children seemed quiet but they were contented, and they had all that they needed. The scent of flowers filled the air, and in the distance she could hear the gentle chatter of the stream. Everything was just perfect. The garden had always been Rhianna's favourite place to sit and think; her own little paradise.

And yet…

Max and Livvy left their game and came running towards her. Livvy bounced into her lap, and Rhianna, smiling, kissed her daughter's hair.

'Have you finished your game, darlings?' she asked.

'No,' Max said, flopping at her feet. 'It's too hot to play today. Anyway, it's not so fun without Aunty Brooke and you and Nana.'

'Would you like me to play too? I can if you want.'

'That's OK.'

'Mummy, when will we go home?' Livvy asked, kneeling up to look into her face.

'We are home, sweetheart.'

'I mean, home to see Nana and Aunty Brooke.'

'I think… not for a while.' Rhianna hugged Livvy to her, pressing her face against the little girl's hair as if the scent of it could give her strength. 'Aren't you happy here? You've got lots of nice things, and you don't have to miss Daddy any more.'

'I'm glad Daddy's here,' the little girl said slowly. 'But now I miss Nana and Aunty Brooke as much as I missed Daddy when we were at their house. So it's like swapping one missing for a different missing.'

'You'd rather be here though, wouldn't you? With your lovely big garden, and all your nice toys, and your riding and ballet lessons, and Daddy to play with?'

Livvy didn't answer. She just shuffled round to throw her arms around her mum's neck, hiding her face on her shoulder.

'Daddy isn't here to play with now,' Max murmured. 'He's hardly ever here. He's always at work.'

'Well, he's busy making money for you to have nice things,' Rhianna said. 'You have to remember that while it's school holidays for you, adults still have to go to work.'

Max shuffled to look at her. 'We'll be going home in time for school again, won't we? And my birthday party on Sunday?'

'You'll be going to Lennox House in the autumn, with your old Abbotleigh friends. It's a very good school – it's where your daddy went. Won't you like that?'

'I want to go to Ravenswood with Zach and Cara,' he said, flushed and peevish from the heat. 'What about my party? Aunty Brooke said I could have a chocolate fountain.'

'Now, Max, don't whine,' Rhianna said, pressing her fingers to her temples. 'My head's throbbing today.'

'Is dinner ready?' Livvy asked. 'Lunch, I mean. It's fish finger sandwiches on Thursdays when it's holidays.'

'No fish fingers, I'm sorry. Ursula's making a salad or something. She's going to call you in when it's ready to eat.'

Livvy shuffled round as if preparing to make a case against such brutal treatment, when suddenly her eyes went wide. She shrieked, then bounced off her mum's lap to run towards a stranger entering the garden through the gate.

Rhianna shielded her eyes from the sun. 'Who is it, Max? Is it Daddy?'

Max stared, then he jumped up too.

'It's Aunty Brooke!'

He ran off towards her. Brooke, laughing, had already swung Livvy up into her arms by the time Max cannoned into her legs.

She waved to Rhianna, who stood up.

'Brooke,' she said in a low voice when her sister joined her, still carrying Livvy and with Max gripping her belt as if worried she might disappear again. 'What are you doing here?'

'Visiting.' Brooke gave Livvy a kiss before putting her down again. 'Gosh, I've missed you monsters. Do you know how quiet it is without you causing chaos? I can hear myself think and everything. Honestly, it's horrible.'

'We missed you too!' Livvy yelled, bouncing on her heels.

'Is Nana here? Are we coming back to your house?' Max asked breathlessly.

'It's just me today. Sorry, Maxie.' She glanced at Rhianna. 'I came to talk to your mum.'

There was the sound of a throat clearing, and they looked around to see Ursula on the terrace with her arms folded.

'Lunch is ready,' she said, not quite concealing a disapproving glance at Brooke's exposed tattoos.

'Ursula, this is my sister,' Rhianna said. 'She's come to pay us a surprise visit.'

Ursula looked as if she approved of this state of affairs about as much as she approved of Brooke's tattoos.

'Will she be wanting to eat with us?' she asked, in a tone that said she'd better bloody not do.

'Don't worry about that. Just take the children inside,' Rhianna said. 'Brooke and I will sit out here. We can fetch ourselves something to eat if we want to.'

Ursula nodded, and beckoned to Max and Livvy. Reluctantly, they followed her to the house.

'Don't go without saying goodbye,' Max whispered to Brooke.

'I promise, Maxie.'

Max and Livvy disappeared into the house. A second later, Livvy came running out again, flung her arms around Brooke's waist, then ran back in.

Brooke laughed. 'I think they might've missed me nearly as much as I've missed them. I didn't think that was possible.'

'What are you doing here, Brooke?'

'Is James here?'

'No, he's at work.'

'Good.' Brooke gestured to the garden furniture. 'Can we sit down? I was hoping we could talk.'

'I said all I had to say on the phone. My life's here now. I've made my decision, and… I'm not going to change my mind.' She softened her voice when she saw her sister's hurt expression. 'I mean, don't think I'm not grateful for everything you've done for us. You've been a gem, you and Mum both. It did the children so much good, occupying a different world for a while, and it taught me some lessons I badly needed to learn. But eventually there has to come a time when reality kicks in. I can't be hanging on to your skirts forever, and… well, this was my only other choice.'

'Please, sit down,' Brooke said. 'There are things I need to say to you. Things I didn't want to go into over the phone.'

Rhianna frowned as they both took a seat. 'Mum's all right, isn't she?'

'Mum's fine. Still loved up with Martin. This is about me and you.'

Rhianna shook her head. 'If you're planning to try and talk me out of it, you're wasting your time. I've thrown my lot in with James now. For better or worse, as our wedding vows say.'

'"Forsaking all others" is another thing they say.'

Rhianna winced. 'That's behind us now. This was the right thing to do, Brooke. It's what's best for all of us.'

'Are you trying to convince me or yourself?'

Rhianna turned her eyes away. 'I don't need to convince myself. This wasn't a spur of the moment thing, Brooke, whatever you might think. I've been weighing it up ever since I walked out in the first place. Five days ago, I came to a decision and I stand by it.' She gestured

355

around the perfectly manicured garden. 'You see how happy the children are? Everything they have here? James has promised to get them a pony.'

'And yet the first thing they said to me was that they couldn't wait to come home.'

'It'll take them a little time to settle into the old ways again, yes, but they'll soon get used to it.'

'And what about you?' Brooke said gently. 'Will you get used to it? What about your self-respect, Rhianna? Is that worth selling off to the highest bidder?'

Rhianna flushed. 'Self-respect is a lovely thing to have, but when you're a mum, it takes a back seat to your kids the same as everything else. Besides, James has sworn it won't happen again.'

'And you believe him?'

She twisted her wedding ring around her finger. 'I don't have a choice.'

'That's what I came to talk to you about.' Brooke took out her mobile. 'I wanted to bring you something.'

'What?'

'A choice.' She showed Rhianna a photograph: three signatures on a sheet of paper. Brooke Padgett, Jane Padgett... and Nick Weyborough. A line for a fourth signature, under Brooke's and her mum's, had been left blank.

'What is this?' Rhianna whispered.

'It's a contract. Between us and Willowtree Taverns. All it needs is your signature, then the sale of The Highwayman's can go ahead and you'll be £400,000 richer. That wanker Nick's waiting for you to call him up and arrange it.'

'But... why? Why would you do that?'

'Why do you think? For you, Rhia. To give you the independence Dad wanted for you.' She pressed Rhianna's hand. 'I'm sorry it's taken me so long to realise what a selfish bitch I've been. I should've done this as soon as you told me you needed money. I've been beating myself up ever since you left, knowing I was responsible for forcing you back here.'

'But you love that place.'

'I love *you*, Rhia. The pub's just a pile of bricks, in the end. I don't want bricks, I want you and the kids back.'

Rhianna shook her head. 'I can't let you sell the pub.'

'You'd bloody better.' Brooke set her mouth into a firm line and pointed to it. 'See? This is my mind-made-up face. You're not going to be able to talk me out of it, or Mum either, so you might as well just agree.'

'Brooke, I... I don't know what to say.' Rhianna leaned over to peck her sister's cheek. 'That's the most generous, wonderful thing anyone's ever done for me. Thank you.'

'Then you'll come home?'

A cloud came over Rhianna's face. 'No. No, I... I'm sorry. It's not just the money. I signed up for this and it has to be my life now.'

'No it doesn't!' Brooke took her hand. 'Rhianna, you can be free,' she said softly. 'Don't you get that? You can be free. You don't have to be dependent on James, or on anyone.'

'He's my children's father, Brooke,' she said in an expressionless voice. 'To tear them away from him was a wrench the first time around. To do it again... I can't keep moving them from place to place, school to school, while I'm dithering about my feelings. It isn't fair.'

'He cheated once, Rhianna. He'll do it again.'

357

'He swore to me he wouldn't.' Rhianna's lips flickered with a smile. 'He's been so attentive since we came home. Treating me to meals, buying me presents. It's like it was in the early days, almost.'

'Almost. Because unlike in those days, you don't love him any more. Do you?'

'That's… not true.'

'Yeah? Look me in the eyes and swear to me you do.'

Rhianna turned to look at her. 'I do. I… I love him.'

Brooke laughed. 'You've always been the worst liar, Rhia.'

'Well, it doesn't matter. I'll learn to love him again, with time. We just need to rebuild the trust between us. The main thing is that he's Livvy and Max's father.'

'Are you sleeping with him?'

Rhianna flinched.

'You're not,' Brooke said, sounding satisfied. 'I didn't think so.'

'It just… takes time. We've had a long break. Things can't just snap back to how they were.'

'Has he booked you onto that postgrad course he promised he'd pay for?'

'Not yet. It's too late to get in for next term. He will though, he promised.'

Brooke rested a hand on her shoulder. 'Come back, sis. You don't have to make yourself do this. The kids are better off out of a home where their parents are trapped in a loveless marriage. It damages children, something like that, especially if they feel their parents' unhappiness is their fault.'

Rhianna shrugged the hand away. 'Brooke, please. Just go, will you? Go back to The Highwayman's. It's yours now; I'll sign my share over to you if you want, and maybe one day you and Hayden can run the place together. I've made my life here and I'm determined to see that through.'

Brooke lowered her gaze. 'Hayden's… it's still off. I can't get hold of him. I think I burned more than one bridge that day I drove you away.'

Rhianna sighed. 'Well, I'm sorry. Still, one way or another, it ought to be your name over the door of the pub.'

'I don't want the bloody pub. I want my big sister back.'

Rhianna patted her arm. 'And you've got her. But I belong here, Brooke. This was the life St Mary's trained me up for. I ought to stay and make the best of it.'

Brooke examined her face.

'Where did you say James was?' she asked.

'At the office. Why?'

'Been spending a lot of time there, has he?'

Rhianna flushed. 'It's Thursday afternoon. Where else would he be?'

'Evenings too, though. Am I right?'

'Well, yes, a couple. But that doesn't mean anything. It's a demanding job, and he's on deadline.'

Brooke nodded to Rhianna's mobile phone, sitting on a glass table between them. 'Is that thing still synched to his Fitbit?'

'I guess so. I haven't deleted the app.'

'Why not? If you trust him then you may as well, right?'

Rhianna shrugged. 'I just didn't think of it. I forgot it was on there, to be honest.'

'So you haven't checked it.'

'Well, no. Why would I? He swore to me it was over and I believed him. We start couples' counselling next week.'

'You weren't even slightly tempted to look?'

Rhianna turned away. 'Why would I be? I told you, I forgot I had it on there.'

'That's a whopper if ever I heard one.' Brooke picked up the phone and held it out. 'I dare you.'

'I don't need to.'

'All right, then for me. If I'm going to walk away and leave you in this place, I want to know your recently cheating spouse is managing to keep it in his pants.'

'No.' She folded her arms. 'I won't. I can't throw myself back into married life while there's an atmosphere of distrust.'

'Is that it? Or are you afraid of what you might find out?' Brooke asked, raising an eyebrow. 'If he's got nothing to hide then you've got nothing to fear.'

'Fine.' Rhianna snatched the phone from her and unlocked it. 'If that's what it takes to prove it to you. But after this, you have to promise to go back home and let me live the life I've chosen, all right, Brooke?'

'If that's your decision, fine. I can't make you leave him. I'd just like to be able to tell Mum he isn't up to his old tricks.'

Rhianna felt a churning in her stomach as she watched the Fitbit app load. She tried to ignore it. It was going to be fine. There was going to be nothing there to see.

She tapped on the icon that would bring up James's last seven days' worth of heart rate statistics. For a moment, there was silence.

'I'm sorry,' Brooke said quietly.

'How did you know?' Rhianna whispered, turning the phone off again.

'It's like Mum always told us. Cheats don't change.' She stood up to pull her sister into a hug.

'Oh Brooke,' Rhianna whispered, letting out a sob. 'I've been such a fool. For the second time, that man's made a complete fool out of me.'

'No he hasn't. You were trying to do what was best for your kids. Don't blame yourself when you could be blaming that cheating prick.' Brooke held her back to look into her face. 'You're not going to stay now, are you?'

Rhianna gave a damp laugh. 'Are you kidding? I didn't pawn all my self-respect when I came crawling back here. There's still a sliver left.'

Brooke pulled her back into the hug. 'Thank God for that.'

'Just give me the rest of today,' Rhianna murmured. 'There are a few things I need to do.'

'What?'

'I need to get the kids packed and… go through some bits and pieces.'

'Anything I can help with?'

'Not really. I saw a letter on James's desk this morning and it made me think… well, I don't want to say anything until I know. I'll fill you in later.' Her brow knit with determination. 'But most importantly, before I leave I need to tell that piece of shit I'm married to exactly where he can fucking go.'

Chapter Thirty-Four

'Where's Aunty Brooke?' Livvy asked when Rhianna entered the dining room.

Rhianna went to kiss her head. 'She had to go, sweetheart.'

Actually, Brooke had been keen to stay. She hadn't wanted Rhianna to confront James alone. But Rhianna had been adamant this was something she needed to do for herself.

Max blinked. 'But she promised she'd say goodbye first. I wanted to ask her about my party on Sunday. She *promised*, Mum.'

'She didn't really go without saying goodbye. We're going to see her again a bit later.' She glanced around. 'Where's Ursula?'

Livvy pulled a face. 'She went into the kitchen for more horrid salad. Mummy, why does she always use radishes? I hate stupid radishes. I told her I hate them and she *still* puts them in.'

'Because they're good for you, I should think.' Rhianna crouched down so she could speak in a low voice. 'Are you two able to do something for me this afternoon? It needs to be done very quietly and calmly, but as fast as you can.'

'What is it?' Max asked.

'I need you to pack your favourite things in your suitcases for me; whatever toys and books you like best. Not

362

too many, because we need to save space for your clothes and things. I'll help you.'

Livvy's face filled with hope. 'Are we going to see Nana and Aunty Brooke?'

'That's right, Liv. We're going home.'

'Is Daddy coming too?'

'No.' Rhianna stroked her hair. 'No, Daddy isn't coming. You'll come to visit him though. Will that be OK?'

Livvy looked thoughtful. 'I wish he was coming and we could all live together. But I'd rather live with Nana and Aunty Brooke than live here with stupid Ursula.'

'Now, Livvy, you mustn't be rude.' Rhianna smiled. 'But I'm glad you're pleased about it.'

Max was bouncing in his chair.

'That means we can have my party!' he said. 'And I won't have to go to Lennox House, will I, Mum? I can go to Ravenswood with Zach and Cara.'

'That's right.'

'Can I go pack my things now?'

'Finish your dinner first. We've got a few hours until Dad gets home, and besides, there are some things I have to do before we go.' She lowered her voice. 'Anyway, I don't want to tell Ursula where we're going. So keep schtum, you guys, OK?'

Max nodded, holding a finger to his lips.

Rhianna left them whispering together and went to seek out Ursula in the kitchen.

'Ursula, how would you like the rest of the day off?' she said with a bright smile. 'I can tidy up the lunch things.'

Ursula looked wary. Rhianna had suspected for days now that the new au pair, knowing which side her bread was buttered, was sneaking tales about her to James.

'I haven't booked any time off,' she said.

'I know, but I'm sure you could make use of a free afternoon, couldn't you? Do some shopping and things. On full pay, naturally.'

Still Ursula hesitated.

'Do you have plans then, Mrs Garrett?' she asked.

Rhianna had told the au pair on numerous occasions to call her by her first name, but Ursula just couldn't seem to bring herself to do it.

'That's right,' Rhianna said, casually examining her nails. 'My sister's just popped to the shops to get a few picnic snacks, then I said we'd have an outing to the river. We can easily cope with the children between us, and it'll be nice to spend some time together as a family. There's no need to waste your afternoon when I'm sure you've got better things to do. Go out and enjoy yourself, eh?'

Ursula still looked suspicious, but she gave a nod of acknowledgement.

'Right. I'll see you tonight then.'

As soon as Ursula had left the house, Rhianna set the children to packing their cases and shut herself up in James's office. There was something on his computer she needed to find.

–

'Good evening, darling,' James said when he came in, tossing his suit jacket and briefcase onto a chair. He cast an approving look over Rhianna's light summer dress and her loose hair, cascading naturally over her shoulders. 'You look absolutely glowing. Are the children with Ursula?'

'No, I gave her the afternoon off. Max and Livvy are upstairs. I asked them to stay in their rooms until I called them.'

James frowned. 'Is something wrong, Flops?'

Rhianna winced. 'Can you please drop that nauseating nickname?'

'I thought you liked it.' He took her in his arms. 'My flopsy bunny. It used to make you giggle.'

'Well, I'm not twenty-one any more.' She extricated herself from his embrace.

'Rhianna, what is it?'

OK. This was it. Time for her carefully prepared speech. Rhianna took a deep breath.

Not that she was nervous, really. She wasn't even hurt by his betrayal, which in her heart she'd always known was going to come. This afternoon, as she'd calmly helped the children pack their cases, her dominant feeling was relief. Relief that she could go, now, with no recriminations from the voice in her head that liked to whisper she was a bad mum for taking the children away. She had her independence, she had her self-respect and she had the support of her family, which were all that she needed.

Still, she steeled herself before she made her speech because, if nothing else, it was momentous. Before, when she'd left James, it had felt like she was in a sort of limbo state; no longer living with her husband, but still hovering, wondering if her marriage was really over. This time, it was the end.

'Are you familiar with the term gaslighting, James?' she asked him.

He frowned. 'Gaslighting?'

'Yes, you know. It's what they call it when someone psychologically manipulates or belittles their partner, to the extent that they start to doubt their version of reality. These people, the ones who get gaslighted, have their confidence chipped away bit by bit so that eventually they start to question everything they think or do. They come to believe they must be as stupid or incapable as this person – this person who claims to love them – has made them think they are.'

'Rhianna, what's this about? You're surely not saying that I—'

'It can take a lot of forms, this gaslighting,' Rhianna went on. 'Perhaps the person might make their partner think they're foolish or childlike, unfit to cope with adult life on their own. This might be easier if, say, their partner was quite young when they met them, especially if there's a significant age gap. They might do things like persuading the person they're gaslighting to sign a legal document that would prevent them being an equal partner in a marriage. They might convince them that they're not fit to have a career, so they'd be reliant on the gaslighter to provide for them.' She laughed. 'Some would even go as far as timing their spouse's pregnancies to stop them doing the training they might need for a professional career. Can you believe that?'

'You're not accusing me—'

'Sometimes, the gaslighter tries to isolate his victim from her family. He tries to get her to make changes to the way she speaks and acts, even to her body, in his quest to make her into the person he wants her to be. And the ultimate insult, the real humiliation, is when, having made the other person completely dependent on him, he betrays her by being unfaithful. The gaslighted partner, of course, has nothing of her own, so even if she finds out about the infidelity she's in no position to object.'

He took her hands. 'Rhianna, I don't know what gossip you've been listening to but I can promise you—'

She yanked her hands away.

'Sometimes, though, the gaslighter's plans backfire,' she said, keeping her voice calm. She didn't want the children to hear anything that sounded like a row. She just wanted to quietly say her piece and get out. 'Because sometimes, the gaslighter can't make the other person dependent on him entirely. Maybe his partner's got a family who won't give up on her. Or maybe...' She took a piece of paper from the table. '...maybe he just got stupid one time.'

'What is that?'

'I printed it off this afternoon.' She unfolded it for him. 'It's a statement. From my account on that investment website – you know, the one you set up? I think it was some sort of tax dodge, using my name. A way to get a slightly bigger slice of the pie. Thank fuck men like you are as greedy and entitled about money as you are about sex.' She turned the sheet towards her and regarded it complacently. 'I'm rich, James. There are investments here adding up to £200,000. I've already put in a request to have the lot transferred to my bank account.'

'What?' James's face was starting to turn a lovely shade of purple. 'You can't do that! That's my money. I invested it.'

'It's got my name on it. I think that makes it mine, don't you?' She pecked his cheek. 'Thank you, darling. It was ever so generous of you.'

'But what the hell... why are you doing this?'

'I just thought it was best if the children and I moved on. You'll still see them, of course, but I'd rather not stay another night under this roof. Apart from everything else I just listed, the fact you're still fucking Shari is a pretty big deal-breaker for me.'

'Don't be ridiculous.' He softened his voice, taking her hands again. 'Is that what all this is about? Another attack of jealousy? I told you that you could come to work with me if you wanted, didn't I? It's over between me and Shari, Flops. It's been over for months.'

Her hand slid up his arm to push up his shirt cuff, revealing his fitness watch.

'Get a good number of steps in today?' she asked.

He blinked at the abrupt change of subject. 'Er, yes. I suppose so.'

'You certainly got a good workout anyway. I mean, a hundred and forty beats per minute, phew! You know, you should watch yourself at your age. Maybe let her go on top next time. Is it Shari or is this someone new? No, never mind, I don't care.'

'Rhianna, what are you talking about?'

She laughed, pulling her hands away. 'Your fucking watch is synched with my phone, James. That's how I knew before, and it's how I know now.'

He stared, gaping at her like a startled codfish.

'But...' he managed.

'James, it's over. You're not going to be able to talk your way out of this one.' She shook her head. 'Christ, and I was going to have plastic surgery for you! What the hell was I thinking?'

'I only wanted...'

'...to model me. To shape me according to the image in your head, like you're bloody Lord God Almighty. Well at heart, despite your best efforts, I'm still the same common Yorkshire lass I always was, and these...' she held up her scarred arm to him, and he flinched '... these are mine, forged in blood and fire like the stretchmarks that gave me my babies. They're a part of me. They remind me of what I've beaten. That I've struggled but I've survived, over and over. I've survived *you*. And I'm never going to forget that again.'

'Rhianna,' he whispered, looking defeated now. 'Don't go. Please. I… I need help. It's like an addiction or… I couldn't help myself. You have to admit, your libido's never been a match for mine.'

Rhianna snorted. 'Yes, you're right. Of course I forced you into having yet another affair when I pleaded off shagging you, didn't I? I mean, I've only actually been back for four days, but…'

'That isn't what I meant. Just… please. Please stay, and we'll make it all right again. I'll get help for it, check myself into one of those rehab places, and… we'll fix it.'

'Come on, James,' she said with a wry smile. 'You've been in business long enough to know when it's time to cut your losses.'

She went out of the sitting room and called up the stairs. 'Max! Livvy! Time to go home.'

The children came bounding down. Their suitcases had already been loaded into Rhianna's car.

'Say goodbye to Daddy,' Rhianna instructed them. She glanced at James. 'You'll see him in a few weeks' time when you come for a visit.'

A dazed James gave his children a hug and kiss as if he was on autopilot.

'Be good, my loves,' he mumbled, like that was all he could find to say. He looked so utterly defeated that Rhianna couldn't help feeling just the smallest amount of pity, even though he didn't deserve it. He did love the children, despite his faults.

'Bye, Daddy. We'll miss you loads,' Livvy said, oblivious as usual to anything wrong. 'Come and see us, but don't bring Ursula, though. I love you.'

But Max submitted to his hug in silence, not meeting his father's eye. At nearly eleven, he understood a lot more about the state of affairs between his parents than his little sister did. As Rhianna watched him, she felt how right Brooke had been. Raising children in a home with a loveless marriage affected them more than adults could know.

When they were done, the children ran out to the car without looking back.

'So. I suppose this is goodbye,' James said quietly.

'Yes.'

'I'll call you about the children.'

'I'll call you.' Rhianna turned to go, then stopped at the door. 'Oh, by the way. I forgot to mention earlier but I shredded all your suits with the breadknife.' She smiled brightly. 'Bye, then.'

Chapter Thirty-Five

Brooke was in the living room, staring at her phone, when her mum came up from the pub.

'She's not back yet?' Janey asked.

Brooke shook her head. 'And not a word from her. Mum, you don't think he's managed to talk her round again, do you?'

'After what she found out? Rhianna's stronger than that.' Still, Janey looked worried.

'Who's on bar?' Brooke asked.

'Mark. He was good enough to stay on and do an extra shift. God knows, me and you are going to be no bloody use down there. I'm twitchier than a ferret.' She sat down. 'He doesn't like working nights, though. Now Rhianna's gone, it's difficult to make the rota work without...'

'Without Hayden,' Brooke murmured. 'Ironic, isn't it? I tried to convince you we didn't need him, then we ended up coming to depend on him.'

'I don't suppose there's much point recruiting for someone else. Not with... you know.' Janey looked around the room. 'I'll miss this old place. I watched my babies grow up here. Did you consider that offer to stay on as landlady after Willowtree take it over?'

'I don't want to stay on under them. It'll only frustrate me, feeling like it's my pub but not my pub. I'm better off taking the money and making a fresh start with a little

371

freehold of my own.' Brooke glanced at a framed photograph showing the pub in the 1920s, old black motor cars and charabancs parked outside, back when the first generation of Padgett landlords had owned it. 'It'll be no Highwayman's, though.'

'No.' Janey sighed. 'It's a shame.'

'But it'll be worth it, if we get Rhianna back.'

Janey straightened at the sound of a car pulling up outside.

'It'll just be a customer,' Brooke said. 'I've been the same, jumping in my seat at the sound of every car.'

Still, she followed her mum as Janey went to peer out of the fire escape door.

Three figures were walking through the beer garden, weaving through the tables with a case in each hand.

'Nana!' a little voice yelped as the smallest figure started waving frantically.

'Oh my God!' Brooke turned shining eyes to her mum. 'It's them! They're home!'

'Thank God,' Janey said with a sigh of relief.

Seconds later the little family were reunited there on the fire escape, hugging and laughing and crying, no one quite sure whose arms belonged to who but embracing whichever body they found themselves nearest to.

'Oh, my love,' Janey whispered to Rhianna. 'You were so brave. We're so glad you've come back to us.'

'You've saved our lives, Mum. Both of you.'

'Come in, all of you. Come and get unpacked so I can feel like you're really back to stay.'

Janey shooed them inside, like a mother duck teaching her babies to swim.

'Max, Livvy, do you want to go put your things back in your bedrooms?' she said. 'Mum could do with a glass of wine, I should think. It's after bedtime, but I suppose tonight you can be allowed to stay up late. I've been saving some chocolate for just such a special occasion.'

'And so the bad habits begin,' Rhianna said after her children had run off to unpack.

'Spoiling them has always been the nana's prerogative,' Janey said, smiling.

'Speaking of bad habits, let's get the wine open.' Brooke headed into the kitchen to pour them all a glass.

'Rhia, I can honestly say I've never been so happy to see you,' Brooke said when they were all furnished with a drink. 'I mean, I don't want you to get carried away and think I like you or anything, but welcome the fuck home.'

Rhianna smiled. 'OK, stinkosaurus.'

'Stinkosaurus Rex.'

Janey laughed. 'Rhia, tell us what happened.'

'There isn't much to tell. I sent the au pair out, packed the kids up, told James exactly what I thought of him and walked out. Honestly, I was so calm I surprised myself. You know when you're so angry that it sort of passes through anger and into a sort of mellow resignation?' She took a sip of wine. 'Mind you, I'd already taken a lot of it out on his suits.'

'What did you do to his suits?' Brooke asked.

'Shredded the lot with a kitchen knife. At least a dozen, all designer, and not one costing less than eight hundred quid.'

Brooke laughed. 'Oh my God! Rhianna, you're my absolute hero.'

'Well, chicken, welcome back,' Janey said. 'In case you haven't worked it out by now, we're pretty pleased to have you home.'

Brooke glanced at the old photo again. 'For as long as it is home. I do think we did the right thing in selling, and I wouldn't ever wish it undone now we've got you back, Rhia, but I'll miss this old place.'

'Oh, that reminds me,' Rhianna said. 'I still need to ring Nick about that contract.'

Brooke nodded. 'Has to be done.'

'I'll do it now. Get it over with while I'm feeling brave.'

She took out her phone and pulled up Nick's number.

'Hi, Nick? It's Rhianna.' She paused. 'I'm absolutely buzzing, thanks for asking. I was ringing about the contract.' Pause. 'No, Monday's no good for me. No, not Tuesday either. Actually, I just called to tell you you can shove it up your arse. I'm not signing.' She smiled. 'No, you heard right. Nothing you can do to… no, well, it's no good to you without all three of our signatures, is it? Nope, definitely not going to change my mind. Thing is, Nick, this place belongs to my family. It has done since 1928. If it's all the same to Willowtree Taverns, we thought we'd quite like to hang on to it for at least one more generation. OK, bye. Bye then.' She hung up.

'Tell you what, I'm having a great day,' she said to Brooke and Janey. 'It's cathartic, telling off all the men who've ever done you wrong. I might see if my ex from uni's in the phone book, just so I can make it a hat trick.'

Brooke stared at her. 'Rhia, what the hell did you just do?'

'The right thing.'

'But… what about your independence?'

'I can have my independence without us having to lose the pub.' She took out a piece of paper. 'This is a statement from the company James uses to manage his stock portfolio. He's very kindly invested money in my name to the value of two hundred grand. It's winging its way to my bank account as we speak.'

'Two hundred grand!' Janey said, her eyes widening. 'Why would he do that?'

'He didn't mean to. It was some loophole to do with tax, and paying as little as he could get away with. The main thing is, the money's in my name and there's nothing he can do to stop me claiming it. It was only when I spotted the company logo on an envelope in his in-tray that I remembered the account and it occurred to me I might be able to claim the cash.'

'But...' Brooke's head was spinning. 'But you could've had twice that again if you'd signed Nick's contract.'

'I'd rather have the pub.'

'Rhia, you didn't need to do that just for me.'

'I didn't.' Her gaze wandered to the old photo. 'I did it for me. I care about this place too, Brooke. I still want to do things with my life and career – I want to fulfil my ambition to practise as a barrister. But there'll always be a part of me invested in The Highwayman's Drop. Well, it's Dad's, isn't it? That means it's ours.'

Brooke leaned over to give her a hug.

'Thanks,' she whispered. 'I won't forget this.'

'You won't be able to,' Rhianna said, smiling as she returned the hug. 'You're stuck with me now, sis. How does it feel?'

'Wonderful. Absolutely wonderful.'

—

The Sunday that followed was the day of Max's eleventh birthday party. The pub's function room had been reserved for the occasion, with a table-top chocolate fountain hired, plus a face-painter and an entertainer who was going to teach the kids circus skills. All of Max's Leyholme friends and a couple of the boys he'd been close to at Abbotleigh had been invited. Brooke could hear the sounds of merriment from her bedroom.

She was flicking through the image gallery on her phone, looking at the few selfies she had of her and Hayden. He was still ghosting her. Brooke was starting to wonder if it was time to give up and accept that he'd made his decision – except she couldn't bring herself to give up, although it had been over a week since their big row. Not without at least talking to him one more time.

If he'd only pick up! She could tell him, then, how wrong she'd been. Apologise; tell him she'd changed her mind. And hope, hope to God, he'd be able to forgive her…

There was a knock at the bedroom door, and Rhianna's face popped round.

'Aren't you coming down?' she asked. 'We're having the funnest good time ever downstairs. Max's words, not mine.'

'No, let the kiddies enjoy themselves,' Brooke said. 'They don't want old crumblies like me hanging about.'

'Yes they do. Max asked for you, that's why I came up. He wants to see you eat a chocolate-covered strawberry.'

Brooke sighed. 'Will he be upset if I don't?'

'I think so. Well, you were the genius behind the chocolate fountain idea.' Rhianna came in and squeezed her shoulder. 'Come on, sis, cheer up,' she said gently. 'I hate seeing you out of it like this. We've made a little breakout room for the parents where the wine's flowing. Come and join us, let your hair down.'

'I'm not in the mood for talking to parents. What can I talk to them about? It'll be all OFSTED inspections and chickenpox outbreaks, or whatever the current thing is.'

'Just come for a bit, for Max. One glass of wine and a chocolate strawberry and we'll let you escape up here again.'

'Well, all right. For Max then.' She swung her legs off the bed and followed Rhianna down to the function room.

'Aunty Brooke!' Max yelled when he saw her, running up. He was grinning from ear to ear, his face painted like Spider Man and his mouth smeared with chocolate. 'You were right. Chocolate strawberries are the best way to have strawberries.'

She forced a smile. 'Told you, didn't I?'

'I dipped one for you.' He ran to the fountain table to get it and bore the paper plate to her solemnly. Brooke smiled as she popped the strawberry in her mouth.

'Yum,' she said, rubbing her tummy. 'Definitely the best. You should try them with white chocolate, though.'

Max's eyes widened. '*White* chocolate!'

'We'll make them one day, shall we? We can give them choc–chip eyes to make strawberry ghosts.'

'Ooh, yeah! I want to make strawberry ghosts.'

A little girl with her face painted like a tiger ran up and tugged his sleeve. 'Max, come on. We're going to learn how to juggle.'

Brooke flinched as she recognised the kid under the paint. It was Cara. Of course Cara and Darcie would be invited, as friends of the birthday boy.

'Um, hi again,' she said.

Cara blinked at her. 'Hello.'

Rhianna hooked an arm through her sister's. 'Come on, Aunty Brooke. Come have a glass of wine with the mums and dads while this lot practise their juggling skills.'

'Right.' Brooke watched Cara trot back to the group of kids with Max, then followed Rhianna into the small adjoining room where the buffet was laid out.

She frowned when she walked in.

'But there's no one here,' she said.

'Yes. I may have told a naughty fib. Most of the parents are down in the bar.' Rhianna put her hands on Brooke's shoulders and turned her around. 'All except this one.'

She blinked. 'Hayden?'

He smiled awkwardly. 'All right?'

'I'll leave you two to talk.' Rhianna gave her sister's arm a supportive squeeze before leaving them.

Hayden rubbed his neck. 'Um… so.'

'So,' Brooke said.

'I think one of us has been a bit of a prat, haven't they?'

She sighed. 'I know. I'm so sorry.'

'I meant me.' He stepped forward, as if he was going to hold her, then thought better of it. 'Er, your sister tells me you've had an eventful week.'

'Yes.' Brooke felt like she was half in a dream. 'Well, I lost my boyfriend. Then I lost my sister, and my niece and nephew. Then I came within a gnat's whisker of losing my pub.'

He whistled. 'That is eventful.'

'It kind of worked out. I mean, I saved my sister, and then she paid me back by saving the pub.' She met his eyes. 'But I'm still miserably single, so it hasn't all been happy endings.'

He flushed. 'I'm sorry. I should've answered your calls. I've been… kind of sulking. It really hurt me when you said you thought I was just using you to get a mum for my kids.'

Brooke winced as she heard her words repeated back to her. 'God, I'm sorry. I never should have said it. I know how you feel about your kids, and what an honour it was that you were so keen to make me a part of their lives. I was angry that you'd pushed me into that situation before I was ready, so I lashed out and said things I didn't mean. I've been trying to ring you all week to apologise.'

'You're right, I shouldn't have pushed you into it. The girls were excited, and… well, you're an aunty. You know how hard they are to say no to when they get like that.' He lowered his gaze. 'Still, I knew better. Sorry.'

'Do they hate me now?' Brooke asked quietly.

'No. They're just puzzled. I wasn't sure how to explain it to them.'

She summoned a watery smile. 'We've missed you at the pub.'

'I've missed being here.'

'Will you come back?'

He met her eyes. 'To the pub?'

'Well, I kind of meant to me. And the pub. I think you know by now that we come as a pair.'

She caught his hesitation, and her heart sank.

'I mean, if you don't want to after what I said then I understand,' she said.

He laughed, finally taking her in his arms.

'I wasn't hesitating over the coming back to you part,' he said, kissing her hair. 'It's the pub. I have missed it, but this past week, rediscovering what it's like to be more than a part-time dad, playing games, helping with home-work… it made me realise I needed to make more time for the girls. I can't keep working every second God sends.'

'I understand.' She tilted her face up to kiss him. 'What about one shift a week on Saturday nights? Just so we can have the old gang back together.'

He smiled. 'Deal. Now how about we go have a drink downstairs while we wait for the kids? I'm buying.'

'Hayden…' She leaned back to look into his eyes. 'Um, could we…'

'What? Nip down to the beer cellar?'

She laughed. 'Not right now. I was going to say… can we say hi to your girls before we go down? I'd like to start as I mean to go on.'

He looked into her eyes. 'You mean it?'

'Yes. I'd love to get to know them better. I mean, I'd be proud to, really. I know already that they're a great pair of kids, and, well… they're yours.'

'Aren't you frightened? I know how you feel about big, scary, terrifying children.'

She smiled. 'Not any more. You can thank Max and Livvy for that. I don't think I realised quite how much those two had come to mean to me until I discovered they were gone.'

'I'd love for you to get to know the girls,' he said softly. 'Hey, are you busy this afternoon?'

'No, why?'

'I told them we could have rounders practice on the rec after the party. How about joining us, with Rhianna and the kids if they're free? We'd love to have you all.'

'That sounds… perfect.' She kissed him. 'Just perfect.'

Epilogue

Eight Months Later

'Brooooke!' a voice wailed from the en suite bathroom in their Venice hotel. Brooke sighed as she twisted Cara's hair into waves with the straighteners.

'What is it, Darce?' she called back.

'This bridesmaid's dress is rubbish! You can see my knickers! I'll have VPL in all the photos.'

'Did you put those no-snag tights on that I packed for you?'

'What?'

'They're in your case, you banana. Go look.'

A little white hurricane came hurtling in and dived head-first into her suitcase.

Brooke rubbed a bit of mousse into Cara's hair to finish it off. 'There we are. You're gorgeous, Car.'

Cara went to admire herself in the mirror.

'Ooh, I love it!' she said, patting the sophisticated waves. 'Brooke, you're the best at doing hair.'

'Well, I learnt from the best.'

'Who?'

'My mum,' Brooke said, smiling. 'She's the queen of hair.'

Cara twisted round to admire herself from a different angle. 'I look hot. Hey, are any boys coming to Janey's wedding?'

'Just Max. Oh, and Martin's grandson, but he's only three.'

Cara shrugged. 'Well, Max'll do, I guess.'

There was a knock at the door.

'Are you girls decent?' Hayden's voice called.

'You ought to know by now,' Brooke yelled back. 'You can come in, though.'

He came in and whistled as Brooke stood up and twirled to let him admire her hot-pink cocktail dress.

'Wow,' he said, looking her up and down. 'I mean… wow.'

'Thanks.' She nodded to his suit. 'Looking pretty sexy yourself.'

He wrapped his arms around her and planted a soft kiss on her lips. Cara put her fingers down her throat and gagged.

'Brooke, I can't wear these!' Darcie said, holding a pair of tights aloft. 'They're elephant-leg size.'

'Oh. Those are mine. Sorry, I must have yours in my case.' Brooke extricated herself from Hayden's embrace and went to take them from her. 'Elephant-leg size. Cheeky madam.'

'Not what you signed up for that first night in the beer cellar, eh?' Hayden whispered.

'No.' She kissed him again. 'But I love it.'

He offered her his arm. 'Well, shall we go?'

'Hang on. Me and Darce still need to put our tights on.'

When everyone was wearing all the undergarments they needed, the group headed to the lobby to wait for a taxi. It deposited them in front of a lavish, cushioned gondola moored by an arched bridge.

A gondolier and violinist in white and gold livery stood one at each end of the boat, while a celebrant in the middle waited for the bride and groom to arrive. On the canal bank some chairs had been set up for the guests. Rhianna and the children were already there, along with Richard, Rhianna's boyfriend and fellow postgraduate law student, who looked thrilled to have been invited as her plus-one. On the other side of the aisle sat the groom's family: Martin's son and daughter with their partners and children.

Livvy clapped her hands when she saw Cara and Darcie dressed in bridesmaids' dresses identical to her own, and ran over to be made a fuss of by them. Max, too, sidled over to the girls, but far more hesitantly. The sight of his friends in their posh dresses seemed to bring out his shy side.

Rhianna stood up when she saw her sister. She plucked her elbow, and they drew a little to one side while Hayden sat down next to Richard.

'How do you feel then?' she whispered.

'I don't know.' Brooke's eyes drifted to the family group awaiting the bride and groom. 'Happy. Sad. Thoughtful. Wistful. Lots of things. I'm feeling everything today.'

'I know what you mean. It feels like… everything's starting afresh.'

'Yes. It does feel like that.'

'I brought you a wedding present.'

Brooke laughed. 'I'm not getting married, Rhia.'

Rhianna cast an arch look at Hayden. 'Well, not yet.'

'Oh, don't tease me today. I'm liable to laugh and then promptly burst into tears, with the emotional rollercoaster I'm on. What's this present, then?'

'It's really for both of us.' Rhianna reached into her clutch and handed something to her.

Brooke looked at the plaque, which was engraved with the words:

> *Brooke and Rhianna Padgett. Licensed to sell all intoxicating liquors for consumption on or off these premises.*

'Always a Padgett over the door, right?' Rhianna said, smiling.

'God, Rhia.' Brooke dashed away a tear, laughing. 'I told you I was primed to go off, didn't I?'

'I know. It feels more real when you see it in writing.'

'I bet we'll be the only pub in the area with a Cambridge graduate for a landlady. We should put that on the chalkboard instead of Dick Turpin.'

Rhianna laughed. 'You'll have to let me be quizmaster, then.'

'Deal.' Brooke looked at her watch. 'They're due any time. We'd better take our seats.' She gave her sister a quick hug. 'Thanks for the sign, Rhia. It's perfect.'

They shepherded the children into their chairs and sat down. A few minutes later the violinist started to play, and everyone turned to watch the bride and groom walking down the aisle.

Janey looked radiantly happy, beaming at them all in a figure-hugging pale blue dress that Martin struggled to keep his eyes off. The groom was in a suit of pure white, and looked so happy and proud that Brooke decided to spare him the *Saturday Night Fever* gag she'd been planning to unleash on him later.

All eyes were on the couple as they murmured their vows, looking deeply into each other's eyes, while the beautiful Italian violin music played softly in the background. When the service ended, Martin planted a soft kiss on his new wife's lips and they stepped hand in hand onto the gondola. Brooke smiled as she watched it float away, not caring a jot about the tears pouring down her cheeks.

'You soppy mare,' Hayden muttered.

She snorted. 'Says you.'

He took out a tissue and dabbed his eyes. 'A lady would've pretended she hadn't noticed.'

'A gentleman wouldn't have had his hand on my thigh throughout the service.'

'Well, what do you think?' he said, nodding to the gondola disappearing into the horizon.

'About what?'

'You know.'

She smiled. 'You asking, are you?'

'I might be. You answering?'

'I might be.'

'Right.' He paused. 'And, er, how exactly would you be answering?'

'I'd be answering… I'll think about it.'

'That's the best I'm getting, is it? I mean, I'm here in bloody Venice, asking you to marry me on the banks of a canal as we watch a gondola full of blissful newlyweds float off into the distance, gorgeous violin music all around us, and the best you can manage is—'

She rolled her eyes. 'Oh, all right. Yes, then, if it'll stop you going on.'

'My God, you're romantic. I might just swoon.'

'You're a lucky man.' She slapped his leg. 'Come on. Let me buy you a drink.'

A letter from Lisa

Hi everyone! Thanks so much for choosing to read *The Sister Pact* and join me on this third trip to the pretty Yorkshire village of Leyholme. It was wonderful to be back in this community and join Brooke, Rhianna and Janey on their journey, and to catch up with some old friends from the previous two Leyholme-set books, *The School of Starting Over* and *Friends With Benefits*. The core themes in this story are love, family and never giving up on the people we care about: topics that resonated especially at the time of writing, as the world fought against the effects of the Covid-19 pandemic. If you enjoyed this story, I do hope you'll consider checking out the previous books too.

I'd also absolutely love to hear your thoughts on this book in a review. These are invaluable not only for letting authors know how their story affected you but also for helping other readers to choose their next read and discover new writers. Just a few words can make a big difference.

If you would like to find out more about me and my books, or contact me directly, you can do so via my website or social media pages:

Facebook: LisaSwiftWrites
Twitter: @LisaSwiftAuthor

Web: www.lisaswiftauthor.co.uk

Thank you again for choosing *The Sister Pact*.
  Best wishes,
  Lisa

Acknowledgments

As always, huge thanks to my agent, Laura Longrigg at MBA Literary Agents, and to Keshini Naidoo, my editor at Hera, for all their hard work on this book.

Big thanks to all my supportive writer pals: Rachel Burton, Victoria Cooke, Rachel Dove, Sophie Claire, Jacqui Cooper, Kiley Dunbar, Helena Fairfax, Kate Field, Melinda Hammond, Marie Laval, Katey Lovell, Helen Pollard, Debbie Rayner, Rachael Stewart, Victoria Walters, Angela Wren, and many others! Thanks, too, to the Romantic Novelists' Association for being such a wonderful and supportive organisation and its members. I'm also grateful for the support of the RNA's Rainbow chapter, which provides support for RNA members who identify as LGBTQIA+ and/or write novels featuring LGBTQIA+ characters.

Special thanks go to Victoria Dowd, not only a talented crime writer but also a former barrister, for her advice on the passages in this book relating to routes to entering this profession.

As ever, thanks to my family, friends and colleagues – my partner and long-term beta reader Mark Anslow; friends Robert Fletcher, Amy Smith and Nigel and Lynette Emsley, and Firths, Brahams and Anslows everywhere.

And finally, thanks to Keshini, Lindsey, Dan and the gang at Hera for everything they do!